"For everything there is a seaso[...]
to die......... A time to kill and a t[...]
a time to laugh......... A time to [...]
time to love and a time to hate.[...]
happened before, and what will happen in the future has happened
before, because God makes the same things happen over and over
again". Ecclesiastes 3; 1-16 NLT

*Almost without exception, the woman's point of view has been
ignored in Western historical fiction. This was true even of the
best writers, such as Louis L'Amour and Zane Grey. The movie
"Tombstone" showed how fleshing out the roles of the wives of the
Earps and Doc Holliday made the story fresh and timely. Cindy
Smith and T.B. Burton likewise have given us another look at both
sides of the sexes in "Time in Contention". The love story takes first
billing, but It lacks not for action with plenty of blazing gunfire.*
Jim Dunham, Director of Special Projects/Historian
Booth Western Art Museum, Cartersville, Georgia

**When T.B. asked me to do the photography for these books, I thought it
would be something special. After reading it, I understood just how special!
The characters really come to life. TIME IN CONTENTION is action packed
historical fiction at its best!**
Don Contreras, Photographer
We Dance Because We Can - 1996
The Cowboy Way - 2002

***TIME IN CONTENTION** offers an original story as well as a
peek back into history. The characters come to life vividly as
you travel along their journey with them experiencing their
every emotion. As you immerse yourself in the pages you
find yourself falling in love with Mr. Bogardis' gritty charm as
deeply as Mollie has. Theirs is a passion that will withstand the
test of time and will make some history of their own.*
Lynn Hubbard, Western Author, Lemon Press Publishing
Desperado - 2010
Run Into The Wind - 2010
Return To Love - 2009

Printed in the United States.

Photography: Don Contreras

ISBN: 978-0-9829006-4-2

Time in Contention

The Trilogy

A Western Love Story

The Return from Prescott

The Trouble in Tombstone

BY

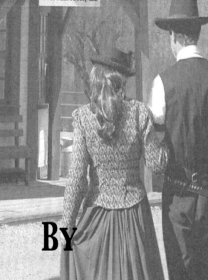

CINDY SMITH AND T.B. BURTON

INTRODUCTION

The **TIME IN CONTENTION** series is written in 'two-part' chapters. Separated by different fonts, Mollie's version is spoken through the eyes of a compassionate young woman, spirited and courageous in an uncertain world. From the wild, unsettled region of southern Arizona, Mr. Bogardis tells his side of the story with the sharp raging keenness of a true western hero. Blended together, **TIME IN CONTENTION** is an unpredictable story full of passion, revenge, life and death.

Although Mollie and Bogardis are fictional, we have composed our story to recount certain events, locations and legendary figures in history. Contention City, Arizona was ten miles away from Tombstone. In October, 1881, a historical street fight took place between the Earps and the Cowboys. We have intricately woven truth with fiction to entangle the lives of Mollie and Bogardis with Wyatt Earp and Doc Holliday, and the events of 1880-1883.

Gunfights, bloodshed and turmoil of the old west prevail in **TIME IN CONTENTION**, but it is the relationship of Mollie and Bogardis that will not allow you to rest until you have read the complete story.

When Mr. Bogardis, a former Texas Ranger turned bounty hunter arrived in Contention, his only concern was unfinished business with the Gorch brothers. Mollie left her troubled past behind her, but struggled for the strength to claim the life she so much desired.

Timing is very important for love to transpire. Some people may never know true love because of this misfortune. Although true love may last a lifetime, or a short season in your existence, true love is no accident. It had been waiting for Mollie and Bogardis on the sidewalk the very first day their eyes met. True love waits for it's believers ...... and this is a story of that kind of love.

Mollie's side of the story / Mr. Bogardis' side of the story

Time in Contention

A Western Love Story

by

Cindy Smith and T.B. Burton

CHAPTER ONE

It was late in the year 1880. I felt the wooden sidewalks of Contention City crackle under my feet from the hardened mud. The air tasted stale, as it always did blowing from the mills. It left a gritty taste in my mouth as I swallowed each breath.

I was not here in Contention City because I liked the town. Things happen out of necessity. Sometimes you are where you are, at the right moment in your life, for a reason.

Contention City was a fairly new town, bustling with strangers coming and going. Most everyone who settled here found work at one of the three stamp mills. The rest of the town folk either owns or earns their wages from local shops here on the main thoroughfare. The proprietors of the shops, who are referred to as the "Town Council", seem to have some kind of an understanding between themselves and the owner of one of the mills, who's rumored to hold sway over the town.

Things are never fair that way. I had begun to accept the way that life isn't fair, especially for a woman, when I felt the winds of change blow across my face and raise the hair on the back my neck. I was living my life as barren as possible. I knew that the existence of happiness in my future was as indefinite as the unpredictable climate of Contention City in late November.
That was, until the first day I saw him.

I had a few errands to run for my employer before my work day was ended. I had stopped just outside the Mason Hotel and knelt down to feed some scraps to a stray cat.   When I stood up, I caught sight of him. I couldn't help but watch his gradual approach down the crowded dirty street. it was sometime around late afternoon.   The sun was setting low in the sky, giving off a reflection of an orange colored glare just behind his back. He appeared larger than life and everything around him seemed a blur.

I stood motionless as my eyes were drawn to an unfamiliar figure riding tall in the saddle, coming towards the hotel on a coppered colored bay. His face had the look of prominence, distinct and in control. He scanned his surroundings as if looking for someone, or something.   His eyes slowly moved from side to side, until I could feel his vigilant stare upon me. I can still feel the very moment our eyes met. I just stood there, starring back at him, our eyes locked into each others.
Shivers ran through me as I drew my woolen wrap closer to my body. It was as if I was sensing the presence of something happening beyond my control.

I continued to watch him as he moved deliberately in an unhurried manner. He dismounted, walked into the hotel and checked in.

My cheap one room residence faced the hotel on the opposite side of the street. But, being a lady, going over to the hotel and introducing myself was out of the question.

Still, the luminous image of that first sight of him burned in my memory, and soon he was all I could think about. My mind would dwell on the intensity of his blue eyes until I felt my heart thumping in my chest. He was just a stranger that day. I had no idea of what was yet to come.

I was beside myself with uncertain emotions and incapable of communication with him. Days went by until I decided I had to write him a letter, improper as it may suggest. I began impulsively writing to a stranger with informal words of passion that I could no longer hold inside myself. I can't remember just how many letters I wrote him those first few weeks, it seems like so many. It was almost as if the letters were writing themselves.

The quill in my hand would flow with passionate words for a man I knew nothing at all about, but felt like I had known him forever. How could this be? My world was stable, and although lacking in vitality, I was content.

I forgot all rationality as I sat at my desk with a blank sheet of paper in front of me. I starred out the murky window facing the hotel, thinking of fate and destiny. I was hoping to catch a glimpse of the man responsible for my reckless manner. As the ink laid drying on the finished letter, I re-read my words that began this raging, impetuous relationship.

"My dearest stranger,
I feel that my affection towards you increases each moment my heart beats throughout the day. I am thinking of you now, as you read the words that my heart has written. I fear my life will never be the same since I saw you. I know you may not understand this now, but when our eyes met, I felt as if my prayers were answered. You do not know me, but I saw your shadow through the window
last evening as you moved about. I reached out my arms as if to touch you. Then, I closed my eyes, and dreamed of you."

It gets cold this time of year, even in southern Arizona. It seems like I've been on the trail for a month, maybe I have. Time has a way of running together, or standing still, when you are always watching your back.

As I rode into Contention City, I felt eyes on me. Not unusual. Everyone looks at strangers in these two-bit mining camps. But this was different.

I saw her on the sidewalk by the hotel. A beautiful lady, standing there wrapped in her coat, her cheeks flushed red from the cold. Our eyes made contact, for what seemed like an immeasurable amount of time as I walked into the hotel. Why would this woman even look my way? Could it be just accidental, or perhaps just idle curiosity?

Nonetheless, I was not here to socialize. I had come to Contention on business. I intended to keep a low profile and stay only as long as necessary.

As the days passed, I began to receive letters. They were delivered by a boy who works at the Chinese laundry down the street. At first I could not believe they were to me, but the passion was undeniable. They were, I believed, from the certain lady I had seen as I first rode into town. What could I say to her? Though she knows nothing about me, she writes like she actually knows me.

But, does she know all the bad things I've done? Does she know why I ride the back-trails, only venturing into remote, isolated camps and towns? I don't want to bring my trouble to her, yet I find myself longing for just a brief look in her direction.

I learned long ago that to survive I must stay out of the day light. Don't talk to people or do anything that might call attention to myself. I'm always looking at strangers, trying to be sure that they are strangers. I can't afford to run up on someone who might know me. I was a good man, once. Now, death seems to follow me wherever I go. I have a job to finish here, and I need to avoid this distraction.

But this lady causes me to forget everything but her. I see her during the day, sometimes walking from the dress shop to the general store. She is always in order, refined and lady-like. I see her entering a room, alone, just across the street from the hotel. I read her letters over and over. I am sure I don't know her. I have never seen her before I rode into Contention.

When I read the words she writes, I want to bolt across the street and pull her into my arms and hold her. I haven't felt this feeling in a long while. I have never spoken to her or even been close enough to tip my hat. It would not be proper for her to come in the saloon where she would find me, let alone make a visit to my room. If I could just meet her, on the street perhaps, could I be bold enough to ask her for her name, or to dine with me? Should I?

I have to remember that I don't need any more trouble in my life, and from what I was beginning to feel already, this woman would only be a burr under my saddle.

I needed to take a walk, get out of this enclosed room for a while. The cool evening air might help clear my head. I might even see her image through her window. Hell, why do I care! Why does this woman rule my thoughts, even haunting my dreams?

CHAPTER TWO

Night after night, I dreamed of the stranger who sleeps across the street from me.   My waking hours were infused with thoughts of what he must be thinking about my continual letters.

On this particular evening, the wind was howling through the tiny cracks around the window glass as I peered out into the darkness. From the window, I saw the same stray cat that seemed to be following me home at night.   I gathered some dried bread pieces and wrapped them in a handkerchief.

It was as if I was existing only for the glances I would catch of the man as he wandered from the hotel door to McDermott's Saloon or Hopkin's diner up the street.   Garbed in black from hat to boots, he conveyed the impression of an experienced gunman striding with certainty in his steps.

I knew it was foolish, but still I moved effortlessly as I dressed to confront the elements outside my room.   I needed more.   What was it about him? I wanted a closer look, so I tucked the folded handkerchief into my coat pocket.   I took in a deep breath as I opened the door and closed it behind me.   With intentions only to feed the cat, I would be closer to what had become my hearts desire.

The wind was blowing cold and crisp and made my cheeks glow and burn like fire. My steps were long and eager as I attempted to cross the uneven frozen tracks in the street that separated us. The moon, dangling like a half circle, gave off just enough light to define to the sparkling frost setting in for the night. I was being careful not to trip and fall into the ruts made by the wagons hauling ore from the mills. As I approached the sidewalk, with my head bowed down to see my way, I heard the hotel door open. I looked up without thinking, and there no more than a few feet away, he stood.

I cannot describe the feeling that overwhelmed me, as I found myself for the second time, starring into those piercing blue eyes of the stranger.   "Ma'am", he said softly, his hand on the brim of his hat, being careful not to lose contact with my eyes. Feeling somewhat embarrassed, I quickly looked away. My eyes dropped to the stranger's lips. They were parted just as if he was about to say something else, but a fierce blast of wind blew from behind me and I almost lost my balance. He reached for my arm and with the ease of a gentlemen, his hand was tenderly grasping the sleeve of my cloak.

"Ma'am, if I may ask, what are you doing out here on such a cold night as this?"   "I..........", stumbling over what to say, nothing more than "I" would come out.

"Come inside, you need to get out of the cold!", he warned as he guided me through the door of the hotel. Cornelius Crane, the desk clerk, had already retired for the evening, so the small front lobby was bare. My heart was stomping in my chest, my knees were weak and trembling. Breathing hard and trying to catch my breath, I blamed it on the bitter night air. When I felt his hand upon my shoulder, I wanted to turn around, look upon his face, but I was powerless!

I realized that we were now alone. My letters! He must know that I am the author of the intimate letters he has been receiving since he arrived in town!

Slowly, his hand drifted downwards toward the center of my back, as if he was actually feeling my body through several layers of heavy winter clothing. Standing still, not wanting the moment to end, I exhaled and closed my eyes.

Before I knew what was happening, I was thrown to the floor with the strangers powerful body covering mine. Against my head, I felt the cold steel of a pistol in his grip which I knew without a doubt, he was ready to fire. I could hear the gunshots blasting just outside the hotel doors! A rapid fire of three, maybe four, I can't remember.

The commotion outside turned out to be nothing more than just some rowdy conduct from a couple of cowboys. They probably had too much to drink, as that is what all the men around here seem to do all night. When it was all over, I was peering into soft spirited eyes, the color of the Arizona sky in early spring.

I could have stayed there forever, but he gently helped me to my feet. I couldn't take my eyes off him. From under the wide brim of his hat, strands of light brown hair dangled around his forehead. His face was somewhat weathered and tanned but seem to soften when he looked at me. His lips were covered by a mustache that appeared to be well groomed and waxed so that it curled up on the sides, like a present with a bow on top. I was close enough to smell his scent, fresh and masculine, so carnally appealing as it drifted into my body.

For a moment, I thought he would kiss me. But, instead, his expression changed quickly. His eyes narrowed as he spoke sternly, "This is not the time or place. I am taking you back home where you belong. Tomorrow....... we will talk".

With the promise of tomorrow, he left as I walked into my room.

He offered no explanation of why he was so anxious when the shooting began. No mention of his name as we crossed the darken street side by side. I knew nothing more of him than I did the day before. Nothing more than the fact that I had become entranced by a man whom I longed to be touched by.

When I took off my coat, the handkerchief fell out of the pocket scattering bread pieces into the floor. In all the excitement, I had forgotten to feed the cat!

*   *   *   *   *

What a night! Wind blowing up the street and howling between the buildings. Not a night fit for man or beast. But as it has become my habit, I always get out in the evening. I need to know if anything is going on in town. So far, no one has yet to question my being here. And with the weather so damn brutal, I don't expect much to be going on. Still it is wise to get out and take a look around.

When I went through the lobby, I noticed that the old man who runs this dump has already called it a night. Good, I don't like his demeanor. It's as if he suspects something.

As I stepped out onto the sidewalk I almost ran into someone. Bundled up against the cold, head down and face almost hidden by the hood of her cloak. Still, I knew that this was what had become my yearning obsession. As she looked up the hood slid backwards, revealing waves of auburn hair glowing in the moonlight. Our eyes met for a moment, just as they did that first day I rode into town.

A gust of wind caught her from behind and I had to reach to keep her from falling, at least that is probably what she thought. Little did she know that I constantly think of her and would go to any extreme just to touch her. I asked what she was doing out on a night such as this. She started to answer, then stopped. What a contradiction, the lovely lady who wrote all those letters so full of passion was suddenly speechless!

I guided her through the hotel door and closed it behind us. We were alone in the lobby. I placed my hand on her shoulder to turn her around. I could feel the warmth of her body all the way through to her bones.

As she turned, I heard three quick gunshots in the street. Had they found me? All I could do was throw her to the floor with my arm and half my body across hers. My gun was already in my other hand. Immediately, I could hear the Marshal and his deputy warning a couple of errant cowboys not to shoot within the city limits. It was nothing.

She was face down on the floor with my body against hers. I gently rolled her over and looked into those eyes filled with both fright and passion. I leaned closer to her, our lips only inches apart.

As I looked into those green eyes, it seemed as if the world had come to a stand-still. She looked back into mine, her lips slightly parted. I wanted to kiss her and hold her in my arms, but instead, I helped her to her feet. She deserves more than a kiss from a stranger that she knows nothing about.

We crossed the deserted street and I took her home without further delay. I
promised that we would talk tomorrow. But what can I say to her?

We were lying on the floor with my body touching hers, and I don't even know her name. She has never signed her letters to me. All I know is that this woman, within a matter of just a few short weeks, has captivated my heart and soul. It will be a long night thinking about her across the street, so near and yet so
far.
I should be honest with her, but how can I ever explain who and what I am.

CHAPTER THREE

The hours passed like days. The sun had disappeared, sinking below the hazy horizon, and still he had not come to call on me. What could have happened in the last twenty-four hours?

I could barely concentrate on my work at the dress shop today.

Mrs. Sara May Marks, the owner of the shop, was a harsh older widow woman. I was so grateful to her for giving me the job when I needed it, that I tried to overlook her compelling ways to interfere with my life. Mrs. Marks was from a prominent family in Arizona. She was known by everyone, she knew everyone, and she made it her business to keep up with all the gossip and happening for miles around. All day long she was talking about the stranger, making her speculations on who he was and what he was doing here. I had to keep my thoughts to myself, not letting her become aware of my hidden feelings.

The shop was busy this time of year. People coming and going, orders that needed to be filled. Mrs. Marks didn't pay me much for all I did, but at least she had been a friend to me since I moved into town several months ago. She knew somewhat of my past, my situation, but she also let me know she disapproved.

I tried to listen in on some of the conversations I overheard while finishing the hem of an eloquent ball gown I supposed was being made for the town Christmas dance. I took my time with the needle and thread between my fingers so I could cling on every word. Mrs. Marks said she thought the man was from Wyoming, on the run from a bank robbery in Cheyenne or something. Others said they heard that he once rode with Jack Taylor's gang of outlaws. Seems they had kinfolk around here at one time. Maybe they still do.

Unconfirmed gossip. That's all they know. This whole town is like that. People here seem to thrive off of what they don't know so they can fill in the blank spaces of the truth with their own made up lies.

I accidentally pierced the tip of my finger with the sewing needle and a tiny bit of blood seeped into the satiny material of the gown. If Mrs. Marks thought I had been listening and not concentrating on my work, she would take some out of my pay this week. So, I moved the gown to the back room to continue sewing without the distraction of the idle talk in the shop.

The back room has a small lower window adjacent to the alleyway between the hotel and Marshals office. I overheard talk coming from somewhere near by and left the needle in the dress to walk towards the window. Two men were in the alley talking to the Marshal. I couldn't recognize the men, their faces were turned away from me. Fortunately, it was quiet in the back room and I could hear a word or two through the glass of what they were conversing among themselves. They were pointing at the Mason Hotel, precisely at the window where the stranger has been staying. I don't know why, but I didn't have a good feeling about what I observed.

After the shop closed, Mrs. Marks had invited me to dine with her over at the boarding house. I declined, and swiftly walked away so that she would not question my decision. Later, alone in my room, I lit my oil lamp and waited as the hours passed on. With no knock upon my door, I sat pondering the question, had he changed his mind?

I paced the floor back and forth making myself sick with a frightful knot growing in the pit of my stomach. What if he did have second thoughts, he doesn't know me, just as I don't know him. The only difference is that for me, it was too late. The stranger was obsessing my life now.

Something, or someone, kept him from coming to me tonight. I fell into a restless sleep praying that he was at the very least safe, where ever he was.

*   *   *   *   *

It was a long night. Not much sleep. All I could think of was that lovely lady looking up at me with those beautiful penetrating eyes. I convinced myself that I only had two choices as far as she was concerned. Either I need to sit down and talk with her about my situation, or pack my saddle bags and hit the trail. I know what I want to do. I want to hold her in my arms for the rest of my life. But is that fair to her? I never know how long the 'rest of my life' might be. Besides, when she finds out who and what I am, she may want me to leave. I wouldn't blame her.

I just know that I cannot abide seeing her from a distance and wanting her with me. I have been to who knows how many cattle towns, mining camps, and even some pretty large cities. They all had their share of women, but I never wanted any like I wanted her. Why does this one captivate and torment me so?

Earlier today, I put two of the town kids "on payroll." They are supposed to watch for strangers or anything unusual, and get two bits if their information pleases me. I also have the Chinese laundry boy, 'Hey-You', on a similar deal. Hey-You came and told me he saw two men come into town this afternoon. I could not get much more out him, since he doesn't speak our language very well.

Bad timing.

I had almost built my nerve up enough to visit the lady and lay everything out on the line for her. Now I don't want to do anything that might cause anyone to think that we are friends. Friends! What a word. I want so much more from her.

One of the boys came by with more news. He saw a couple of cowboys and managed to hide behind some barrels in the alley while they talked with the Marshal. According to what the boys overheard, I could piece enough together to understand what was going on. The men did not exactly lie to the Marshal, but they did not tell the whole story. By using half-truths and stretching things a little, they made it sound like I was murderer. It didn't take much sense for me to realize they were the Gorch brothers, my reason for being in Contention.

There was no love lost between the Gorches and myself. The Gorch family lives just outside of Contention and owns one of the stamp mills in town, probably through some kind of a botched poker game or something like that. They're the kind of men who carry a knife up their sleeve for killin' and use the dead man's coat to wipe the blood off their crooked hands.

These small town Marshals, like in Contention, usually don't care what you did somewhere else, as long as you are straight while in their jurisdiction. I just don't know how much the Gorches have to do with running this town, or who they may have in their pockets. I have to be careful how I approach this.

Still, it might be best for me to go to the Marshal and tell him who I am and what I'm doing here. I would have appreciated that back when I was a lawman. When I was a lawman..... that seems like a hundred years ago now.

I cannot go to the lady (I don't even know her name) until I clear things up with the Marshal and end this trouble with the Gorches.

It has taken all of my will power to not cross the street today. The thought of her thinking that I don't want to see her is unacceptable, but necessary. I thought I might knock on her window this evening, but the risk would be too great. I knew the first time I laid eyes on her that the likelihood of me getting to know her was like unto a lion getting to know a lamb.

CHAPTER FOUR

During the following days the weather had let up some. I was able to see the stars again, piercing through the dark sky like diamonds on black velvet. Not a moment passed throughout the wasted hours of my days and nights, that I was not overwhelmed with thoughts of where he must be.

Yesterday, coming home from the dress shop, I ventured on the opposite side of the street. I slipped in through the curtain door of the Chinese laundry and motioned for Hey-You. I asked the boy if he would be out later in the evening to stop by my room, I had another letter I wanted him to deliver for me. Hey-You lived with his aging father, Po-Mo-Sang, and did much of the work in the laundry. So much responsibility for such a small boy. He had no schooling and spoke very little English, but my heart went out to him. His mother died on the boat and his older sister had been sold into slavery. Most likely for prostitution. They lived in a little shack behind the store front. For having so very little in life but hardships, Hey-You made a special effort to always lend a smile to me from behind his slanted troubled eyes.

I did not know what had happened to the stranger, but I was sure he would come for me, if only he could. I saw the look in his eyes when he lay over me just a few nights ago, intense and full of fire. The talk at the dress shop was still the same. Rumor after rumor, it would never stop until they knew the truth. But what is actually the truth in their minds, would be nothing more than what they choose to believe.

I thought if I wrote him just one last letter, a letter of explanation about myself, he might understand why I constantly dwell on the perception of him.

My Dearest Stranger,

I must know who you are. I feel that I may have frightened you with my letters by appearing so bold and strong. That would not be the case. You see, I have so much I want to share with you. I knew this the moment our eyes first met in the street and it was confirmed on the floor of the hotel lobby. And, so with this letter, you will now know who I am.

My name is Mollie Lewis, a dressmaker from the Northern States. I have not always been as this, though I will tell you more as time goes on. I do not know your name, but I do know that I have been waiting for you, lingering in existence between reality and dreams.

So many evenings by candlelight I would pray to God for Him to send me someone to hold on to. Someone to make my life more bearable. The world is such a vast place, and my fear was that I would not know who God would send me if I saw him.

But there you were. It was as if God had spoken to my heart when I stared into your eyes. I am sure you felt it too. I am writing to tell you that I do not care who you are or what your past is comprised of. I want to consume your future.

avec mon ame, Mollie

*   *   *   *   *

I finally decided to speak with the Marshal. As I made my way to his office, I hoped that I would not see my beautiful angel. If anyone saw me look at her, they would know my heart. And that cannot happen. One must not show weakness on any level if he chooses to be perceived as a man not to be trifled with.

The Marshal invited me to sit in his office. He seemed like a fair man. I told him no lies, but I did not tell him more than I thought was necessary for him to know. I explained about the killing of the other Gorch brother and their father, and that I was not charged with murder or anything else. Of course the remaining two Gorchs would have preferred that not to be the case. They have made it perfectly clear, they will not rest until I am dead. They believe I used the badge to obstruct their interpretation of justice.

I have since taken the badge off my chest. I became a man that I have grown to dislike, hunting down fugitives with a price on their head. I do this not for money, but for my own peace of mind, to rid the world of worthless dregs of society like the Gorches. For years, I have tried to avoid confrontation with them, I am not a killer by any means. But, I am not a coward either, and they will not let this rest. They're not known for being brave, just ruthless. They would not be above hurting someone that I cared for if that was the only way to get to me.

I know their family holds some kind of grandeur here, though I am not impressed. I came here looking for them, as they have been looking for me. They are in their element here. They will make their move soon enough, probably in the back, and I intend to be ready.

After about an hour or so in his office, the Marshal thanked me for the particulars. Though I couldn't tell if he was bought and paid for, at least my conscience was content.

Hey-You brought another letter tonight. At last, I know her name. Mollie. A beautiful name for a beautiful lady. It is as if I can read between the lines of her letters. I know she is unaccompanied and alone, and has come to accept it. Nothing would suit me more than to cross the street, take her in my arms, and wipe away any loneliness and hurt from her heart. But I can't, not yet.

I should write her back and tell her something about me, not everything, somethings should be talked about in person. But she should understand that I have only the finest of intentions when it comes to her. I have nothing to offer but my honesty. I cannot even portray the truth to her without implying the worst. Such a complicated mess. Hey-You seems to be trustworthy so I will send a letter back by him.

My Dearest Mollie,

Please accept my humble apology for not writing to you sooner. As I am sure you have surmised, there are reasons why I have avoided public contact with you, not the least of which is your reputation. Though it cannot be now, please believe that we will properly meet soon.

There were two men in town a few days ago who know I am here and it is important that they never see me socialize with anyone. For your safety, Mollie, please understand this. This will be over soon enough.

I should tell you a few things about myself, Mollie.

I was born in Georgia dirt poor. When the war came, my brother and father enlisted. We know my brother was killed at Shiloh Hill. We had to assume my father was killed, because we never saw or heard from him again. But the old man may have used the war as a means to escape from his responsibilities. He wouldn't be the first one to do so. My mother, being an educated woman, held intentions of me one day becoming a doctor. Instead, while still young, I enlisted in the Confederate Army in 1863.

When the war was over I came home to find my mother gravely ill. She had grieved over the loss of my father and lost interest in life. She died a short time after my return. Being younger and from the North, you may not realize how bad things were in the South after the war. We were punished harshly. But, that is all in the past. There is so much in the past.

With nothing to hold me, I came west. I rode with the Texas Rangers for a while. In the course of that duty, an incident happened which is partially responsible for the reason I am here in Contention City. I will tell you more about that when we are able to talk.

Please know that you are forever in my heart and mind. The first time I saw you I knew that something special had happened too.

Until we meet, I Remain Your Humble Admirer ~
Mr. Bogardis

CHAPTER FIVE

It really didn't matter who he was, except now I had a name for the stranger across the street. I would just wait in shadowy existence until the day Mr. Bogardis could come and call for me. I carried his letter in the crease of my breasts, close to my heart. I would see him as he walked the street, or through the window as he paced the floor in his room. Still, I did what was necessary and kept my distance. Just seeing him in passing would have to suffice for now. He knew what he was doing, and I understood that he wanted me safe. I did not care about his past, everyone has a past.

I try to forget, but running away doesn't allow you to forget anything, not even your own past. You just try to cover up your failures with invented justifications and lie to yourself, all the while hoping for a future. Until the moment I saw him, I did not think of any tomorrows for myself. My life was over before the day I arrived in Contention.

I will someday reveal my afflicted soul to Mr. Bogardis. But for now, I will just count the hours and days that we are apart.

The town's Christmas Dance was just a week away. Probably everyone within traveling distance would be there. I had no reason to attend. Though the folks of this town spoke to me in passing, I knew they also talked about me behind my back. Especially the men. I learned long ago that if you don't give a man what he wants, when he wants it, he will plot his revenge against you. I just wanted to be left alone, start my life over again, if that was possible. But, men tend to believe that a woman's life depends upon a man. Maybe it does, but I know not all men are dependable.

I wake up early each morning and stir the embers in the cast iron stove. Left unattended in the night, they become dark and cold. Once they are stirred, they begin to glow with hot red heat. I have been cold for too long. I came to Arizona to get away from the coldness, in more ways than one. The winter will be over soon enough and in time, spring will bring a fresh renewal of everything. It's the waiting that's the hardest part.

My responsibilities at the dress shop include arriving before Mrs. Marks, so I walk to the shop about thirty minutes after sunrise. The sidewalks that early in the day are usually vacant except for the barkeep at McDermott's sweeping out broken glass and sawdust into the street. Occasionally, I see Po-Mo-Sang preparing to open his store, with his young son not far behind him.

It would be busy in the shop these next few days, with all the special orders that needed to be completed before the dance. I was thankful for the diversion, it would help me take my mind off things. I find myself thinking about Mr. Bogardis more than I probably should.

This morning, as usual, I unlocked the front door of the shop and released the window blinds to show the "open" sign. I took the cloak from my shoulders, walked to the back room and placed it on the iron hook. I felt something crush beneath my feet. Looking down, I saw tiny pieces of shiny broken glass scattered on the floor and in the corner where the material was strewn. I felt a cold shivering breeze and noticed that the window facing the alleyway was broken! Why would anyone want to break into Mrs. Mark's dress shop? Frightened, I grabbed my cloak from the hook, turned back around and headed out the front door. I must inform the Marshal what had happened before Mrs. Marks arrived.

Running as quickly as I could, I reached the Marshal's office in no time at all. I pulled the handle on the heavy wooden door and it didn't open. That's strange! The Marshals office was never locked. I pounded several strong knocks and still no one answered. Not even his no account deputies were any where around.

As panic formed in the pit of my stomach, Mr. Bogardis appeared from somewhere out of the early morning shadows. "What is it, Mollie, what's happened!" He had such an intense implication in his voice like he was protecting me that I almost forgot what had happened back at the shop!

Briefly, I explained the window and the broken glass, stuttering and confusing my words, still just a little out of breath. I told him that something must be terribly wrong, that the Marshal never locks his door, and that at least one of the deputies should have been on duty. He tried the door himself, still it refused to budge.

"Get back to the dress shop, Mollie! Stay off the streets and I will find the Marshal and let him know what happened." I hesitated, I could have asked a million questions, but he frightened me with his forceful sense of urgency.

I did what he said. Once back inside the shop, I rested my back against the door. I then realized, that Hopkins Diner had their "closed" sign in the window when I ran by. Again, this appeared very strange to me. The man who ran the diner was like all the rest of the town folks and just out to make a dollar. Many of the other business proprietors congregated at Hopkins early in the morning before their own places actually opened up. I couldn't imagine why he would chose to be closed on the same day.

I could only hope Mr. Bogardis knew what he was doing. I tried to compose myself, hung up my cloak and picked up the broom. I cleaned the shattered glass from the floor and table and did my best to secure the window with scraps of wood from a broken chair. Peering out the busted window, I remembered the two men talking with the Marshal in the alleyway the day before. I should have told Mr. Bogardis what I saw. The complicated secret emotions inside of me were tormenting my mind with worry and causing me to not think straight.

Just as all the muddle in the back room was cleaned up, I turned to find Mrs. Mark standing in the doorway. I didn't notice the time it had taken me to clean, so I felt fortunate that Mrs. Marks was late in her arrival. Her rigid stare was fixated on me, with a blank expression on her face. For the second time that morning, I tried to explain what I had discovered earlier. When I told her the part about the Marshals office being locked, she coldly looked away. I almost felt as if she knew something that I didn't.

The rest of the morning carried on as usual. No word from Mr. Bogardis. No gossip in the shop regarding the Marshal or his deputies. I tended to my duties and finished the gowns, then stepped back to admire my workmanship. I allowed my imagination to drift away for a few seconds. I could see myself, in the bright red ball gown trimmed in delicate black lace, dancing across the floor in the arms of Mr. Bogardis. I could hear the music playing softly as we waltz oblivious to all around us. It is a wonderful scene playing out in my mind, but I realize that was not to be. At least not yet.

*　　　　*　　　　*　　　　*　　　　*

As I rounded the corner in the early morning chill, I once again met the woman who has captivated my heart and soul. When did I first see her? Was it yesterday, or the day before, last week, last month? I no longer have any perspective of time, only that my lovely Mollie passes through my life all too briefly.

She looked frightened. She explained the broken window in the dress shop and that when she came to report it to the Marshal, his office door was locked.

I already knew where the Marshal and his deputies were. One of my young little spies had overheard a conversation in the alley yesterday between the Marshal and the Gorch brothers.

They had made the Marshal an offer that was hard to refuse. They fully admitted that they were here for me. The Marshal would give his deputies the day off, and then leave town himself. When they returned, the Gorches would have their business concluded. Only one person would get hurt. And after all, I was just an expendable stranger in a town owned by dirty money with the Gorch name written all over it.

The Marshal was actually an honest man, to some degree, but he knew that he and his deputies were no match for the Gorch brothers. If he didn't cooperate, he would lose the authority of his badge. They threatened the town council as well. They informed the Marshal to relay the message that if anyone intended to help me, the town would be used as a shooting gallery.

The Marshal went to the Town Council and explained the ill-fated situation to them. The Council was made up of several business owners, including the lady who owned the dress shop where Mollie works. It didn't take them long to decide that the fate of one stranger was not as important as the safety of the entire town.

So everyone agreed that the Marshal and his deputies would be out of town, and the Gorch brothers would take care of me and leave everyone else alone. The Marshal had the decency to come by and inform me of what was to take place. He was giving me the opportunity to run for it.
I no longer feel the need to prove my courage or myself.

What I do now is strictly business. Some call me a 'Bounty Killer'. I prefer the term 'Bounty Hunter'. I usually go to great pains to give the men I hunt every opportunity to go with me peacefully. I say 'usually' because there was that drunken Yankee soldier who kidnapped a twelve year old girl. I caught him, but he did not go back for trial. I still can't get that memory out of my mind. When you put your hands on a child, all you get is dead. Like I said before, worthless dregs of society!

So why not run? One very good reason. Mollie Lewis. There is nowhere I can go that could ever erase her from my memory. I know she feels something for me, even though we have hardly touched, and never kissed.

I will not leave. And if I survive, I will do everything in my power to make her mine.

What am I thinking? When she knows what I am, she will shun me like the rest of polite society. Yet, I have to try. There is still a heart that beats inside of me. There is hope in the back of my mind that Mollie feels the same for me as I feel for her.

I would have expected the Gorch boys to have come at me head on, since they had already arranged to have the law out of town, but so far, there is nothing out of the ordinary.

I changed my routine very little, but I also paid even more attention to my surroundings. After running into Mollie this morning, I went out for breakfast a half hour later than usual. Lunch was an hour later. If someone knows your schedule and are waiting for you, being a little bit later gives them the fidgets. Just one way of perhaps gaining a little edge.

I saw nothing out of the ordinary at any time. But I know that as it gets later in the day, the odds of a confrontation increases. I just hope that Mollie takes heed to my words this morning and stays off the street.

So far they have had everything their way. Yet they still are reluctant to do what they came for. The Gorch family was never known for nerve. They prefer to look down the side of a shotgun at someone's back.

I spent a little more time in the saloon today. I could back a chair up to the wall and see anything coming. Nothing. Damn the waiting for the unknown.

Its gets dark early this time of year. As I head for the diner down the street, I try to stay alert to my environment. That is increasingly harder to do because of Mollie. I long to walk arm in arm with her close by my side. To let everyone in this town, everyone in the world know that we belong to each other. Will it ever be? Instead, of eating alone at my table, I want to be able to sit next to her. When I look into her eyes, I can see the reflection of my own desires.

I ate sparingly tonight. I find that food slows not only the body, but the senses. I have to stay sharp if I want to survive. And I do. Mollie has given me something that I want to carry as far as we can take it.

As I walked back to the Mason hotel, the hair on the back of my neck was standing up. I could feel eyes on me. I just didn't know where they were. As I crossed in front of the alley between the dress shop and the hardware store, I don't know if I heard something or saw something move. A damn gray cat screeched and jumped up from out of no where. I jerked back as two bullets hit the corner of the hardware store by my head. My hand was already by my gun in anticipation of something like this. My gun came out smoothly and I leveled it and fired five shots rapidly, trying to sweep the alley. I heard a groan and a crash. As the echo of the gunfire died away, I heard movement at the other end of the alley and caught a glimpse of someone turning the corner. One or both of them had escaped. I holstered my fired pistol as I reached for my second. I learned long ago that reloading is when a lot of men die.

You would think that the town would pour out into the street to see what had happened. No townsfolk showed up. A few men from the saloon, mostly drifters and drovers, ran out to see the commotion. I asked one of them to bring a lantern before I entered the alley. He ran across the street and returned quickly. I thought I would be on my own, but he offered to enter the alley with me and hold the lantern. Although I did not know him, he had been in town off and on since the first day I rode in. From listening to the talk in the saloon, I knew that he worked on ranch a few miles outside of town. It was just a feeling, but I thought I could trust him.

As we moved slowly down the alley, we saw a pair of boots sticking out from behind a row of boxes. It was the younger Gorch brother. Although I could not see my targets, one of the bullets had hit him in the throat, pretty much centered under his chin. There was still a slight gurgling sound coming from the wound. But it was obvious that nothing could be done for him. He had bled out.

We walked on down the alley and found nothing else. The other Gorch had left his kid brother dying alone in the dark. Like I said, the Gorch family was not noted for their willingness to stand up and fight.

Some of the boys from the saloon tried the Marshal's office, but could not get anyone to the door. Of course, I knew why. I suggested they go get the undertaker. He was there in what seemed like only a moment. He looked shocked as he stared first at me, then the dead man. I am sure he knew what was supposed to have happened. I am not sorry to disappoint him.

As my blood cools down, I think of Mollie. What is she going to think of me now? How can I explain this?

Then the cold reality of fact sets in. The last Gorch brother got away. One of the boys from the saloon said he heard a horse heading out of town in a hurry. Far from being over, he is without a doubt going for help. I have whittled down the Gorch brothers and their old man, but who knows how many cousins, uncles, whatever they may have.

This means I may have a few days to get ready. I know the townsfolk would have preferred for me to be lying in that alley. At least this thing would be over for them. Should I take the Marshal's advice and leave town? I know they will find me, and thats all right. At least I would not endanger the only person I have come to care for. Yet I know if I leave, I will never have her. And if I stay, and survive, will she ever be able to love me?

I know it is selfish of me, but I have to at least explain things to her in the hope that she will understand. I should try to talk with her tomorrow. Will she even want to talk to me after tonight? I can only hope.

CHAPTER SIX

Everyone in town is talking about what happened last night! A man was shot dead in the alley way as gun fire rang out of the still darkness. I am not sure anyone has told the whole truth, but I think I have put together the pieces here and there to make out the gist of it. From what I gathered, the men I saw talking in the alley to the Marshal a few days ago were the Gorch brothers. I have never actually met the family, but they own one of the largest stamp mills in Contention. It seems a Texas Ranger shot and killed one of their brothers and their father a few years back and they have sought revenge ever since. I don't know who they would want to kill around here, but word has it that it is the stranger, Mr. Bogardis. I have even heard a rumor that he was the Texas Ranger who did the killing!

It's hard to say, I need to hear the truth from Mr. Bogardis himself. All I know right now is that the grave is being dug for one of the brothers, and Mr. Bogardis is still alive!

Being Sunday, the shop is closed. I did what was expected of me yesterday and finished the gowns like Mrs. Marks wanted. It's just as well, I did not care to see Mrs. Marks today and hear any of her gossip. There's just too much going on around here for my taste. Since seeing Mr. Bogardis is not a possibility today, I have a hundred other things that I can tend to.

Idle hands are the devils hands, that is what I was told as a child, so I intend to take heed. I can never find time to mend my own clothing when working at the shop all day. I have an old dress that I seldom seem to have use for anymore, so I am going to sew a few yards of lace and crinoline to it, maybe even add a few fancy stitches of gold colored string to brighten it up. It would be perfect for a Christmas dance! I will also fill the ink bottle with fresh black fluid, just incase I feel like drafting another letter today. I have some store bought flour and pig lard on the shelf, I could make a fine batch of biscuits for the jar of molasses I've been saving. It would warm up the room, and you never know when someone could stop by.

What am I doing? What am I thinking! All my thoughts seem to dwell around the man across the street! Just down the road and up the hill, a pile of cold, fresh dug dirt waits for a man who was shot and killed last night. It could have been intended for Mr. Bogardis instead! I have no right to hope for a future. No reason to believe there is a future.

I have to keep my thoughts logical. I am a sensible woman, rational and reasonable. I am independent and practical, so how could this be happening to me? I have fallen in love with a man I know only in passing! And, love, what is love anyway? Nothing but Pain in disguise waiting to inflict it's wounds into your bleeding unsuspecting heart.

I felt one small tear roll slowly down my cheek and drop onto the needle I was threading with gold string. Without pausing, I closed my eyes and imagined what the dress would look like when I am finished.

Although I can occupy my hands, my mind still wonders aimlessly towards Mr. Bogardis. My fingers become sore from tiny needle pricks. Not concentrating on the dress has caused me to spend more time on it than necessary. But, I must say, the gold thread and black lace gives it an exotic look.

The town seems to be at rest, even after the death of a man they are burying in the cemetery today. Everyone is preoccupied with themselves. The mills in town close down on Sundays. The streets are mostly deserted with the exception of Hey-You and a few other children playing with sticks and rocks.

Many of the businesses are closed, and most of the self-professed decent people around here attend the Union Fellowship Church meetings in the back room of the furniture store. I myself thought about becoming one of the members of the church when I first came here. I sought the sanity and wisdom that worshipping the Good Lord is supposed to bring a person in need. Eventually, I discovered that the lies and gossip I heard around town, were actually started by the righteous members of the Union Fellowship Church.

There was an incident not long ago when an outlaw cowboy, on the run and laid up drunk in Contention City, went into the church meeting. By gunpoint, he made the preacher dance a jig and no one in attendance was brave enough to do anything about it. What a Sunday Service that must have been!

I found myself wanting to take a walk again. That old gray cat that no one seems to claim is probably wondering around the streets tonight. I have started to call him 'Littlefoot'. He's been following me around for a while leaving tiny footprints in the dust outside my door. Everyone needs someone, even an old stray cat. I suspect he should be hungry right now.

I did not expect to see anyone on the street. Almost instantly, there he was, Mr. Bogardis, standing in front of me! He must have been watching my door. I had no time to think or to consider the consequences of my actions. He touched my face and I was overcome with desire. I impulsively slipped my arm in his and he steered me towards the other side of the street. We stopped just outside the hotel doors, and his eyes were immersed into mine. His cold, callused hands were firmly gripping my shoulders.

He started to make a sincere plea for my approval of whatever it was he wanted to tell me. "Mollie,..... let me explain...".

I didn't care. I couldn't waste the time we may have together with trifling words seeking to justify the necessary measures he has had to take. I took his hand and urgently pulled him inside the hotel doors and locked the entryway behind us. He responded aggressively, and before I knew it, I was pressed up against the flowery wallpaper of the lobby. His body was so tightly leaning into mine, I could feel the outline of his taut chest muscles through his loose canvas overcoat. Without hesitation, he forcefully mounted my lips with his mouth. "Hmmmmm...." Warm and roaming, he explored my hunger for him. It was at that very moment, I knew that I wanted him more than I had ever wanted any man in my life.

When he finally released me, his eyes were closed as if he was drawing a mental image in his mind. I held on to him with the very essence of my soul. Without the opportunity for any other words to exchange between us, our brief spellbound entanglement was interrupted!

Corney Crane had been watching from the top of the stairway. The look on his face was manifested condemnation! Mr. Bogardis wasn't aware of him immediately, as his back was facing Corney. But, I saw him, and his judgement! He is a twisted man and I knew what he was thinking. I reluctantly dropped my arms and quickly lowered my eyes away from the face of my beloved Mr. Bogardis. Upon feeling my sudden uneasiness, he swiftly turned to confront the unknown situation behind his back. His hand gripped the revolver at his side. I held my breath, uncertain of what would happen next.

*   *   *   *   *

Today is Sunday. The town is pretty much shut down for the Sabbath. I feel certain that the Gorch who got away will not be back until he gets plenty of help.

I had determined I would stand outside across from Mollie's room. Perhaps if she saw me, she would come out. I didn't know what I was going to say to her. I didn't know if she would even give me the opportunity to speak to her. Had I known that the day would come when she would enter my life, I would have lived differently in hopes that there would be no obstacles in our path. Too late for that now.

I had been out for a little over an hour, and had seen only two people. I was ready to give up when Mollie came out and started to cross the street in my direction. I couldn't wait on her. I rushed to met her before she even got started. Neither of us spoke, I was lost in her eyes. I reached up and touched her cheek. She put her arm in mine and we walked back across the street. When we reached the sidewalk, I stopped and turned her towards me. "Mollie,..................."

I had no sooner gotten the word "Mollie" out of my mouth when she took my hand and pulled me into the hotel parlor.

As the latch caught in the door, I took her in my arms, pinning her lovely body to the wall. As I squeezed her tightly, my lips found hers. There was no doubt that each of us wanted the other completely. The wild abandon of her kiss, so warm and soft, yet so bold and flaming with desire. Could this really be happening?

As our lips parted, I started to speak. But I could feel someone behind me. As I turned, hand already on my gun, I could see old man Crane, the hotel clerk, at the top of the stairway. I had noticed Crane before, when I was sitting in the lobby reading and Mollie would walk down the sidewalk across the street. It was obvious that he lusted after her. A man can sense that about another man. I was also reasonably certain that his affection was not returned. I sometimes make my judgments quick about a man. In my line of work that can be important. I considered Crane to be a weak, sniveling little man. Not the kind that you would expect to cause trouble, not in a stand-up way. But he had certainly seen enough in that brief moment to cause Mollie a lot of grief.

"Crane, come down here", I said. He took one step and stopped. "Crane, now!" I ordered more sternly. He slowly came down the stairs and stopped. "Over here by the door, Crane." He stopped a few feet from us and I asked him a question, "Crane, did you see the wagon that they use as a hearse go by on its way to the cemetery today?" I knew the answer. Not much went on within sight or hearing that Cornelius Crane did not have his nose into.

"Yes," he answered. I knew that the whole town knew the results of last nights gunfire.

I explained briefly and in a very matter-of-fact way that the man in the pine box in that wagon was a man who had tried to come between me and something that I wanted.

" Crane, I know that in your little mind, you think you have witnessed something that you can spread around town and impress everyone with how you caught Mollie in a slight indiscretion. But what you really need to know is that if one word is spoken about this, if one person says anything derogatory about this lady, or if she even suspects that someone may know something by their actions toward her, I won't go to the Marshal, or to the Mayor, or to the City Council. I WILL BE COMING TO YOU! Do you understand Crane, is that perfectly clear to you?"

Crane was speechless, but his head was nodding up and down. To make things even more clear to him, I turned to Mollie. "Mollie, if for any reason you come to think that Mr. Crane here may have opened his mouth about you or us, all you have to do is let me know."

As Mollie was nodding her head, I glanced back at the sheepish hotel clerk. He was pale as a ghost and he was beginning to shake. I looked down and saw the yellow liquid running across his shoe and onto the floor.

"Don't let us hold you up Crane, I'm sure you have things to do." He was gone in a flash. As I turned back to Mollie, she had noticed the puddle on the floor and was trying not to laugh. I put my hands on her waist as she looked up at me. "Mollie, I don't think anyone knows you are here except our new friend. Would you like to come up to my room?" I can't believe I just said that! What if she says no? What if she says yes?

"Mollie, I'm sorry. I should not have......"

CHAPTER SEVEN

Yes! That was all I wanted to say! My feet would have carried me up the stairs, but I knew in my heart it wouldn't be right. And, so did he. I couldn't even allow him to walk me home. I was so weak at the moment, I doubt I could have turned him away if he had asked to come in. And, I had forgotten to feed Littlefoot again last night. Poor little cat!

Mr. Bogardis may never know just how much I wanted to follow him to his room that night. But, my life was changing, taking a different path, unexpected, something I did not bargain for.

I couldn't sleep again last night. I can barely make myself believe what actually happened. I acted so forward pulling Mr. Bogardis inside the hotel. I don't understand why he has effected me like this! His kiss, his consuming kiss, has only made me want him more.

He promised to see me tonight. He said he didn't know how or where, but he would see me when the sun disappeared and the shadows possessed the night.

But, for now, I find myself dreading the day at the dress shop with Mrs. Marks. With just days before the big dance, every woman in town will be coming in to pick up their garments. I wasn't in the mood to socialize, and Mrs. Marks always has plenty to say to everyone.

After working over an hour on a single garment, I must have stopped sewing and was gazing into my memory again when I heard, "Mollie, where is your mind today!"

"I'm sorry, Mrs. Marks, I didn't sleep well last night". Luckily, just as Mrs. Marks was about to inquire the reason for my loss of sleep, the door opened. Upon seeing the frail figure in the door way, my mouth dropped and I could feel the blood rush to my face.

It was Cornelius Crane! "Morning, Mrs. Marks, Morning, Miss. Mollie." I couldn't imagine what he was doing here! Without waiting for a response, he slithered closer to Mrs. Marks and bravely stated, "I feel it is time I stopped by and cleared up a few things in regards to you and the rest of the town council." His voice was a little weak as he continued, "I no longer have a concern as to who or what, uh, what I mean is, uh, what he's doing here in town." Mrs. Marks looked at Corney like he had just been kicked in the head by a mule! I could tell Corney was getting very intimidated. "I don't owe any of you an explanation. I will handle my own business without the concerns of..." Mrs. Marks interrupted him saying, "Speak up, Cornelius, for Pete's sake, what are you talking about!"

Corney kept glancing over in my direction as if he wanted my validation. He almost looked as if he could cry at any given moment. Mrs. Marks stood up, grabbed Corney by his shirt and warned him, "I don't know what has gotten into you, but you are just as much a part of this as I am. How dare you come into my shop and talk to me about....." I think she must have suddenly remembered I was still in the room! She lowered her voice, let go of Corney, and told him to leave, that it wasn't over. She then looked at me with loath in her eyes, and told me I had work that needed to be done. She gestured towards to the back room, indicating that I should finish my day away from her sight and out of her way.

I only need to make it through the day. I am existing in this world only to see Mr. Bogardis tonight. He has become my reason for being alive. As soon as the night arrives, and I see my beloved, I will not care what has happened in here today. Nothing else will matter.

*   *   *   *   *

I can't believe I placed Mollie in such an awkward position last night. I don't know what came over me........ that's not true! I know exactly what came over me. Her! Her eyes, her lips, her scent, everything about her compels me to reach out for her.

What might have happened if old Crane hadn't shown up? I know in my heart now that she wants me as I want her. Her kiss doesn't lie.

As the town starts to move this morning, I can tell something is going on. The "Pillars of the Community" are running around having little meetings with each other in some kind of panic. If they only knew what is about to come down, they would panic. Maybe the Gorch family has gotten to them.

I had a visit early this morning from an old friend, Texas Jack Vermillion. It's strange, but it seems that some of us who roam the West always seem to run up on each other. Texas Jack and I have known each other for quite a while, through some mutual friends. He came to bring some news to me. He has been up in Tombstone for a while and it seems that the last Gorch brother has been up there recruiting some folks to help him take care of me.

He has assembled quite a little group of supposed bad men. The funny thing is, none of these "bad men" would want to face a man down one-on-one. But put them in a big group and they all get real brave.

One of these so called gunmen, according to Texas Jack, had been snooping around Contention the day of the Gorch attack. Probably in cahoots with the Gorches. My guess is that he is probably to blame for the broken window at Mollie's dress shop. I don't know why a gunman would want anything in a dress shop, but you can never get into the mind of a killer.

Unfortunately for Gorch, he tried to recruit some friends of mine, Wyatt Earp and John Holliday. There was that time when Doc, that's what they all call John Holliday, saved Wyatt Earp's life in Dodge City, Kansas. Wyatt was unarmed and surrounded by a bunch of cowboys. Doc pulled his pistol and shot one, it caused the others to back down. Well, Docs' six gun didn't hold enough cartridges to scare off that many cowboys.   No one but Wyatt, Doc and some of the cowboys saw me standing at the corner of the building with a sawed off double barreled ten gauge covering the whole show. Afterward, Doc, Wyatt, and I became good friends. Good enough that they feel like they owe me. They are both in Tombstone, just up the road, along with two of Wyatt's brothers.

Texas Jack came down to let me know that I had all the help I would need, all I had to do was ask. Now all I need is some advance warning of when and how they intend to strike. According to Texas Jack, it would probably take them a while to get their courage up.

I promised Mollie I would see her tonight. But how? At least it has warmed up in the past few days. There is a storm on the horizon, I can smell it approaching. I think I will wait at my usual vantage point across the street at sundown. It does not take long this time of year for the darkness to close in. Twilight is very short. Perhaps we can meet, if for nothing more than a few moments. Could I hold her for only a few moments? No! I want her more than anything in my life. I am afraid that the next time I touch her, I will not be able to turn her loose until our desires are fulfilled. I am afraid, yet that is what I long for.

Maybe not tonight Mollie, but soon.

CHAPTER EIGHT

For the last two nights, I have prayed and thanked God for the rain storms! Lightening bolts flickered across the blackened sky allowing shadows to disappear in the darkness. Thunder, roaring louder than a lion's hungry stomach, was all that could be heard in the deserted streets. No one was aware of the two figures in the alleyway. Soaked and drenched from head to toe, pressed up against the bricks between the two buildings. Our only protection from the pounding flurry was the narrow channel above us, something the hotel used for gathering rain water.

It's a wonder that both of us haven't caught our chill of death, being out late at night in such a storm, but it was as if God Himself had granted us a gift. Mr. Bogardis and I were able to be in each other's arms completely oblivious to the rest of the town, moaning with eagerness and passion that was heard by no other's ears but our own. It wasn't for very long each night, but long enough to hold us and bond us closer to each other.

The storms have now passed and blown over the mountains. Everyone else couldn't be more pleased, as these were dangerous storms. Lightening killed a man over at Blinns Lumberyard in Tombstone! Mr. Bogardis hasn't explained everything to me, seems our time together was used for things other than talking, but he says he is taking me to the dance tonight. He has told me that he has good friends in nearby Tombstone. Friends he can rely on. He told me not to worry, that we will get through this and we will be together. That he will be mine and I will be his.

I still can't understand why, but I believe him when he tells me these things. And I, Mollie Lewis, should know better! Haven't I heard all the lies before? I am going to have to tell him! He needs to know the truth about me. How can I be his, when I belong to someone else? I may call myself Mollie Lewis now, but not long ago I was known as Mollie Fisher, wife of Sam Fisher.

No one in town knows my secret. I just arrived one day, alone, and they assumed what they wanted. When Mrs. Marks hired me on, and I told her where I was from up north, and that I had run from a man in my past. Of course, she questioned me further, but I gave such evasive answers that she was more confused than anything else. Occasionally, she would suggest an available gentleman of her liking for me to associate with, lecturing me that a woman should not live alone. Then, became disgusted with me when I declined their offers.

I know what I did was right. I did what I had to, to save myself and what was left of a broken life. I took only what was necessary when I ran and took the stage here. I was told this was a booming town, more employment opportunities than in Tombstone. I will explain all this, the truth, the whole truth, to my beloved soon. He will forgive me and understand.

But, for now, I hear the music playing in the distance. The fiddle players are warming up to the tune of "Oh my Darling Clementine." Wagons are heard coming and going from both directions and multi-colored gowns are seen on either side of the street.

Mr. Bogardis will soon be here for me. My instinct was to beg him not to take any chances on his life and be caught off guard during the dance. He has assured me that this is his desire, to hold me in his arms, to publicly display his affection towards me. Something no man had ever done for me in the past.

I have no looking glass in my room large enough to see my overall appearance, but I know my dress is glittering with gold threads and black lace. It has taken me an hour to wind and pin the hair on top of my head so that it falls gently around the side of my neck. I proudly placed the tortoiseshell comb my mother had given me before she died, high on top of the curls. I pinched my cheeks and dotted on a light scent of lilac oil behind my ears just before I heard his knock on my door.

Tonight, we are together for the entire town to see. Tonight, I will feel beautiful in the arms of a man I have waited for all my life. Tonight, is the beginning of forever.

*   *   *   *   *

This night has been a long time coming. I knew Mollie wanted to go to the dance, and I would do anything not to disappoint her. As I tied my tie for the fourth time, I wondered if I should have told her of the precautions I took to insure that tonight would be free of trouble for both of us.

It's time to pick up my sweet Mollie and set this town on its ear. More out of habit than dread, I check the street before I cross. Every thing appears to be in order. As I knock on Mollie's door, it opens immediately. She must have been waiting just inside. She is .....beautiful! Her hair is pulled up and secured with a tortoiseshell comb and falls gently around her neck. That same neck that I have pressed my lips against while hiding in the alley in the cold rain. Her dress shimmers, her lips seem to shine, but, as always, it is her eyes that captivate me. When she looks at me, I know that I have something that most men only dream of.

"Are you ready," I asked.

"Are you sure we should do this," she replies. "I don't want to endanger you by taking your mind off those men."

"Darlin', those men are the last thing we have to worry about tonight," I tell her as we start down the street arm in arm. "You know I would never do this if I thought there would be any danger for you."

A couple of days ago, I took a short ride out of town. I was gone most of the day preparing for tonight. Again I wonder if I should at least prepare Mollie for what was about to happen.

The only person in town who knows anything unusual may happen is old man Crane. When I got back from my ride, I asked him if there were three empty rooms in the hotel. He replied that there were. I instructed him to keep three rooms, side-by-side, available for Saturday night. I paid for them and gave him the names of the people who would be coming in. I also advised him that since he was the only person in town who knew about my guests, I would be "very disappointed" if the word got out. He just turned a little paler than usual, but at least he didn't piss in his shoe again.

As Mollie and I arrived at the town hall, I pulled her back into the shadows just inside the door. I wanted to see what might be going on. Out on the dance floor, I glanced at a good looking young man with a lovely young lady. Mollie asked if I knew them.

I explained to her that the young man's name was Morgan, and that his wife was Louisa. I told her to look toward the table with the punch bowl at another man, taller and leaner with an attractive lady. They had quite a crowd gathered around them. I knew that he must have already introduced himself and the others. "Mollie, that man is Morgans brother. His name is Wyatt."

"Wyatt Earp?", she exclaimed.

I confirmed that it was indeed Wyatt Earp and his wife Mattie. "The slim man on the bench against the wall with the grey coat is a dentist from Georgia. You may have heard of him. His name is Dr. John H. Holliday, but most folks call him "Doc"."

I took Mollie's arm and we stepped out the shadows. At that moment, Morgan saw us and let out a big whoop, grabbed Louisa, and ran over to us. He put his arms around Mollie and swung her in a circle, her feet off the floor. As he sat her down he gave her a big kiss on the cheek. "Mollie, you look great", he declared, and commenced shaking my hand while Louisa hugged Mollie.

As soon as Louisa turned to me, Wyatt had come over. Being much more restrained than Morgan, Wyatt put his hands on Mollie's shoulders and leaned down and kissed her gently on the forehead. "Mollie, if we had realized you were this close, we would have come to visit sooner," Wyatt said in a voice loud enough to be heard by any bystanders, especially since the music had stopped and you could hear a pin drop except for our conversation. As Wyatt and I shook hands, Mattie was making a fuss over Mollie.

Before we knew it, Doc had arrived with his companion, Kate Elder. Doc reached for Mollie's hand, put his arm across his waist, and bowed, kissing Mollie's hand. "Mollie darling, you look ravishing," he commended. Again loud enough for anyone to hear. Ole Doc, ever the southern gentleman.

As I looked at my Mollie, I could see her eyes roaming over the crowd. Every man and woman in the place was looking at us. The town that had cared nothing for Mollie or the stranger that they hoped would soon be dead in the street, had to stop and rethink their position. They still might not like us, but I would be willing to bet that they would not be as quick to show it in the future.

Morgan broke the silence. "Let's get this ball started," he yelled. With that, the fiddles started back up.

CHAPTER NINE

Just to comprehend what Mr. Bogardis has done for me, to make this night happen, is beyond my imagination. Seems that Mr. Bogardis traveled to Tombstone a few days ago and invited his friends, the Earps and Mr. Holliday, to come to Contention tonight. The plan was for them to claim they "know" me, like I am someone important, a friend of theirs. I was speechless at first, not knowing what to say. I hope the surprised look on my face didn't let on to the act.

Everyone greeted me so politely, so respectful. No one in their rightful minds would have the nerve to make a scene with this assembly of flesh and blood in their presence. Mr. Bogardis wanted to insure we would be safe tonight to enjoy each other and the dance.

Of course, everyone in town knows who the Earp's are! Their reputation is like a store bought paper book, some truth with exaggerated passion and falsehoods. Town folks stared at them in awe all night long, whispering speculations and hearsay. No one was brave enough to even look them in the eyes, let alone approach them with questions. They just talked around them and pretended to be decent and hospitable. Their dauntless stories of tonight will begin tomorrow, well after the Earps are back in Tombstone.

Just a month or so back, I remember hearing them talk about Wyatt and his other brother, Virgil. They said that back In October, when Virgil was assistant Marshall in Tombstone, Wyatt was in a saloon late one night and heard gun shots. He ran out into the street where Marshall Fred White was trying to arrest a rowdy cowboy. The cowboy accidentally shot Marshall White between the legs, setting his pants on fire! Wyatt put the shooter in a make-shift jail. The cowboy went by the name of Curly Bill. He turns out to be the same drunken cowboy that was in Contention making the preacher dance at the church meeting! Marshall White died a few days later and Virgil took over being Marshall, but he resigned two weeks later when the town elected Ben Sippy instead. News travels fast from Tombstone to Contention.

Wyatt's no longer in law enforcement either, thats what I overheard when Wyatt was talking with Mr. Bogardis tonight. He said that just a few days ago, he was out scouting water rights on the east slope of the Huachuca Mountains. I couldn't understand all the story, but it was something about his missing horse and who stole it, a young kid, a trouble maker, named Billy Clanton. His tone sounded like he was particularly irritated about it.

I liked the Earps. Apparently Wyatt was at no loss for cash, as he paid for all the refreshments, in spite of Mr. Bargardis' persistence.

He explained that he had recently sold some land and mines for a large profit. He said he was hoping to make some more investments in the town of Tombstone.

Wyatt is a little clumsy and rigid as a dancer, but Mattie didn't appear to mind it so much when he stepped on her toes quite often. I spent some time talking with Mattie and Morgan's wife, Louisa. Mattie was wearing a plaid gown, with ruffles across the sleeves and hem. She wore her hair in many rows of curls over her forehead, and longer curls at one side. She's not much of a talker, but smiled politely as Louisa swayed the conversation away from Wyatt's business ordeals. Wyatt mainly congregated with his brother, Mr. Holliday and Mr. Bogardis all evening, which I could tell bothered Mattie. She excused herself and sat alone the rest of the evening, complaining she was getting a headache, as the music was too loud.

The band played 'Aura Lea'. One of my favorites from years ago in my other life. I had to stop and swallow hard, as a glimpse of fear and pain seeped past my eyes. No one noticed. I thought it would be a good time to talk with Morgan's wife and distract myself to regain my disposition.

Louisa, or Lou, as she asked me to call her, is a little smaller than Mattie, a little more outgoing and refined. I could tell she really admired her husband, Morgan. She told me they had been living in Montana and moved to Tombstone only nine months ago. Lou's shorter hair, lighter colored than Mattie's, swept gently to one side, away from her face. Her eyes sparkled when she talked about Morgan, reminding me of how I feel about Mr. Bogardis.

Then, there was Mr. Holliday. He insisted I call him "Doc", like everyone else. A striking, good looking man, who kissed my hand as a greeting. His southern drawl sounded a little flirtatious and caused my face to flush. I got a sense that Mattie and Lou didn't care much for Doc, maybe because their husbands spent so much time talking and laughing with him. Doc was there with a quite handsome woman, hanging constantly on his side. She introduced herself as Kate. She was very brazen, gutsy when she spoke. She often looked towards me and smiled, like she understood in some unspoken way. I could also tell that she approved of my choice in a man. For a moment, I thought she was going to ask Mr. Bogardis to dance with her, but instead, he reached for my hand and guided me out onto the dance floor.

We danced and danced and danced! When I looked into his eyes, I saw my own reflection. It has been a wonderful evening. I didn't know my life, as this, could even exist. But, as I look around the room, everyone who hasn't already left is saying their goodbyes. The Earps and Doc and Kate are staying at the hotel tonight and leaving in the morning. Doc has had too much to drink and is leaning heavily against Kate. Mattie still has a headache and Lou and Morgan left arm in arm just minutes ago. I don't want this night to come to an end. As Mr. Bogardis walks me back to my room, my only fear is that tomorrow, when I awake, that this evening in all it's splendor will have only been a dream.

*　　　*　　　*　　　*　　　*

I only hope is that my darling Mollie has had a time to remember tonight. Doc and the Earps sure put this town on its toes. Everyone minding their mouths. I am sure everyone in town was thrilled to have this assembly of "known" men in their midst. It probably made them think that they (the town) were important.

Imagine the surprise they must have felt when Mollie and I walked in! First Morgan, then Wyatt, and finally Doc all clamor over to pay their respects to Mollie. Mollie, the sad lady that this town has looked down on ever since her arrival, became someone this night. Although I am sure the town will never take Mollie or me into their arms, I am equally sure that they will be very careful of how they treat her in the future. After all, Tombstone is only ten miles away. They must know that their guests of tonight could very well be here on short notice and would frown on any of their friends being treated disrespectfully. Imagine a drunk, pissed off Doc Holliday running around town looking for anyone who might have, in some small way, insulted one of his friends. No, I think Mollie, while not being totally accepted into the fold, will be treated somewhat better than she has been in the past. I can't help but believe that Mollie, like myself, has no real desire to be accepted into anyone's fold. I hope that I can someday be enough to fill her life and her heart, as I know she could fill mine.

Mollie has danced me to death tonight! I am not a dancer at all, but it did not take long to figure out that Mollie loves to dance. She seemed so happy when we were dancing. I only hope that her happiness, like mine, was not totally contingent on the dance alone, although it gave me the proper opportunity to hold her and touch her. Everything is winding down, Wyatt, Morgan and Doc and getting ready to escort their ladies to the hotel. Won't old Crane have a tale to tell! Wyatt Earp, Morgan Earp, and Doc Holliday all staying at his hotel. He really should thank me.

I managed to speak with all three of them briefly tonight. I wanted to thank them for coming down and making this a night for my sweet Mollie to remember, as well as for me. If Mollie is happy, I am happy. All of them assured me that they will be there if "we" need them.
It is time to walk Mollie home now. It is a surprisingly warm night for this time of year. We can take our time and walk slowly. I treasure every minute that her arm is around mine.

While we have had a brief break from the troubles we have, it is not over. There are still things that must be done if we are to have a life together. It will not be easy, not for either of us. But I will do whatever I have to do to give us the chance to make a new start to our lives. "Our" lives. I never thought I would use that term.
What should I do tonight? I want to take Mollie to my room and hold her all night. Hmmm...... If Doc and the Earps are going to stay up a while and drink back at the hotel, I am sure everyone would think that Mollie and I were with them. I wonder.....

CHAPTER TEN

Mr. Bogardis and I were one of the last couples to leave the dance. Neither one of us wanted to accept the fact that it was over. I wasn't ready to be taken back to my room, where I would be alone for the remainder of the night.

"Mollie, would you like to stop by the hotel and join the Earps and their wives for a drink before we end this evening?", he asked, more like an invitation than a question. I was sure Mr. Bogardis knew the answer would be "yes" since he was already leading me towards the hotel instead of across the street to my quarters.

I paced willingly beside him, smiling, looking up into his shadowy face covered by the wide brim of his black hat. I couldn't see his eyes in the darkness, but I knew he was looking straight ahead at the hotel door as we walked. The corners of his lips were hidden by his curled up mustache, displaying the same smile he had worn all evening.

After entering the lobby, we climbed the narrow stairs of the hotel to the second floor, and walked first to Wyatt and Mattie's room. As we approached room number five, we could hear blaring voices. The thin, cheap walls of the hotel left much to be desired for privacy. "I don't care, Wyatt! Why do you have to act like you do? Just leave me alone, I have a pounding pain in my head!". Just then, Mr. Bogardis and I flinched when we heard what sounded like something being thrown across the room. The crash was followed by a few choice words from Wyatt. I turned to look at Mr. Bogardis. He grabbed my hand and we headed down the hallway to Doc and Kate's room.

Doc and Kate were in room number seven. We paused for just a quick contained kiss on the cheek before Mr. Bogardis gave a gentle rap on the door. As we stood waiting in the hallway for the door to open, we could hear movement inside the room. It was a pulsed, thumping commotion and what sounded like an occasional moan.

Again, Mr. Bogardis reached for my hand and lead me away from room number seven. "I think Doc and Kate are having a private party of their own tonight, Mollie." His eyes twinkled, then he winked and let out a muffled laugh as he escorted me onward down the hallway.

Mr. Bogardis stopped and leaned against the door of room number ten. "Mollie, this is where I stay. I feel like I can't go on like I am, leaving you each time and feeling this emptiness. There should be something else..... something that is missing." I starred blankly at him, but I knew what he was about to say, because I felt the same way. His bottom lip was slightly quivering as he spoke. Still holding my hand in his, he caressed it tighter as he continued, "I have to tell you..... Mollie, I have to tell you....... I love you."

The words hung thick in the air. I seized them and tucked them away for safe keeping deep inside my heart. He loved me! I whispered in return, "I love you, too."

Mr. Bogardis pulled the key out of his coat pocket and opened the door for me to walk through, then bolted the door behind us. He held my face in the palms of his hands and pressed his lips to mine. Our eyes were open, fearful of missing a single moment.

He pulled the tortoiseshell comb from my hair and enabled the locks to fall on my shoulders. He ran his fingers across the loose strands and chills ran up my back. I watched as he carefully unbuttoned the front of my dress and slid the fabric slowly away from my skin. White cotton undergarments covering only my torso, silhouetted my frame, making a shadow on the wall.

Moon light trickling in through the street side window caused his face to glow like a halo. Impatiently, he yanked his coat and shirt off and tossed them feverishly onto the floor. Pulling my body tight against his, he lowered me gently on to the bed.

"Mollie, I don't want to do this if you're not ready", he said, speaking softly into my ear. His tongue ran along the ridge of my neck. The feel of his mustache tickled and caused me to sigh. I was afraid I couldn't breath. I could hear my heart pounding and throbbing against his body.

The hairs on his chest glided through my finger tips as my hands roamed instinctively downwards. I opened my mouth to speak, to assure him that I wanted him as much as he wanted me, but nothing came out. It was our eyes in the pale moon-lit room that did all the necessary talking.

There is a lapse of time in my memory........... minutes, hours.......... I can't distinguish. Desire overwhelmed us, and we became as one.

Lying side by side, he held me in his arms as our breathing resumed to a slower rate. Resting my face against his warm, damp skin, I can finally close my eyes and not be afraid. I will not allow my other life to creep into my thoughts tonight. There will be no fear, no guilt, and no remorse to destroy what was happening to me. I fell asleep knowing that this was real, this night, this feeling, his love, it was all real.

As we strolled arm in arm in the cool midnight air, I could feel her body against mine, our sides touching with the gentle sway of her hips. I was feeling the dread of having to leave Mollie at her room and spend the rest of the night wishing I was with her. I gambled and asked her if she would like to stop by the hotel and visit with the Earps and Doc before we called it an evening. Somehow, I knew she would accept.

I would have used both of my left feet forever to please Mollie dancing tonight. Her smile, the glow in her eyes, made me feel like the evening was so important to her. I could not understand why she did not have that many suitors to count, as I am sure she has had plenty of offers. Why she chose me, a stranger off the street, is beyond my understanding.

When we arrived at the hotel, there was no one in sight. Crane had already gone to bed. I don't even recall seeing him at the dance all night.

We climbed the stairs to the second floor and proceeded to Wyatt's room. Before I could knock, we heard Mattie screaming at Wyatt. Something about the way he treated her. There was a loud crash, something probably broke against the wall. At that point, we heard Wyatt tell her to shut her damn mouth and take another drink of Laudanum, if that was all that would satisfy her.

I decided not to interrupt. I pulled Mollie on down the hall, to Doc and Kate's room. As we stopped at the door, I bent down and kissed Mollie gently on the cheek. Damn this woman! I feel like I have to be touching her all the time. Anywhere I can put my lips on her skin sends shivers through me.

I had barely knocked on the door when we realized that Doc and Kate were preoccupied. It was not hard to figure. The sound of what appeared to be the headboard banging against the wall told the story pretty well.

Morgan and Lou's room was further down the hallway, but I stopped just as we reached room number ten, my room. As we stood together, pausing with a little awkwardness, I pressed Molliehard against the door with my body. The feel of her beasts against my chest was making it hard to concentrate. There was something I had to tell her, but I was unsure of how she would respond. After a few moments of stuttering and stammering, I finally blurted it out. "Mollie, I love you." There was a brief pause, then I felt her lips against my ear as she whispered, "I love you, too."

I could not get the key out of my pocket fast enough! I opened the door and gently pushed her quickly inside. I used her body to shove the door closed and hurriedly bolted it. As I held her face in my hands, we kissed, long and deep with our eyes open. If I could have nothing else, the look in Mollie's eyes when we kiss is worth any price I would have to pay.

When I lowered her gently onto the bed, I could feel her body quiver. I managed to muster up enough decency to ask her if she was sure about what we were doing. She answered by placing her hands eagerly on my body.

Because of all the things I have seen and done, perhaps life is now more precious to me. Death was my companion in that damn war, then through the Ranger years fighting Mexican bandits, Indians, and outlaws. After that, death continued to ride with me as I hunted down those with a price on their head. But what better way to savor life than the act of making love?

Mollie felt my passion, my intensity. My every touch, every move, was to share these things with her. I have loved her with my lips in ways that the Parish Priest would probably not be able to grant atonement for. We kissed as we writhed on the bed, our bodies already joined together, breathing in uniform.

We loved as long and as hard as our strength would allow. My final thrust caused Mollie's body to shudder, then her throat let out a sound that was familiar to me. The prim and proper "Yankee" lady, from somewhere up north, let out what to me sounded like a "Rebel" yell!

As we lie there in each others arms, I know to whom my heart belongs. I still have trials to face, but I know I have a reason to go on. I was in love with Mollie.

CHAPTER ELEVEN

Things were moving very fast. Especially time. Maybe because time is something you can't hold on to, you can't control, and once it's gone, you can never get it back.

Time has passed so quickly since I first met Mr. Bogardis. The past two months since I have been with him have been like another lifetime. He makes me forget that I have another life somewhere outside of Contention. I still haven't confessed my past to my lover. The truth is always on the tip of my tongue ready to be spoken, but "dirty" like the stamp mill air it breathes upon. I lie and tell myself, I will explain everything to him tomorrow, but later when tomorrow comes, I am convinced that the truth will make no difference in how we feel about each other. So it remains unspoken, but never forgotten.

Since the dance in December, a perpetual smile has graced my face. Just the thought of seeing Mr. Bogardis causes my heart to race and my legs to become weak. But, this love that I feel for him is what I blame for this veil of deceit that tortures my soul. How long can I keep my serene composure and hide the truth he needs to know?

I did leave a lawful husband up North, if you want to call him that. Sam is a spiteful man who I know will never forget what he thinks I have done to him. My life was so different back then. I married with the intentions of loving Sam for the rest of my life. But, it wasn't long before I figured out I was not what he wanted for a wife. His comfortable home, his land, his possessions, his money, they were not what I wanted either. Especially how he came about these holdings. By the time I found courage to run, I was already in too deep with what I knew. Sam won't forget. The notches on his gun reminds him everyday of what he has done and what he must do. I fear he will come looking for me and take back what belongs to him. I pray each night that he will never find me.

Regardless of what I have done, life does go on. Time does not stop for anyone or anything. The city paper is full of news about the railroad coming to Contention. They are already making plans to build a new two story depot on the other end of town. Talk is that Contention will prosper more than Tombstone in the next few years. Last week, it was announced that we now reside in the newly formed "Cochise County", with Tombstone becoming the county seat. Time will bring prosperity to Contention. Time will bring changes to everything.

Mr. Bogardis has been busy these past few weeks. We see each other as often as possible, but he has his business to settle, and he prefers to keep it at a distance from me. Sometimes, it is like Mr. Bogardis is actually two different men. The man who is waiting in Contention City with a hand always on the grip of his Colt's revolver, and the man who kisses me with consuming desire. I wish I could separate them from each other, the good from the bad. But, I suppose one is needed to balance the other in this wicked world.

Earlier tonight, Mr. Bogardis met up with Wyatt and Doc Holliday over at McDermott's Saloon. Two other men were traveling with them from Tombstone, Dick Clark and James Leavy. Seems they just filed for water rights in the Huachuca Mountains. Wyatt told Mr. Bogardis that he and his brothers are doing real well with all their recent land purchases and mines. They will soon be moving into separate housing. He said once they are settled in their new homes, he would be pleased if Mr. Bogardis brought me to visit with the wives.

And, so it seems, the Earps, the dentist from Georgia, and even the town of Tombstone are all doing well with the time that God has granted them. Who could ask for anything more than time?

After the meeting at the saloon, Earp and his friends left town allowing Mr. Bogardis and I to have some private time of our own. We walked just before sunset to the diner and ate supper sitting side by side. It had been raining again, and more storms were just off in the distance. It took me back to the nights Mr. Bogardis and I were in the ally way and we were soaked to our hides! Even the remembrance of those passionate nights seem lost in a gap of isolated time. There is just never enough time.

After supper, we walked back to my room, stepped just inside the entrance, leaving the door cracked just a few inches. Our lips were against each others and his hands were gently stroking the side of my face.

We both heard it at the same time! It sounded like a shotgun blast. At first, I thought maybe it was a close bolt of thunder striking within spitting distance of my front door. But, the storm was still a mile or so away. Mr. Bogardis was never without his gun, and his hand is frequently positioned and ready to draw at any given moment.

"Stay inside, Mollie! Don't open the door no matter what you hear."

Just like that, he was gone in an instant and disappeared out of sight in the dark uninviting streets of Contention. I locked the door behind him and lowered my lamp to dim glow. I was so confused about what just happened, all I could do was catch my breath.

In a town like Contention, it could be anything, rowdy cowboys, drunk miners, even malicious boys. I know Mr. Bogardis can not take any chances, especially when it comes to me. People in this town speculate about the relationship between me and Mr. Bogardis, and there is just no telling what they are thinking. Neither of us have much of a welcome here, we're both outsiders, even after the events of the dance. It is apparent that they would like nothing better than to be rid of us both.

If he doesn't find the culprit of the explosive sound, Mr. Bogardis may be up all night safeguarding my door. He is like that, he would do anything in his power to protect me. It will be a long night, not the first and not the last.

All I want is to sleep peacefully beside him. Every night. To press my body against his as we rest untroubled side by side. Is it too much to ask? I have waited for him so long, I don't want to wait any longer.

But, the time is not right. There it is again..... time...... ticking...... and ticking away. leaving, gone so quickly, and yet I'm always wanting more.

I dressed for bed with a heavy heart, with mixed emotions clouding my mind. I knelt beside my bed and prayed. I pleaded to God to bring him back to me and give us more of what we need............ time.

*   *   *   *   *

My intentions were to stay with Mollie long into the evening, even though it would probably not be prudent in our situation. The sudden shot we heard changed that. I ran out and told Mollie to lock the door behind me not to open it for anyone but me.

As I stepped out into the night, it seemed like I was walking in a dream world. It has been this way for me for a long time. I sleep very little and then only for brief periods. The nightmares are always there. Mostly the past, sometimes the present, and even into the future, the images in my mind haunt me. The worst part is when I awake in the night, and the dream continues. I once heard it told that a nightmare when you are awake is called a delusion, or something like that. It doesn't matter what you call it, it is terrifying. I can't make it stop.

My salvation from this hell is Mollie. It should be me protecting her, as far as physical harm is concerned, but it is Mollie who has pulled me from the abyss. Her kiss, her touch is enough to hold me in the real world. The world we want together.

There is usually very little going on this late. As I ventured out into the darkness, not far from Mollie's door, I spotted two miners running eastward down the alley. Their argument with each other was barely perceived by my ears, cuss words muddled in the stagnate breeze. The shotgun still in the hand of one of them as they ran out of sight.

I wanted to go back to be with Mollie, but I knew I should stay away, especially after knowing what Clark and Leavy told me tonight in the saloon. It's better I hang out in the shadows and keep an eye on her place until sunup.

It gives me time to think.

At a campsite, just west of town, seven men are drawing their plan for Bogardis' last days on earth. I couldn't tell Mollie. I hate to keep so many deliberate secrets from her, but it's best she does not know every thing. Maybe I was with her tonight hoping she could distract me from the inevitable.

Along with the last Gorch brother, Elvin, there were two Gorch cousins, three so called hard-cases found drifting in and out of Tombstone and one Texas gunman whose name I did not know. Clark and Leavy say he looks like the devil himself. He's rumored to have beat a man to death in Yuma over an insult during a Faro game. But, as any gambler will admit, tempers sometimes flair while bucking the tiger. Hard to say what kind of a man he is and why he's riding with this bunch. Last they heard, the man was in the Fairbanks jail before he joined up with Gorch a few days ago.

Texas Jack had already warned me of Gorches

scheme to kill me when I last met up with him. I've been aware of what they were planning for some time now. I am grateful they have waited this long to make their move. The Christmas dance is over and Mollie and I have had some times to remember! If they kill me tomorrow and I'm lying cold in the ground, I would die knowing that I have been loved by my Mollie. That will be all I would ask of my wasted life.

As the sun began to climb it's way up into the Arizona sky, it brought a hazy luminosity over Contention City. I had been outside all night and again sleep has evaded my body. The cold air must have frozen my senses, I could hardly feel my feet inside my boots. I'm thankful that the storm passed in another direction, at least it wasn't wet.

I dragged myself into my room at the hotel to warm and clean up a bit. I wondered if this Gorch thing would ever end as I washed and shaved my hardened face. The mirror on the wall didn't lie. I didn't feel much like a man right then, especially one that the likes of Mollie would want.

My stomach rumbled from hunger, it had been awhile since I last ate. I figured the diner would be open by now, as the morning hours progressed to sometime after six o'clock. Mollie would be up dressing for the day and would soon be on her way to open the dress shop. I can't help but to think of her every movement, whether I am with her or not, she is never far from my thoughts.

I crossed the empty street and walked to the diner, not many folks out this time of day. The winds are blowing in from the north and there's a smell of death in the air. I pulled the collar of my coat up closer to the back of my neck. Strange, how last night it was much colder than this, but I don't recall the bone chilling temperatures with Mollie's safety on my mind.

There were very few people in the diner when I arrived. Maybe it's too early for breakfast. Old man Hopkins called to me from behind the counter and asked me what will I have. I heard myself ordering coffee, black and strong.

I just finished my first cup and was deciding on how

many eggs to order when a familiar face walked in. It was Bill Davis from Tombstone. He was susposed to have been riding with Wyatt's bunch from yesterday, but for some reason, he chose to stay behind. I could see the look on his face as he approached my table. In a concerned compelling tone, I heard him say, "Bogardis, we need to talk."
This can't be good.

CHAPTER TWELVE

It was a chilly night, but the embers in the fire started to liven up with flames when I added the morning log. I washed and dressed hurriedly before I sat down to eat a bite of sweet bread.

I should have been more fearful for myself when we heard the gunshot last night, but it is Mr. Bogardis that I am afraid for. Maybe the gunshot had nothing to do with him, he does keep a tight eye on his surroundings. I don't know everything about what his business is, it's better that way. I would only worry for him more than I do. But, I can never be sure the shotgun wasn't intended for me.

I picked up the brush to comb my hair and there on my desk in front of me, I starred at the blank sheets of paper I had used to write Mr. Bogardis those intimate letters. It feels like so long ago. Somehow, I had courage to reveal my intimate feelings to a man I didn't know.

Wait! What am I doing?

Suddenly, a wave of guilt rushed through me like a hurricane and literally made me sick to my stomach! I'm a married woman! Though I have not entirely lied to Mr. Bogardis, I now find myself hiding the truth from him - the man I love! This has gone too far. I am not who he thinks I am.

I could hardly breathe! I was so stunned by my abrupt thoughts of reality that I couldn't even cry. If Mr. Bogardis knew who I was, or that I was married to Sam Fisher, I couldn't blame him if he never wanted to see me again. I cannot face that thought!

I don't know how long it took to compose myself, but when I regained my thoughts I was holding the quill in my right hand. Looking at the sheets of paper, It was time I told him the truth. I am too full of shame to confront him so my only recourse will be in letter form. Oddly enough, our relationship had started with my letters and now a letter will end it.

Since I was not thinking within reason, I thought this was the only choice I had left. I could confess and hope for his forgiveness and continual love for me. But, I could not see that happening. I am not worthy of him. I knew then what I had to do.

I had to leave.

I guess I had always known that this day would come. I had little to pack. I could be gone and out of town when the first stage arrived this morning. No one would care. No one would notice. Of course, Mr. Bogardis would search for me, but his efforts would be exhausted as soon as the letter arrived and he knew he truth.

I could have Hey-You deliver my letter later tonight. By then, I will be miles away and out of his life. It will be better this way, for him and for me. I have only been deceiving myself, believing I could be with the man I love and settle down with happiness. My life was over when I left Sam, and the sooner I accept this, the sooner Mr. Bogardis can get on with his life.

But, I do owe Mr. Bogardis an explanation! My love for him was no lie. I have to do this, I have to write him one last letter. God, please steady my shaking hand and give me the words to justify what I am doing.

*　　　　　*　　　　　*　　　　　*　　　　　*

Bill Davis was an acquaintance of both the Earp's and myself. I was surprised to see him, especially that early in the morning. "Bogardis, we need to talk", he said as he pulled up a chair. "I got some bad news." Already my heart was pounding.

He was supposed to be riding with Wyatt and his bunch up into the mountains, but stayed behind in Tombstone to assist Virgil Earp. It seems that Virgil asked him to come find me as soon as possible. There was an arrest made last night of one of their town drunks. He was sober enough to make a deal with Virgil to save himself. The fellow overheard Gorch discussing a murder to be carried out in Contention. It only took Virgil a second to put two and two together. He dispatched Davis to come and warn me. Since Wyatt, Morgan and Doc were still out of town, and Virgil himself guarding three prisoners, I would be on my own. I thanked him for the information and asked him to send my gratitude for all the help that the Earp's have given me since my arrival in Contention. I told him this was no time to be sticking around town, but if he would, also relay another message to the Earps for me. Ask them, in case of my demise, to kindly check in on Mollie for me from time to time.

We shook hands to bind the commitment and I watched as Davis rode out of town. I wasn't sure if Hopkins had eavesdropped on our conversation or not, but it didn't matter. I knew there would be no help from this town in regards to the Gorch gang and me.

I thought it wise to drop by the Marshal's office and inform him of the coming trouble, if for no other reason, for his own protection.

I trudged down the dirty sidewalk and sticky clay street with only one thought on my mind, Mollie Lewis.

When I arrived at the Marshal's office, it was unlocked with a note attached to the door saying that he was out of town for a few days. Hmmm, how convenient! Again, no surprise. I presume this tells me it could be anytime now.

Well, the way I figure it, even if the Marshal himself won't help, I don't see any reason why his office can't. I stared at the row of rifles and shotguns along the back wall secured in a rack. I looked inside the desk, and luckily came up with the key to the lock on the chain guarding them. I slipped it inside my pocket for safe keeping. I plan to "borrow" a couple rifles and few shotguns when it gets dark tonight, if I'm still alive by then.

I need to see Mollie, even if it means going into the dress shop today.

I hurried about my duties and kept a faithful eye on the entrance of the dress shop. Unfortunately, Mrs. Marks showed up first. Mollie must have woke late, it was probably a long night for her.

I shouldn't be seen with her right now anyway, it's too risky. Gorch could be anywhere. I wish I could explain everything to her. I would change the world for my Mollie, if only I could. I'd like a chance to hold her once more, maybe even tell her goodbye. Seven to one ain't likely odds. There's not much of a chance I will survive.

I head back to the saloon, put my back against the wall, and wait.

CHAPTER THIRTEEN

It didn't take long to gather my things and place them into my carpet bag, but I was over an hour writing the final letter to Mr. Bogardis. I am a coward, running from my past, preventing a collision of tears and emotions if I stayed. I will miss the life that I made here in Contention. I will even miss Mrs. Marks and the dress shop. I will miss Hey-You and his father. I really wanted to be more of a friend to them both, maybe even teach Hey-You to read. But, most of all, of course, I will miss Mr. Bogardis. I will miss his tender touches, the way he stares into my eyes, and.....

But, this is not the time to be regretting the decision I have just made. I need to stay strong and move swiftly. I counted the money I had saved, rolled it up and hid it securely inside my bustle. As I took one last look around the room, I could feel the familiar pain of my heart shattering deep inside my chest.

Carrying only one bag, I checked the street to be sure no one was watching before I hurried off to the Chinese Laundry to give the letter to Hey-You. I moved quickly, peering into every pathway and alley along the way. The likelihood of seeing Mr. Bogardis was a long shot, I knew he'd been up all night watching my door and probably asleep by now. Still, I needed to be careful.

Hey-You and his father were attending to their usual morning chores. I explained to the boy that I needed the letter to be delivered to Mr. Bogardis around eight o'clock this evening. It was very important that he have it then. I handed him two bits and before I walked away, I bent down and kissed him gently on the forehead. We exchanged a brief smile, and I turned quickly away before the tear fell down my cheek.

I was the only passenger when I arrived at the Kinnear Stage Line office. I asked for the first stage out of town. I was told it would be arriving within the next half hour and on it's way to San Francisco. I paid the ticket fee and began to pace the floor. San Francisco was a large city, easy for one to disappear into the hustle and bustle of all the ongoing chaos.

I was thinking about the letter I wrote. I explained everything. Maybe one day, Mr. Bogardis will forgive me for the pain I have caused. But, I cannot dwell on that now.

What is done, is done.

*   *   *   *   *

83

Dooley, the bartender, is not a very likable fellow. But, then again, I haven't ran across many who are very likable here in Contention. None the less, Dooley keeps the coffee coming to my table and doesn't ask any questions.

It was getting late in the afternoon. Still nothing was happening. Not a single drifter in here today. A few men from town come in for an afternoon drink to wet their whistle, but nothing suspicious. Hell, maybe I am wrong. Maybe it's a setup, a scheme to throw me off course to defer my attention from something else.

I started to feel a little light headed, and remembered that I still hadn't eaten any food. I called for Dooley and asked if he served anything other than cheap whisky and coffee. He said he would see what he could scrounge up.

With this empty time on my hands, I can't help but sit here and reflect on my past. My regrets are many. When I rode as a Texas Ranger, the star upon my chest proudly represented my belief in the justice system. My mother would have been proud of me. But, I just don't know anymore. When did it all change? When did I become so cold?

I think back on the day my conflict with the Gorches began. I was down in Maverick County, Texas, just across the Rio Grande River from Mexico. First Lieutenant Hall placed me in charge of escorting a couple of men back to Austin for a murder trial. A Texas outlaw gang had been rustling cattle and stealing horses, killing dozens of men in the process. The men I was escorting were caught from that gang, most of the others escaped and sought refuge at a family ranch near by.

It was the third day out, I think, I was ambushed at camp just as the first light of morning made an appearance. I felt the weight of a man coming out of the darkness as he landed squarely on top of me. I pulled the gun from my holster and began spraying lead. After the smoke cleared, three people lay dead. Two of them named Gorch. I took a bad hit that day and lost a lot of blood, but you can bet that the men I was escorting arrived promptly in time for their trial. I hauled the dead men back on the supply wagon and Elvin Gorch came to claim the bodies.

He didn't take kindly to the killing of his brother and father. He overlooked the fact that they were trying to kill a Texas Ranger and liberate a couple of fugitives before they went to trial. Gorch offered a hundred dollars in gold to any man who would gun me down on the spot. He thought his money was enough to cross over the border of right and wrong. I left the Rangers shortly after that.

From that day on, Gorch and his younger brother have been persistently threatening my life. That is until a few weeks ago when I shot one of them dead in the alley. Dooley sat a plate down in front of me on the table. The smell of a half rare piece of steak brought me back to the present. Without a spoken word, I nodded my appreciation to Dooley. I needed my strength. This could be my last meal.

CHAPTER FOURTEEN

I watched the hands of the clock on the stage office wall move in slow motion. There it was again, that ticking of time! It was following me where ever I went. When will I ever stop running? I have to remember that I am doing this for Mr. Bogardis, for I have hurt him enough, deceiving him as I have.

"Miss, are you alright?" I turned around and saw the ticket clerk motioning for me to sit down. "Ma'am, Coach number 74 is running on schedule. Maybe you should rest your feet some before it arrives, you look a bit peaked."

I guess maybe I did look somewhat frightful. "Thank you, but I think I will stand." I wanted to stay by the window and watch the streets. I couldn't allow Mr. Bogardis to find me here.

Finally, I saw dust rising in the distance from the gallop of the stage horses. The ticket clerk was correct, the stage was on time.

There were a few other travelers on the stage as the driver helped me board. Two gentlemen in suits were on the seats facing front-wards. They greeted me with "Good day, Ma'am". I sat on the bench facing the gentlemen, sitting beside a frail looking woman, head bowed, dressed in black mourning attire.

Within minutes, the driver was back up front, and I felt the jerk of the stage leaving Contention. We were on our way. The first stop would be just a few miles up the road in the town of Fairbanks.

*   *   *   *   *

I waited in the saloon, only departing the chair to relieve myself. Sundown had taken it's time. I took my pistol from the table, rolled the chamber a time or two, and placed it back into my holster on my hip. It was time to take a walk to the Marshal's office.

Unlocking the chain from around the weapons, I helped myself to a couple of rifles and three shotguns. I grabbed enough ammunition to load them all. Now, if I can just carry out my plan without anyone suspecting what I am doing.

I hid one of the rifles inside the Marshal's office, near the door which I left partially cracked. The other in the alley by the general store. One of the shotguns, the sawed off ten gauge double barrel, I hid behind some bushes in the alley by the dress shop. Then, another shotgun around the corner by McDermott's Saloon, the last one out of sight behind a hay bale at the livery stables.

It was just after eight o'clock. I was sure no one had seen me. I started walking back toward the saloon to sit it out, when I saw Cornelius Crane running in my direction. "Mr. Bogardis, Mr. Bogardis!".

"What the hell is it, Crane?"

"This was delivered for you just a short while ago. The Chinese boy said it was very important." He waved a piece of paper at me, an envelope addressed to me. I took the envelope from Crane, who looked like he was having trouble breathing, and walked into the saloon.

It was Mollie's handwriting.

I tore open the paper and removed a letter. I could feel something was wrong. I knew I was tired, I hadn't slept in over two days, so I had to read the letter twice to make myself believe it.

My Dearest Darling,

Please forgive me for what I have done to you. I couldn't bear it if I thought that you would regret your love for me these past few months. Please allow me to explain.

My name is actually Mollie Fisher, 'Mrs. Sam Fisher'. Being a former Texas Ranger, you are correct if you assume Sam is kin to the outlaw, John King Fisher. Sam rode with his cousin, King, out in Texas in the later part of '77. He stole horses and rustled cattle across the river to Mexico. He and King earned a reputation for gunning down any man who got in their way. When King was arrested, Sam left the family ranch on Pandencia Creek and fled up north into the Ohio Valley.

That would be where we met. I didn't know about Sam's past when we married. King was never charged with any of his murders, and his gang was growing stronger everyday. Sam wanted us return to Texas, he said King was a powerful man. He said no one in the entire country would testify against King Fisher or his clan. He said they had it made, he and King could have whatever they wanted.

I did not want to live like that. I didn't want to live with a killer.

While Sam went to wire King to expect us, I took my belongings and left. I knew Sam would never let me go, he considered me his property. I took only enough of the stolen money to buy stage fare. I ended up in Contention City when the money was gone.

I was content to live out my life alone, hiding from Sam and never knowing if there would be a tomorrow.

Then I met you.

For a short while, you caused me to forget my burdens and heartache. You gave me passion with your kisses and tenderness with your touches. You made me feel loved like I have never felt it before in my life. I will never forget you.

But, it is too late for us. I can no longer lie to you. I belong to another man and he will see to it that it stays that way as long as he lives. I am hunted like an animal. When you read this letter, I will be far from Contention and out of your life. You must not come looking for me. Please understand that it has to be this way.

Your forever in my heart~

Mollie

I sat in the saloon with the letter crumbled up at my feet and the pistol in my hand. An empty bottle of whisky rolled off the table in front of me. Mollie was gone. I wanted to die.

"Gorch come and get me!" I yelled, half drunk and loud enough for the entire town to hear me. The most dangerous man in the world is a man who has no reason to live.

CHAPTER FIFTEEN

It was close quarters inside the coach. I couldn't help but listen to the other three passengers' conversation.

The woman beside me was introduced as a recent widow, Mrs. R. W. Todd. The two gentlemen in suits were her brothers-in-laws, Walt and Oliver. They were on their way to Fairbanks to identify and claim the body of her husband.

Apparently, Mr. Todd was in Fairbanks last week on business and decided to sit in for a game of poker. They said he wasn't much of a gambler, and most likely couldn't win at playing cards even with a marked deck! From what they were told, the ante was upped and Todd's small fortune lay on the table in front of him. When Todd lost the hand, he accused the fellow he was playing with, a drifter, of cheating. He'd lost everything he had to take back home. Before he could defend himself, the drifter pulled his gun and shot him dead. He left him lying in his own pool of blood and went on to continue playing the card game.

The Marshal in Fairbanks arrested the gunman and locked him up in city jail. But, later that night, six men wearing kerchiefs partially covering their faces, broke him out. Almost destroyed the entire jail doing so.

When the stage arrived in Fairbanks a short time later, the driver informed me that there would be a delay in traveling onto San Francisco. He said work was required on the coach, something about a king bolt needing to be repaired. He directed me to where I could get a meal and rest up and wait until the departure.

I wasn't tired or hungry. As I looked around, the street was full of ladies, smiling and walking arm in arm with their gentlemen. Not something I wanted to see right now!

With time on my hands, I thought maybe I could be of assistance to the grief stricken family I had met on the stage. I offered them my condolences as they were about to walk away.   The brothers asked, if it wouldn't be an inconvenience, would I so kindly assist them with their sister-in-law in this occasion of sorrow. By all accounts, she was taking the death of her husband pretty hard.

"Of course," I answered, and slipped my arm around the thin waist of the woman as I followed them to view her dead husband's body. In a way, I was also feeling the loss of the man that I loved. Though Mr. Bogardis may still be alive, I would never see him again. My heart was breaking right along side Mrs. Todd's.

We were approached by the local lawman, Frank Carter, along the way. We paused as he explained he had organized a posse to look for the gunman and the other six men who broke him out of jail.

He said, although the men were masked, one of them was identified as Elvin Gorch. Gorch lived nearby and owns one of the stamp mills in Contention City. He said, although Gorch controls the law in Contention City, this murder and jail break was in his jurisdiction. Carter said he would do whatever was in his power to see that the men were brought to justice. Though Carter knew Gorch, he explained that he didn't know the connection between him and the man who killed her husband, known as Sam Fisher.

I was so light-headed, I couldn't stand. Did he say.... Sam Fisher? My jaw dropped and I felt faint...dizzy.....frightened. I backed away from Carter and Mrs. Todd, carrying my carpet bag as I moved. I said not a word.

Sam Fisher was here.

*   *   *   *   *

I had sobered up and denied my body of any rest. What the hell do I need sleep for anyway! My eyes burned from the smoke rising off the rolled tobacco leaves Dooley had lit between his teeth. My mouth was dry, maybe I did need another drink. As I slammed the empty bottle back down onto the table, Mollie's stray cat jumped down from the chair beside me and rattled my nerves a bit. Damn that cat!

Dooley had his eyes on me since I came into the saloon last night with Mollie's letter in hand. It appears Dooley himself doesn't care for sleep much either, as he went in his back room for only a few hours before sunrise and returned. It would be a long day of waiting.

It was coming up on three o'clock in the afternoon when I heard the call. It was Gorch in the street outside the saloon calling me out. I got up slowly, no use in hurrying. Dooley glared in my direction, I shot him a look back. He dropped his bar towel and made a run for the back door. I edged up front and peered out the saloon doors. I could see

Gorch and two men beside him, I knew there was seven all together. I needed to get a heads up on the others.

People seemed to be running in all directions, getting off the street. I surveyed my surroundings. I spotted one stranger standing near Wells Fargo. A rough lookin' character, twirling his pearl handled pistol with his right hand. Another fella with his foot propped up on a chair outside the telegraph office, trying to look inconspicuous. Both of these men would be behind me if I walked into the street to face Gorch. That leaves two missing, they could be anywhere or anybody.

Hell, might as well get this started and over with, I said to myself. I moved closer to the door and looked out at Gorch. Gorch and his two friends were watching me, waiting for me to make a move. I walked out and stopped at the edge of the sidewalk. I had no intention of walking into the street just yet.

Gorch taunts me, shouting, "Come on out, Bogardis!"

No point. One of them will get antsy soon enough and come after me. I assumed correct. The one on Gorches right went for his gun. I was ready and I got the first shot off. I hit Gorch in the shoulder. He was my target. My second bullet wiped through the center chest of the man who drew his gun all too slow. He staggered a bit and hit the ground lifeless. The man on the left ran to the other side of the street. I didn't see which direction Gorch went. I turned and emptied my first pistol towards the man by Wells Fargo. Bullets were flying and nipping at his heels as he moved for cover. I got him, down he goes for keeps. The one by the telegraph office ran and ducked inside a store front.

I hit the dirt, sliding near the saloon corner and grabbed the hidden shotgun.

I saw the gunman just inside the door, cocked both barrels and let him have it. He dropped dead on the sidewalk, breaking a few boards as he fell. I turned lose the shotgun and made a low run for the Marshal's office. I dived in the cracked open door and retrieved the loaded rifle as the bullets slammed into the door frame.

The man from the street was now behind a water

trough. He rose up and and fired two shots in my direction. I returned fire hitting the side of the trough. Water came pouring out in different directions. He came up again, fired, and I fell to the floor as if I'd been hit.

Lying still, I held the rifle in a steady position, aimed at the top of the trough. When he came up the third time, I shot once, hitting him between the eyes. He fell backwards, the force of the bullet shoving his head against the wall behind him. Four down, three to go.

Gorch was still out there, wounded but alive. No one else in sight. The only thing left to do is try to draw some fire. With the rifle at my hip, I walked out the Marshal's door and down the sidewalk with my back to the wall. A bullet hit high on the corner post and I dove into the alley by the general store. I had no idea where it came from. I looked for the other rifle I had hidden and it was gone! Whatever is left in this one is gonna have to do.

Lying in the dirt, I saw Hey-You and another kid, hiding under the sidewalk overhang. One of the kids was pointing upwards towards the building across the street. I moved into a position to better see what they saw. There was a rifle barrel sticking out past the facade. I can see where he is, but it's a long shot. When his head came into my rifle sight, the poor fellow never saw the 44-40 bullets coming! I emptied the rifle and he rolled off the roof like a sack of grain.

There's still Gorch and one other man out there. I cautiously step out into the street. A bullet whizzed by my ear. I saw Gorch, soaked with blood, coming at me. I dropped the rifle, drew my second pistol and begin firing. Walking toward him, I unload all the lead my six gun held and blasted it into his chest. His only shot hits me in the thigh and I go down, but Elvin Gorch will trouble me no more.

It's a bad hit, there's a lot of blood. I guess that is what this town would want, to see me dying in the street. I felt someone walk up behind me. I tried to get up, but I'm kicked back down. I brought my pistol up to fire but all I had were clicks, I had emptied the gun into Gorch. The man walked around and stood in front of me. He looked hard at me, vengeful and full of rage. He spit a wad of tobacco out of his mouth. I wondered what he was waiting for, why don't he just finish me off!

"Well, what the hell do we have here!", he smirked as he watched the tobacco splatter on the tip of my boot. "If it ain't the fearless Texas Ranger Bogardis! You and I had a run-in a few years back. You recall... Marshall County, Texas? I was riding with King Fisher when you killed Marvin Gorch and his son. You thought you could arrest me and King and haul us in. Gorch wanted to hire me to kill you then. You'd been dead already if I hadn't rode up north instead. Just to tell you now, nobody arrests Sam Fisher! But, this must be my lucky day........ it seems that we both have a mutual interest."

So this is Mollie's Sam Fisher! I wanted to kill him with my bare hands!

"I had a little reunion with my wife, Mollie, yesterday", Fisher continued with a cold stare in his eye. "I always thought I would just kill her when I found her, but I changed my mind when I figured out about the two of you. She belongs to me and I'm taking her with me to Texas. She's gonna remember she made a fool out of me for the rest of her life. Just thought you might wanna know that before I kill ya." My guns are empty and I don't have enough strength to charge him. I don't care that I die, my only regret is that I cannot avenge my sweet Mollie. He raised his gun with a sick smile on his conceited face. I saw his finger tighten around the trigger. Then, I heard a loud blast in my right ear. I watched as Sam Fisher bent over, his gun going off into the ground.

I jolted around. Behind me, up the street a good ways back, was Mollie. The sleeve of her dress was torn, but in her arms she was carrying the sawed off ten gauge I left in the alley by the dress shop. Not at her hip, but at her shoulder. Mollie was deliberate! The first barrel hit Fisher in the stomach, but the barrels were too short for the long range, and only proved to slow him down. Mollie continued to walk towards us at a fast pace, shotgun still high on her shoulder and her hand on grip. She was twenty feet away when Fisher straightened up and aimed his pistol.

"Shoot Mollie!" I yelled. "Shoot him!"

The ten gauge bucked and Fisher took the charge full in the chest. When he hit the ground, he twitched only once before his last breathe. Mollie threw the gun down and ran to me. I could see her eye was blackened and her lip swollen.

I tried to smile at Mollie's bruised face. That's the last I remember before I passed out.

CHAPTER SIXTEEN

I sat by Mr. Bogardis' bedside for three days. He lost a lot of blood and only regained consciousness for a few minutes at a time. Fever had set in and he was oblivious to what had happened in the street.

I wanted so much for him to wake up! I rubbed his forehead with a damp rag while talking to him as if he were listening to my every word. It was what I had to do to keep my sanity through all this confusion and pain. I covered his body with another warm blanket, then held his hand and ran my finger along his knuckles, speaking softy as I continued on with my story.........

"That morning after I left Mrs. Todd, I walked back to the stage office to pull myself together. I sat down on the bench outside the door and buried my head in my lap. Sam must have been watching, maybe even following me because when I sat up, he had grabbed my arm. He began dragging me down the alley to where he had tied his horse. I struggled the best I could, but he threw me on the horse and we rode out to a campsite a few miles out of town. I was scared Sam and the other men would have their way with me, but their hateful obsession towards you preoccupied their minds. Sam bound my wrists and ankles with rope so I couldn't escape."

"At sunup, Sam brought me back to my place, pulled me inside and bolted the door. He said I should have never taken that money from his stash, no matter what amount it was, it was his! Then, he wanted to know where you were. He wanted me to watch as he put an end to it all..... and end to you and me. But, I wouldn't tell him anything."

"Sam told me that he had known where I was for some time. He said he broke into the dress shop one morning and had planned to kill me then. The only problem was he had seen you that same morning and recognized who you were. He kept on eye on every move we've made since then and realized how strong our feelings were for each other."

"He knew the Gorches from their association with King Fisher. He said you were familiar with King Fisher too. He mumbled something about how Gorch and King had wanted to kill you for a long time."

"Sam said Gorch confronted him in the saloon in Fairbanks that night he killed Mr. Todd over a card game. Gorch told him that he had the opportunity to finish something he had started a long time ago, kind of a two for one deal. When Gorch busted him out of jail, they laid up just a ways out of town and waited to make their move."

"It was just before three o'clock in the afternoon when Sam started to get restless. I watched him as he checked his guns in preparation. He grabbed my hair in his hands, came closer and whispered into my ear saying that today was a good day for 'Contention'. Today was a good day for the vendetta to end. He struck me a few times, reminding me of my life before I ran. When he pushed me against wall, I must have fallen and hit my head. When I woke up he was gone."

"I knew he'd come looking for you, so I ran across the street and over to the hotel. I pounded on your door to no avail. I called your name over and over again. Corney heard me yelling. He said he hadn't seen you in two days. He didn't know where you were."

"I didn't know what else to do. I thought maybe if I went to Mrs. Marks, with her influence, she might persuade the town council to help us. Someone needed to do something! I ran to the dress shop. Mrs. Marks took one look at the condition I was in and proclaimed I was in need of a doctor."

"I begged her, 'Mrs. Marks, please hear me out! Sam Fisher will not only be back for me, but also for Mr. Bogardis. The town needs to help us!'"

"I didn't expect Mrs. Marks to respond the way she did. I saw fear in her expression and concern in her eyes as she blinked back tears. She wanted to make it clear as she spoke, 'Mollie, you don't understand.'"

"'The town council has always been fighting against the Gorch family', she went on. 'Gorch has threatened to put us six feet under if we didn't pay him off. When Mr. Bogardis came to town, we'd heard he'd been a Texas Ranger and thought maybe we finally had some hope. Gorch found out about our intentions to hire him to protect us, to make our town a safer place to live. The Marshal had his instructions to come and tell us, that if we didn't conform to Gorch's authority, Gorch would shut us all down. We tried, Mollie, but there is nothing anyone can do for you..... I'm sorry.' "

"I left her scared and crying, and slammed the door as I ran out. As I passed the alleyway, I noticed what I thought was a shotgun barrel, obstructed from view by a few pieces of tumbleweeds. At the same time, I heard Gorch in the street calling your name, demanding you to come out and fight."

"That's when I stepped into the alley and grabbed the shotgun. I was horrified when I watched the the gunfire blasting from one man to the other. It all happened so fast, I didn't know if you were alive or dead. When I saw Sam step out into the street, I knew he was ready to kill you. I put the shotgun to my shoulder with no doubt about what I was about to do."

"I guess you know the ending, Mr. Bogardis", I said, finishing the story for now. I was tired and I needed to rest.

It was three days ago and still hard for me to think about. I prayed for Mr. Bogardis to wake up, for the fever to break and the wound to heal. There will be many more wounds to heal after this. I ran my fingers through my tangled hair and lowered my head down on Mr. Bogardis' chest as he slept. I listened to him breath as I closed my eyes .... and cried.

I had killed my husband, Sam Fisher.

*   *   *   *   *

Maybe it was the scent of Mollie's hair, or the sound of her muffled cry that caused me to wake up. When I opened my eyes, Mollie lifted her head off my chest, the tears still wet on her face. I saw her look of relief when she realized I had awakened. Her crying got louder, but this time I'm sure it was out of joy. I held her in my arms and we clung to each other for what seemed like forever.

"It's gonna be alright now, Mollie" I said trying to comfort her. "It's gonna be alright".

I was able to get myself up and start moving around after a couple of days. Mollie never left my side. She kept trying to explain everything, but I told her it wasn't necessary. I just smiled and kissed her tenderly. We looked into each others eyes, just like that very first day on the sidewalk. In Mollie's eyes I saw everything I needed to know. I told her not to say a word, that our time in Contention together was all that mattered.

Everything was different now. Cornelius Crane and Sara May Marks come by together every day with well wishes. They bring us food, canned fruits and fresh roasted pork. There's a twinkle in Crane's eye when he looks at Mrs. Marks, who appears to be dressing mighty fit these days! Crane says, now that Gorch is out of the way, the town council will reorganize and elect new city officials. They even asked if I'd be interested in becoming the new sheriff.

Neither Mollie nor I am very attached to this town. We've got places to go. As soon as I'm able to ride, I promised Mollie I'd take her to visit the Earps. Wyatt checked in on me just yesterday. Said Doc is on one of his three day drunks but sent along his good wishes for Mollie and me.

I asked Mollie if she'd consider leaving with me, maybe traveling up to Prescott and find a nice place to settle down, call our own. Hell, I even told her we'd take that damn gray cat of hers with us if she wanted!

Prescott's a good town to start a new life together, if she'd say 'yes'. I know we've been through so much in the last few months, and there is so much she doesn't know about me. But, I told her I would explain everything to her about my past, anything she wanted to know.

She didn't say a word. Holding her hand in mine, I looked down into her smiling face as she gave me a tender kiss.

And, in Mollie's eyes, I saw everything I needed to know.

CHAPTER SEVENTEEN

Mr. Bogardis was ready to leave Contention City as soon as the doctor told him he had recovered enough to travel. Instead of visiting the Earp's in Tombstone, Wyatt had made arrangements to gather us all together in Prescott. The wives had been wanting to shop in the city while the men had business to conclude at The Palace.

It was a wonderful reunion, but only lasting a few days.

Mr. Bogardis and I had thought about going back up North and retrieving any gold Sam may have hidden. But, we didn't want to start our new life together with tainted money. We will make do with what we have. Mr. Bogardis and I settled in a small but quant home near Gurley Steet. We began living under the assumption of man and wife.

On warmer evenings, Mr. Bogardis and I stroll arm in arm, crossing over the foot bridge at Granite Creek. The stars reflect in our eyes as the crickets sing, and I am happy. Without the threat of Sam in my life, I seem to be laughing at any given moment, giggling and glowing!

I have made a friend in Prescott, her name is Lilly. She works at one of the dress shops. She's younger than me, almost like a sister that I never had. Mr. Bogardis has found pleasure in teasing me about Lilly. He says I would make a fine mother someday.

The last few days, I have been a little indisposed, mooning around like a lovesick lass! Maybe the change in climate has contributed to my delicate condition. Still, I have never been happier! I wake each morning with Mr. Bogardis by my side. From the moment we open our eyes neither of us want to move! I only hope it continues like this.

Only time will tell.

*   *   *   *   *

Prescott is a bustling little city. With all the mining going on in southern Arizona, Prescott has become a supply hub.

Mollie and I settled in easily after the long stage ride. The doctor in Contention hold told me that I would have a pronounced limp for the rest of my life. But it's only been a few months and the limp is barely noticeable. So much for that old sawbones!

Between the two of us, we had saved up a fair sized poke. Not enough to buy a ranch by any means, but enough so that we can take our time and just enjoy each others company for a while.

With my sweet Mollie by my side, I sleep later than I can ever remember.

We're always touching each other all through the night. Even the nightmares that have plagued me for years, have since subsided, displaced by Mollie's touch.

One of Mollie's favorite places in town is the dress shop. She had gone to the shop her second day in Prescott to make a minor repair in her traveling dress. It seems that as she was climbing out of the stage at one of the rest stops, her dress caught on the door and tore a small hole in it.

There was a young girl in the dress shop who Mollie immediately took up with. Mollie says the girl reminds her of herself when she was that age.

I have to find work soon. I have some leads and know a few men who are influential in Prescott. John Fremont, the Territorial Governor, resides not far from us. Maybe I'll make a visit and call up a favor or two.

If all else fails, I have been offered an opportunity, if you want to call it that. It seems that a small but brutal gang has been terrorizing the farmers and ranchers in Arkansas, Texas and Oklahoma. They always manage to escape pursuit by going deep into the Indian Nations.

It would be worth a lot of money if I could put a stop to them. It's not a good time to leave Mollie, and I haven't told her yet. Having her in my life causes me to weigh decisions that I used to make on the spur of the moment. I want to make Mollie happy, any way I can. I plan to do whatever is necessary. She is the love of my life.

I won't let anything stand in my way.

Time in Contention 2

Contention 2

The Return from Prescott

by
Cindy Smith and T.B. Burton

CHAPTER ONE

It is hard to leave Mollie behind in Prescott. We have been together so long now that I may have forgotten how to look out for myself. The months of having her take care of me may have spoiled me. But, at the same time, I realize that she looks to me to secure our future together. My mother passed on some fifteen years ago, and I have not had anyone dependent on me since. I thought I would never want to provide for anyone other than myself. Mollie has brought so much joy into my life that all I can think about is providing for her well being.

We still have money on deposit in the bank, but not enough to last a lifetime.

I have spoken with Governor Fremont on several occasions, and he hinted he might have plans for me in the making. But, instead of waiting, I decided to head out for Tucson. I thought I'd see if I could find anything to make a living at. I took just enough money out of the bank to take care of my expenses, which left Mollie enough to last for quite while.

I know there is a gang that is causing a lot of trouble up around Fort Smith, Arkansas. They do pretty much as they please and run into Indian Territory when things get hot. I understand that the rewards for all ten of them totals more than four thousand dollars. That could really set us up! But, Fort Smith is such a long trip. I couldn't be away from Mollie that long even if I thought I could earn the money. The odds aren't real good in my favor.

Mollie took it pretty hard when I told her my plan, but she is a strong woman and knows that we will need money. She even mentioned trying to get some work in the dress shop while I am gone. I think it would be good for her and I am sure she would enjoy Lilly's company. They make quite a pair! Besides, Mollie has been acting kind of strange these past few weeks. She would do well to have more female company.

*   *   *   *   *

Mr. Bogardis had his mind made up when he told me he was leaving. He is such a hard headed man and I understand that he is only doing what he thinks best for us. I just sat on pins and needles in the arm chair, in the parlor of the house I had tried to make our home. I blinked back tears and looked away as he explained about going to Fort Smith, Arkansas. He couldn't look directly at me. He paced the floor in front of the window, stopping only long enough to glance outside at the carriages rolling by.

He was wearing his traveling clothes. His dark canvas trousers, his suspenders and pocket vest. I knew there was no use in trying to sway him from leaving. I couldn't tell him. I have only known for six weeks or so, but inside me rests the unborn child of Mr. Bogardis. I had been waiting on the perfect time to make the announcement to him, hoping he would be filled with joy. But, now is certainly not the 'perfect' time. It will have to wait.

I gathered my thoughts and told Mr. Bogardis that I would be all right here in Prescott on my own for a while. I told him I suspected Lilly may have more work than she could handle at the dress shop on occasions and this would give me an opportunity to offer my help. He told me he thought that was a good idea, to keep myself busy. Mr. Bogardis said there would be enough money in the bank for any expenses while he is gone. Again, I assured him that I would do just fine.!

It seemed that Mr. Bogardis had thought his plans out precisely, as he had already bought a stage ticket and was leaving within a few hours. He was already packed and I had been oblivious to his intentions. I placed my hand on my abdomen and forced a smile for Mr. Bogardis, hoping that he would not see my sadness.

I had our mid day meal already prepared, so Mr. Bogardis and I dined together as usual, our unadorned wooden chairs positioned side by side. From the beginning, Mr. Bogardis and I have enjoyed our meals sitting next to each other. It was not unusual for his left hand to glide softly along my right knee and travel upwards on my thigh. I would acknowledge the gesture with a smile and place my hand behind his back and softly rub his shoulders. These simple acts of passion between us was an every day occurrence in our new found lives together.

After we finished our meal, Mr. Bogardis said it was best that I did not accompany him to the stage. It was better we say our farewells here in private. He took me in his arms and held me so tight, I was worried he might feel the extra weight I have gained! He loves me so much, I know this, but part of me feels lost without him around me.

We kissed, knowing that it would be a long while before our lips would touch again. His forceful eager kisses, hungry with desire, left me lingering for more. I watched him go into our bedroom to collect his hat and baggage and walk out the front door. I called out, "I love you", and he turned and walked back for one last kiss.

This time, I allowed the tears to escape my eyes and wet my face. I watched his strong, muscular silhouette walk toward Granite Creek and eventually out of site. I stood at the doorway for what seemed like hours. Maybe I thought, or rather hoped, that he would change his mind. Maybe, It was only a dream, that he wasn't really gone. Perhaps when I awake in the morning, he will be lying beside me, curled up with his leg over mine and his arm around my waist.

No. No, I knew better, he was gone.

CHAPTER TWO

I decided to go by stage from Prescott to Tucson, taking my saddle with me. I could always pickup a good horse in Tucson. I rode in the company of two women and two men. Common folk, probably out and about for a journey to visit kinfolk or something. It doesn't take very long for me to get bored with their conversation. All I could do was stare out the window and think of Mollie. What is she doing right now? Is she thinking of me? Does she miss me the way I miss her? I hated to leave her, but some things are just necessary for a man to do.

Four quick shots immediately bring me out of my daydreamin'! The stage comes to a halt as three men on horseback surround the stage with guns drawn. We were probably half way between Phoenix and Tucson, so there wasn't gonna be much help available. While still mounted, one of the men ordered everyone to throw their guns out the window and climb out with their hands up. I obliged, to a point. When travelin', I always keep my second pistol strapped high behind my hip so my coat covers it completely.

As we all get to the ground, two of the robbers were on our side of the coach, still mounted. The third jumped down from his saddle, walked toward us and ordered everyone to produce all jewelry, money, and wallets and drop them in the bag he was holding. He said 'if anyone was wearing a money belt, they could take it off themselves or he would take it off after they were dead.' Somehow, I didn't like the sound of that.

One of the men started trying to produce his money belt when the leader shot him. All three of them laughed at the bleeding man laying face down in the dirt. One of 'em suggested that they might ought to search the ladies.

I heard a few frightened cries as their attention was turned to the woman-folk. This was the opportunity I was waiting for! Reaching behind my back, I swiftly drew my Colt. I fired off a shot towards the gunman on the ground. Hit him in the side of the head. Before he hit the dirt I pulled the trigger twice and shot both men who were still mounted. One fell immediately while the other tried to ride away.

His horse bucked and made it about a hundred feet before the outlaw fell dead on the ground. I knew the first two were done for, so I ran to the third man. My bullet had caught him in the side, going through on an angle. Pretty painful and a fair amount of blood, but he would survive.

During the excitement, I had forgotten about the driver and shotgun rider. I looked up and both of 'em were still sittin' on their seat with their hands in the air. I couldn't tell from the look on their faces if they were shocked or scared half out of their wits. Maybe both. When they realized the fightin' was over, they climbed down and began checking out their passengers.

One passenger was dead, two bandits were dead, and we had one wounded bandit to worry about. One of the women became hysterical and wouldn't stop cryin'. It was most likely her husband that lay dead on the ground.

With the help from the drivers, we tied all three of the dead men to the horses. I patched up the wounded bandit, who looked a little too old to be in this line of work, and tied his hands together. I explained to him that as long as he behaved and did exactly what I told him to do, he'd be given over to the first lawman we could find. If he did not cooperate, I wouldn't waste a lot of time tryin' to keep him alive. We could always just leave him, with or without a bullet in his head. Wouldn't make much difference this far out.

We finally calmed the grieving woman the best we could and situated her back into the stage. I thought about Mollie. What would she do if somethin' would happen to me.

The rest of the trip was uneventful. We arrived in Tucson and I told the shotgun rider to take the wounded man to the Marshal. I then secured a room, had a hot bath and shave, and proceeded to the nearest saloon. It had been a long day!

*　　　　*　　　　*　　　　*　　　　*

Mr, Bogardis had only been gone a day when a Mr. Bill Williams knocked on my door. He was sent by the Territorial Governor. Mr. Bogardis knew Mr. Williams and for some undeclared matter, he did not approve of him. I could only wonder what he was here for as I stood face to face with him at the door.

"Good day, Madam", he announced. I nodded in response, leaving a crack in the door of about twelve inches wide. I did not like Mr. William's demeanor. I watched his eyes roam up and down my torso as he paused between his words, causing me to shutter with disgust.

"I have come at the request of Governor Fremont to speak with Mr. Bogardis".

John C. Fremont was the Arizona Territorial Governor since '78, he lives not far for here on Gurley Street with his wife, Jessie. He has quite a reputation as a man who gets what he wants. I have heard Mr. Bogardis speak of him in business matters quite often. Since a young girl, I have heard tales of Mr. Fremont and his adventures with the late Kit Carson.

"I regret to inform you that Mr. Bogardis is not available. He has left town on business," I answered him. "Is that so", he replied. Mr. Williams sounded as though he was grateful for Mr. Bogardis' departure. "Do you know when he is scheduled to return?"

I wanted to lie and say 'any day now', but I just shook my head.

"Then I will advise Governor Fremont on the situation".

I thought Mr. Williams lingered a little longer than required after his last words, so I ended the conversation with a 'good day, Sir' and shut the door.

Later in the afternoon, I answered another knock at the door. This time it was Governor Fremont himself! He was dressed in a gray tweed doubled breasted suit with a large black velvet bow tie. His hair was a little unkept, but his beard was well groomed and trimmed. His eyes were deep set, and at first appearance, looked sorrowful. I was much surprised to see a man of his authority come calling on his own accord! "Mrs. Bogardis, I presume?" he asked.

I am Mollie Lewis", I confirmed. "What can I do for you?"

Narrowing his eyes and titling his head just a little, he asked, "It is my understanding that Mr. Bogardis is out of town, is that correct?" I see that Mr. Williams must have reported back to the governor accurately. Strange, how both Mr. Williams and Governor Fremont reminded me of children's puppets! The kind with painted wooden faces and strings that dangle and get all tied in knots after they are played with.

"When do you expect him back?"

"Mr. Bogardis has business to take care of and I do not know when he will return. May I inquire as to the nature of these questions, Governor Fremont?" I was being bold asking such a direct question, especially after declaring myself not be the wife of Mr. Bogardis.

"Miss Lewis", he stated looking directly into my eyes, accentuating the name 'Lewis', "As you are aware of, I am John C. Fremont, Arizona Territorial Governor. Can you get word to Mr. Bogardis to contact me immediately? I assume you do know how to reach him."

Men! And men with power are the worst. They think they can talk down to women, women like me and it is acceptable. If only Mr. Bogardis was here!

"Yes, Governor Fremont," I hesitated to answer but that was what he wanted to hear. "I will certainly try to reach him as quickly as possible". He then spoke of the State of Georgia, where both he and Mr. Bogardis were from. I thought I heard him say he once knew Mr. Bogardis' father. He mumbled a sentence that I did not fully understand, but I believed that he intended it that way.

He then left without so much of a 'good bye' or 'good day'. He just turned and walked back to his expensive black carriage waiting, parked at the edge of the street. His servant rushed to his side and extended his hand to help him board. The Governor accepted and I thought, Mr. Bogardis would never allow himself to be assisted in such a manner!

The sun was beginning to set and I did not like to be out on the streets of Prescott this late in the day. It would be best if I waited to walk to the telegraph office first thing in the morning. Our little cottage of a home was within walking distance from Whisky Row. Many times we set out for an evening stroll and crossed the foot bridge that separates the rest of the town from the roughage of Whisky Row. Mr. Bogardis and I would hold hands and gaze up at the stars, and all the while a drunken brawl could be heard just a block away outside one of the many drinking establishments on Whisky Row! I promised Mr. Bogardis I would be all right, so I must not take any chances on my safety. Besides, there is another reason to take good care of myself these days! I will get up early in the morning and walk to the telegraph office.

As I undress and prepare for bed, I wonder what my life would have been like if I had never met Mr. Bogardis back in Contention City last November. I was content on living the rest of my days alone. I would not hesitate to let any man know that I didn't need anyone! Now, I can't imagine my life without him. Even though he is not here tonight, I can still feel his presence. I never doubt his love for me, but I wonder, does he know just how strong my love is for him?

I looked down at my growing stomach. "I wish I had told him", I whispered to myself. But all in good time. Mr. Bogardis will be back soon enough.

I awoke the next morning well rested despite the absence of Mr. Bogardis at my side. As I opened my eyes, I saw the first ray of sunshine fighting for an appearance between two tiny pin holes in the curtains. I immediately rose up, gathered water for my morning bath and prepared myself for the day. I wanted to arrive at the telegraph office when they first opened.

It was a beautiful spring day! The birds were chirping from the tree tops, flowers were blooming in the gardens and the sky was the color of Mr. Bogardis' eyes! If only Littlefoot were here! Mr. Bogardis offered the idea that Littlefoot could make the trip to Prescott with us, but I knew he wasn't taken with the stray cat like I was. Besides, she has a new home. Mrs. Marks was very kind to volunteer and give Littlefoot food and shelter in my absence.

As I walk on Gurley Street, I slow my pace when I reach the Governor's house. It's not a large house, but rather smaller then expected for a Governor and his wife. It has two tones of paint and sitting porches on each side. Mrs. Fremont has servants who work in the yard during the day. It is pleasantly shaded by tall towering trees with buds that have already begin to bloom.

Spring is so beautiful! The early morning breeze is blowing just enough to gently sway the flowering stalks of day lilies near the sidewalk. I can smell their fragrant scent as I pass by the still sleeping house of the Governor, his wife and daughter.

Mrs. Jesse Fremont appears to be a very highfalutin woman in town. Lilly says she will not wear the dresses in her shop, but insists that she order them all the way from New York City! She speaks the French language as well as any refined lady who lives in Paris. I sometimes see Mrs. Fremont with her long flowing hair, adorned with jewels that her husband lavishes her with, passing by in her private carriage. With all due respect, she rather seems polite to me, even greeting strangers as they gawk at her appearance. I do suppose most women could be resentful of her beauty and outspokenness. She is said to be a lady by her own means, writing books and being a respected author. I've never read any of her books, but I would like to, given the opportunity.

As I approach the telegraph office, I ponder what my words will be to Mr. Bogardis. I miss him terribly and it has only been a matter of days!

"Miss Mollie! Miss Mollie!" It was Jimmie, Lilly's younger brother. He's an early riser on a school day! "Miss Mollie, Lilly says for me to tell you to come by the dress shop this morning." I bend down just a little to pat Jimmie on the head. "Off to school, young man!", I tell him. I see Lilly standing in the dress shop door entry and I wave at her, a confirmation that I will come by after the I visit the telegraph office. It will be good to have a friend to talk with today!

CHAPTER THREE

Feeling somewhat refreshed, and more or less cleaner than I was, I entered the nearest saloon I could find. I saw a small table over in the corner. Perfect for me. I put my back to the wall and waited for a drink. One of the girls came over and I asked for a cup of coffee and a bottle. Wearing a frilly red dress, low cut and tight at the waist, I thought she looked too young to be working in a saloon.

There were several people at the bar for the time of day. Things seemed to be getting pretty lively real quick. I saw a large man come through the door and head in my direction. He was a mountain of a man and had star pinned to his vest.

"You Bogardis ?" he asked. I said I was. He introduced himself as the town Marshal, and asked me a few questions about the attempted stage holdup. There was not much I could tell him, other than what happened. I knew none of the bandits. He informed me that there had been a series of holdups in that general area, and the three men I brought in fit the descriptions of the bandits. Of course, the stage company had not told any of the passengers that. That would not be good for business. The Marshal also informed me that there was a hundred dollar reward being offered for each of the bandits, dead or alive. He stated that the stage company considered the matter closed, and I could come by at my convenience and pick up my money. Not bad. I made three hundred dollars for just trying to stay alive.

As the Marshal left, I sat there and pondered my good fortune. I am still alive, I gained three hundred dollars, and the most wonderful woman in the world is mine. I am a lucky man.

The noise and commotion from the bar brought me back to the present. The young girl who had brought my coffee and whiskey was being handled roughly by an old codger who appeared to have had a little too much whiskey. A younger man who had his eye on the girl told him to release her. He did, but snarled that 'no one told him what to do!' I watched the drunk man's hand move slowly down toward his gun. The kid told him "I don't want no trouble".

But the old man replied that it was a little too late for that, as he intended to kill him.

The kid held his hands out from his sides, showing his intentions of not wanting to fight, and said that he was leaving. As he turned his back, the old man yelled "I'm gonna kill you boy" and started to draw his pistol. The kid spun around, his Colt coming out faster than the eye could see. One shot rang out and the old man hit the floor, one hole centered dead square in his chest. The kid looked around before holstering his gun. You never know who else might want to take a turn. He didn't need to worry about anyone jumping in. My own Colt was in my hand. I would not have let anyone interfere.

Something about this young fella seemed mighty familiar to me. I have seen him before, but couldn't quite place him. He holstered his gun just as the Marshal reappeared. The Marshal asked the kid, the bartender, the young girl and couple others what had happened. He saw that I was still sitting in the same place and came over. "Did you see what happened here, Bogardis?" he asked.

"Yep," I said. "If the kid had not killed that old man, he would be dead himself."

The Marshal allowed how that was good enough for him. Before he left he ordered someone to clean up the mess and get the dead man's body out of here. Bad for business.

The kid looked my way and I motioned him over to my table. "Fancy running into you here, Mr. Bogardis," he nodded and said. I explained that although I was sure I had seen him before, I could not quite place where. "You remember a dark night in Contention City when you needed someone to hold a lantern?" he asked. Of course! He's the kid who held the lantern and went into the alley with me the night I killed the youngest Gorch brother. I stood up and held out my hand. "I didn't get a chance to thank you that night, so let me buy you a drink," I offered. He declined the drink, shook my hand saying that he only allowed himself to indulge two per evening, and he was already there.

He said his name was Zack Blade. He explained

that he and his brother had gotten tired of working on his folks ranch just a few miles outside of Contention City and decided to look for something else. We talked a good hour while I drank weak coffee chased by a half bottle of Dickel. I asked him to have breakfast with me at the diner next door first thing in the morning, as we might discuss the need for both of us to secure work and make money, if he was interested. It must have intrigued him as he agreed before he left the saloon.

I swallowed the last drink in the bottle, just as I watched the young saloon girl in the red dress head up the stair case, her arms wrapped tightly around the waist of a drunk cowboy with coins jingling in his pocket.

*   *   *   *   *

"Good Morning, Lilly"! She and I hugged liked old friends who have been apart for years as I entered the dress shop. "I just left the telegraph office", I continued. "I had to wire Mr. Bogardis that Governor Fremont had been inquiring about him."

I didn't want say too much, and I tried to sound petty, and hoped Lilly wouldn't ask too many questions of me. I was right in my assumption, Lilly had paid no attention to what I had said. She had her hands attached to a large bolt of material she couldn't wait to show me!

"You must look at this Mollie. Wouldn't this be just divine for a maternity dress! You and I could sew a gathered false front panel and it would be just perfect!". I ran my fingers across the fabric Lilly was holding. It felt like expensive silk from across the ocean. "Lilly, this is much too elaborate for me. I think we have plenty of time for sewing a maternity dress." I shook my head and let out a muffled laugh. I loved Lilly's excitement for me!

Lilly was somewhere close to the age of twenty. Her parents had both crossed over and she was helping to raise her younger brother, Jimmie. Lilly lives in town, she rents a small space with two rooms just a few doors down from the dress shop. Jimmie stays with a old widow woman who already has six young'uns of her own. He is somewhere around the age of nine years old, and he reminds me of little Hey-You in Contention City.

Lilly's a beautiful young girl with mounds of wheat colored hair that she braids and twists around her head. Her blue eyes do not have the same deep intensity as Mr. Bogardis, but are more the color of a robin's egg. She has a big beaming smile, and is innocent to the ways of the world.

Lilly has a beau, his name is Joseph. He's from a good family here in Prescott. He's not well off, but he's suited for taking a wife and raising a family. He's a mighty handsome boy, sparkling eyes and shiny white teeth. Why, every time I see him, he's smiling and grinning at everyone! He hasn't asked Lilly for her hand in marriage yet, or even to be properly court'in, but she is expecting it any time. I think the reason she is so trilled with me having a baby, is that she hopes to be a mother herself someday.

Losing her homestead and family hasn't been easy for her. From what Lilly has told me, Jimmie was inflicted with the same sickness that killed their parents. It was some sort of fever that spread throughout the county a few years back. Lilly tended the bedside of her father while her mother cared for little Jimmie. Just as Jimmie was showing signs of recovery, their mother took ill and never recuperated. A few days later, their father passed on. It must have been very hard on both of them, losing their parents so suddenly, especially for Lilly. She and Jimmie had to leave their home and take up separate residences in town. But Lilly is strong and she did what was necessary to go on. Mr. Bogardis is always saying that she reminds him of me!

"Lilly", I commenced, "Mr. Bogardis will be out of town for a while and I have some time on my hands. I was wondering if you and Miss Nancy are in need of my services here at the store? I would be glad to give you some time off, maybe to spend a day with Joseph," I hinted. Lilly's face blushed and she looked downwards, embarrassed at the proposition.

"Lilly, you know that you and Joseph never have enough time to spend together. Pack up a lunch and ask Joseph to take you to the countryside! I can handle the shop for a day and besides it will do me some good to distract myself from missing Mr. Bogardis."

"Oh Mollie, do you really think we should! What would people think if we were unaccompanied on a picnic outside of town? I do desire to spend more time with Joseph. We both have so much to do all week, I barely get to see him except on Sundays. Do you really think we should, Mollie?" Lilly wanted my approval, like a mother figure, so assured her that Joseph appeared to be a gentleman and that no one who knew her like I did would think anything the contrary. Lilly hugged me and said she would speak to Joseph on the idea. "Now, we must decide on the material for your new maternity dress, Mollie!" Once Lilly has a notion in her mind, she is very determined to follow through with it! "All right you win Lilly, let's see what we have here." I agreed and followed her to the back room where the excess bolts are kept.

As we sifted through the fabric, Lilly suggested that I should probably acquaint myself with a bona fide midwife. She just happens to be Lilly's Aunt Polly. "Aunt Polly lives on Garden Street, you should come with me one day soon and meet her! She has brought many babies into this world and I intend for her to deliver mine one day as well."

To my estimation, I am only about ten or eleven weeks along. "Lilly, I don't think I will be requiring the services of your Aunt any time soon, but I'm sure she will be just fine! I will meet with her in due time." I really wasn't ready or prepared for people in town to know my condition. Although, most people were under the assumption that I was Mrs. Bogardis, I had just announced to the Governor himself that I wasn't!

I had finally chosen a modest fabric for Lilly and I to design a maternity dress from, a pink and white gingham cotton. "Mollie, I am so excited for you! Just to think that out of this fabric a dress will be made to display the greatness of a baby in waiting. I hope it shall be a baby girl, Mollie. We will have so much fun sewing little dresses and knitting shoes and socks. You are such a fortunate woman, Mollie!" I smiled thinking the same thing myself! We then said our goodbyes and I told Lilly to let me know when she would be needing me to tend to the shop. I reminded her to speak with Joseph about the picnic. "Take every opportunity to be happy, Lilly. Life is very unpredictable."

"Thank you, Mollie, I will."

I turned and reached for the door and almost ran into a woman on her entrance. She was very well dressed and obviously wealthy. She was an ample woman, well rounded and appeared nearing the age of forty. "I have come to see Miss Nancy", she announced as she nodded towards Lilly. "I am Elizabeth Fremont, I have a dress to pick up for my ma, mother, ah.. a special order that was placed through Miss Nancy about a month ago."

"Yes, Miss Fremont, I am sorry but that dress has yet to arrive", explained Lilly. "It should be delivered any day now."

"Oh dear! My.. my mother was expecting to wear that dress to a dinner we will be hosting this evening. I'm afraid I will have to inform her of the dreary disappointment."

"Pardon me, Ma'am", I interrupted. "Did I hear you say you are Elizabeth Fremont?   You must be the Governor's daughter. I'm Mollie Lewis. I had the pleasure of meeting your father last afternoon. He came to my home to call on Mr. Bogardis."

"Miss Lewis, pleasure to... to... meet you", she said softly as she reached for my hand in a sophisticated-like gesture. I detected a slight stutter as she spoke. "I have heard my... my... father speak of Mr. Bogardis. Someday soon we should have dinner, as...sss... my guests, so he and my father may conduct their business. I will have Ah Chung, our house cook, prepared something ss...special for you." Miss Fremont then turned her attention back to Lilly, "Please be sure to deliver the dress as soon as it arrives. My ... my mother will appreciate that. She has been ailing and I was hoping this new dress would brighten her spirits for the dinner tonight."

"Yes, Ma'am, I will see to it," Lilly assured her.

Lilly and I watched as Miss Fremont boarded her carriage. I thought it must be the same carriage the Governor traveled in yesterday when he arrived at my door. "Poor Miss Fremont,"   Lilly commented, "she is a spinster, you know! She has been all over the world, and yet she has never married. She remains here in Prescott to care for her mother and tend to her father's business ordeals. She doesn't like it here, she thinks of us as uncivilized. I feel pity for her!"

"Oh, Lilly!" I scolded. "She seems very charming to me. I like her. But, I wonder who they are expecting for dinner tonight at their home. I'm curious if it has anything to do with the Governor requesting the whereabouts of Mr. Bogardis."

Although, I was in no hurry to return home, I once again bid farewell to Lilly. It would be a pleasant walk with the weather being quite comfortable this time of year. Everything seemed so fresh and renewed. Unfortunately, it is our home that seems barren and lifeless without the presence of Mr. Bogardis.

CHAPTER FOUR

It was a lonely night thinking of Mollie. I got dressed and headed towards the telegraph office to wire her. I needed to let her know that I had arrived safely in Tucson. I should tell her something about the stage incident, as she might hear about it in the newspapers, but I didn't think she needs the worry. I would tell her about running into the young man who helped me in the alley in Contention.

As soon as I entered the telegraph office, the old man who works there told me he had a wire for me. He said it had just come in and he had not had time to find me and get it delivered. It was from Mollie, of course. She said that John Fremont, the Territorial Governor, had come to call on me.

She explained to him that I was out of town of business. Mollie mentioned that he told her that he was from Georgia, and had briefly spoken of some of my father's family. Although, she said she had no idea of what he wanted with me, she did promise the Governor she would wire me as soon as possible.

It was nice to read Mollie's words, just knowing that she was alright, it wouldn't have mattered what the wire was about. I confirmed to Mollie that I would contact the Governor directly. Of course I told her that I miss her and am already anxious to return. I do not like to go a day without her.

I should find out what Governor Fremont wanted. I drafted a wire to Governor Fremont that was short and to the point. "How can I help you, Governor". I told the old man to come find me as soon as the Governor responded to my wire. I heard my stomach make some rumbling sounds as I walked around the corner to the diner. I hope Zack hadn't changed his mind. I'd be nice to have a friend with me I could trust.

Zack was right on time. I had just taken a few bites of eggs, when I saw him come in. Zack walks tall and proud, he keeps a sideways grin on his face, showing off his youth and good looks. He was with a slightly older gentleman whom he introduced as Ben, his big brother. While Ben is clean and well mannered, I can tell that he probably doesn't have the sand of his younger brother. Ben's light colored hair covered his forehead and hung low in his eyes when he sat down at the table. Hard to read a man without getting a good look at his eyes.

Within minutes, I was notified that Governor Fremont's reply was waiting for me. I excused myself while Zack and Ben ordered their meal and said I'd be back in a minute. I had previously told the Governor while meeting with him back in Prescott, that I would be at his service if he needed me, that is if the money was right. I was anxious to know what the Governor had in mind for me.

Apparently, the Governor had recently hosted a dinner at his home for an Atlantic Pacific railroad agent and a Wells Fargo stage representative. Seems that the railroad agent was aware of my reputation. I have been requested to handle a situation, and the Governor wishes that I grant the request.

North of Tucson is a town called Canyon Diablo. The railroad had come to a halt there waiting for a bridge to be built across the canyon. The bridge would require considerable planning and would take quite a while to complete. In the meantime, the residents, mostly miners, railroad men, drifters, outlaws, gamblers, and the like had nothing to do but cause trouble. The Governor said that according to reports, there were fourteen saloons, ten gambling houses, four brothels, and two dance halls. Wedged in somewhere were a couple of eating establishments, a grocery, and a dry goods store.

The Stage ran a regular route to Canyon Diablo from Flagstaff, carrying various payrolls and items of value. It was becoming a problem to get the stage through without a hold up. Since the closest law enforcement was over fifty miles away, the stage company pressured the Governor to send help.

The Governor decided that the stage as well as the freight office, which did double duty as the bank, needed more security. He advised the railroad and the stage owners that security could be provided, but they would have to pay for it. Just like a man of politics. But he convinced the railroad and the stage line that if they would kick in together and pay for the added security, it would be money well spent. When they suggested me, he mentioned that I might be available for the job.   The fact that I had just rid the stage line of three bandits didn't hurt. The offer was three hundred dollars per month for me, and I would have to pay any additional help out of that. That's a lot of money. But it is also a lot of risk. It sounds crazy to me. There are probably several hundred people up there with no law.

I   need some time to think about this. Number one, I would not consider it as a permanent arrangement. I am not going to take Mollie to that kind of place. And I have no intention of spending any more time without her than is absolutely necessary. It's more than a one man job, and where do you get people you can trust? Zack, of course. It sure couldn't hurt to have someone as fast as him if I took the job.   He did not drink excessively, and would avoid trouble if possible. Plus, I already felt I could trust him if things got tight. And he is looking for work. Yeah, this might work out good for both of us.

Back at the diner, I explained the Governor's offer in the telegram to Zack and Ben. When I asked them if they would be interested, Zack almost jumped out of his chair in eagerness! Ben nodded and said to count him in as well. I explained that while the Governor had forwarded the offer, I was not exactly pleased with it and wanted to try to get a little better deal. This was something we needed to think about for a few days.

*   *   *   *   *

All I think about these days is how Mr. Bogardis was going to feel about the baby. It would be a surprise, although it shouldn't be! I would like to think it will be a girl. I already have a name chosen for her, Miriam Kay. She should be named after my grandmother. She died when I was just a child, but those few memories I have of her I hold dear.

I do not know much about Mr. Bogardis' family line. He seldom speaks of his father. All I really know is what he told me early on. His father left and went to fight in the War between the States. He never returned, leaving his mother and him behind. They lived a very hard life without his father, never having much, and what they did have was a struggle. He tried his best to provide and care for his mother, but she died not long afterwards. I don't believe he ever forgave his father for leaving and getting himself killed. !

Lilly and I used most of the pink and white colored gingham fabric in the back room of the dress shop. We've have been sewing my maternity dress for days, in between the regular customer orders. It appears that I suddenly have a small but proud bulge projecting from my abdomen!

Spring time has come with a vengeance, it's been nearly eighty degrees this week. Workers at the Courthouse plaza have had to dig four new city wells, one at each corner. I watched their progress as I walked by each day. One morning, one of the wells had sprung a leak and there were children dancing in the cool spraying water. They looked like wet bumble bees running around in circles, flapping their arms and laughing. Children are such a joy! !

I stayed a little longer than usual at the dress shop than I should have these last few days. I suppose it makes me feel less lonely. I am considering routing my walk home tonight to include Garden Street. I had told Lilly I would wait and meet her Aunt Polly at a later time, but actually I was not telling the truth. I am in full of anticipation of meeting her!

Aunt Polly is a well respected mid-wife here in Prescott. She had offered to take on Lilly and Jimmie after the death of their parents. But Lilly refused to impose on her, saying that Polly had too much on her plate as it was. I am sure Aunt Polly would do anything she could for her dead brothers children. Lilly often speaks so kindly of her.

I said goodbye to Lilly and left the shop early enough to acquaint myself with Aunt Polly. Just as I was approaching Garden Street, I passed a wagon with a young couple in the seat. I thought how much the young man looked like Joseph, Lilly's beau. They stopped just ahead of me and I watched as the man helped the girl down from the wagon.

It was Joseph! He didn't notice me, but I stopped and waited inside a store front just a few feet away. They were laughing, smiling at each other, and his arm was around the small of her waist. He called her Vera. She was beautiful! Richly adorned in a store bought dress that clearly didn't come from Lilly's shop. She was wearing a brooch on her breast, an elegant array of rubies and pearls that stated the fact that there was money in her heritage. Joseph was teasing her, rollicking in a playful spirit that one does with their mate.

So, this is why Joseph did not have time for Lilly! I wondered if Vera knew there even was a 'Lilly', the way she was staring into Joseph's gleaming eyes.

How could he mislead Lilly! Sweet, trusting Lilly. I watched as the couple swayed carelessly into the mercantile store. I knew I shouldn't but I watched through the window as the two of them inspected the wares. There was no doubt in my mind as to what I was observing.

It would not be my place to inform Lilly of Joseph's indiscretion. Oh, if Mr. Bogardis was here, he would know what to do!

I gazed through the window for only a few minutes and turned away so I would not be seen. I hurried down the sidewalk towards home, forgetting about my earlier decision to go to Aunt Polly's house.

Once I arrived home, the air had cooled and my excitement for the baby had been replaced by anxiety for Lilly's situation. What ever I do, I must not allow Lilly to spend the day with Joseph and get her hopes up for something that may never happen. Poor Lilly, to trust someone with your heart and have it trampled on is like looking into a broken mirror. You see all the shattered pieces spread about in a tangled maze and suddenly nothing makes sense anymore. You begin to think that it can never be repaired. !

Then before you know it, the heart looks into a different mirror and it's better than it was before. At least, that's how it was for me with Mr. Bogardis, and I'm sure it will be the same for Lilly. She is young and beautiful, and maybe Joseph isn't the man for her, but she will one day find someone who is.

As I sat on the porch in the cool evening breeze, watching the carriages roll by, I felt the baby move for the first time!

I try so hard not to show my enthusiasm for the baby at the dress shop in front of Lilly, or we would both be acting like a pair of giggly little school girls all day long instead of working! Now, I can't wait to tell her about what I just felt!

Everything is so real to me right now. The baby moved, our baby! She wanted me to know she was there. I can almost see her little hands and feet. Oh, Mr. Bogardis! We're waiting for you, please come home.

CHAPTER FIVE

I spent the next few days thinking about the proposal I would make to the Governor. Although it was not his money, he was arranging it for the stage line and the railroad. I finally settled on a deal. I would need to receive two hundred dollars per week. I would furnish two assistants and there would always be at least one person on the stage. When the freight office had payrolls or other funds, one of us would guard it. We would need a room in Canyon Diablo that would sleep up to three people, as well as a nice hotel room in Flagstaff. All expenses incurred by the three of us would be paid by the company. I would keep a log of expenses and turn it in weekly. Should any robbery end with the capture or death of the bandit or bandits, a bonus of a hundred dollars would be due. While the bonus might be collected often at first, as soon as word got out that it was no longer safe to rob the stage or the office, the bonus probably would not be collected as often. I wonder just how desperate they are! They may laugh at my proposal, but it is going to be rough, dangerous work. I sent the offer to the Governor and pretty much said the company could take it or leave it, and explained why.

From there, I had a stop I'd been planning on making. It's funny the kind of things a man on the move might carry with him. For over fifteen years I have carried my mothers amber and gold cameo locket rolled up in a handkerchief in my gear. Don't know why, I guess just as a remembrance of her. I had been thinking about giving it to Mollie, but I wanted to do something special to it that would make it hers. I've heard of a jeweler here who can write on almost anything, engraving is what he calls it. What I like about it is that it is permanent.

I showed him the locket and he said he's see what he could do. I told him to write these words, "In Omne Tempus". Latin for 'into all time'. Forever. I can't wait to present it to Mollie. I suppose the cameo is the most valuable thing I have to offer her.

Upon leaving the jeweler, I half expected to receive a telegram telling me where I could go with my offer to the Governor. I didn't hear anything for a matter of days, but then my terms were confirmed. Governor Fremont must have done a good job selling it, or perhaps the company knows that if it doesn't work, they won't have to pay us for very long.

I met with the Blade boys and explained that we had a job if we wanted it. We had already discussed the danger involved. They were up for it so we started making plans to head on over to Flagstaff. The Governor had told me to contact a Mr. McEvers when I got to Flagstaff. He would be our contact and would help with anything we needed from the stage line. I sent a wire to him at Flagstaff and explained that we would be there in a few days, as soon as we closed out some business in Tucson. I had explained to Zack and Ben that we were going to Canyon Diablo first, without anyone else knowing about it. Mr. McEvers may be a good man, but I'm not sure enough to bet our lives on it. We'll poke around Canyon Diablo, scout out the area and then follow the stage route back to Flagstaff. Nothing wrong with getting a good idea of the terrain and possible ambush sites before we become sitting ducks in a shooting gallery.

It's about a hundred miles from Tucson to Canyon Diablo. And of course there's no easy way to get there. The boys had horses, but I needed to buy one. I settled on a bay gelding about fourteen hands. Next we provisioned ourselves with food, water, and the items necessary for a ride of this distance. I had brought my two Colt's revolvers with me, and a little something extra. I had broken down the sawed-off ten gauge that Mollie had used to save my life back in Contention and carried it in my bag. I got it out and assembled it. I had vowed that it would never be far from me. Since we would be traveling across some pretty inhospitable country, I decided that I should purchase a rifle. The Colt's and the sawed-off are good for close-up, but out in the open a rifle can make a lot of difference. I got a dandy '73 Winchester that had belonged to an unfortunate young man who had purchased it new in St. Louis when beginning his trip west. I say unfortunate because just before arriving in Tucson, he was riding ahead of the wagons when his horse reared and threw him. Not usually anything to worry about, but in this case he landed on his head and broke his neck. Yeah, there are a lot of ways to die out here.

The boys were ready. They have good mounts, saddles, and weapons. So tomorrow morning, right after a good breakfast, we will head north toward Canyon Diablo. I have always looked forward to new country and new adventures. But now I find myself only wanting it to be over so I can return to Mollie. I am going to have to keep my head on straight if I want to get back in one piece. I know Mollie will want me to keep my concentration on the job at hand so we can be together when this is over.

Now, I need to wire Mollie and let her know where I'm headed. Soon Mollie, soon.

*   *   *   *   *

I received a letter from Lou, Morgan's wife, this past week. She wrote to tell me about Doc. She says there is talk in Tombstone about Doc robbing a stage out near Contention. Although she and the other wives are not fond of Doc, she really didn't believe he was responsible. Seems he and Kate have been at it again, drinking and fighting. Kate told Sheriff Behan that it was Doc who held up the stage. Behan knew it wasn't, but he'd use any excuse to arrest Doc and throw him under the jail. Wyatt formed a posse and went out looking for the real outlaws and already has one fellow jailed.

She said that Morgan and Virgil have been consumed with their friend Bat Masterson since his arrival in Tombstone. Spending all their time in the Oriental, neither one of the wives saw their husbands much. She was glad to hear that Masterson just left for Dodge City yesterday on the stage. She closed the letter stating that she hoped all was well with Mr. Bogardis and myself and we were welcome to visit at any time. I must write Lou back, I have so much to tell her!

There's not much going on here in Prescott. I'm afraid my letter to Lou won't be as exciting as hers was to me, until I get to the part about the baby! Hmmmm, where do I start?

147

My dear friend Louisa,

What such pleasure it was to receive your letter today! I must say that Doc and Kate find themselves in perplexing predicaments! Hopefully, Wyatt will apprehend the true culprits and Mr. Holliday will be exonerated.

While Mr. Bogardis has been away procuring employment, I have found work at a local dress shop. It keeps me busy during the day, but the evenings are much to lonely for me. When I sit on my porch at night, I can hear all the commotion just across the bridge on Whisky Row. Mr. Bogardis tells me there are so many saloons and drinking establishments all lined up so close together, that is it hard to tell where one stops and the other begins!

I remember that you and Mattie were looking at window shades when you were here in Prescott a few months ago, and I found a beautiful pair at George S. Potter's Fine Furniture Store you would just love! They are hand painted with a delicate floral design that would match the fabric in your curtains. I wish you could see them. Mr. Potter says they are straight out of Godey's Ladies Book!

On a brighter note, I have a wonderful announcement to share with all of you. I am expecting and will deliver Mr. Bogardis' baby in the fall! I am hoping it will be a girl. Unfortunately, Mr. Bogardis left before I could tell him of the news. He should not be away much longer, and I know he will be delighted with the surprise!

Please give all my best regards,
Respectfully, Mollie

CHAPTER SIX

Talk about solitude. There ain't much of anything else out here. We made camp and ate supper, then just sat and talked. The boy's family have a small ranch north of Tombstone. Just a six hundred acre tract that was hard to make much of a living on. The rest of their family consisted of their Ma and Pa, and a younger sister, Lacey. Both of the boys seemed to adore their blue eyed baby sister and spoke real highly of her. Always smiling with the mention of her name. Maybe a little sadness from missing her as well.

Ben and Zack had worked hard but wanted more than the broken down ranch could ever provide. They said a local rancher had been trying to buy out the family for a couple of years now. They had both advised their father to sell and move on to something not so remote and hard. But their Ma and Pa had said this is where they would stay. They gave their sons their blessings and encouraged the boys to head out on their own. I got the impression that they may have felt a little guilty about leaving.

We got an early start the next morning. We had a quick breakfast and some good, strong coffee. Before we had gone ten miles, we came upon a wagon with a woman, a small girl, and a boy maybe twelve years old. There was no road, and they had cut too close to a wash and the rear wheel had slipped into a hole. It did not appear to be too serious, but the two mules would never pull the wagon out of the hole unless it was unloaded or they had some help. As we rode up, the little girl hid behind her mother's skirt. The boy stood out and was unafraid. It was easy to tell that the mother was uncomfortable. I asked if her husband was about, and that seemed to upset her. I explained that we were going to Canyon Diablo to serve as guards on the stage. She seemed to relax a little.

I told Zack to tie onto the mule team. Ben, the boy, and me would try to lift it up and take some pressure off of the wheel in the hole. A few pulls and the wagon was free. I checked it over and could see no apparent harm. I told them we were about to stop and eat and would be happy to share our meal with them. I caught both Zack and Ben looking my way. We had no plans to stop until nightfall, but something told me these folks were hungry. The woman thanked me and everyone pitched in to get a fire going and get it set up. It was nothing fancy, but we managed to get some biscuits and beans going.

After we ate, they loosened up a bit so I asked what they were doing this far out alone. The woman explained that they had come from Illinois with her husband, Mr. Pryer, almost a year ago. They had a small piece of property that they intended to make into something one day. Since the day they arrived, they had nothing but bad luck. It was hard to grow enough to live on and keep their few head of cattle and pigs alive. They were offered money to sell out and move on. A man by the name of William Lawrence owned thousands of acres and was willing to buy their land. Coming west and running a ranch had been a dream of theirs, so her husband refused sell. After convincing Mr. Lawrence that he would not be interested in selling out, strange things began to happen. What little water they had was supplied by a creek coming off Mr. Lawrence's property. One day they got up and there was no water in the creek. Mr. Pryer ventured upstream to see what had happened. A few hours later Mr. Lawrence's foreman, a man named Harvey, rode up with two of his hands. Mr. Pryer was strapped across the saddle. Harvey had explained that they found him lying by the creek bed. They did not know what had happened to him, only that he was dead when they found him. They stayed long enough to bury him in what was once the garden. Harvey suggested it might be a good time to move on, since there was no water and no man to help her. He implied that things could continue to get worse.

So she packed what she could, the boy hitched up the mules, and they headed for Tucson. From there they hoped to make arrangements to get back to Illinois.

We gave Mrs. Pryer some of our provisions and let them go. For the first time since we met up, I saw the little girl smile. I thought of Mollie as a child. I then told the boy how to find their way in to Tucson. They would most likely make it by the following evening.

It's very easy to get lulled into thinking that everything is o.k. out here. You lose your focus for a split second and you end up dead. Your horse can step in a hole and break a leg, even your leg. Rattlesnakes can come outta nowhere and rile up your horse. Everything out here will either stick you, bite you, or sting you. So we traveled pretty much in silence the rest of the way. The horses' steady hooves echoing the beats of my tattered heart.

I had noticed that Ben and Zack kept glaring at each other while Mrs. Pryer was tellin' us her story. When we stopped for the night, I inquired about what they might have had on their minds. Zack asked me if I had ever heard of John Chisolm, of New Mexico. Of course I had. He seemed to own half of New Mexico. Zack went on to say that the story going around was that William Lawrence wanted to be Arizona's equivalent of John Chisolm. Lawrence was buying up everything he could get his hands on, and sometimes just taking over land abandoned by settlers. I asked if he was one of those eastern millionaires who came west and tried to take over everything they saw. He said he didn't know a lot about him, but he came to Arizona after the war and started building his empire. There was talk in southern Arizona that he bought and traded cattle and horses from the Clanton family and the group known as the "cowboys". Most folks believed them to be nothing more than thieves and rustlers, and probably murders if the need arose. Yeah, I knew of the cowboys and their reputation.

The boys and I rose early and got a good start on the daylight. It took a few more days of travel, but when we finally topped a small ridge, there it was, Canyon Diablo. It sure don't look like much. But, it is easy to see how the place got its name. The Devil's Canyon is really something, deep and foreboding. And they are gonna try to build a railroad bridge across it. I'm glad my job doesn't have anything to do with that!

We checked our gear, primarily our six guns, and rode in to check it out. Not many folks out on the street, but from the noisy commotion we heard, we could tell most of the population was inside the walls. We spied a couple of rough looking characters engaged in a fist fight out on the edge of the street, but they were mostly minding their own dealings.

Not only does the canyon have the right name, but the town does too. If there was ever a place on the earth that the Devil would claim for his own, this is it. The stench was horrid, the filth was sickening. There is only one street, with several brothels, assorted gambling houses, and numerous saloons. The name of the street, why "Hell Street" of course. Yep, being this far out and with no law, this is probably as close to hell on earth as you will get.

We were interested in the freight office because that is where the stage will leave any shipments, payroll or otherwise. Most of the town is shacks or tents, but the freight office appeared to be the sturdiest in town. It was built out of logs and appeared to be solid. While there is enough small timber around the canyon to build it, it would take a lot more than that to span the canyon with a bridge. I can see the three of us hold up in there surrounded by the entire town. Yeah, this could really get interesting.

Although we got some stares, no one questioned our reason for being there. I had already warned the boys about trying to make friends here. Better to consider everyone a potential enemy. We pitched camp just outside of town. We will get a good nights sleep tonight and backtrack the stage route to Flagstaff. Of course one of us will be awake all night, just in case. We drew sticks, Ben took first watch. We woke early and left with the sun, headed west towards Flagstaff.

Today is Saturday and there is not a freight shipment today. I don't want to accidentally get involved in a holdup until we have a chance to look the trail over from an outlaw's point of view.

It appears that this route is an outlaws dream. Plenty of places to ambush a stage. Lots of rocks and rock outcroppings to hide behind. Now I can see where the timber is going to come from to build the bridge. The farther west we go, the more Ponderosa Pine we see, which adds another element to the outlaws advantage. And, the stage is constantly going up and down hills and canyons. Many places the horses will probably slow to a walk. Yeah, the bad guys seem to have everything out here on their side. The stage has to remain on the trail, but bandits can pick and choose their spots. But we will have our own advantage, surprise.

I told the boys that we would split up, the two of them taking the north side of the trail and I would take the south side. We need to stay just out of sight of the trail, yet follow along with it. We are looking for campsites, lookout posts, or anything that would give a clue as to where the favorite ambush sites might be.

I noticed a narrow passage between two large rock walls. Not quite big enough for a horse, but plenty big enough for a man. At the beginning of the passage, on the side away from the trail, I found a whiskey bottle and a place where at least two horses had been tied up. I walked through the passage and had a perfect view of the trail from a place that had good cover in case there was some shooting. Just as I was finishing, Ben walked across the trail and said that Zack wanted to show me something. I walked back with Ben and walked into pretty much the same setup on their side of the trail. This was definitely one of the ambush sites. Now we need go on toward Flagstaff and mark the trail so we will know that we are coming up on the ambush site. We continued to do the same at each site that we could tell had been used, as well as several sites that just made good sense to be wary of.

After two days we arrived in Flagstaff. While the boys took care of our horses, I went to pay a visit to Mr. McEvers of the stage line. He was a short heavyset man who looked completely out of place. He should have been back east working in a dry goods store. When I introduced myself, he jumped up and stuck his hand out. I nodded to him, but did not shake his hand. That is a custom I do not routinely approve of, but save for those that I trust. I asked that he tell me about the previous robberies and approximately where they happened. I did not mention that we had already inspected the stage route and had a pretty good idea of where a robbery was likely to occur. He explained that it had gotten so dangerous to try to fight off the bandits, that the stage usually gave them what they wanted, or at least appeared to. Each shipment had the payroll or other valuables hidden in the stage. They carried a strongbox with cash and sometimes gold that was given up when they were robbed. It seemed to me that was like paying the bandits to let the stage go through, and I voiced that opinion. Mr. McEvers agreed, and that is probably why we are here. As well as they are paying us, it is probably a small amount compared to what they are paying the bandits.

The next payroll shipment was to go out on Thursday. That gives us a couple of days to get ready. I told Mr. McEvers that I would like to know how many passengers the stage would be carrying that day. I would check with him before he closed on Wednesday. I was planning a big surprise for Thursday. Mr. McEvers told me what hotel to go to and that everything there was already taken care of. I reckon now me and the boys can start planning the party.

*   *   *   *   *

It had been so busy today, I didn't realize how fast the time had passed! The sun had already begun to set low in the sky. I promised Mr. Bogardis never to be out on the streets alone at nights. We live to close to Whisky Row, the side of town where the drinking never stops. Prescott is a dangerous town after sunset!

Although, Mr. Bogardis wires me occasionally, I am sure he does not tell me everything! I have lost track of days and weeks he has been gone now. My belly seems to grow larger each morning I awake! I am afraid that if he doesn't return soon, he will have two of us waiting for him when he does! Still, there is plenty of time. Months before she will show her face.

I pulled my shawl up closer to my neckline as I locked the dress shop door for the evening, barely enough light left for me to see the keyhole. I felt a cool crisp breeze blow down my back. I have been managing the dress store alone these last few days. Lilly hasn't been herself lately since finding out about Joseph. She has been coming in the shop late and leaving early each day. Her spirits are down, and I understand. I wish I could convince her that this all will pass. That one day her heart will be healed. But, I guess time is the only thing that cures a broken heart.

At least I didn't have to tell Lilly about finding Joseph with Vera. I am glad that Joseph was a man and expounded the truth to Lilly before it went any further. It was the day that Lilly finally got her courage up to ask Joseph to accompany her on a ride to the country side. After church that Sunday morning, Lilly lingered behind hoping to kindle Joseph with her proposed idea. But, Joseph had disappeared through the church's double doors as soon as the last 'amen' was heard. Lilly searched him out only to find Joseph escorting Vera to her wagon, climbing aboard and preparing to leave with her. Lilly called out to him, but no words of explanation were necessary when she saw the looks on their faces. Lilly told me that later that day, Joseph did call on her to apologize. He claims he had no intentions to hurt her and did not realize that Lilly felt that strongly for him. He said that although he cared for Lilly, it was Vera who held his heart. She cared not to hear his excuses or reasons, she just wished him happiness in his new venture. I think she felt in some measure a little foolish. She was trying to be brave and nonchalant, but inside she was aching.

I carried my newly finished gingham dress in my bag and walked as quickly as I could homeward. My free hand lay upon the bottom ridge of my swollen tummy holding my baby girl in place as I stride with a sense of dignity. Although the air tonight tasted like stale liquor, my mind was thinking about all the fragrant flowers blooming on Gurly Street. The flowers are in full bloom now and the sun stays in the sky a little longer each day surrounding each petal with it's warmth.

I could almost smell their scent, fresh and intoxicating like exotic perfume from France, only better. I must remember to pick a bouquet for Mr. Bogardis and place them in a vase the first day he arrives back home!

I guess my mind was so preoccupied, walking so fast and thinking about Mr. Bogardis that I wasn't paying attention to all the commotion just ahead of me. I have passed this area each night on my walk home, but never so late in the evening as this.

Then, it all happened so fast! Practically in slow motion. I heard a gun shot first, at least I think I did, then I saw the doors swing open from the Diana Saloon. Two men with bright red sashes tied around their waist came out in a tangle, falling and stumbling, fists flying in the air. After the men staggered out onto the sidewalk just a few feet in front of me, several other men followed through the doors cheering on the drunken brawl. Bottles and broken glass were being scattered in the street, crashing and exploding like tiny pieces of rainbow colored lights against a blackened sky.

As I stopped, suddenly aware of what was happening, I watched in horror as one of the tumbling men's boot tip plunged straight into my abdomen. I reached for the wooden lamp pole beside me and balanced myself from loosing foot. I dropped the bag I was carrying and both my arms immediately surrounded my stomach. I heard myself let out a scream that would awaken the dead. I felt like I was in a nightmare! My Baby! My precious unborn baby!

CHAPTER SEVEN

There is a timber yard on the edge of town where Ben, Zack and I gathered and talked over the plans. It was about an hour before sunset but the yard was closed and no one was around. I still like to talk about important matters where I know there are no ears listening. Especially about matters that have lives at stake.

I suggested that Zack and Ben go out the day before the stage run. They would camp just outside of town, far enough that no one in town would notice, and off the trail. I would be a passenger on the stage. They would follow well behind the stage, off the trail and one on each side. It is important that they are far enough back that the bandits do not see them until the robbery has already begun. Then they ride in behind the ambush, one on each side of the trail. It's my job to hold ground until they get there. They close in behind the bandits and open fire. It is not a game. These men will kill you without giving it a second thought. We only stop shooting when everyones hands are in the air, or they are all on the ground.

I suggested that they each begin the fight with rifles. If they are lucky they can stay out of pistol range and pick the bandits off. I will have my Colt's and will put the 10 gauge back in the bag until we are underway. Yeah, this is going to be real interesting. On Wednesday I wired Mollie that I was in Flagstaff and was looking forward to seeing her soon. Although I had already told her that Ben and Zack were with me, I neglected to go into any detail about what we were doing. No point in making her worry. All the worry in the world won't protect me, so best just get on with what I have to do. If it works out, she need never know of the danger. If it doesn't work out, well, we just have to be careful and make sure we have everything covered as best we can.

In the afternoon I checked in with Mr. McEvers. There were to be no passengers on this run. I told him I would be riding the stage as a passenger. Ben and Zack headed out as planned that evening. Soon we would be in action. Sleep was hard to come. If only I could have dreamt of Mollie.

The next morning I packed the bag with my 10 gauge. I also had plenty of shotgun shells and cartridges for my Colt's. Since there were to be no passengers, I decided I would throw my rifle in. I pulled the driver and the guard aside and explained to them that I was working for the company. I also told them I expected them to perform as normal. If we were held up, they would stop, throw down the box, and be ready to get down. I told them not to shoot unless their target was within shotgun range and wearing a mask. I don't want to get Ben and Zack shot. Told them they didn't have to shoot, but not to move the stage until I told them to. If they start moving too soon, I may start shooting at them! The guard said it was alright with him to fight back if he had some help. But, there were usually four or five bandits. I told him things might be different this time, just make sure the horses don't run. The driver and guard looked at each other and smiled. They were getting on up in years, but I could tell by looking at them that they had seen and done their share in the old days.

It was a beautiful morning as we pulled out of Flagstaff. I could only hope that things had went according to plan with Ben and Zack. There was no way to contact them. The next time we would meet would be at Canyon Diablo or on the trail.

It was easy for me to stay alert regardless of how little sleep I had the night before. I have too much to live for now to start getting careless. I moved from one side of the stage to the other quite often. I was glad there were no passengers on this run. Somewhere about half way through, we started slowing down due to the roughness of the trail and the terrain. I thought I caught a glimpse of a lone rider crossing ridge into a small canyon. It might have been Zack or Ben checking on our progress, or it may have been nothing.

As we rounded a bend with a rock outcropping on one side and a stand of Ponderosa Pines on the other, I heard the driver start to whoa the horses. I looked out and there were three men in the road, all wearing masks. They had picked a good place. The road was rough, we were going slow, and immediately in front of us was a steep grade that would slow the horses even more. Well, once the shooting starts, we won't be able to get away. I hope Ben and Zack are close by. As the stage halts, one man tells the guard to throw down the box, another starts walking to the stage door. As he opens the door, I give him one barrel of the 10 gauge. There is a moment of silence, as the bandits can't believe someone is actually resisting. By the time they realize what has happened, I put a .45 slug into the nearest one. I rolled out of the stage and headed to the edge of the rocks. I brought everything with me, the shotgun, rifle, and the bag of ammunition. Now bullets seem to be coming from everywhere. The third man who was in the road is down now, a victim of the guards shotgun. I glance at the stage and the guard is hunkered down, reloading, with the biggest toothless smile you have ever seen.

Shots are coming from both sides of the trail, mostly at me. There is no way to tell how many are out there. I start returning fire with my rifle, just shooting at puffs of smoke. I see one man stand up from behind a rock to aim. I don't aim, but lever off three quick shots in his direction. I see a splatter of red as he goes down. I quickly reload my rifle and again I am shooting at smoke. There is a short lull, and I hear a rifle from across the trail, but at a greater distance than the others. Then a rifle from my side of the road, but farther away. It must be Ben and Zack. The bandits have turned their attention from me to the boys. I leave the rifle, pick up the shotgun and start heading for the pines. I almost run over one man who is crouching down. When he turns and swings toward me I let him have a 10 gauge load in the chest. Just ahead I see a man down with blood everywhere.

Ben got that one. The shooting seems to have stopped on this side of the road. I see Ben stand up and wave. "That's all of them over here", he yelled. I motioned for him to come on. I turned and started back towards the stage. We need to cross over and help Zack. Just then I heard a shot behind me.

I turn in time to see Ben fall, the gun still in his hand. It was like his body bent backwards and his knees collapsed from under him. The man behind him falls as one of my bullets hits him high in the chest. I run to Ben, he's lying face down in the dirt. I roll him over. He was shot in the center of the back. He makes a weak smile and says, "Take care of my little brother". Then he is gone. I ran over to his killer to finish him off, but he is already dead. I quickly grab my shotgun, reload my Colt's and head across the road. I see the driver slumped down and the guard holding his own arm. He appears to be alright, he waves me to go on.

As I start through the rocks I catch movement on my left. The shotgun comes up in time to take a bandit who was to slow. The shooting has slowed down considerably now. I eased on very slowly. I saw movement just ahead.

A man was lying on his stomach with a large rock between him and Zack. I could not quite see enough of him to take a shot, but I took a chance. I took careful aim a spot on the rock just above and to his right. If this works, I can shoot the rock and he will raise up and turn my way. But I will have to be ready when, and if, he does. The shot hits just right, and he realizes there is someone behind him. When he came up I put one shot in his lung. It may take a while to die, but he should be out of the fight. I closed in carefully. He is still trying to breathe, but there ain't much left for him. I threw his guns far enough that he would not be able to reach them and proceeded on. I am concentrating on some rocks to my left, when I hear loose rocks rolling down from above and to my right. As I spin around, a man is aiming his rifle at me, but before he can fire I hear a shot and the man folds up and falls off the little cliff. I look around and there is Zack. "I think that's all of them," he said. I think so too.

Zack walks on over and asks about Ben. I shake my head, "I'm sorry Zack, Ben caught one in the back. It must have killed him instantly", I lied. "Ben moved up too quick and bypassed one of the bandits, who then had an easy shot at his back." I told Zack to go tend to his brother. I went back to the stage to check on the guard and the driver. The driver was dead, but the guard only had a wound in the arm. He would be fine.

Zack carried his brother back to the stage and laid him down. He took his blanket from his bedroll and placed it over Ben's lifeless body. Zack's face was in his hands but he composed himself enough not to shed any tears, at least for the moment. I stayed busy gathering up all the dead bandits. It took a while to get them all drug out to the road.

There were the two in the road that I shot and one that the guard shot, one Ben killed in the pines, three I killed in the pines, two I killed in the rocks, three that Zack killed, including the one that was about to do me in. That made an even dozen. Very unusual. Most stage robberies are pulled off by two or three bandits. While if everything went according to their plan, only three of them would have been seen. It was almost like they had an army waiting as backup. It makes me think there is more to this than what meets the eye.

I felt real bad about Ben. Even though he was the oldest, I could tell that Zack was a lot handier with a gun. Maybe I should not have brought Ben along. I hope Zack does not hold it hard against me. I haven't known neither of them for very long, but both Ben and Zack have become trusted friends and companions. I hated to loss one of them.

We made a big enough splash that I don't think there will be another robbery for at least a while. Zack may want to go home and bury his brother, unless he wants to do it here. I would think his folks would want him resting on their own place.

All of the bandits had horses. I tied them on their mounts securely, so they had a ride back to Flagstaff. The guard said he could probably handle the horses on in to Canyon Diablo. I asked him to not divulge exactly what had happened. Just say some strangers jumped in and helped out. I told Zack I would appreciate it if he would ride in with the stage to Canyon Diablo. I would use his horse and take everyone else back to Flagstaff. Once the payroll was unloaded in Canyon Diablo, he could come on back to Flagstaff.

It was quite a sight when I rode in town with thirteen horses, each one carrying a dead man. I went straight to the livery when I got there and told the old man who ran the place to send for Mr. McEvers right away. He arrived in a few minutes and was taken by surprise at what he saw. I explained that one of the dead was my friend, but the rest were bandits who attempted to rob the stage. He looked at me and I could read the question in his eyes, "Now What?" I told him he should contact his superiors and explain that the stage would arrive safely with ALL of the payroll intact. Advise them that my group killed an even dozen to prevent the holdup, and that I had lost one man in the process. They could decide what to do with the bodies, other than my friend. They could have the horses and saddles, and I would keep the weapons. If there was any reward for any of the bandits, other than what the stage company offered, I would get that. I would expect payment immediately. Throughout the conversation, Mr. McEvers just nodded his head in agreement. "And I do need a notarized statement regarding the deaths of the bandits", I stated matter of factly. Mr. McEvers left in a hurry. I am sure he wanted to pass the information to his superiors as soon as possible.

As for me, I can't shake the feeling that there is more than meets the eye with the stage holdups. Each holdup had only had three to four men pulling it off, but apparently there were an even dozen involved. Was it just a group of outlaws working together, or was there something more behind it? It would bear looking into when Zack and I had time, assuming that Zack would even want to continue our partnership. But, we can worry about that after he takes Ben home to be buried and I get to see my sweet Mollie.

I asked the old man in the livery if he had a large box I could buy. "How large?", he asked. I explained that it needed to be big enough to hold all the guns and gear of twelve men and it needed a lock on it. He said he had just the thing and would be glad to put all the items away for me.

Next stop, the Funeral Parlor. I went directly to the only Funeral Parlor in town and spoke with the owner about Ben. I told him that Ben was from farther south and would it be possible to prepare him for burial here and then take him down. He assured me that it would, so I escorted him to the livery to turn over Ben's body.   I told him that his brother would be by tomorrow and make the arrangements, and that I would be responsible for the bill. I went ahead and gave him twenty dollars.

I thought I might wire Mollie and check in. She is probably worried because she has not heard from me in a while. But, since I will be leaving for Prescott tomorrow I think I will wait and surprise her. Right now, I am going to get a drink, a bath, another drink, and something to eat. I am sure I will be ready to turn in early tonight.

*   *   *   *   *

I must have become unconscious after the accident.   I cannot remember anything that happened after I fell on the sidewalk. My last memory is of my arms clutching my abdomen and feeling the horrific pain.

When I awoke, I was lying in the bed, the lamp on the bedside table lit and flickering, almost out of oil. Amber colored shadows danced on the wall like demons escaping from hell. Gasping for air, I called out for Mr. Bogardis. But, only Lilly, accompanied by the sad face of a white haired woman, charged through the door to my bedside.

"Mollie, you must take it easy! Lie still, you cannot get up yet!"

"What happened? The baby!   Is she alright?" I started to cry, maybe I didn't want to hear the answer. I already knew it. My stomach was in pain, but my heart was grieving like no other suffering I have ever felt before in my life.

"Mollie, I'm sorry."   The woman, whom I gathered was Aunt Polly, spoke softly, "I promise you, there will be other opportunities for you and....." I couldn't hear what she was saying, I hurt so badly! Lilly was holding my hand but I jerked it away and grabbed my stomach. How could it be so empty? She was there just yesterday! Or was she, how long have I been here in bed? I have to see Mr. Bogardis, I need him here with me!

"Mollie, I know how you must feel", Lilly said trying to comfort me. But it was no comfort. I asked them both to leave me alone. Aunt

Polly said it was best that I try to rest anyway.   I watched them wipe tears from their cheeks as they turned and left the room.

I tried to sit up but the pain was excruciating. I saw a bowl of red stained water in the corner of the room. I heard whispering coming from beyond the bedroom door. My head was spinning, I was weak and queazy. Fever raced through my body and caused my hair to stick to my neck and back from sweat. I tasted the salty tears that soaked my face. I reached for a glass of water Aunt Polly had left on the bedside table, but my throat was raw and it was hard to swallow.

The last drop of oil burned out and the flickering had stopped. The room was completely dark. I couldn't tell whether my eyes were open or closed, because I couldn't see nothing. Nothing at all.

No one, no one in the world could understand how I felt! I wanted to fall asleep and I didn't want to wake up anymore.

CHAPTER EIGHT

Zack had gotten an early start and arrived in Flagstaff about noon. I explained to him the arrangements I had made. I also told him we would talk after he got his brother home and buried. I will certainly understand if he wants no more to do with me or my crazy ideas.

I stopped by to see Mr. McEvers and confirm that he had done as I asked. He assured me everything was taken care of and that a deposit had been made in the bank in Flagstaff in my name. I asked how much, and was shocked when he told me three thousand dollars! That is a little more that we contracted for and I asked why. He explained that the company was sorry that we had lost one of our own and wanted help out. They also wanted to stay on good terms with us so they might avail themselves of our services in the future.

I purchased a buckboard and horse to carry Ben's coffin home and to transport our box of gear that came from the bandits. Zack and I decided to leave immediately and put as much ground behind us as we could before dark. We would ride together to Prescott, and he would continue on to his folks ranch to bury Ben. That night as we sat around our campfire, I told him I expected to stay in Prescott for a short while, so if he wanted to contact me he would know how. I apologized for getting his brother killed, and I told him I would understand if he did not want to continue with me. He assured me there were no hard feelings, that I wasn't to blame. His brother's death was just one of those things that happen when you deal with bad men.

We got an early start the next morning and I am sure Zack knew I was impatient to get home. I would have never wanted to be away from Mollie for this long. Who am I kidding? I don't want to be away for even one night. By sundown I will be holding her tight and we will try to make up for the time we have lost. Maybe I would give her the locket tonight, a token of how much I have missed her and love her.

When Prescott came into sight, Zack told me to go on ahead. He would stop at the livery as he needed a fresh horse. He didn't have to tell me twice. I rode ahead at a fast gallop thinking of how surprised Mollie was going to be.

I rode into the livery and told Fred to take care of my horse and that my friend was behind me in a buckboard. He was to help him in any way he could. Although I was dusty and dirty from the trail, I headed straight for our home on Gurly Street.   I unlocked the door, expecting to see Mollie. No one was there. Oh well, she might be out with Lilly. I went down the street to the dress shop just as it was closing. The lady was not Lilly, but I figured she probably knew Mollie so I asked if she had any idea where she was.   "Are you Mr. Bogardis?" she asked, turning a little pale. "Where is she", I shouted.   She pointed down the street and said I should first go to the Doc Ainsworth's office. I left running not knowing what may have happened. I nearly tore the door down getting into the Doc's office. He met me half-way across the floor. "Where's Mollie", I demanded to know. "What has happened?"

He said, "I think Mollie is going to be just fine, but I'm afraid she lost the baby."

Baby! ....What Baby!

*   *   *   *   *

Since the accident, I have remained in Lilly's bedroom much of the days and nights. Lingering in and out of consciousness, I was unaware of the amount of time that had passed. I refused to eat so often that Lilly said she was going to tie me down and force feed me like a orphaned calf.

Aunt Polly came by daily to check on me, as well as Doc Ainsworth. I may have refused the food that was offered but I did help myself to the laudanum bottle.

"Mollie, you must snap out of this! Mr. Bogardis will be home any time and he must not find you in this condition", pleaded Lilly. Her words would go in one ear and out the other. I just wanted to stare at the ceiling, drink the laudanum and be left alone.

Miss Nancy, owner of the dress shop, called on me a time or two. She would ask Lilly when she could return to work at the store. Lilly refused to leave me alone, even if it meant losing her position at the store. Lilly would simply answer Miss Nancy replying, "Soon".

One occasion, when I decided I had the strength to move about, I saw the bag I was carrying the night of the accident. I opened it to find the pink and white gingham dress which took me weeks to finish. I held the fabric against my face. I wanted to cry, I needed to cry, but every ounce of molten tears that was in me was drained, emptied. Nothing but weeping sounds remained.

Lilly would reassure me that Mr. Bogardis would be home soon. I knew I needed to compose myself and go back to our home on Gurly Street. How long has it been? I walked over to the wash bowl on the dresser and splashed my face with the lukewarm water. Grateful there were no mirrors in Lilly's bedroom, I patted my face dry without looking up. I pulled my hair back and secured it with a comb and called for Lilly to gather my clothing.

"Mollie, you're up!' rejoiced Lilly. "Let me help you", she pleaded, leading me out of the bedroom and into the sunlit adjoining room. I followed, reluctantly. Maybe it was time for me to go home, for Lilly to reclaim her own room again. Maybe I would feel closer to Mr. Bogardis in our home, and less vacant inside.

Lilly helped me dress, but I was not quite ready to attempt the walk home. Lilly said that Doc Ainsworth would be by in the morning and maybe I should stay until then. I nodded, prompting Lilly to feel as if I was consenting to the notion. I told Lilly I would now take a bowl of the the potato dumpling soup she made for me. She scampered off so quickly to retrieve it I thought she would stumble over her own feet.

While I waited, I walked over to the window. I pulled the yellow lemony colored curtains back and the streaming sunlight poured in and hurt my eyes. I stood starring outside at the stillness of the budding leaves on the tree branches. All was quiet, as if the world had turned to stone. I couldn't move. I suppose I just wanted to see what life looked like without our baby.

CHAPTER NINE

I no doubt terrified the Doc, as he kept patting me on the shoulder, trying to assure me that Mollie was fine. He was unware that I knew nothing about a baby. There had been an accident and some drunk cowboy had kicked Mollie in the stomach as she walked home one evening about two weeks prior. She had lost the baby and was doing quite well, except for the fact that she had contracted scarletina. He said it was hard to determine just how long Mollie had been afficted with the illness, but that he was quite certain that she was suffering with it now. He told me that although she would make a full recovery, that it was unlikely that she would ever be able to carry a child again.

He finally calmed me down enough to get through to me. He hadn't told her this yet, as he thought it was too much for her to handle in her condition. I told him to not mention it to anyone, that I would tell Mollie when I thought she was ready.

Since the accident, Doc explained that Mollie had been staying with Lilly. He said she lived just a block over from the dress shop. He assured me that Lilly was doing all she could and that Mollie was well taken care of. I thanked him and left in a hurry for Lilly's house. My poor Mollie. I should never have left her alone for so long. As soon as I am sure Mollie is alright, I must ask the Marshal about this accident. I want to know who is responsible.

I must have ran the entire way to Lilly's house. It didn't take long and just as I was approaching, my sweet Mollie was coming out. When she saw me threw her arms around me and began to cry. All I could do was hold her tight and tell her how sorry I was for not being there when she needed me. This was all my fault.

I picked up the bag she was carrying. I would have picked up Mollie too, and carried her all the way back to our house, but Mollie said she was fine now. She could walk on her own. I have never had to take care of a woman before, this was something I didn't know how to do. In my haste to get Mollie home, I forgot to thank Lilly for taking care of her in her time of need.

We spent a good deal of the evening talking about the events that had transpired in each others absence. She told me why she had not mentioned the baby before I left for Tuscon and then about the accident in front of the Diana Saloon. I did not question her much, I will take it up with the Marshal. I told her a short version of what had happened on our first stage run. No need to make more out of it than necessary.

I think both of us were just excited to be back in each others arms at last, peacefully sleeping side by side in our own bed. But in the early morning hours, some time around half past three o'clock, I woke up in a cold sweat. My body was trembling, my heart racing. I managed to regain my composure to prevent Mollie from wakening. It was only a nightmare! I remember them all too well. I dreamt that Mollie and I were together and in danger. No matter what I did, I was unable to protect her. Not the kind of thing I want to think about, especially after all we have been through. Eventually I drifted off again, peacefully holding Mollie as close as possible, and dreading the day that I have to tell her we may never have a child.

*   *   *   *   *

He was home. He was finally home! I was the first to awake this morning. My immediate thought was disbelief. Was the nightmare finally over? All I knew for sure was that Mr. Bogardis was lying by my side, one arm under the back of my neck, the other around my waist.

There was a lot of explaining to do last night, the baby, what happened outside the Diana Saloon, everything. He briefly told me about his journey to Canyon Diablo, of meeting up with Zack and Ben, and the misfortunate occurrence of Ben's death.

He told me he made a good amount of money while he was gone, that I need not worry about anything from now on, that he would never leave me again. He told me how much I scared him, the fear he had in his head when Miss Nancy told him to go see Doc Ainsworth about me. He said he was more afraid at that moment than he could remember feeling in his entire life!

Aunt Polly said we could try to conceive again one day, and I will rely on that notion. For now, I am just grateful to be in the arms of Mr. Bogardis. I watched his face as he slept, peaceful and serene. I heard his heart beat, a slow steady rhythm, like rain falling on a spring day. I hated to move, but I was anxious to get the day started. I had to get back on my feet and tend to my daily chores since I have been out of commission for so long.

As I walked to the kitchen area to make Mr. Bogardis a hearty breakfast, I spotted a letter addressed to me on the hall table. It was from Tombstone. Another letter from Louisa. When did this arrive? My days have gotten away from me, it was now mid way through the month of June.

I tore open the envelope and slid the paper out. I skimmed over the first part of Lou's letter exclaiming how happy the Earp's were for Mr. Bogardis and I about the baby. I am going to have a hard time confirming the heart breaking reality when I write back to her. The letter was lengthy, three pages in size. I sat down and started reading.......

"........I have so much to tell you, Mollie, I don't know where to begin! Morgan is all in a rage about Jim Wallace shooting Curly Bill Brocius in the face. Apparently, he and Wallace were on a drinking binge in Gayleyville when it happened. Morgan says Wallace should have been a better shot and we would all be rid of Brocius for good.

Ben Sippy has resigned being Marshall and has left town. There are rumors he owes hundreds of dollars in gambling debts. Virgil has been appointed Marshal in his place. They should have appointed Morgan instead, he is better qualified! Virg had to show his authority right away by arresting Wyatt for fighting, charged him with 'disturbing the peace'. Can you believe that! Mattie had some fine words for Virgil that day!

Virg then goes on to arrest Mayor Clum. He charges him with riding his horse too fast inside the city limits. I wish you were here to see these amusing exploits for yourself.

Wyatt has intentions of being elected sheriff. I heard him talking with Morg about making a deal with Ike Clanton, something about the Wells Fargo robbery. He says if the deal plays out, he would for sure win the election. Mattie is at her wits end with him, he constantly yells at her in front of all of us. She suffers from her headaches much more frequently now.

We have moved again. Our new residence is at the corner of First and Fremont Streets. A larger home then our last, but still across the Dead Line, in the Mexican area of town. Allie and Mattie have taken in sewing jobs to bring in extra money. They are always contemplating something together, while Bessie and I prefer to keep the house in order.

Mollie, I wish you and Mr. Bogardis would move back to Contention once the baby is born. A baby would be such a delightful distraction from all the everyday mayhem around here!

With hope that this letter finds you well, I close your friend,
Louisa"

I must let Mr. Bogardis read this letter after breakfast. I am sure he will want to know all the happenings with the Earp's.

"Mollie....... Mollie, where are you!"

"Calm down, my Darling, I am here!" I jumped up and ran back into the bedroom. "I was up to surprise you with breakfast", I told him, running my fingers softly along the side of his cheek. "I don't want any damn breakfast," he grumbled, gripping my arm and pulling me closer. "I want you back in this bed with me where you belong!"

CHAPTER TEN

Mr. Bogardis had planned to meet Zack for breakfast, but that was before he found out about my condition. Lilly knocked on our door bright and early. She was so excited for me she couldn't wait much longer to come over and visit, making sure I was doing alright. Mr. Bogardis had just pulled me back into bed when we heard her knock. He then remembered his plan to meet up with Zack at the diner.

While Mr. Bogardis was dressing for breakfast, I invited Lilly to dine with us and she accepted. We had just been seated at the diner when Zack walked in. Locks of his sandy blond hair fell out from under his hat as he quickly removed it and nodded acknowledgment to Lilly. The smile that spread across his boyish face a mile wide was certainly not meant for Mr. Bogardis or myself. In fact, we were almost oblivious in his sight.

If I could have seen my own face the day I first saw Mr. Bogardis on the sidewalk in Contention, I am sure it would have looked liked Lilly's! Her chin was slightly dropped, her eyes sparkled and shined like twinkling stars and her words were mumbled like a stuttering child. All of this within the first minute of seeing Zack Blade when he walked in the diner for breakfast.!

I didn't really recall ever seeing Zack Blade in Contention, but Mr. Bogardis explained how they first met that night in the alley. The remaining conversation at the table that morning was saddening, as we heard about Zack's brother, Ben. Zack told us that he was only staying in Prescott long enough for breakfast and then he'd be traveling back to Contention. Mr. Bogardis told Zack not to forget to take the box of weapons back with him.

Saying goodbye to Zack was difficult, especially for Lilly. We all wished he could have stayed in Prescott for a few days, but we understood his immediate need to leave. Mr. Bogardis said they would stay in touch with each other, as there was more work available for them as partners. They'd just take a break for a while while Zack tended to family matters. I could tell Zack really admired Mr. Bogardis and looked up to him.

During the next week or so, I noticed that Lilly seemed not as dishearten as she had been. Joseph seemed to be a distant memory for her, and she spoke not of his name anymore. The gleam was still in her eyes as she continued to daydream about the handsome young Zack Blade. I began feeling a lot stronger and back to my old self again, sleeping with Mr. Bogardis by my side was all I really needed.

The day before the Fourth of July celebration in Prescott, Lilly and I were busy making the final preparations on the assorted gown orders in the shop. After the fireworks in the evening, there is going to be a Grand Ball. Mr. Bogardis and I have decided not to attend the Ball, since Lilly had no escort.

Mr. Bogardis knows a fellow at the Prescott Hook and Ladder Company. They are in charge of the celebration fireworks. He has told Mr. Bogardis about all the wondrous sites to expect. Parachute rockets bursting in mid-air sending down colorful balloons! Union Candles flying upwards and exploding into cascading dazzling stars! And for the finale, a thirty foot magnificent meteoric balloon, illuminated with thousands of tiny light showers! I have never seen fireworks, so this is going to be a grand occasion for myself and Mr. Bogardis.

We got a good night's sleep, the night before the celebration. We have been so tired with all the excitement and commotion around town, we needed the rest. There is so much that must be done today! Mr. Bogardis had asked me to make us a picnic. Seems he has planned an entire evening for us to relax in a nearby meadow just outside of town. He claims we will be able to view the fireworks just fine from that location, but without the crowd in the city.

Lilly helped me made a mess of fried chicken and biscuits, slice some fresh cheese and bake a blackberry pie. Mr. Bogardis had made himself scarce most of the day, but he arrived promptly on time, driving with a carriage.

"And where are you taking me, my dearest?", I asked, but I really didn't expect an answer. Mr. Bogardis seemed amused with all his secretive plans for me today! He just grinned and kept the horse at a steady pace. He looked very elegant for a country side picnic. A pressed white shirt, gray vest with a black ribbon tie, dark trouser pants and polished boots. Even his hat appeared to be freshly cleaned and shaped.

He spoke very little until we reached a meadow full of green grass gently swaying in the evening breeze. We finally stopped near a tree with branches spread out and covering the sky in all directions. He helped me down from the carriage and we spread the blanket under the tree. I could hear the somber chirping of baby robins waiting on the return of their mother high up in the tree top. It was their supper time, and I'm sure they could smell the scent of our fried chicken and blackberry pie when I laid it out.

The meadow was beautiful! The sun was just beginning to sink behind the mountains, and the sky was the color of a King's robe blazed with bands of yellow, red and orange. I sat on the blanket while Mr. Bogardis stood to remove something from his vest pocket.

"Mollie, I have something I have been meaning to give you", he spoke in a
low voice, a gold chain dangling from between his fingers. He opened his hand to reveal an amber colored cameo locket, glistening in the fading sunlight. "This was my Mother's locket, Mollie. She wore it around her neck since I could remember. I've carried it with me for many years, perhaps the only attachment to my past that I have. I wanted to make it special for you, so I had it engraved while I was in Tucson."

I couldn't say a word. He walked behind me to slip the locket around my neck. As it fell upon my chest, I took it in my hand and opened it. I couldn't read the words inside, they looked foreign, in another language of sorts. Confused, I asked Mr. Bogardis what it said.

"Before we left Contention, Doc Holliday jokingly told me something in Latin. He was drinking and talking about ......uh, something about how he felt about a girl he once knew back in Georgia. 'In Omne, Tempus'', he called it ...... it means 'for you, forever."

He took my hands in his and gently pulled me up to where I stood in front of him. "It's the most precious thing I have ever had", I whispered.

He pressed his lips to mine and gently wrapped his arms around my shoulders. It has been a while, I have missed him so much! The heat in the late hours of the day was sweltering and causing our skin to sweat and dampen our clothing. I watched as he removed his vest and hung it on a nearby limb.

"I need you, Mollie", he mumbled in my ear. He was taking his time, kissing my neck, caressing my back. Carefully and tenderly gliding his hand closer to the inside of my garments. We had refrained from intimacy because of the the accident and I knew he was worried that I might not be ready.

We embraced in each others arms and I rested my face against his chest. I paused just long enough to look up and stare into his eyes. As if granting permission, I leaned my throbbing body in as tight as possible against his. Then, trying to sound humorless, I teased him, "Are you gonna draw that gun you're carryin' or just keep it in the holster?"

Mr. Bogardis threw his head back in laughter! He smiled and grabbed a hold of me with both his hands. Passionate and eager, he began to fumble over the tiny buttons on the back of my dress. "Damn!", he grumbled, "How many buttons are on this dress!"

I distracted his concentration by placing my hands on the mid section of his trousers, unleashing his manhood and desire for me. Forgetting the array of buttons down my back, he swiftly lifted me off the ground and positioned my body on the blanket. Impatiently he laid on top of me, strong but gentle with every touch. At the very moment his consuming urge was unbridled, I opened my eyes to witness an array of multi-colored lights bursting in the distant sky, exploding and replicating my senses. It was fireworks! Beautiful, passionate fireworks!

*   *   *   *   *

Mollie was getting stronger every day. After only a week or so, she seemed more like her old self. There was going to be a dance on the fourth of July, and I figured Mollie would want to go. Even though I am not much of a dancer, I would take her. Surprisingly, she decided we would sit this one out. I think she did not want to go because Lilly would not have had anyone to take her. Some fella broke her heart it seems and Mollie figures Zack may be the cure.

The news of President Garfield being shot at the Washington Railroad Station doesn't appear to be dampening the festivities for the fourth in Prescott. Makes one question the reasons behind Garfields dealing with the railroads.

In any case, I have my own plan for the fourth. I happened up on a meadow a short distance from town one day while out for a ride. Nothing really, just tall grass, a few trees and a small creek running near by. I had met a man who's a volunteer with the fire department, and is in charge of the fourth of July fireworks. I asked if he knew the meadow and would the fireworks be visible from there. He said Prescott had never seen fireworks like this before, and he guaranteed they would be visible high up in the sky. The plan was coming together. I asked Mollie to make us a picnic for the evening of the fourth and get us up some blankets. She asked if Lilly could come along but I told her this one was just for us.

I arranged to rent a carriage and spent a good deal of the day spiffing myself up for her. Even paid for a hot shave and a haircut. The crowning touch to all this would be the special gift I had been saving for Mollie. I've been waiting for the perfect time.

I picked Mollie up on time and she sure was surprised to see the carriage. She was beautiful. She had a glowing smile on her face. It was like those first days back in Contention when I could just sit and look at her. Lilly had helped her with her hair, swept it back off her face the way I like it.

We arrived at the meadow after a short ride, and we spread out our blankets. Mollie busied herself getting our picnic laid out, and I just laid back and admired her. What could she ever see in me? She had fixed fried chicken, biscuits, and a blackberry pie. It was all delicious but I had another hunger on my mind. When we had finished our meal I stood up to get the locket out of my pocket. I fumbled around for a few moments, thinking I might have lost it. A little nervous, I guess. I explained that it had belonged to my mother as I put it around her neck.

I pulled her up and gently pressed my lips to hers. The evening was hot and sweaty, as so were we. It has been a long time since we shared our bodies with each other. I tried to be gentle, as I was not sure she was inclined to be taken. I was willing to just lie on the blanketed ground beside her, if she spurned my proposition, but I wanted Mollie something fierce.

Any doubt I had was put to rest when she responed with agressiveness, a little out of character for my sweet, proper Mollie. All I could do was burst out laughing and pull her tight against me. The aprehensiveness I felt was gone as we fumbled with each others clothing. Close enough to see the reflection of the last rays of sunlight in her eyes, I whispered, "I love you".

I was on top of her in a moment and we were consumed by our desire. Our heated bodies stuck to the blanket as we lay against the cushioned ground. Not anything in the world would have brought me out of the trance of my passion for her .... or so I thought! Just then, the sky burst forth in all the colors that one could imagine. "It's fireworks, Mollie!" I told her, but meaning more what I sensed than what I saw. I rolled over beside Mollie and saw her eyes light up like a childs! We lay on the blanket and watched the sky for what seemed like an eternity. With Mollie's head resting on my arm, I watched her thrill in seeing the display of bright lights. It was the end of a perfect day.

CHAPTER ELEVEN

Our fourth of July evening seems to have put us back where we were before I left. Being with Mollie every day, and especially every night, has relieved my concerns and I think Mollie feels the same.

I checked with the Marshal about the accident that injured Mollie. He said it was just one of those things, a couple of cowboys had too much to drink and one of them stumbled into Mollie. Just an accident. I wanted to know who they were and where they were from. The one who kicked Mollie was named Luke Bradshaw, and worked off and on for the Circle L Ranch. I inquired about the Circle L and found that it stretched from north of Flagstaff down to Contention. It was not a solid strip of land, but the owner, William Lawrence was taking up land in Arizona just like John Chislom in New Mexico. I decided I would check more into the Circle L later.

I received a letter from Zack that was filled with bad news. When he arrived at his ranch, the house was deserted. No note or anything to tell him where everyone was. He walked out back and was shocked to see three fresh graves. No markings telling who they were, but his gut told him they belonged to his family. I can't imagine the restraint it took to dig a fourth grave for Ben, but that is what he did.

Upon closer inspection, it appeared that there had been some kind of struggle in the house and outside as well. Some of the furniture was out of place and it just did not look like the way his mother would have left it. Upon checking the barn, he noticed that the pick and shovel still had the fresh dirt clinging to them from digging the graves. Since the sun was already going down, he decided to get some sleep and go into town the following day.

When he arrived in Contention the next morning, he went straight to the Marshal's office. Upon his entrance, the Marshal stood up with a shocked look on his face. "Zack, we thought you and Ben were dead. Killed somewhere around Flagstaff." Zack explained what had happened and that he had just come from his parents ranch and no one was there. He also told the Marshal about the three fresh graves. The Marshal told him to have a seat and he would tell him what he knew.

Three men from the Circle L Ranch had ridden through and found his parents and sister dead. They said the house was ransacked like someone was looking for something.   They straightened the house up as best they could and buried his family. Then they rode into Contention to inform someone of what they had found. "We had just received word that you and Ben were dead, so we didn't know what to do", explained the Marshal. "One of the men who found them was Harvey Gaines, the foreman at the Circle L".

"Your parent's ranch borders the Circle L and they said they would take possession of the livestock and move it in with theirs since there was no next of kin." The Marshal went on, "I contacted the county sheriff and he agreed that there was not much we could do".

The name Harvey struck a bell in Zack's head. He asked about the Circle L. The Marshal explained that it was owned by William Lawrence, a wealthy rancher. Just about everything around bordered his land, some saying it stretched well to the north towards Flagstaff. Zack told the marshal he was going home, and that if he saw anyone from the Circle L to tell them to bring back the livestock. If not, he would pay a visit to Mr. Lawrence.

Zack did not come out and ask, but I sensed he could use a little help right about now. I explained to Mollie what had happened and that perhaps we needed to return to Contention and be of whatever help we could. I did not tell her about the Circle L, not yet.
She agreed and said Zack certainly needed his friends near him. I decided we would buy a small wagon and then sell it when we got to Contention. The next day we were making preparations for the trip, and Mollie asked my permission for Lilly to leave with us. I told her I could not see why Lilly would want to go, but that was up to them. There would be room for her in the wagon.

We have our few belongings packed. I'm glad now that I sent that box of guns we got from the bandits back with Zack for him to keep up with. More room for Lilly's things. I do seem to sense some excitement from Mollie. I'm not sure if it's because Lilly is coming with us or because she longs to return to Contention. Either way, I'm pleased she's up for the journey. Our last time in Contention was certainly an adventure. I just hope we are not getting into something that will cause more grief and heartache for any of us. But this thing with the Circle L has left me a little unsettled.

* 　　　 * 　　　 * 　　　 * 　　　 *

Life was almost back to the way it was before Mr. Bogardis left for Tucson. Even my everyday chores were joyful. I find myself singing while scrubbing the floors! And the nights, the nights are better than I would have ever hoped for.

A few days ago, Mr. Bogardis received a letter from Zack Blade. It seems that upon his arrival in Contention with his deceased brother, he incurred a tragic homecoming. He discovered that his mother, father and sister were killed, murdered he suspected.

Zack wrote Mr. Bogardis explaining the circumstances. Although, he did not come right out and ask for help or assistance, Mr. Bogardis has been pondering the idea of going back to Contention. Zack is now alone on the ranch, and way too young to have already buried his entire family.

I would love nothing better than to return to southern Arizona. I'd be closer to my friends, the Earp's, and to tell the truth, I miss Mrs. Marks and Mr. Crane. I wonder if old Littlefoot is still roaming the streets. I dare not mention my thoughts to Mr. Bogardis as I do not wish to impose my wants or wishes upon what he feels he should do. He must make his own judgement on going back to help Zack.

I watched him this morning, contemplating what to write back in a letter to Zack. Each time he attempted an answer, he took the paper, crumpled it in his hand and threw it against the wall. I think he is angry at the men who would commit such an act. He won't tell me what he already knows, if anything, about the killings. I know that he has also visited the Marshal here in Prescott and inquired about the accident. He asked about the men in the red sashes who were drunk and fighting that night in the Diana Saloon. Mr Bogardis, always thinking he needs to protect me from the horrors of this world! aI have spoken with Lilly. I considered how alone she would be without me in Prescott. She has nothing to keep her here any longer. Jimmie is growing up a fine young man, living with an upright widow woman in town. Joseph has moved on with his life. We have heard rumors that he and Vera will be tying the knot soon. I think Lilly is happy for him. Now that she has met Zack, I think she understands. I reckon she just wanted someone in her life to care for her, and Joseph was a plenty handsome enough fella to wish for! I have asked Lilly if she would consider leaving with Mr. Bogardis and me, if the chance presents itself. Bearing in mind that Zack is in Contention, and knowing what he has had to endure, she didn't hesitate the notion. Thank goodness! I couldn't leave here without Lilly. I firmly believe she started packing her belongings as soon as I left her!!

CHAPTER TWELVE

Once we were loaded and under way, I tried to keep my mind on what was around us. Not only did I have Mollie to care for, but Lilly as well. Both of them were doing fine. It was not a particularly arduous trip, but there were moments I was side tracked. My mind wanted to dwell on the recent events regarding Mollie's accident and Zack's misfortune with his parents. Something did not sit right. I managed to keep it pushed out of my mind for the most part, so I could concentrate on getting us to Contention safely. It is never good to let your guard down for even a moment. Things out here can turn deadly in the blink of an eye. I know that all too well.

I had decided that we would book rooms in the hotel as soon as we arrived, and rest up a good bit before I rode out to see Zack. I am sure Mollie and Lilly would want to go, but I thought it best that Zack and I talk in private first. When we entered the hotel, Mrs. Marks was behind the counter. I guess her and Crane must have hit it off pretty well. She was apparently glad to see Mollie and started rattling off about something before I even got the bags unloaded. Mollie is much more understanding of Mrs. Marks and the rest of townsfolk than I am. Mollie has a good heart and finds it easy to forgive, even if they almost cost both of us our lives. I don't share her forgiving nature. I tend to remember wrongs done to me. And my memory is long. I wasn't interested in small talk with Mrs. Marks or anyone else.

Since we left Prescott, we've had to behave ourselves because of Lilly! Now nothing restrained us. Mollie unlocked the door to room number ten, but I told her wait a moment. I pushed the door open and sat our bags inside. I turned to Mollie and lifted her over the threshold. As soon as the door closed, I threw her on the bed as an old memory replayed through my mind. And her smile told me everything I needed to know.

Later, as we lay side by side with her head on my chest, I began to consider recent events. Zack and I would have much to talk about in the morning.

*   *   *   *   *

The wagon ride through the rough terrain of Arizona was not easy. Lilly had never ventured this far from her home place before. She was, on one hand amazed with all the new sights, and yet still worried about seeing Zack again in such sorrowful circumstances.

We slept nights under the what cover we could find, but the desert heat of the day and the cold stinging air of the night were not what bothered Mr. Bogardis. He had two women in his charge, and tried his best to keep a calm manner about him through out the journey. But I could see through him. Something was troubling his soul. Of course, I could only think that it must have been Zack's ordeal that preoccupied his mind.

Before he rode out to Zack's place, Mr. Bogardis wanted Lilly and I to settle in at the hotel in Contention. We all three needed a restful night of sleep in a bed somewhat terrible. We didn't really have a plan as to where we were going to be residing once we arrived in town. I think Mr. Bogardis had intentions about us staying at the ranch with Zack, but he wasn't sure this was the proper time to impose. He said once we get situated at the hotel, he'd leave and head out to Zack's place alone.

What a surprise to see Mrs. Marks behind the hotel check-in desk! She barely recognized me. There is so much to catch up on, she tells us. She inquired about what we were doing back in Contention, but Mr. Bogardis replied 'all in good time.' He just wanted to rent two rooms and take a hot bath.

Mr. Bogardis carried our bags, as well as Lilly's, up the familiar staircase to the second floor. At the same time, running down the steps and across the tip of my shoe, was an old gray cat. Littlefoot! I tried to grab him and gather him up in my arms as he hurried by, but he was to swift. Mr. Bogardis, shaking his head called out to me, "Never mind with the cat, Mollie, get the door unlocked so we can get unpacked." I looked up to tend to the door, and saw it was number ten! The room Mr. Bogardis rented when he first came to Contention. The same room we came back to the night after the Christmas Dance!

"Is everything alright, Mollie?" Lilly asked when she saw the way I looked at the door. "Everything is wonderful, Lilly! We are very acquainted with this room." I stood in the hallway as Mr. Bogardis carried Lilly's bags to her room, three doors down. He returned with

198

empty arms, lifted me over the entry way of the door and into room number ten. He used my body to push the door closed behind us and bolted it shut. He kissed me long and hard, eagerly and forceful. Playfully stoking the side of my cheek, he smiled and whispered, "You do remember what comes next, don't you, Mollie!"

CHAPTER THIRTEEN

I got up early and thought I'd get a good breakfast before I headed out for Zack's ranch. I left Mollie sleeping peacefully in the bed, locks of her damp tangled hair stuck to her cheek. I dressed quickly and sat down on the edge of the bed for one more look, hoping to burn the vision of her into my memory. The sun was just breaking and allowing golden rays to parade through the curtains, glistening upon Mollie's exposed skin.

I glanced at the bedside table where I had emptied the contents of my pockets the night before. Funny how a man's life can be summed up with a few coins, a pocket watch and a handful of lead. Then I noticed the locket. There'd been a lot of blood spilled these past few months and nothing was making sense anymore, until that very moment. It was all for her...... everything I've done, everything I do, it's all for her.

I left expecting to be at Zack's place well before noon. The trip was uneventful except for a very large diamondback that I almost stepped on while I was off my horse answering natures call.

I topped a little rise and saw the ranch down below. It was close to the mountains but had plenty of open space around it on all sides. The house itself appeared to be pretty well kept on the outside. I could see where there had been a vegetable garden, a couple of broken fences around a patch of recent tilled up soil. While there was some grass, it was easy to see why it took so much land to keep up livestock. Cattle would have to range far to get enough to eat. That's pretty much the situation in New Mexico, too. The big land barons like Chisolm were the only ones who could make much of a living with cattle.

I rode up to the house, careful to keep my eyes moving, just in case. The door opened and Zack stepped out holding his rifle. He was also being cautious. He greeted me with a smile and asked me to come on inside and have some coffee. That sounded good. We went into the main room of the house, which was the parlor, dining room, and kitchen all rolled into one. The house was even smaller than it looked from the outside. I pulled up a chair and sat down as Zack poured up the coffee.

I told him how sorry I was to hear about his family and asked him if he had learned anything else about their passing. He explained the town Marshal was pretty vague, only stating that Harvey Gaines of the Circle L found them, buried them, and reported it to him. For some reason the Marshal had thought that both he and Ben had been killed up north. He buried Ben next to the rest of his family and just settled in to see what would happen. That's why he came to the door with a rifle. I told him I thought that he should certainly take every precaution. After all, three of his family members were murdered here in this house.

I told him to hear me out. There's some things that just don't make good sense. Nothing I can back up, but it don't seem right. The man who found Zack's family was named Harvey. "Zack, do you remember Mrs. Pryer, the woman we came across on the trail, the one who lost her husband?" I asked him. "They were told they should leave their land before something else happened. Remember who told them that? His name was Harvey".

Could he be the same one? If so, what would he be doing ranging out so far? We need to check on this Circle L Ranch. All I know is that it is owned by a man named Lawrence who is trying to round up as much property as he can. He already has holdings up around Flagstaff and as far south as here. I suggested that Zack pack up a few things and ride back to Contention with me. We can shake the tree and see what falls out. Besides, there's this pretty little girl by the name of Lilly who came with us. I told him that Mollie has it in her head that she is sweet on him. I saw a quick flash of red in his cheeks, but he stood and said he would be ready to leave as soon as he put his gear together.

We rode back to Contention is silence. I guess both of us were wondering what possible connection there could be between a displaced family from around Flagstaff and the deaths of his family outside of Contention. If nothing else, there was a man named Harvey involved and I don't think I like him. I know you should not judge people that quickly, especially someone you haven't even met. But quick judgments have kept me alive more than once.

I think I should have a little pull in Contention now. After all, if it were not for me, the Gorch family would still have the town under its thumb. Mrs. Marks, Cornelius Crane, and quite a few others should be willing to at least fill in some of the blanks for me. I also need to feel out the county Sheriff. Whatever is going on, it is not a town matter. But human nature being what it is, I would guarantee that some people in town knows something about what is going on. And Mrs. Sarah Marks would be a good place to start. I should probably let Mollie in on my suspicions. She might get more out Mrs. Marks with honey than I can with rock salt. But on the other hand, the town knows that I do not give up on a cause once I take it on. They know a little of what I am capable of. And of course, they all remember that sweet little Mollie put two loads of buckshot into her husband, Sam Fisher. Yeah, I think there just might be some people willing to talk.

*   *   *   *   *

"Hurry, Lilly! I want to walk down to the Chinese Laundry and see Hey-You. Remember, I've told you about him before. He's about Jimmie's age and I was so attached to him before we left. I can't wait for you to meet him and his father!" I watched Lilly prepping herself in the mirror and tried to scutter her up. Without looking away, she asked, "Mollie, do you think Zack will be coming back with Mr. Bogardis today?"

"I don't even know if Mr. Bogardis is coming back to town today," I told Lilly. "You look just fine. Now, if you do not leave this room and follow me into town, you will be on your own today!"

As I waited for Lilly in the hall way, I stepped back inside my room to retrieve my cameo locket from the bedside table. I only take it off my neck before I go to bed for sleeping purposes, as not to harm it. I slipped the gold chain over my head, pulled the locket open and looked at the photograph I had placed inside. Beside the photograph are the words Mr. Bogardis had engraved for me. I must have read the inscription a hundred times over. I would love for Mrs. Marks to observe the piece and give me the opportunity to gloat and praise Mr. Bogardis' affection for me!!

I saw Lilly put her hair brush back on the dresser and run out of her room in time to catch up with me before I entered the lobby. Cornelias Crane! He looked different, maybe not quite as frazzled as he was before. It seemed that Mrs. Marks must have informed him that we had arrived yesterday. 'Miss Mollie! How good it is to have you back in Contention!", he shouted from behind his desk. "Mrs. Marks has asked me to inform you that she will be serving breakfast at her place for you and your lady friend this morning".

I'm sure that Mrs. Marks is exceedingly curious about why we have returned. But that is alright, I also want to know what has been going on around here since we left. Breakfast at Mrs. Marks would be fine, but first, I wanted to take Lilly by Po-Man-Sang's laundry.

Just as I thought, Hey-You was hanging clothes on the rope line behind the laundry door. When we saw each other, he ran and wrapped his arms around me like he would never let go. His father rushed to greet us, hugging Lilly and then hugging me. Hey-You was talking so fast, I couldn't make out all the words. I finally told him that I would be here in town for some time and that I would come back and see him again soon. His father looked as if he was ready to cry and said a few words in Chinese. I introduced Lilly to them both, told them we were staying at the Mason Hotel and that we were late for breakfast. I kissed Hey-You on the forhead which left a big smile on his face as we left. We said goodbye and walked towards Mrs. Mark's home.

I had only been to Mrs. Mark's home a time or two. She had been my employer at the dress shop and one of the only friends I had in Contention after I arrived. Although we had our differences, I understood the way she was. She's a widow woman set in her ways and sees the world as if it under her aurthority. I do believe that Mr. Crane is now in direct influence of her and I don't think he minds it one bit!

Mrs. Marks has a very elegant home. Expensive oil paintings hang on her wall behind a velvet upholstered sofa in her sitting room. Upon our entrance, she served Lilly and I freshly baked sweet bread and steamed tea from the south of France. We sipped from dainty porcelain cups with tiny lilac flowers painted on both sides. As we ate, Mrs. Marks told us she and Mr. Craine have been keeping company these past few months on a regular basis. They were even considering the idea of marriage. She said that she was now doing his books for him at the hotel and tending to his profits as well as hosting the guests. She went on and on about how she could not believe he could have managed his business before without her help. Money was a very valuable asset to Mrs. Marks.

"Mollie, I was wondering if Mr. Bogardis has made an honest woman of you yet?" inquired Mrs. Marks, blount and to the point. I was a somewhat taken back with her impudent question, but that is just how Mrs. Marks is. "Mr. Bogardis and I are very happy, Mrs. Marks, and I thank you for your concern". I uncomfortably twisted the gold chain between my fingers, the cameo locket dangled against my breasts. That was as close to a straight forward answer I could give and still remain respecful!

"And you, Miss Lilly, are you spoken for?" Mrs. Marks continued, but now directing her questions at Lilly. "I know a few eligible young gentlemen who would love the opportunity to sweep you off your feet. A woman should never be without a man, you know. I have had several husbands and have outlived them all. I suspose Mr. Crane will be my last."

Poor Lilly! I have been in her shoes, ambushed by Mrs. Marks questions. 'How long will you be in town?' 'does Mr. Bogardis have a job appointment?' and 'have you heard about so and so?' We barely managed to break a word in edgewise! I told Lilly I would ask Mrs. Marks about possible employment at her dress shop. Lilly mentioned that she had brought a letter of recommendation from her former proprieitor in Prescott, Miss Nancy. Mrs. Marks assured us that there was plenty to be done these days and that we shall discuss it further next time we talk. I promptly thanked Mrs. Marks for her hospitality and breakfast. She escorted us to the door, still rambling on to no end. The morning was over and the afternoon had quickly approached. Our first day back in Contention was quite a mouthful, to say the least! Lilly and I enjoyed the peaceful quiet of our walk back to the hotel.

CHAPTER FOURTEEN

We arrived back in Contention around dusk. We got our horses taken care of and set out for the hotel. Of course I was anxious to see Mollie, and I think Zack did not mind that we brought Lilly along. When we entered the hotel lobby, Cornelius Crane was behind the counter. He spoke and wished both of us a good evening. I nodded and told him I would like to have a few words with him when the opportunity presented itself. He swallowed hard and just blinked his eyes. I assured him it was nothing for him to worry about, and would only take a few minutes of his time. I did not want to cause him to make a puddle in the floor like a previous time we had a talk.

Zack said he would wait in the lobby in case Miss Lilly came down. I smiled as I turned my back and started up the stairs. I bet a stampede would not prevent either of them from seeing the other, at least if Mollie is half right. I tapped on the door to room number 10 and waited for Mollie to acknowledge the knock. In an instant she had jerked the door open and threw her arms around me. I asked if that was the greeting everyone who knocked on the door got. She certainly did not check to see who it was. She called me a silly man and said that she knew it was me by the sound of my walk. We kissed briefly and I told her that Zack was downstairs wondering if Lilly would come down and visit with him. Mollie was down the hall and knocking on Lilly's door in what seemed like one leap. Lilly's face lit up as soon as Mollie told her that she had a visitor. We followed her down the stairs and tried our best not to laugh at the two of them. They were both bashful and just said hello softly to each other. Lilly offered her condolences on the loss of his family. At that point I suggested that we all walk across the street and get a bite to eat.

It appeared to be a slow evening in the diner. We took a back table that was secluded enough that I thought we could talk. And of course, I took the corner seat. That way I could see anything and anybody that might be a threat. When Mollie and I first got together, I think she was sometimes amused and sometimes annoyed at my precautions. She came to realize that vigilance was required in order to remain safe.

The waiter appeared and Mollie and Lilly each ordered a bowl of stew. Zack and I had a better appetite and we each ordered a steak. We had coffee all around. I explained briefly to Mollie and Lilly about the man named Harvey who had supposedly found the husband and father dead, brought him in, and told his widow she should move on before something else happened. A man named Harvey Gaines found Zack's family and buried them. He's a foreman for the Circle L Ranch. The ranch is owned by a man named William Lawrence, and the land stretches over a lot of territory. I asked Mollie if she would talk with Mrs. Marks to see what she knew about William Lawrence or Harvey Gaines. I asked Zack to hang around the saloon some tonight and tomorrow. A lot of information passes through a saloon when the liquor begins to take hold. First he should come back to the hotel and we
will get him a room before he goes out. We all agreed to meet the next morning for breakfast. When we got to hotel, Zack was quick to put up his gear and head out to the saloon. He bowed to Lilly and Mollie, and then he was gone. I was not too worried about him in the saloon. I already knew that he was not a hard drinker and would keep his head in the event of trouble.

Lilly went on to her room to turn in. Mollie and I took a short walk down the street, past her old room where she was abducted, past the alley where the Gorch brothers had first tried to ambush me, and for some reason, we had to walk down the alley where we met secretly so many times. Even in the storms, we would meet and hold each other in the shadows. When we got to our special place in the alley, we stopped and looked into each others eyes like we did then. I leaned down and kissed her gently as her arms went around my neck. "Is that the best you can do?" she asked. "Just wait until I get you back to our room!" I threatened. We both smiled and walked back to the hotel arm-in-arm.

Even with Mollie sleeping softly beside me, I could not stop my mind from trying to piece things together. It was like a puzzle with a few pieces missing. My gut told me that there was a connection somewhere, but I just could not grasp it. When I finally fell asleep, I had that nightmare again. Mollie was in danger and I could not protect her. It made me wake with an uneasy feeling in my stomach. But after all, it's just a dream.

*   *   *   *   *

Zack seemed to be pleased that Lilly had come with us. Last night, I watched them gaze into each other's eyes over supper at the diner. He's not much at conversation, but Zack just doesn't know what to say to Lilly yet. I think it's because he has so much on his mind. He and Mr. Bogardis have made plans on uncovering the truth about Zack's parents. They explained to Lilly and I that we must keep our ears and eyes open.

Mr. Bogardis tells me that he will be riding into Tombstone in the next day or so. He thinks maybe Wyatt or his brothers may have some information for him. I asked to go with him, but he didn't think much of the idea. He says that Tombstone is in shambles right now. A couple of weeks ago, a fire broke out in front of the Arcade Saloon on Allen Street. Burned down a lot of businesses and made a mess of the town. Virgil's looking into it, but says it was most likely an accident. Anyway, Virgil's more concerned over the mess Doc Holliday is in. Kate signed some kind of affidavit that accused Doc of the stage robbery in Contention a while back. This ain't the first time she blamed him for something, they get drunk and fuss at each other somewhat terrible. I think this time, she's a little more embittered with him.

I'd love to see Louisa and the girls. I'd like for Lilly to meet them. But since we will be staying in Contention, we will occupy ourselves in other ways. Perhaps Lilly and I will venture about town today and talk with Hey-You and his father. I did notice that there were red tinted sashes laundered and hanging among the other items of clothing on the rope line yesterday morning. I remember seeing the same red sashes tied around the waists of certain men in Prescott, as well as on the drunk cowboys at the Diana Saloon.

I saved a few leftover crumbs for Littlefoot from last night's supper so I stepped out into the hallway to call for him. When I did, I heard Mr. Crane talking with a couple of men in the lobby. I tiptoed to the edge of the stairway to listen in as much as I could. They were talking about men named 'Clanton' and 'Lawrence'. Then I heard the name 'Harvey Gaines'. I think that's the same name Mr. Bogardis told us about. There were a few other words I caught, but I couldn't make out the gist of it. I should probably tell Mr. Bogardis.

I went straight to Lilly's door and knocked. She seems to require more time perparing herself for the day, so I thought I should make sure she was awake. She should have been up by now, but there was no answer. I pounded several times on the door. In panic, I called out, "Lilly! Lilly! Are you in there?"

CHAPTER FIFTEEN

Mollie came running in telling me that Lilly was not in her room. She did not answer the door. I pretended that I was unconcerned and that Lilly was able to care for herself. I did not really believe that and told Mollie I would see if I could locate her. As I turned the corner on the stairway, I could see Crane talking with two men. Crane looked and addressed me as I approached the desk. He told me that Miss Lilly had left a message that she was going on to breakfast over at Hopkin's. The larger of the two men introduced himself as Roy Flores, and the other man as Phil Thomas. They said they were both Pinkerton Detectives and would like to talk to me about the Flagstaff to Canyon Diablo stage route. I explained that I needed to check on something but would be glad to meet them in about an hour. They said they had a room in the hotel and suggested we talk there.

I went out and headed toward the diner but did not have to go very far. I met Lilly and Zack walking back to the hotel. I did not let on that Mollie was in a worry fit about Lilly. I only offered a good morning and let Lilly and Zack do the talking. Lilly said she rose early and was very hungry so she went to the diner for breakfast and met Zack on her way, so they had breakfast together. They both had that silly "hand in the cookie jar" look, but I did not press them. I told Zack there were two Pinkertons at the hotel wanting to talk about the stage robbery, and that I was out looking for him. We walked back to the hotel together and retired to our own rooms. Mollie was pacing the floor, but I told her Lilly was fine. I explained their "story", to which Mollie just rolled her eyes and smiled. "Yep, sounds like you two really do have a lot in common", I teased. She slapped me hard across the upper arm and laughed. I think Zack will be keeping a close eye on Lilly, and her on him. I also explained about the two detectives who were down stairs

Mollie said that she had heard them talking earlier but forgot to tell me because Lilly was missing. She said she could not understand everything they said, but she caught a few names, one being Harvey Gaines. Interesting. I told Molly I was going for coffee if she wanted to go. She declined saying it would take her too long to get ready. I'm sure she just wants to get to Lilly's room and tittle-tattle about Zack. I told her she could find me and Zack down at the diner for a while.

Over coffee, I explained to Zack about the Pinkertons and the names they had dropped. He said that the only thing he knew about Gaines and Lawrence was what we already knew. But he did know a little about the Clanton family. They were part of a loosely configured group known as the "Cowboys". You could always tell a cowboy by the red sash they all wore. There were rumors that they dabbled in rustling, both horses and cattle, but nothing was ever proven. We decided we would finish our breakfast and go back to the hotel and see what the Pinks had to say.

When we arrived at the hotel, the lobby was deserted except for Crane. I walked over and told him it was time for us to have a talk. I thought if he knew anything, I might could get it out him. I asked about Gaines, Lawrence, and Clanton. He knew the Clanton brood was a little ways out of Tombstone. He had heard of William Lawrence and the Circle L. He had also heard about Harvey Gaines. He said some say that Harvey Gaines is a violent man who was used to having things his own way. Some say that he was nothing more than a hired killer until he went to work for Mr. Lawrence. Well, it's a start at least. And all without scaring the wits out of him this time. I asked for the room number of Flores and Thomas, and Zack and I went on up.

I knocked once and the door opened. They invited us in and I introduced Zack. Flores immediately asked if this was one of the young men who was with me at Canyon Diablo. I replied that he was and followed up with a question of my own. What and how did they know about Canyon Diablo?

Flores invited us to sit and told us that while we were working for Wells Fargo Stage Company they were employed by the Atlantic and Pacific Rail Lines. For some time, they had suspected that the stage robberies were just one of many problems that someone had designed to stop the progress of the railroad beyond Canyon Diablo. I asked what kind of other problems. Thomas said there had been mysterious fires, explosions, theft or damage to railroad equipment. In fact three employees were killed when a powder magazine blew up.

They congratulated us on our success in foiling the stage robbery between Flagstaff and Canyon Diablo. The story was spreading about the three men who had taken out an even dozen bandits. I explained that while we did put some research into our plan, we were extremely lucky to come out of that with only one dead. Thomas mentioned the story they heard, was that two of the defenders were killed, not one. In fact, two brothers from around the Contention area. They had just recently become aware of the actual truth, but said they'd keep the public under the impression that both Ben and Zack were killed. It might work out better that way.

Flores offered Zack and I a drink. We declined, a little early in the day for me, and Zack as well. I wanted to know who William Lawrence was and what part he played in this show. They explained that he was the owner of the Circle L and that it had been steadily expanding for the last twelve or fifteen years. No one really knew much about him prior to his arrival in Arizona shortly after the war. He did most of his business through his foreman, Harvey Gaines. He was another story. Harvey Gaines had somewhat of a checkered past. It was thought that he had been charged with murder on more than one occasion, but was acquitted each time because the witnesses refused to testify. There was no doubt that he was quick with a gun and no slouch with his fists. He seemed to rule Lawrence's empire with an iron hand.

The Clantons, however, came off as being just rowdy cowboys who liked other peoples cattle. They never had much of a herd, at least not for long. They would build up a herd and then it'd be gone and they'd build up another.

I told them about the Pryer family, less the husband, who we met as they were headed for Tucson. The woman said a man named Harvey had found her husband dead and brought him home and had his men bury him. He then told her it might be best to move on before something else happened. Zack told them about his parents and sister's demise. Harvey Gaines had been the one who found and buried them. Could it be the same Harvey? It was a pretty good distance between, but both areas were around the Circle L property.

We agreed to keep in touch. I told them I would be based here in Contention. I would be going up to Tombstone soon to check on other matters. They asked if they could be of assistance. I thought " why not"? They would have more pull than a stranger in some of the land offices.   I told them I would like to know the extent of William Lawrence's holdings, when he began acquiring land on a large scale. Also, anything they could find on Harvey Gaines. I would check out the Clanton family and we could swap information. We all shook hands and Zack and I left. Zack started to say something in the hall, but I put my finger to my lips and motioned him down the stairs and outside. We walked down the street rather than on the sidewalk. Harder for someone to overhear you. What Zack was going to say was that he knew that the Circle L was close to his parents ranch. I told him I suspected as much, and that I would be going to Tombstone tomorrow to see some friends. He asked if I wanted him to go along. I told him no, that I would feel better if he stayed here in Contention with the ladies. He smiled and nodded.

*   *   *   *   *

Zack and Mr. Bogardis have been preoccupied all day. Just as well, I've been a little worn since we arrived and decided to take the afternoon and rest. Lilly stayed with me in the room for a spell, but I told her it wasn't necessary. She has her own suspisions regarding my ailments.

"Mollie, do you think perhaps you are with child again?" Lilly asked, sounding over anxious. "There has been enough time and it would be simply wonderful! I realize it may only be a few weeks, but Aunt Polly has told me that a woman can feel these things right away."

What a lovely thought, but I explained to Lilly that it was more likey just fatigue from the journey. A little rest and soon I would feel like my old self again. After Lilly left, I laid down on the bed but couldn't close my eyes. I day dreamed about what our children would be like. I was hoping the next time we could have a son. Mr. Bogardis would construct a wooden horse for him when he got of age to walk. I can imagine him in his daddy's boots and cowboy hat rocking back and forth, pretending he's a Texas Ranger.

I must have drifted off to sleep. When I awoke I heard the key turn in the door and saw Mr. Bogardis in the shadow of the hallway light. I jumped up before he could notice I had been resting. I quickly poured water into the washing bowl, splashed my face and refreshed my appearance.

Mr. Bogardis began telling me about his day with Zack and the Pinkerton men I had heard in the lobby. He didn't go into that much detail, which was quite alright with me. I just sat and ocassionally smiled in his direction. It seemed that his words were just wondering in one ear and out the other .... I was still away in another place, watching our 'son' ride on his wooden horse.

CHAPTER SIXTEEN

I explained to Mollie last night that I would be riding over to Tombstone today. Of course she wanted to go visit with Lou and the other girls, but I told her I was going alone and making a quick trip out of this and would not have time to linger.   She said wasn't feeling well again, anyway. I should tell her what Doc Ainsworth said back in Prescott, but now is not the time. I don't know much about scarletina, but the doc did say it could take a while for her to get back to feeling proper again. She handed me a letter she wrote, asking me to deliver it to Louisa.

I got on the trail early and had to force myself to concentrate on my surroundings.   I keep trying to put it all together.   There is just something missing. As I rode into Tombstone I could tell that the fire had done a lot of damage.   People were busy either tearing down the carnage and rebuilding.   I had no doubt that they would have everything operating normally in the near future.

I tied my horse at the Marshal's office and walked in. Virgil was sitting behind the desk and Wyatt was sitting across from him.   They both jumped up and met me, shaking hands and extending greetings. I congratulated Virgil on him being elected Marshal. He laughed and said he was not sure that congratulations were really in order. I asked where Morgan was, and was told that he was up pretty late last night and had not made it out yet, and that Doc had been with him. They told me about the charges brought up against Doc for robbing the stage coach and killin' the driver. He and Kate had been fighting and she invented the story, "you know how she gets when she's drunk with the barbaric temper of hers!" But it's all settled and over now, Doc was acquitted a week or so back.   Doc might be a lot of things, but robbing stage coaches was not his line.

Wyatt asked about Mollie and I gave him an abbreviated version of her accident. I also mentioned that I had done some work for the stage line between Flagstaff and Canyon Diablo. They looked at each other and smiled. They allowed as how they heard something about me and a couple of boys taking on a dozen bandits. Wyatt said it was a shame that both of my boys were killed. I told him that was only the rumor and that Zack was still with me. I also told them about Zack's family. They both said if there was anything they could do for Mollie and I and also for Zack, all I had to do was ask.

I told them I have been trying to tie some folks together and I need a little help. I asked what they could tell me about the Clanton outfit and the group known as the "cowboys". They lit in quickly explaining that the Clanton bunch were part of the cowboys, and the group tried to run southern Arizona. They also explained about old man Clanton's mystery herd. Sometimes large, sometimes small, and then back large again. It didn't take much to figure that they were stealing and reselling cattle.

Virgil said that he and Wyatt had been trying to keep an eye on them, as they caused considerable trouble in town. But any rustling they might be doing was out of Virgil's jurisdiction. I asked if they had ever heard of William Lawrence of the Circle L and his foreman, Harvey Gaines. They said they knew that the Circle L had be expanding and was really stretching out over Arizona, and that William Lawrence was a very private man. They also suggested I ask Doc about Harvey Gaines.

I invited them to the saloon for a drink, as I intended to wait a while until Doc got up and about. They both declined due to work, but again offered any help I might need.

I walked in the Oriental and looked around. Just a few shirkers at the bar who looked like they had been at it hard all night. I picked a corner table, put my back to the wall and ordered coffee and a bottle. I had not been there long when the swinging doors flew open and in came Doc Holliday and Morgan Earp. Doc looked as if he had never taken a drink in his life, but poor Morgan looked like he had been run over by a wagon. Keeping up with Doc would make an old man out of a youngster. They both came over and shook hands. They said they had been by the Marshal's office and Virgil had told them I was in town. Doc could not resist a sarcastic comment and asked if I could not have found a bigger gang to take on. After all, me and two more against a dozen did not seem quite fair to him. We laughed and I told Doc that he shouldn't talk much, seems like he's been in a pile of trouble himself. 'Never mind bout me', he said, 'what the hell are you doin back in Tombstone'. I asked if he could fill me in on what he knew about a man named Harvey Gaines. Doc's face went sour and I could see his lip curl under his mustache. He said Harvey Gaines was no man. He was spawned of the Devil to torment the innocent. It wasn't that he only picked on the weak, he picked on anyone. Doc had been in the same saloon with him on a few occasions, and regretted he had not sent him home to the Devil. He said if I was looking for Gaines, I better be careful. He was fast and was afraid of nothing in this world.

At that point Wyatt stuck his head in the door and told me there was a cowboy in the Marshal's office who wanted to speak with me. I said goodbye to Doc and Morgan, and remembered to give Morgan the letter to Louisa. Doc told me that if I had to go up against Gaines, he would be happy to help out. Whatever I needed.

I walked into Virgil's office and saw a young man with a faded red sash in his hand, wait'in in a chair. He looked nervous and would not look directly at me. I told him my name and asked what I could do for him. He said his name was Luke Bradshaw and that he was the man I was looking for. He went on to say that his friend Adam and he were in Prescott a while back and having a few drinks in the Diana Saloon. He said that they were the ones who accidently hurt my wife. Before anyone could stop me, I was across the room and had him by the throat. Virgil and Wyatt pulled me off of him and got me in a chair. Luke said that someone had mentioned that I rode into town that morning so he knew I had tracked him down. He was afraid to approach me so he came to Virgil. He said they were just having a little fun and got too rowdy. When they came through the saloon doors, Adam had tripped him and pushed him at the same time. Neither of them even saw my wife until she was lying on the sidewalk.

I asked him what the hell did he think I was going to do to him! He explained that he had worked for the Circle L and rode with the Clantons. He was a cowboy, but since the accident he took off his sash and was trying to do the right thing. His friend Luke had been killed in a stampede right after the accident, and he was afraid God was going to get him too. He figured if I killed him or not, he did not want to spend eternity in hell. I always thought it strange that a man would fear death. Whether a man believes that there is a heaven and hell, you're going to one place or the other after you leave this world. There is no way this kid can bring back our lost baby. So his after-life is none of my concern.

I had been full of hate for the men who caused Mollie to lose our child, and would not have a second thought about killing both of them. But this young man seemed to be genuinely sorry for what had happened. I knew in that moment that Mollie would have told him she forgave him. I don't forgive, but I reckon I can let him live. He kept repeating that he would do anything to try to help make up for what he had done. I told him nothing he could do would ever undo the pain he had caused.

He started out the door and I took a chance. I asked if he would be willing to tell me what he knew about the Circle L, William Lawrence, Harvey Gaines, and the Clantons and "cowboys". He responded that he would be glad to do so, although much of it might incriminate him. I looked at Virgil. He shrugged his shoulders. If what you know helps me, your part of it will stay in this room, I told him.

It was as if he could not talk fast enough. This boy wanted clear his conscience. While he had never been along when anyone was killed, some of the others had talked about visiting small ranches from Contention to Canyon Diablo. They said Harvey makes them one offer to get out. If they don't, then the next time someone dies. And when Harvey gets bent on killing sometimes there is no stopping him. He will sometimes have his way with the women and enjoys inflicting pain. I made a note in my head to not tell Zack about that part.

He did not know a lot about William Lawrence. He owned the Circle L and was Harvey's boss. He was also trying to get as much land as possible into the Circle L. Sometimes when some of the men were out on a job without Harvey, they would talk about things they had seen or heard. Adam and some more men had spent a week one time between Canyon Diablo and Flagstaff. Their job was to rob the stage when it carried the railroad payroll. Some of the men with them were there to cause the railroad trouble in any way they could. They were supposed to slow down the progress of the railroad.

Hmmm....., I had assumed that someone had wanted to stop the railroad. When I questioned Luke further he said that Mr. Lawrence's intent was not to stop the railroad, but to delay it so he could acquire more property out ahead of the railroad. Now the puzzle is starting to come together.

I asked about the Clantons and the "cowboys". Luke said that as Circle L grew, it was in constant need of stock. Old man Clanton, along with the "cowboys", supplied that stock by rustling anything they could find. Sometimes they even went into Mexico to rustle. In fact, he'd heard talk about a scheme to raid the cattle herd near Guadalupe Canyon near the Mexican line. This was due to take place in the next week or so.

I told Luke that if I had known he was the one who hurt my wife (I saw no reason to correct his assumption) that I probably would have killed him on the spot. I said I hoped he was sincere in his efforts to turn his life around. I could not believe I was saying those things, but I knew in my heart it was what Mollie would have done.

As the door closed behind Luke, all I could do was lean back in my chair. I felt totally drained. I had come to Tombstone to try to find out a little about the Clantons, and ended up breaking this whole thing wide open. I now knew that William Lawrence was behind everything, and that Harvey Gaines was his trigger man. The Clantons no longer concerned me much. If you cut off the snake's head, the rest of it will die. It may be time for Zack and I to meet Harvey Gaines and William Lawrence.

*   *   *   *   *

I sent along a letter with Mr. Bogardis, addressed to Louisa, for him to give to Morgan. I hadn't answered her last letter and I needed to inform her about the accident. It wasn't much of a letter, but I figure we'll be meeting up with each other one day soon. Before we left Prescott, I went down to George S. Potter's Fine Furniture Store and purchased those window shades I thought she might like. She's gonna be plenty surprised when I present them to her!

Mr. Bogardis left at daybreak this morning for Tombstone leaving Zack here to look after us. Last night, he told me that he thought my intuitions were correct. He can see that Zack and Lilly are smittened with each other and understands why Lilly wanted to leave her home and follow us to Contention.

Lilly and I have plans to spend some time with Mrs. Marks and Mr. Crane today. Lilly is hoping Mrs. Marks will employ her at the dress shop. She is going to be in need of income soon to support herself. Mr. Crane charges us almost the sum of fifty cents per day for living expenses. Of course, that does include fresh water, toiletries and breakfast if we have a notion to eat his cooking. It seems that Mrs. Marks fired the cook that he used to keep on duty for preparing the morning meals. He says his new rates are at the request of Mrs. Marks. 'Profit', she says, 'is the backbone of every man!'

Zack arrived around mid morning and asked if we were in need of his services. I told him that he could accompany Lilly and I on a walk to the dress shop if he so desired. Of course, he was pleased to do so.

Mrs. Marks was once again in a chatty mood as we arrived. She was pleased to meet Zack and thought she might have met his family on ocassion when they happened into town. She was aware of his family's untimely deaths and doubted that anyone from Contention could have committed such a deed. She said that there has been some shady charactors drifting in and out of town these last few months and she was rightly appalled. I asked Mrs. Marks if she noticed if any of these 'charactors' ever wore red tinted sashes around their waists. Taking a moment to ponder the thought, she said she reckoned a few of them did. They may not have all been red in color, but sure enough, some of the men had worn the sashes. Zack had a few questions of his own, and Mrs. Marks did the best she could to answer with what she thought she knew.

Before we left the company of Mrs. Marks, she asked if we would care to dine with her and Mr. Crane later in the evening. I looked at Zack and Lilly and told Mrs. Marks I believed that perhaps we will accept her kind offer another day.

On the walk back to the hotel, I informed Zack that I was feeling a little out of sorts. Maybe another afternoon of rest might suit me well. I suggested that Lilly should not be left unattended and asked Zack if it was possible to spend some time with her today.

Hmmmmmm...........He smiled and nodded.

CHAPTER SEVENTEEN

I said my goodbyes quickly as I wanted to get back to Contention that day. Again it was hard to pay attention to the trail because my mind had a lot going through it right now. At least we have a direction to go in. But it will take cool heads and a plan if we want to come out of this. The Circle L has a lot of hands, as well as a lot of friends. I'm sure William Lawrence could get the Clantons to do anything for him for money.

I arrived back in Contention in time to have dinner with Mollie. She'd been resting, probably had a busy day with Lilly. I washed and cleaned the trail dust off as best I could and we headed out to the diner.

When we walked in and sat down, I noticed Lilly and Zack were already here. It was hard for Zack to take his eyes off of Lilly, but he motioned for us to come join them at their table. He wanted to know if I had found out anything useful in Tombstone. I told him I had found out a lot and could pretty well put together what had been going on. But we should wait and talk about it in private. They had already ordered so I called the waiter over and ordered a small, rare steak and some beans. Things may start happening quick so I need to watch how much I eat and especially how much I drink.

We made small talk throughout the meal, but I did ask Zack if the Pinkertons were still in town. He said they told him they were leaving this morning, but would get back to us if they came up with anything. That's just as well. I have not decided who we should let in on our latest information. Generally, I only talk to people who need to know or when it is to my advantage for them to know. In fact, I suggested that we rent a two-seat wagon and go for a ride tomorrow morning before the heat gets too much for the ladies. Anyone watching would just think we were out for a ride. And we could be assured of complete privacy. Zack agreed to make arrangements early in the morning for the wagon, and we could leave right after breakfast.

With tomorrow morning scheduled, we took a leisurely walk around town before returning to the hotel. As we said our goodnights, Zack asked Lilly if she might like to sit on the bench outside the hotel lobby for a few minutes before retiring for the evening. She glanced at Mollie, who gave a barely perceptible nod before she agreed.

When we walked into our room, Mollie threw her arms around me and smiled. She asked if I remembered back when we first met. I explained that our situation was entirely different than Zack and Lilly's. I was looking to have it out with the Gorch brothers and she was running from her husband. Not quite the same as Zack and Lilly. But it did get me to thinking.

I blew the lamp out and we laid in the dark, Mollie's head on my chest. She wanted to talk about us having a family. I'm not prepared to tell her the truth yet. All I could think to say was, 'one thing at a time, Mollie, one thing at a time'. I changed the subject matter and asked her what went through her mind the first time she saw me. Whatever possessed her to write those letters and meet me in that dark alley in the rain. I knew pretty much what she would say. When I first saw her I would have never thought that we would ever do more than nod to each other in passing. And yet. here we are. We both fell asleep thinking of our early times together.

We met at the diner and Zack already had us a rig to use that morning. When we finished breakfast and got to the rig, I told Zack to drive and that Lilly could sit up front with him. I helped Mollie into the rear and climbed in beside her. She just looked at me and smiled.

As soon as we got out of town, I started telling them what I had found out in Tombstone. Mollie almost fell out of the wagon when I got to the part about Adam. She leaned over and grabbed my hand. She squeezed it tightly and whispered that I had done the right thing.

I don't know if it was the right thing or not, but Mollie was satisfied with it. Zack listened to the whole story without saying a word, but several times I could see him tense his muscles and knew that he was ready to avenge his family. One thing I find interesting is that everyone I talk to has thought that the entire Blade family had been killed. That left the ranch open to the taking. Maybe we should let Zack move back out to the ranch. I'm sure it would not take long for the word to get out that it was occupied. If Harvey Gaines wanted to finish the job, he might get a little surprise. I laid it out for Zack and he agreed. Zack said that he had not known what to do with the box of weapons we took from the bandits at Canyon Diablo, so he buried the box in a fake grave next to Ben. Maybe someone from the Circle L had rode by and assumed that was the grave of the other brother. There is one thing that I am absolutely sure of. There are going to be a lot more graves before this thing is settled.

*   *   *   *   *

It may have been merely for the intentions of dicussing business, but Lilly and I enoyed the ride this morning so much. I feel somewhat of a relief in knowing the truth about who the men were that caused the accident that night. Not that it makes much of a difference cause no matter how hard I pray, you can't go back and change the past. Our unborn baby is gone and neither of the two men can bring her back. Most people would remember a man but the worst that he done in his life, but I reckon I'll choose to remember the goodness of his honesty.

I am learning to accept what happened as I take each day for what it is. A new beginning. Happiness is all in the moment you find it, and I want to grab on to it every chance I get. My heart is at ease knowing that Mr. Bogardis didn't kill that man, Luke, for his soul is tortured enough. God will forgive him as well.

The air smelled so fresh riding in the country side so early in the day. Contention smells like the stamp mills. Three of them running at one time. The Contention Mill itself has twenty five stamps crushing the ore to powder. They use cyanide to heat up the mercury and the smell is carried into town. I suspose we grow used to it and tend not to notice it after a while.

We rode out a mile or so, stopped the horses and took a brief stroll staying in sight of the carriage. I wish we could have brought along a blanket and a picnic basket. But it was not a good time. Infact, Mr. Bogardis spent most of the trip conversing with Zack regarding the information he found out in Tombstone. Lilly and I sat idlely by and tried to follow what they were saying.

Mr. Bogardis says that Zack should go back out to his ranch. He says he would keep an eye on him out there and he wouldn't be left alone to fend for himself. Just that no one would know that. He says that if Harvey Gaines should return, that'll be just fine. That way they wouldn't need to go lookin' for him. If they played their cards right, Mr. Bogardis says that soon everything will come to a head.

CHAPTER EIGHTEEN

When we got back to the hotel I explained the plan to Mollie. Zack and I would go back out to the ranch tomorrow. I told her I expected visitors, but that Zack and I would be prepared. Of course, I worried about her safety, and Lilly's as well. She says that I cannot always be with her every minute of the day, that she can take care of herself ocassionally too! But the occurrence in Prescott regarding the accident is still fresh in memory. In any case, Zack and I would have to concentrate on the business at hand.

Early the next morning, Zack and I rode into Tombstone before heading to the ranch. Our first stop was the Marshal's office to check in with Virgil and Wyatt. They had wanted to meet Zack, the young man I had spoken so highly of. I told Morgan that I would only be in town for the day and Zack and I would have to head out to the Blade Ranch tonight. I wanted to spell out my plan to them. I told them that I wanted Zack to have a talk with old man Clanton. Virgil said that was impossible, he was killed in an ambush just a few days ago. If we wanted something from the Clantons, then we should probably talk to his son, Ike. They said he was not always a very pleasant person. He's been running his mouth all over town. No matter. They gave Zack directions and he headed out to their ranch on his own.

While he was gone, I further explained the plan to Virgil and Wyatt. Morgan arrived just as I began the briefing. Everyone, including Gaines and Lawrence, had thought that Zack had been killed. That meant they could just absorb the Blade place without any flak from anyone. Zack went to introduce himself to Ike, and tell him that his family had been killed and that he was now going to take over the ranch himself. He would then tell Ike that he was in the market for some cattle, and inquire if the Clantons have any for sale. I expected that Zack would not get out of sight good before Ike would be sending word to the Circle L that the Blade Ranch was still in business.

I was still with the Earps when Zack got back. He said Ike seemed to get nervous when he told his story, and said he didn't have anything right now but would let him know. Everything was going as planned. Zack and I needed to leave and get on back to his place and get ready for a visit. Wyatt volunteered and said he was up to meeting us at Zack's place and stay a few days if we needed him. Virgil and Morgan said they would like to go, but were the sworn peace officers of Tombstone and needed to stay around. I told them I appreciated the offer but I thought the two of us, along with Wyatt, would be enough. Zack and I left to get things ready for our little party.   We went straight to Zack's place and dug up the fourth "grave". We drug the box inside and started to cover the fake grave back up. Then I had an idea. Why not leave it open. An open grave might have some effect on the men who were coming to see us. We checked all the weapons and had them laid out at different points through the house and some hidden on the outside. I did not think we would have company too soon, but we would take turns standing watch through the night.

The next morning, as Zack was cooking up a quick breakfast, we heard horses approaching.   I looked out and could not help but break a smile. It was Wyatt, and he did not come alone. I stepped out on the porch to meet them. Doc dismounted and stumbled a little before he got his balance. Guess he had himself a bottle with him for the ride. But I certainly would not complain about having his gun on our side, sober ot not. Zack cooked up some more eggs and we talked about what might be coming. I figured it would be a group from the Circle L, maybe some Clantons and cowboys, and they would think they'd show up and finish the Blade family off. We went through the locations of weapons and ammunition both inside and out. We then hid the horses in the barn and settled in. Wyatt and Doc suggested that after the party was over, it might be best to not mention their participation. Whatever they wanted was fine with me. Yep, this might be a real interesting gathering.

*   *   *   *   *

With Mr. Bogardis and Zack out at the ranch, Lilly and I have some time to ourselves. Still feeling a little unwell, I told Lilly I would like to make a visit to Tanner's Drug Store.

I browsed the shelves filled with remedies for aliments of any kind and decided on purchasing a bottle of Hufstetler's Stomach Bitters. I preceeded to read the label, '.... invalids who have lost but are recoving vidal stamina declare in grateful terms their appreciation of the merits as a tonic of Hufstetler's Stomach Bitters....'. This may be just what I need.

Upon leaving the store, the druggist called out to me, "By the way, aren't you Mollie Lewis?" I looked at Lilly, turned around and answered that I was. He nodded his hairless head, confirming his notion. "I remember you", he stated. "I watched you, from the window right here, back in January. When I saw you and Sam Fisher at opposite ends of the street, I knew somebody was going to die. I already figured Bogardis was a goner."

Lilly gasped and held her hand across her mouth as he continued. "I watched Gorch gun down Bogardis and Fisher come up behind him. Ma'am if I had a gun on me, I'd of shot him myself! This whole town wanted nothing more than to be rid of the Gorch's and only you and Bogardis stood up against them."

He paused and I heard a muffled laugh before he went on. "You shoulda seen yourself come up the street holdin that shotgun up to your shoulder like an honest to goodness buffelo hunter! I swear, Miss Lewis, I figured that shotgun blast was gonna knock you all the way to Charleston!" The old druggist talked like he was re-tellin a story from a ten cent adventure novel. His eyes got real wide and he showed off his missing front tooth when he grinned, remembering the details.

"Yea, that sure was a day! I ran outside when it was all over and me and Dooley from the saloon hauled Bogardis down to the doc's office. We'd heard about how Fisher kidnapped you. Mrs. Marks told all us on the town council that something needed to be done, but on one stepped up. I would of, but I'm an old man and not much of an aim, if you know what I mean. Why, I couldn't hit the broad side of the barn if I was aiming to hit the barn door!"

I smiled at the old man, told him no need to fret about it, what was done was done. Mr. Bogardis and I did what we had to. He then asked if we'd come back to Contention to settle down. I replied that I hoped that we'd be here for a while. He leaned over the counter and spoke in a much softer voice looking me right in the eyes and said, "Miss

Lewis, if you or that man of your's need anything, why you just let me know and I'll see to it!"

I thanked him. Told him that both Mr. Bogardis and I appreciate the kind words. As Lilly and I walked towards the door to leave, the druggist called out one last time. "By the way, Miss Lewis, you ladies make sure you stay clear from those men wearing them sashes round their waist, you hear? They're no good and always lookin' for trouble anyway they can make it. Ike Clanton, out near Tombstone, has 'em perched out here in Contention snoop'in round. I hear they're cattle rustlers and just plain ol' hell raisers."

The old man had given me something to think about. Lilly and I walked back toward the hotel in silence. I could see that Lilly was a little thrown back with what she had just heard. I hadn't explained all the details of my past to Lilly, and now was really not the time to do so. I just wanted to rest a while and take a measure of the tonic. Then, just as we approached the hotel door, we caught site of a man crossing the street in front of us.

He was wearing a red tinted sash.

CHAPTER NINETEEN

It was all arranged. We decided that Zack should appear to be alone. I expect several men and some of them may hang back to see if there is any trouble. I left Doc in the house with Zack with instructions not to show himself unless needed. Wyatt was in the barn, and I was in the tiny shed that Zack and Ben used to sleep in. Zack would confront anyone who approached. When it became apparent that they were from the Circle L, I would show myself. If there was any shooting, and we knew there would be, Wyatt and Doc would hold their fire until the back-up men came in.

Mine and Wyatt's position were not the most comfortable, but it was important for us to have surprise on our side. Sometime in mid afternoon we heard horses just out of sight of the house. Five cowboys rode in slowly and seemed satisfied that there was nothing amiss. They remained mounted and one of them called for the owner to come out. They said they had a message for him. Zack opened the door enough for them to see that he was armed with a rifle. He told them they could speak their piece and then get off his property. They laughed and said he had made a mistake, as he was the one trespassing. The leader of the five said that sometimes they let people leave freely, but in this case there had already been too much trouble with the Blade family. With that they drew their revolvers and started shooting at the house. Zack was quick to get the leader and one more. I opened up from the little bunkhouse and dropped two more. The last one's horse had gone crazy and was turning circles right in front of the house. That's when Zack and I started to take fire from two different locations. There were two men on foot, one on each side of the house. They were using cover to get close in. A third was running straight up the road levering his rifle at me. I had good cover in the bunkhouse, and picked up my '73 Winchester. I took aim and shot the one in the road. I heard a shot go off in the barn. I guess one of them walked in on Wyatt. Doc couldn't stand it any longer. He had gone out the back door of the house just in time to introduce himself to the third man on foot. He used both barrels of a double to make the introduction, so it did not end well for the cowboy. Meanwhile, the horse in front of the house had finally managed to throw its rider.

Doc, Wyatt, and Zack fanned out to be sure we had not overlooked anyone. I got to the rider just as he was trying to get up. I disarmed him and told him to stay on the ground and not move. Wyatt was first back with a wounded cowboy in tow. Hit through the shoulder, he would live. Wyatt threw him down beside the other cowboy. Doc and Zack walked up and said it appeared that we had all of them. I asked the wounded one how many of them there were. He just shrugged his good shoulder. Doc allowed as how if they were not going to talk, we ought to just shoot them. Or better yet, hang them in the barn. That was all it took. Both of them started babbling at the same time. There were eight of them, so we had them all. While they were in a talking mood, I asked who sent them and why. They were quick to give up Harvey Gaines as their boss. They worked for the Circle L and Harvey ran the show for Mr. Lawrence. They did not know a lot about the reason, just that Mr. Lawrence was taking over land all over Arizona.

Doc looked at me and asked if I thought we ought to kill them anyway. Both of them began begging for their lives. It is amazing what a man will promise to save his skin. I told them I had one simple thing that I wanted them to do. Ride back and tell Harvey Gaines that Bogardis said he would be in Contention anytime he wanted to settle up. After all, he is going to be running short of men if he keeps sending them out for us. Then, they are to find Mr. Lawrence and tell him that Bogardis said as soon as he is finished with his two-bit gunslinger, he will be coming to pay him a visit. They looked at each other and swallowed hard, but nodded in agreement.

I tossed the unharmed cowboy some bandages and told him to fix up his friend as best he could. By the time he was done, Zack and Wyatt had rounded up all the horses and tied the dead men to them. The two that were alive climbed on their horses, and I told them to take their dead back with them. After all, this ain't no damned cemetery here.

All in all, things worked out pretty good. None of us got so much as a scratch. And we accounted for all the cowboys. Not bad. Zack and I thanked Doc and Wyatt for their help. I told them if they ever needed us we would be there. Wyatt said he knew that. I think he was referring to the help I gave him and Doc a long time ago. They were going to head on back to Tombstone unless we needed them in Contention. I thanked them again and Doc took me to the side before he mounted. He said that if I went up against Gaines he would tell me something that might help. Doc said his piece and I nodded, it's always good to have a friend.

Zack and I shut up the house, put the spare weapons back in their "grave", and headed for Contention. I don't which one of us was more anxious to get there.

*   *   *   *   *

The men in the red sashes were everywhere! I was beginning to think that there were more of them than you could shake a stick at. Mr. Bogardis was right, something very odd was going on in Contention City.

I felt somewhat better after a few disbursements of the tonic and a good night's rest, well enough to take a walk about town. No need to bother Lilly, this was something I needed to do on my own. I stopped by Lilly's room to tell her that I'd be out for a while. She was busy sewing a torn dress and most likely had thoughts of Zack going on in her head while doing so. I thought maybe this was a good time to talk a spell and explain a few things to Lilly.

I began by telling her about my husband, Sam Fisher, and what kind of a man he was. His family, their empire of stolen horses and cattle, and they way his eye wondered from woman to woman. I told her how I ran, ending up in Contention City, far from my home up north. I was surviving at best, until Sam caught up with me. Thank goodness for Mr. Bogardis. If it wasn't for him, I wouldn't be alive today.

I told Lilly that she reminds me of myself in certain ways. "Lilly, you are so fortunate! You are in love with a good man, a man who can provide for you and care for you. Any fool can see that he can't sleep a wink at nights without dreaming about you. Zack will be the kind of husband who will put you first in his life, forsaking all others like the Good Book says. I'm so happy for you, Lilly!"

I told Lilly I had things to tend to in town. Lilly said she would be just fine, she aimed to stay in the hotel and maybe dare to eat Mr. Crane's cooking he has prepared. Too bad Mrs. Marks hadn't given him cooking lessons instead of financial advice.

I saw Mr. Crane in the lobby and stopped to speak to him privately. Corney really has changed since we left Contention! He no longer looked as fragile and pale as he had before. By no means was he a 'Mr. Bogardis', but I thought I could now see his backbone protruding from the tail end of his shirt! We had a brief conversation and I was satisfied that if the need arose, that I could count on old Mr. Crane.

Littlefoot followed behind me as I walked to the dress shop. Mrs. Marks was absorbed in sewing a pair of trousers. I heard her mumble something about how tedious the job was and that he should have had his wench who made the tear mend them herself!' She stopped sewing when she saw me, looked up and said, "Mollie, come on in, I didn't expect you in here today." We talked only as long as necessary. I was confident that I was doing the right thing when Mrs. Marks stood and pulled a long barreled .45 caliber Peacemaker from underneath her cutting table. She waved it through the air in front of her, barely able to grip the handle without dropping it. "Don't you worry, Mollie. The folks in Contention are good people. They'll be right beside you in a pinch, you can count on that!" She then gave me a list of the men who made up the town council, mostly local business owners. The first name on the list was the druggist I spoke with yesterday at Tanner's Drug Store.

I made a few more visits and the reactions were all the same. The city of Contention was fed up with outlaws. The Marshal and Sheriff had their hands full, and no one was sure if their hands were dirty. Mr. Bogardis says the lawmen, in all likelihood, are trustworthy. But, sometimes it just becomes necessary to take on the responsibility yourself. Not like vigilantes on the loose, but more like decent citizens protecting what they believe in. May the Good Lord protect us all!

CHAPTER TWENTY

We hit town, dropped our horses at the livery, and we were both off to the hotel. Mollie had seen it from the start, but now even I could see that Zack and Lilly were a pair. I reached number ten and the door flew open before I could even knock. Mollie reached out, grabbed me, and pulled me into the room. Never minding that I smelled like a pole cat and had a coat of dust on me thicker than a jar of molasses, her arms went around my neck. She told me that she had been worried and asked how things went. I told her the story, including the part about Harvey Gaines. I had rather face him somewhere that I am used to than in a strange place of his choosing.

After we had talked awhile, I told her that I had brought her something. While I was going through the box of weapons, I found a .41 caliber Remington derringer. It was small and held two shots. I also found a cut-down Colt revolver. Someone had taken off the ejector and cut the barrel down to just over two inches. It was a .45 so it would still have plenty of knock down up close. I told Mollie they were for her. She smiled and said she did not need a gun, she had me. We laughed, but I told her they would be in the drawer, and that I preferred her to carry the derringer in her purse or in her clothing. She knows how quickly bad things can happen, so she just nodded in agreement.

The next morning, Zack and I walked down to the Marshal's office. Although I did not expect any help from him, I thought we should at least let him know that there would be trouble coming. The office was locked and there was a sign on the door, "Gone to Bisbee". Well, I was used to that kind of response from the Contention Marshal.

We had left Mollie and Lilly getting ready for breakfast, so we went on back to the hotel and walked them down to the diner. The morning was routine, and I don't like that. I had rather know what was coming. The ladies wanted to go down to the dress shop, so Zack and I just walked around town and talked. We went by the dress shop and asked the girls if they were ready for lunch. They declined saying they had promised Mrs. Marks they would finish mending a gown for her.

I told Zack I was going to the saloon for a while. He said he had some things to do and would be to the saloon later. I figured he was going back to the dress shop to be with Lilly. I walked into the saloon and got my table in the corner. I ordered coffee and asked if there was anything to eat. There was nothing, so I just sat and drank coffee. The afternoon went slowly, but I wanted to keep my mind busy. Around four o'clock, a red sashed cowboy walked through the door, slowly looking around. I held my Colt's revolver in my hand under the table. When he saw me, he started my way. As he got closer he raised his hands and said he was unarmed. He asked if I was Bogardis and I nodded. He said Harvey Gaines had sent him to tell me that he would be on Main Street in Contention at three o'clock tomorrow, and if I came out into the street, I would be in hell by three-o-one. I told the cowboy I would be there. He backed out of the saloon and was gone. Now I know what to expect, at least to a point.

I decided I would leave, as I found out what I needed to know. Just as I was going out the door Zack was coming in. We went back to my table and I told him what had happened. Zack said he wanted to take Gaines himself. I told him that when you partnered up with a man, you had to be willing to let your partner do what he could do best. I thought I had a better chance against Gaines than he had. But there was something he could do to help. I needed someone to watch my back. Even though Gaines had a reputation as a fast gun, he might want to hedge his bet a little. Like someone out of sight backing his play.

We went by the dress shop to see if the ladies were ready to go and escorted them back to the hotel. Mollie and I went on upstairs, while Lilly and Zack sat down on the bench outside. I had thought not to tell Mollie what had happened in the saloon, but I knew that she would want to know. I explained everything to her and told her that Zack would be trying to make sure that Gaines did not have any help. Other than that, I would just take it as it came.

We turned in early, as I wanted to get a good nights sleep. That ain't easy when you're thinking about going up against a man like Harvey Gaines. I drifted in and out of sleep, and I think Mollie did the same. We slept a little late, then gathered up Lilly and Zack for breakfast. We ate mostly in silence. Mollie said her and Lilly were going down to the dress shop to help Mrs. Marks again. I pulled Mollie aside and told her I would not meet them for lunch, as I preferred not to eat before a confrontation. I also told her not to worry, that Gaines might not show up once he realized that I would stand up to him. I told her to keep working in the afternoon and I would come and get her shortly after three o'clock. She smiled and we kissed goodbye.

I told Zack I would appreciate it if he kind of wandered around town, taking note of any strangers who looked like they might be part of the Circle L outfit. I would be in my room for a while checking my guns and getting ready for the showdown.

I came down about one o'clock and walked over to the saloon. I went in and saw a man sitting at what I considered my table. I started to take another table, but remembered what happened back in '76 to Bill Hickok when he just changed chairs. So I walked over and told the gentleman, who looked like a drummer of some sort, that I needed that table, and I would be glad to buy him a bottle for his trouble. He accepted and moved across the room. Zack came by one time to check on me. I told him he could best help me by being outside.

Just around three o'clock I heard some commotion outside. A couple of minutes later, I heard Harvey Gaines bellowing in the street. "Get out here Bogardis, or I'm coming in to get you." I walked to the door and looked out. The street appeared to be clear except for Gaines. If looks mean anything, Harvey Gaines looked as mean as I knew he was. I did not see Zack. I could only hope he was not in trouble.

I walked out, not taking my eyes off Gaines. We were only about thirty five feet apart as we faced each other. "Bogardis, I've been looking forward to this", he roared. "Do you think you can do this without your master pulling your chain," I replied. Just then, I heard a familiar voice. It was Molly. Gaines and I both turned slightly toward the sound. What we saw was unbelievable. As we turned to face each other again, Gaines had a sneer on his lips. His face went first white, then red with rage. He went for his gun, but just as he was clearing leather my first slug hit him in the center of the chest, followed immediately by two more. Harvey Gaines was dead before he hit the ground.

I turned as Mollie ran to my arms, a gun in each hand. "That's twice you saved me," I told her. "No", she said, "I saved US".

I looked around for Zack. I had sent him out earlier to keep an eye on anything out of the ordinary. In all the uproar, I had momentary forgotten about him. Then I saw him, leaning up against a pole near the general store. Looking as casual as ever watching the town folks gathered around Mollie, myself and the dead man. I would have never thought that anyone could get the people of Contention to risk themselves for someone else. I guess Mollie can talk anyone into anything. Zack strolled on over, taking his good time, grinning like a rooster in a hen house. "Looks like everything is taken care of around here, huh, Mr. Bogardis!"

"Get a good look at the show from over there, Zack?" I poked at him. "You wouldn't have had anything to do with this, would you?" Zack just smiled at Mollie. "Naw, Mollie there is the one who organized this grand assembly."
The captive cowboys were told to load up Harvey Gaines and take him with them. And not to come back to Contention expecting to have their way ever again. Mollie went back to check on Lilly at the dress shop. Now, I needed a drink. Zack and I walked into the saloon and got my regular table. The bartender had a bottle there before we even sat down. I poured a shot for Zack and one for myself. I could tell that Zack wanted to say something so I told him

just to spit it out.   He said that he thought he was fast himself, but he had never seen anything like the fight he just witnessed. I told him I could not take all the credit as I had a little help from Doc Holliday. He looked puzzled so I asked him if he remembered Doc and I speaking privately before we left the ranch. He nodded so I told him that Doc had seen Harvey Gaines in three gunfights. Doc is a gambler and knows to look for a "tell" when playing. Zack looked confused so I continued. A "tell" is something that a person does that gives away his hand. Perhaps he bites his lower lip if he is bluffing. Or his eyes go from the pot to his cards repeatedly if he has a real strong hand. A good gambler like Doc does not have any "tells". But Doc had noticed that in the three fights he had seen Gaines participate in, each time his right elbow twitched outward just before the draw. Not much, but if you were looking for it you would have an edge. And that's what I did. When I saw Gaines' elbow move I went for my gun. All Zack could say was "who would have thought"? Who indeed.

I asked Zack if he knew what Mollie had planned with the town folks. He told me he had heard the church bells ringing, thought that was a little peculiar. He want to check it out and came across Crane, Hopkins and a few others in the alley. He got the story from them, told them what to do, and they all went out and started rounding up all the cowboys they could find. He made it sound as if there was nothing to it. Good ole Zack!

After two drinks we got up and walked over to the dress shop. There was a pretty good crowd there. Crane, Mrs. Marks, the old druggist, and several more. They were all congregated around Mollie and having their own celebration. They saw us and went quiet as I made my way to Mollie. I took her by the arm and told the gathering that I appreciated them standing up to the cowboys. Then I told them they had not only stood up for Mollie and me, but they had stood up for themselves and their town. Now Contention belonged to them.

We had a good meal that evening, then a slow walk around town. When we got back to the hotel, we said goodnight to Lilly and Zack and went to our room. When you are with someone you love, right after surviving a situation that could have taken that person away from you forever, every touch, every look has a special meaning. Mollie and I savored each other as we had during our previous troubles in Contention. We knew we were alive! We could feel each others heartbeat! We slept as always, touching.

*   *   *   *   *

Lilly was pleased that Mrs. Marks had work for her in the dress shop. She was getting a little fearful that her money might run out before she could replenish it. She was still sending money back to Prescott for Jimmie. She'd confided in me last evening that she and Zack have been talking matrimony. Of course, there will be the decent amount of time passed for the courtship, but Lilly was already thinking about sewing a dress.

Fortunately, dress making was not what I had been thinking about. I spent one entire day, while Mr. Bogardis was at the ranch, talking with the townsfolk. I could see the storm coming, gathering strength with every red sash I'd see. I reminded the men in town about Sam Fisher, just as the old druggist reminded me. I refreshed their memory of how the town council stood by and allowed a couple of bloodthirsty brothers to control and manipulate their every move. Each man told me they'd be willing to do what was necessary. I told them to listen, if they heard the bell in the church tower ring three times, they were all to assemble in the alley way between the hotel and the general store. They were to be armed and ready. There was no question in my mind what had to be done after Mr. Bogardis told me what Harvey Gaines had planned.

I left the dress shop around two in the afternoon. I told Lilly to remain in the shop no matter what, to keep working on her wedding dress and that Zack would be proud of her. She did inquire as to what was happening, why she should stay inside, but I told her not to worry, Mr. Bogardis had everything under control.

I rang the church bell three times, hoping that the men meant what they promised. I stopped by the alter and knelt to say a little prayer before leaving the church. I needed all the help I could get. The

258

building had previously housed a furniture store when I first came to Contention. I remember how the congregation had looked down on me when I attended a few services. Maybe I was wrong about them as much as they were wrong about me. Upon leaving the church, the streets appeared normal. No one running to meet me in the alley, no store signs displaying 'closed' on the doors, nothing.

When I got to the alley way, there was no one there. It was just as deserted as it was those cold wet evenings when I would secretively meet Mr. Bogardis. My hopes were gone. This was something I was going to have to do on my own. Inside my purse was the Colt's revolver Mr. Bogardis had given me when he returned from the ranch. Between the crease of my breasts lay the pearl handle of a small derringer, loaded with two shots that I wasn't afraid to fire. I took in a deep breath before I turned around, dreading to walk out into the street alone.

From the back side of the alley, like a funeral procession all in a line, were several men coming toward me. They were aiming their rifles, pistols and shotguns at men who held their hands high up in the air as if reaching for God Himself to come save them.

The men were all wearing red tinted sashes.

"Miss Mollie, look'a here what we just found! Why if it ain't the dog gone Clanton cowboys themselves." The old druggist's smiled so widely showing off his one front tooth while poking a cowboy in the chest with the tip of his barrel. "We just heard them bells a ringin' and we went to gatherin' up all these no accounts we could find. We sure got us a fine collection of 'em now". I couldn't believe what I was seeing! Behind the druggist stood Cornelius Crane with a shotgun, by his side was no other than Sara Mae Marks with her Peacemaker, shaking in her trembling hands. I saw Dooley, from McDermott's Saloon, and even Po-Mo-Sang carrying a stick in one hand and a pistol tucked down the front of his belt. Mr. Hopkins from the diner still had his white apron on. They were all here, almost the entire town. I could have cried.

Then, out in the street, we heard Mr. Bogardis being called out. I looked at all the nervous cowboys with their hands still raised, and all the proud town folks with their guns pointed at them. They were all looking in my direction. "What'cha want us to do, Mollie?" I didn't see myself at the helm of all this, but I reckoned I was. "Follow me", I told them.

I marched them all, the cowboys out front with the gun barrels at their backs, out into the street. We made plenty of commotion coming out of that alley. I called out to Mr. Bogardis, who by then was facing off a man whom I assumed was Harvey Gaines. What a sight we must have been!

The way I see it, the distraction must have given Mr. Bogardis an edge.

Shots were fired and we saw Harvey Gaines sinking to the ground like a rock in a river. After it was all over, and Harvey lay dead in the street, the old druggist walked over to the bleeding body. He motioned to Dooley, and said, "Don't think we'll be hauling this fella to the doc's office!"

CHAPTER TWENTY ONE

The day after the gunfight, Mr. Bogardis told me he was leaving. He said there was business he had to finish at the Circle L. I wanted to beg him not to go, but I already knew there as no stopping him. I just wanted this trouble over, so we could get settled into a comfortable life together in Contention.

Lilly came to my room in the early morning, shortly after Zack and Mr. Bogardis left for the Circle L. She was glowing, he eyes sparkling and her cheeks pink and rosy. Zack had actually proposed to her last evening. She said they would wait and plan for a spring wedding.

I wished I could have shown her just how happy I was for her, but I woke this morning feeling sickly again. Mr. Bogardis has taken a notice to how peaked I have looked lately. He says there is something that he must tell me, but he has wanted all this cowboy situation to die down first, and then he shall talk with me. He seemed so anixous, but I suspect that he worries about me quite fiercely.

I rested most of the day, but late into the afternoon I decided to take a stroll and find Littlefoot. When I got back to the hotel, Mr. Crane told me that Mr. Bogardis had arrived just a few minutes before. I ran up the stairs in a rush to greet him back home!

When I opened the door, I saw that the room was barely lit. Shadows flickered against the wall in erry movements making the hair on the back of my neck stand up. A half empty bottle of whiskey stood on the bedside table. Mr. Bogardis sat in the dark corner in the arm chair, holding a glass in one hand and his pistol in the other. I moved closer to him. He was starring at nothing, it was almost as if I were invisable.

*　　　　*　　　　*　　　　*　　　　*

We were up early and I dreaded telling Mollie what she already knew. I had one more thing to take care of. William Lawrence. Mollie suggested I let it rest for at least a few days, but she knew that was not my way. I got up with Zack and asked him if he wanted to ride out to the Circle L with me. Of course he agreed. We saddled up and set out. On the way I told Zack that I wanted him to keep quiet and let me do the talking. He said he would. I also told him to keep his hand by his gun, just in case.

The Circle L was a sight to see. The house looked bigger than some state capitals I have seen. As we dismounted, four men walked out of the house and stood by the front door. We tied our horses, stepped up on the porch, and I told them we were here to see William Lawrence. Two of them walked inside in front of us, while the other two came in behind us. The meanest looking one, who appeared to be a half-breed of some kind, motioned toward a door and held his hand up when Zack started to follow. I looked at him and he said Mr. Lawrence wanted to see me alone.

Well, I've come this far. The half-breed opened the door and I stepped in. I barely heard the door close behind me. There behind a big wooden desk sat the would be king of Arizona Territory. He was looking down at some papers and slowly raised his head. "Well Ranger Bogardis, I have been keeping up with you for a long time. I'm glad we finally get to meet in person." As I looked at him, my hand went slowly to my gun. He continued speaking as if he hadn't noticed. "I know this is all a shock to you, but I will be glad to explain everything in time. Right now, it's enough to know that you have nothing to fear from me. In fact, I would like you to consider taking on that idiot Harvey Gaines' job."

I did not know whether to pull my gun or to run. He could see that I was confused. "Take your time Ranger, come back and see me in a few days after you have settled down and we will talk," he said.

I turned and was out the door with sweat running down my face. Zack was right behind me. As soon as we got outside he asked if I was alright. I did not answer. We started back to Contention. We did not talk the entire ride. Zack had been around me long enough to know that if I wanted to say something I would, and if not there was no point in asking.

When we rode in, I asked Zack to take care of my horse. I went straight to the hotel. Mollie was not in our room, which was probably good. I opened the top drawer of the dresser and got out the bottle that I keep there. A thousand things were going through my head all at the same time. On my third drink, Mollie came in. She stood at the door starring at me a few moments before she entered.

"You look like you have seen a ghost!" she let out in a frightened voice.

"Maybe I did." I replied. "I met Mr. William Lawrence today, except I know him by his real name. Bogardis! He's my father, and I intend to kill him!"

CHAPTER TWENTY TWO

Mr. Bogardis still finds it hard to believe that his father is alive after all these years! I can't imagine how he must feel, knowing the wrongdoings of Mr. Lawrence, and finding out all he has about the Circle L. I wish I was more of a comfort to him these past few days, but this is something he will have to come to terms with on his own. He has been somewhat distant towards me and drinking a little more than usual. He says there is only one end to this situation, and he intends to see his father dead!

With Harvey Gaines death, Zack feels satisfied that he has had revenge for his family. He told Lilly he would try his best to keep out of Mr. Bogardis' way when it comes to the ordeal with his father. But he says he will do anything asked of him.

Lilly has accepted Zack's hand in marriage and couldn't be happier. She finally has the love of a good man, something she always dreamed of. I suspect she will be fixing up Zack's ranch to her liking before their spring wedding. Mr. Bogardis and I will need to decide where we will live soon. Of course, Mr. Crane profits well from having us here in the hotel as paying guests! But I would like to find a small home to set up housekeeping in. I've told Mr. Bogardis I was not opposed to living in Fairbank or Tombstone, if he so chooses. Perhaps after this conflict with his father is over we will be able to settle down.

As in the past, Mr. Bogardis does not tell me everything he knows. I am afraid for him. I know he can take care of himself, but this time it is different.

He says when he is ready, he will be seeing his father again, for the last time!

*   *   *   *   *

It's hard to believe. My father has been alive all these years. And no one would have ever known. I remember telling my mother that many men did not return from the war because they wanted to make a new start, without the obligations of a family. She had received word of my brother's death a few months after it happened. When the war was over and I was back home, I asked her if she had ever heard anything from my father. She said she received one letter from him a short time after he left. Nothing else.

No one who knew him or served with him stopped by to tell her what became of him. But, she said she knew in her heart that he was dead. That would be the only reason he would not come back to her.

Her health was not good, and she had suffered from weakness and difficulty breathing for several years. But I believe that the loss of my father caused her to give up. She had lost her oldest son and her husband to the war. I was the only one who returned, and I think she thought I could probably take care of myself. So she gave up and died. That is one more death that my father will have to atone for. To me, he killed my mother just as sure as Booth killed Lincoln.

From our limited conversation, I believe that he thinks he can talk his way out of everything. He said he had kept up with me. If that is true, he should know that I do not bend when it comes to what I believe is right. And, to me, he is as wrong as a man can get.

Poor Mollie! She does not know what to do. There really is nothing she can do.

I am determined that the next time I meet my father, Mr. William Lawrence, I will send him to hell where he belongs.

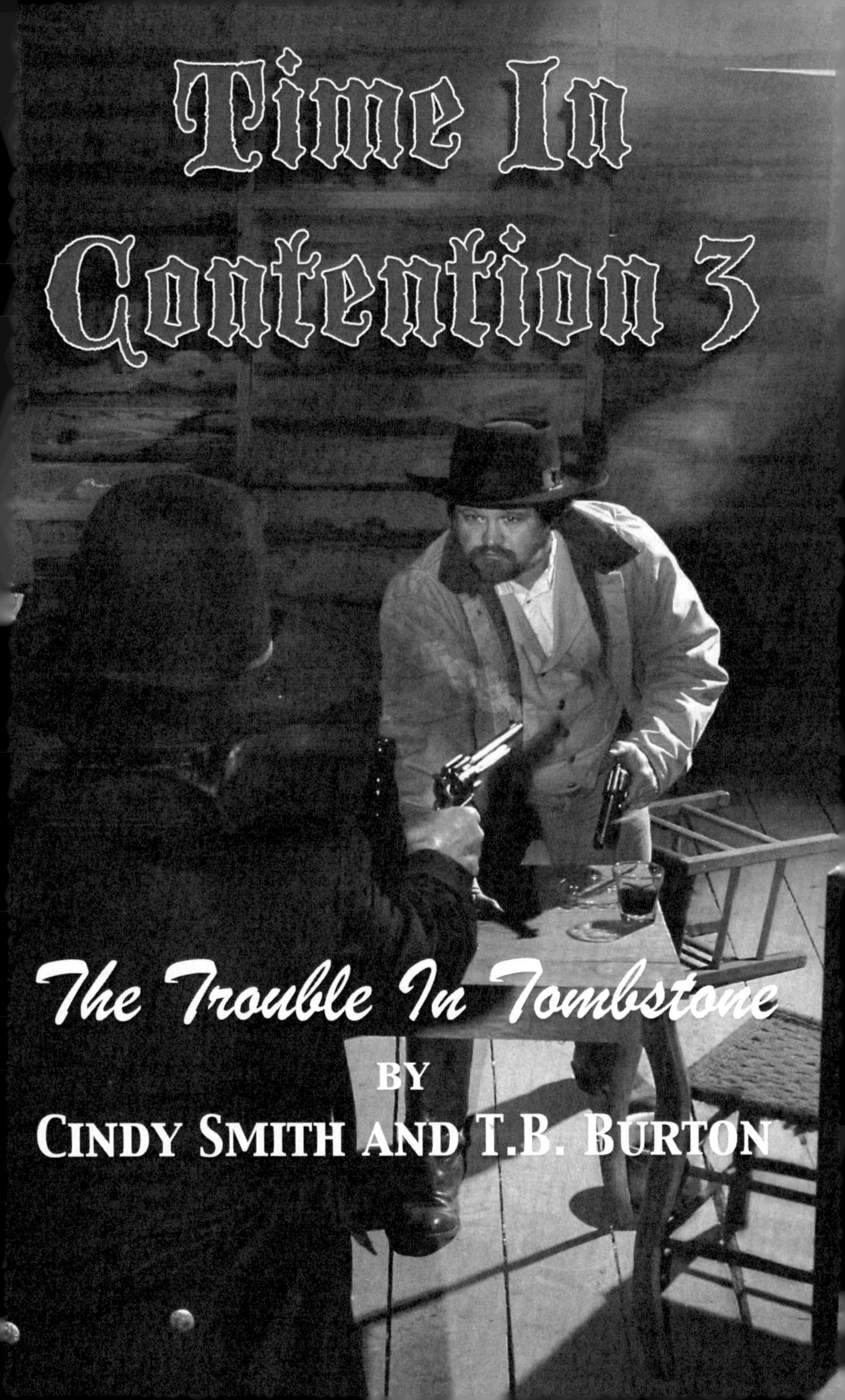
Time In
Contention 3
The Trouble In Tombstone
BY
CINDY SMITH AND T.B. BURTON

CHAPTER ONE

It never occurred to me while we were uncovering the wrongdoings of William Lawrence and Harvey Gaines that it would come home to haunt me. I keep asking myself how I could have been so blind. Truth is, there was no way of ever suspecting that my father was alive, let alone taking over half of Arizona Territory.

Life used to be so simple. I could make split-second decisions based on nothing more than, well, I don't even know what I based things on. Experience, knowledge, gut feelings were all rolled into one. But this new situation with my father has me so confused that I don't know what to do. If my Colt had been in its holster when I first saw him, there probably would not be anything to decide now. I believe I would have killed him on the spot.

Of course there are many things that I should consider. If I had went for him at his ranch, chances are his men would have gunned down both me and Zack. Then Mollie would be on her own. No, there has to be some thought put into this. Not to say that I won't do what I said, but I need to handle this in such a way as to not get anyone hurt but Mr. Lawrence and any of his outfit that want a piece of it.

I have always been very patient when at work. If you rush into things you are more likely to make mistakes that could cost the wrong person their life. I am going to let things set for a few days. Although Zack is a good man that I would certainly trust with my life, I'm not sure he has the experience to offer good advice. The same is true of Mollie. I will discuss things with them as I feel that I need to, but I know that the decision is going to be up to me. There may be as many as fifty to a hundred men on the Circle L payroll. This one is going to take a lot of planning. Just 'cause it's hard don't mean that I can't get it done.

This is the man that my mother loved, and I respected.He will pay for what he did to her. I would never have thought that I could go against my father, but William Lawrence is not my father. He and Harvey Gaines only know how to take advantage of the weak and helpless. I am neither. Soon he can talk it over with Harvey in Hell.

I have spent several days trying to make sense of my situation. I don't sleep much any more. I find myself pacing our room. When it seems that Mollie is becoming fitfull, I go downstairs and pace the lobby, many times going out and walking the deserted streets. This is something that I cannot share. It is my burden to bear, and I will do what I feel is necessary. Of one thing I am certain, I will make my father tell me why. Why did he not come home after the war? Why did he let the world think him dead? Why would he allow my mother to die of a broken heart? Yes, he will answer. And then he will pay.

When Mollie and I sit down together or get ready for bed, I can sense her desire to help me get through this. She knows only that William Lawrence is my father, and that I have said I will kill him. She has no reason to doubt that I will do exactly as I have said.

I see the look in her eyes and know that she would do anything in her power to help me. Sometimes it's as if she is biting her tongue to keep from saying anything. She knows that to offer help without being asked would probably make me more determined to handle this alone. It's just that right now, I need to come to terms with a lot of things on my own.

*   *   *   *   *

How much can a man take? I keep asking myself that question. I look at Mr. Bogardis, and my eyes well up thinking of the pain that must be devouring his soul. If it wasn't for Lilly and Zack, I would lose my faith as well.

"For goodness sake, Mollie," Lilly said as if scolding me as a child. "Mr. Bogardis will do what he thinks needs to be done. But, I need YOU! I need your help with the happiest day of my life!"

"I know, Lilly, and I am sorry for my behavior. It is just all these impending thoughts of what might happen when he sees his father again." There is so much more on my mind, but this was enough for

276

Lilly to understand. We had just finished breakfast at the diner and even before he finished his coffee, Mr. Bogardis had left without so much as a word of goodbye.

Taking ahold of Lilly's hand, I rushed her further on down the side walk leaving Mr. Bogardis in hind sight as he walked from one end of town to the other. I thought I would ask one more time, "Are you sure you do not want to wait until spring to be married like you had planned, Lilly?"

"Oh no, Mollie! The ranch is ready and so empty. There is just no reason to wait. I love Zack so much! It is all we can do to behave ourselves in a decent manner." Lilly went on and on about the ranch and it's decor and her plans, but I was only catching a few words here and there. "........ and we might put up a few........ and we could serve the cake with fresh .... and Mr. Bogardis and a few of the others could ...." She suddenly stopped and asked, "Mollie, you are listening to me, aren't you?"

"Of course I am, Lilly!"

The wedding was only a couple of weeks away. There was so much that had to be done. I volunteered to go into Tombstone and pick up a few items that Louisa and Allie are lending us. It would be a good opportunity to spend the day with the girls. Mr. Bogardis wouldn't mind. He probably wouldn't even miss me. I will tell him later of my plans. I can catch a stage into Tombstone on Tuesday and perhaps spend a night or two with the Earp's.

I glanced back over my shoulder to catch a quick look at Mr. Bogardis, but he was already out of sight. Maybe slipping into the saloon for a morning drink, or maybe venturing to the lumber yard to look for Zack. According to Lilly, Zack had the ranch almost completely overhauled. He wanted it to look more homely for Lilly. He wanted to build new memories and perhaps lessen the sad ones that hover within it's walls. Each day he is reminded of the unthinkable deeds that placed his parents and siblings in their graves just beyond his back door. Lilly is his saving grace.

Lilly and I strolled into the hotel lobby and greeted Mr. Crane. "Oh I forgot, Mollie!" Lilly said. "I received a letter from Jimmie yesterday. You must let me read it to you." She followed me up the stairs with anticipation of reading me the contents of her letter. Jimmie always writes about the latest news around Prescott and of course, about Joseph and Vera.

Jimmie says that Governor Freemont is leaving Arizona. Seems that people are not satisfied with how he handles the affairs of the state. He doesn't know much, only what he hears, so we will have to get the news from the paper to read all about it. Jimmie says that Joseph and Vera were married last week. They had an elaborate ceremony at Vera's home. Jimmie didn't attend, but he was invited. He just didn't think it was a proper thing to do, with Lilly being his sister and the way she felt about Joseph. I don't think Lilly would have minded. She is over Joseph and seems genuinely happy for him and Vera. Jimmie also declined Lilly's offer of moving to Contention and living with her and Zack once they are married. He says although he misses his sister very much, he likes his schooling and the other children who live in the boarding house. Prescott is his home, the place he belongs and wants to settle in when he is grown. He did promise to come visit Lilly and Zack in Contention one day soon. Lilly says he writes like a grown man, not a boy soon to be 14 years old!

Mr. Bogardis walked in the room just as Lilly was folding the letter and tucking it back into her purse. "How was your morning walk, Mr. Bogardis?", Lilly asked, her eyes still fixated on the letter in her purse. Mr. Bogardis walked past her, oblivious to her words. We watched him pour water from the pitcher into the washing bowl on the dresser. He splashed his face a couple of times then stopped and stared into the small oval looking glass that hung above the bowl. The reflection on his face told more than the mirror ever could; sheer torture all the way down to his soul.

CHAPTER TWO

I thought I'd pehaps accompany Lilly to her room when Mr. Bogardis came back this morning. He certainly isn't the best of company these days. But that would not be necessary because Mr. Bogardis had plans of his own. Who knows where he spends his time these days, wondering the streets, drinking in the saloon, riding alone.

As far as I am concerned, he needs to talk with his father and straighten things out. Killing isn't always the answer. Dead men cannot talk. Perhaps if they had a chance to sit a spell with each other in a civil manner, they could somehow mend the strains of hatred that Mr. Bogardis feels right now. If only Mr. Bogardis could just throw his pains in a bucket and lower them on down into the well. But I know that won't hapen. He's a hard headed man, and the gun in his holster is just itchin' to be shot.

It's a good day for me to visit Hey-You and his father, Po-Mo-Sang. I have been trying to teach the youngster to read. He is quite capable. The boy is as bright as a hunter's moon! He is just limited with his time for such book learning. His father needs his help with the chores of the laundry. I am hoping he can manage without Hey-You for an hour or so today.

"Miss Mollie, Miss Mollie!" I could hear Hey-You calling towards me before I even crossed the street to the laundry. The poor boy didn't have many friends. Being Chinese and without a mother, the boy was doomed to a life of labor. I once inquired to his father as to why he is called "Hey-You". According to Mr. Sang, when they arrived here by boat, no one could pronounce his given name of "Guoliang", so folks just refered to him as "hey you". He was born just a year before they had planned to flee from China. His mother had chosen the name because in their language it means "may the country be kind to him". They had hoped for a great future for their son and daughter once they arrived here, but Mrs. Sang died on the boat and their daughter was sold into slavery, most likely for prositution. And the new country wasn't as 'kind' as they had hoped for. Mr. Sang worked for years as a slave to a master and was released when his debt was paid. He spent two more years working in the used up gold mines of California. The Chinese were allowed to work the mines for gold dust after the white men mined them out. He saved his money and brought his son here to Contention to start a new life. He is content here and for the most part, the town people respect his business.

"Mr. Sang, may I please borrow Hey-You for a reading lesson today?" I can't help from smiling when I see the boy's face, glowing

like a June bug in the moonlight!   "No problem, Miss Mollie.   I spare
him for you!". Hey-You grabbed my hand and proudly strolled beside
me, leading me to the living quarters of the laundry.

"I have a new book for you today, Hey-You! I bought it at the
general store for you to keep and practice with. It is called "Nine Lives".
I flipped through the pages of the little book and showed Hey-You the
illustrations. He seemed so eager to know what it was all about, it was
all he could do but to sit still! I explained it was about the mischievous
little cat in the drawings. "Like Littlefoot, Miss Mollie!"

"That's right, Hey-You", I agreed laughing, "just like Littlefoot!".

I read to Hey-You for what seemed to be all afternoon before his
father called his name. He had prepared steamed rice for supper and
asked if I would sit at their table with them. I thanked them both, but
Mr. Bogardis and I always dine together in the evening.

At least we did before....... before he met his father.   None the
less, I should head back to the hotel.

Mr. Bogardis was in the room when I arrived and asked where I
had been. Not so much as he really cared to know, but just for a general
conversation. Small talk. He picked up the gun he was cleaning,
slipped it back into his holster hanging from the bed post and said
he was ready to eat supper. He looked tired, he never slept anymore. His
clothes were wrinkled, and I hoped that maybe he had laid down and
fallen alseep while I was gone. I also noticed that he didn't shave this
morning. Perhaps even two days have passed since he held the razor to
his face.

I thought it best that I discuss my plans to go into Tombstone
on Tuesday   while we ate. Mr. Bogardis doesn't like surprises. I
explained that Lousia and Allie were lending a few things to Lilly that
we needed for the wedding.

Without looking up from his plate of steak and potatoes, he
said, "I'll take you". I explained it was not necessary, that I could take
the stage and spend the night with the Earps, but I was glad that he
wanted to go. He needed to get away and forget his father for a day or
two. Maybe this was just what we needed. The
thought of a romantic few days alone with Mr. Bogardis was beginning
to stir my spirits!

He then announced that while I was with the Earps, it would be
a good time to visit his father at the Circle L Ranch.

I didn't say another word all through dinner. It seemed like he
wanted to be as far away as possible from me when he took me back to

the hotel. He announced that he was going to the saloon for a drink. He should have said, "another drink". He kissed me good-by on the cheek and I told him to be careful. I slid into the cold bed alone.

It was late when I heard shots coming from somewhere up the street. That is something that I can never sleep through, gun shots. It startles me like a rattling of a snake in the bushes, you can hear it but you don't know exactly where it is. In my wild thoughts, I presume the shots came from the saloon. I speculate it is Mr. Bogardis and Mr. Lawrence confronting each other. Fear overwhelms me, and I lay in the bed thinking. Maybe it was just a dream.

My flow is late again. I haven't told Mr. Bogardis. I want to surprise him! He knows how much I want a baby of our own. Not a day goes by that I do not think of our little Miriam Kay. Maybe this time it will be a boy. To take my mind off the gun shots, I lay thinking about what we should name him. "William" is certainly out of the question now because of his father! Maybe a strong name like "James" or "Buchanon", and we could call him "Buck". I like that! Of course, he will look like his daddy and have his blue eyes and dark hair. But I just want him to be healthy. To hold another baby in my arms is all I ever want. When I am completey sure in a few days, I will let Mr. Bogardis in on the secret! If I can wait that long!

I think I will let Lilly know tomorrow. She will be so excited for me. Maybe she and Zack will have a child soon after they are married, and our children will grow up together.

I was trying to calm myself back to sleep when I heard the handle turn on the door. It was Mr. Bogardis, and he was safe and alive! What was in my imagination will stay there. He is right, I worry too much!

I decided to lie still in bed pretending to be asleep. I didn't want to talk about the almost certainty of a baby inside me or inquire about the gun shots I heard earlier. No use. All can wait until a new day tomorrow.

*   *   *   *   *

At dinner tonight, Mollie mentioned that she would like to go to Tombstone and visit with the Earp ladies. It might be a good idea. We decided that maybe I could rent a wagon and drive her up next Tuesday. We could stay the night in the hotel, and I could leave early the next morning to pay a visit to Mr. Lawrence. She would have all day with Louisa and Allie, and Kate if she wanted. Although Mollie may be intimidated somewhat by Kate. She seems a little ill at ease when Kate is around. She thinks that Kate smiles at her too much and maybe flirts a bit with me. She has felt that way since the first time they met at the Christmas dance in Contention. Kate has always been friendly to both of us, but I will admit that both Kate and Doc are a little different from most folks. Hell, they probably think the same about us.

After dinner, I dropped Mollie off at the hotel while I went over to the Saloon for a drink. I told her I would not be long, and yes, I would be careful. When I walked in, I noticed that all the tables were full except for two. The two empty tables were not to my liking because they both showed too much of my back to the door. I walked down to the very end and around the corner of the bar. This I deemed to be safe since no one could get behind me unnoticed.

The bartender brought me a bottle and a glass as soon as he saw me. Once a good bartender knows you, you never have to ask. There was a pretty good crowd, but nobody seemed to be out of line. My eyes always keep moving so I won't miss anything. There were three men at a table, two of them dirty and unkept, drinking straight out of the bottle. They appeared to be talking amongst themselves, but I noticed that they would each cast a glance my way too often to suit me.

After about half an hour, I was ready to go back to the hotel but did not like the idea of walking out and down the street with those three at my back. I stayed, hoping they would be on their way soon. The more they drank, the longer they would stare. Maybe I should say something to them.

I finished my drink, left the bartender a tip and started around the corner of the bar. The youngest of the three stood up quickly and stepped to the side. One of the seated men scooted his chair back and asked me if my name was Bogardis. I replied that it was. "Well", he said, "you must be that Texas Ranger we heard about. Supposed to be fast with a gun. And fought with the Rebs in the war." I allowed as how I had been a Texas Ranger and fought for the Confederacy and was proud of both.

"I was in the war, so I got to kill my share of filthy Rebels", he said. "But little boy Jenks here was too young, so he ain't never kilt him a Reb. We decided that one with a name like yours would be a good one for him to start on." Before I could open my mouth to try to talk him out of it, the one standing up had started his draw. He didn't get to finish it. My bullet took him center chest. As he was going down, I turned to see the one who was doing the talking reaching for his gun while still seated. My bullet hit him high in the chest and turned the chair over backward with him in it. The third man just stood there while slowly raising his hands. I told him to put his gun on the table, which he did. Then I asked the bartender to pick up his gun and the ones belonging to the two dead men. I asked loudly if someone would be kind enough to go get the marshal. This time last year nobody would have been willing to cooperate, but this time two men were out the door by the time I finished speaking.

I told the surviving man to turn around and put his hands as high on the wall as he could reach. He could reach pretty high. Three of the men who had been drinking started to leave, and I asked them to wait until the marshal got there so they could tell him what happened. They shrugged, and one of them said that no one would fault me for the shooting, that it had been self-defense. That's fine I told them. Tell it to the marshal.

The marshal was there in no time. He pushed his hat back on his head and looked at first one, then the other, both lying dead on the floor. He asked me if I knew them. I told him I had never seen any of them, but they apparently knew me. He should ask the one with his nose against the wall, as he was in their company. I told him everyone in the saloon saw what happened, and that I was going to leave. If he needed me, I would be available tomorrow. He nodded, and I went out the door.

My intentions were to go to the hotel and grab Mollie and hold her tight. But killing and loving don't seem to go together very well. I decided to walk around for a little while. The weather has been turning cooler and maybe the cold night air would help calm me down. I did not feel like explaining to Mollie what had happened. She worries too much any way. She would hear about it in the morning, and then I could explain why I did not tell her tonight. Sometimes I feel bad for her because this is not the kind of life I wanted for her. Never knowing whether her man would be dead or alive the next time she saw him.

She never complains, but it still bothers me.

CHAPTER THREE

Mollie and I got up and dressed for breakfast. I sat her down on the edge of the bed and told her I had something to tell her. I saw the blood drain from her face as I am sure she knew it would not be something to her liking. I explained all about the night before, and that there was nothing to worry about. She didn't take it very well, like it was my fault. She mumbled something about going up against three at one time, like that is something I would choose to do.

When she calmed down, we went to the diner. I could tell she was still upset, but there's nothing to be done for it. The marshal came in and asked me if I could stop by his office, no hurry, just sometime at my convenience. Things sure are different around here now. I told him I would come by after breakfast. When we finished, Mollie said she was going to meet Lilly at the dress shop, as they had things to discuss and plans to make. Who knows what those two are up to.

I went directly to the marshal's office, as I was curious as to what he found out about last night. I noticed when I went in that the cells were empty. He asked me to sit, and I did. He asked if I had ever heard of anyone named Tom Evans, Ed Jones, or 'Jenks' Jenkins. I replied that the only time I heard of Jenks was last night. The marshal said that everyone in the saloon agreed that the killings were in self-defense, so no charges would be brought against me. He also said he had questioned the one called Jenks for quite a while. It seemed that Jones, the loudmouth, must have seen me somewhere or knew something about me, but that the three were only passing through on their way to Prescott. Since Jenks had not tried to draw, he had nothing to hold him on. He cut him loose early this morning with the suggestion that he stay away from Contention City in general and me in particular. He seemed happy to leave with his life. I thanked the marshal and went on my way. I have plenty of problems without dwelling on three saddle bums.

I went by Mrs. Marks' dress shop and told Mollie I was going for a ride and would be back well before dark. Her and Lilly could have lunch together, and we could go to supper after I got back. She was as excited as a little kid. She said she had some thing to tell me. She is so silly when she gets like this, and it's good to see her happy. I said we would talk about it when I got back and gave her a kiss on the cheek. She also told me to be careful. I have been hearing that a lot lately.

I went by the livery and got my horse and headed out. I wanted to ride over to Tombstone so I would have to hurry if I was going to get back by dark. The trip was uneventful, although I did keep a sharp eye out. Not because Mollie said to, but because I have learned to never let my guard down.

I dropped off my horse to be fed and watered. He would need to catch a little rest as we would be heading right back to Contention. The purpose of my trip is twofold. I wanted to get out of town so I could maybe think clearer about my problem. But I also wanted to check in with the Earps. Wyatt was in the office when I walked in. After the usual banter, I asked if maybe the ladies could entertain Mollie next Wednesday. I have business to attend elsewhere, but could bring her up on Tuesday and stay the night. He said everyone would be delighted to have us, and I was beginning to feel good about it too. I asked where Doc, Virgil, and Morgan were. He said Doc and Kate had gone to Tucson to attend the San Augustin Feast and Fair. Virgil was already in Tucson for the Stillwell-Spence hearing on the Bisbee stage robbery. He had just sent Morgan to Tucson to fetch Doc back as he needed him for a "special" piece of business. But everyone would be back by next Wednesday. I thanked Wyatt and headed back to the livery.

The ride back to Contention is turning out to be as uneventful as the ride to Tombstone had been. I'm not complaining. The events of last night are still fresh in my mind. I'm just glad that was not some kind of vendetta that left someone alive to continue. It was getting dark, and I promised Mollie I would be back by dark. Guess I'm going to be in hot water again. At least she is pleased to know that we are going to Tombstone next Tuesday and staying the night. Maybe I shouldn't have told her where I am going on Wednesday. Maybe she will be so caught up with Allie and Louisa that she won't even miss me. Although I admit that I am still not sure what I am going to do or say when I get to "Mr. Lawrence's" ranch.

The lights of Contention are in sight. I'm not too late, although I am sure Mollie will not agree. I dropped my horse off and let the stable boy take care of him. I prefer to put him away for the night myself, but I better get on over to the hotel.

When I entered the lobby, Corny Crane was behind the counter. We speak, and this time he is genuinely friendly. I head on up the stairs and just as I get to room number ten, the door flies open and Mollie grabs my shoulders and shakes me, asking "where have you been?" Before I can answer, she throws her arms around my neck. This time she whispers, "I was so worried about you." We hold each other silently for a few moments, then I say, "I'm starved." She pushes me away with a laugh and gets her shawl. As we are walking to the diner, I tell her that everything is planned for next Tuesday and Wednesday in Tombstone. Perhaps forgetting about my visit to the Circle L. She stops, throws her arms around my neck again and whispers "Why are you so good to me?"

"You know why", I replied. "Now, what is your big secret?"

She says she will tell me all about it when we get back to the hotel, as she does not want anyone to overhear us at the diner. I was pretty hungry since I didn't take time to eat in Tombstone, but a thick steak and a plateful of beans solved that problem. I wish everything was that easy to fix. As usual, Mollie had almost nothing. I don't know how she lives eating no more than she does. Mollie was in a hurry to get back so I paid up, and we started walking to the hotel. She was about to bust to tell me her secret, so it didn't take us long to walk back.

As soon as the door to our room closed behind us, she pushed me down into our only chair and jumped in my lap. "Guess what", she exclaimed. I explained to her that I had no idea what she was talking about, and that she should either tell me or forget it. I didn't mean to be short with her, but I have other things on my mind. I could see that my attitude had hurt her feelings so I babied her a little 'till she got over it. It seems that the big excitement was the fact that Mollie thought she was pregnant again.

I need to tell her the truth. The conversation with that old doc in Prescott after Mollie's accident has been haunting me ever since. I tried to change the subject and talk about Zack and Lilly. All the while my mind is still wondering what I am going to do next Wednesday when I ride over to the Circle L. There is too much on my mind to tell Mollie that she can never carry a child. That she will never be a mother. This will break her heart. I need to postpone this conversation until I am sure she can handle it, and I am in the right state of mind. Mollie didn't say another word. I think she thought I wasn't interested in the fact that she thought we were going to have another baby. I'm sorry to make her hurt, but this just isn't the time.

We both were tired. By the time I blew out the lamp and pulled the covers up, Mollie was already asleep. Or at least pretending she was. I didn't blame her, I wouldn't want to talk to me either.

All I could do was lie there in the dark and wonder how I should handle Wednesday. I think it would be easy enough to slip a gun in with me. I may need one to force him to tell me what I want to know. I doubt he will be very forthcoming with the information.

Sometime in the night, I reach over to get my watch from the nightstand. If I hold it just right, the moon shining in the window lets me see the time. It's two- thirty in the morning and I have slept very little, if at all. Sometimes I get so caught up in this thing that I don't know if I am thinking or dreaming. One thing is for sure and for certain, and that is I want to put an end to this one way or another. Not only is this not fair to Mollie, but it is taking its toll on me as well.

I get up, get dressed and walk down to the lobby. The lamps are burning so I just sit in one of the big chairs. There is no one in the lobby so I am still alone with my thoughts.

It's not like I am accomplishing anything. I just keep going over the same things in my head, over and over. There ain't a whole lotta ways for this thing to end. Maybe I am thinking too much. For most of my life decisions have come quickly. Best thing is to just go next Wednesday, be as prepared as I can, and let the game play out. Yeah, that's the best I can do.

As I go back upstairs, I try to be as quiet as possible. No need to wake everyone in the hotel. The stairs creak, the boards in the hall creak, so I take it slow. When I put the key in the lock, I half expect Mollie to be sitting up wanting to know where I've been. But no. She is sound asleep. I get undressed and slide into the bed slowly and silently. As I am trying to get comfortable, our legs touch. She rolls over and puts her hand on my chest. I snuggle in close to her, my arms around her stomach. I must tell her the truth soon. I fell asleep listening to her gentle breathing.

*   *   *   *   *

So much for Mr. Bogardis being excited about having a baby! He didn't even want to talk about it last night. When he quickly changed the conversation to Lilly and Zack's wedding, I knew then he didn't care anymore. Mr Lawrence is the only thing he thinks about these days. Revenge. I despise Mr. Lawrence and the Circle L Ranch and everything they have done! At least Lilly was excited for me when I told her over lunch yesterday.

I arose before Mr. Bogardis. I did not want to see him this morning. I tried getting dressed without waking him, but was unsuccessful. When I turned in his direction, his eyes were open and he was staring at me with a far away look in his eyes. "I have things to do this morning. I must get dressed and leave", I informed him without any emotion in my tone.

He reached out and grabbed my arm. "Mollie, please don't leave. I think we should talk. There is something that I should tell you".

I never like the outcome when a conversation begins like this.

He sat up and leaned against the lace pillows he placed behind his head. He gently pulled me down on the bedside close to him. For what seemed like forever, he just looked hopelessly at my face. "You have such beautiful eyes, Mollie", he began, hesitating as if not knowing what to say next. "I should have told you this before, back in Prescott. I came home that night and ran to the Doc's office looking for you, remember Mollie?"

I nodded my head. Of course I remember, I think about it every day!

"The Doc told me something you should know", he continued, carefully selecting his words. "He said you had a severe case of Scarlett Fever, Mollie. You contracted it early on while you were pregnant, and he discovered it after your accident. He said you would never be able to bear a child again. He wasn't even sure if the baby would have survived if you had carried her full term. That is why you were so ill with fever for weeks afterwards. I told him no need to tell you, that I would do it myself. There was just never a right time to do it. I know how much you want us to have a baby, Mollie, and I am sorry."

So, he has known all along. I wanted to cry, but my pride wouldn't let me.

He wrapped his arms around me, and I felt half dead. My body was limber and motionless.

The last two mornings I have awakened with Mr. Bogardis telling me something he "thought I needed to know". Yesterday it was the saloon killings. The gun shots I heard were real, and they did come from Mr. Bogardis' pistol. He killed two drifters who challenged him to draw his gun.

Will it always be like this? Waking up beside the man I love and never knowing what is actually real or a dream? I have always known he did not tell me everything, but now I will forever fear whatever it is that he keeps from me.

And this hunger he has for retaliation against his father! I thought that when he said he was taking me to Tombstone, that he was going to be with me. I was wrong. It's just his way of keeping me occupied and seemingly safe while he visits his father.

I got up off the bed, continued getting dressed like nothing had been revealed to me. I pulled the strings a little tighter on my corset, there was nothing inside to hurt anymore. I was barren, and I must accept it and never think of it again. Never to dream of a boy child that looks like Mr. Bogardis. Never to imagine what his name would have been.

"Are you alright, Mollie?", he asked from across the room. "I'm fine, but I still have things I must attend to this morning". I lied. I didn't want to be around him or to talk about anything else with him today. My only friends in town were Lilly and Mrs. Marks. I didn't want to bring Lilly down with my situation, so I was left with the choice of Mrs. Marks. I could walk to the dress stop and ask if she could provide me with work today to occupy myself. Only a few more days and we would be off to Tombstone. There, I will share my sad news with Lousia. Maybe then I could cry. I will not allow Mr. Bogardis, Lilly or anyone else to see my pain. Then I will vow to myself never to speak of it again.

CHAPTER FOUR

We got up early on the morning of the twenty-fifth. Mollie can't wait to get to Tombstone and tell the Earp ladies all about the wedding plans. She hasn't been herself since I told her she could never have a child. But, I am sure she will have a wonderful time with Allie and Louisa. Women are like that. I have rented a buggy and put our things in the back, along with my saddle.   I will rent a horse in Tombstone to make my trip. The air is cold this morning, but not bitterly so. We are both dressed for it and wrapped in a blanket. While Mollie is certainly excited about the trip, she knows I have things on my mind. We ride a long ways before she decides to break the silence. She asks what I plan to do in Tombstone, as she knows I will not be around a bunch of silly women planning a wedding.

I said I would just hang around with the Earps and Doc. I didn't want to mention the trip I was making tomorrow. She knows, and enough has been said.

When we arrived in Tombstone, I drove the buggy straight to Morgan and Louisa's house. By the time we were out of the buggy, Louisa was already out to greet us. I told Mollie I would get us a room in the hotel for the night and would carry her things up. She could go to the hotel at anytime, tell them who she is, and they would give her a key. I would go down to the marshal's office and see what was going on with the men.

She gave me a hug,   and they headed into the house, both talking at the same time. I stopped at the hotel, unloaded our bags, checked in, and then drove down to the Dexter Corral. I made arrangements to leave the horse and buggy and also to rent a horse for the next day. I told the stable hand I would be leaving before first light, and he assured me he would be there and everything would be ready. He would even have the horse saddled and ready to go.

I went back to the hotel to organize our things and just think. I stretched out on the bed and tried to get my mind made up about how I was going to handle meeting with my father tomorrow. All I could come up with was to be prepared for anything, and to do whatever I needed to do in order to get him to tell me the things I wanted to know. The things I needed to know.

I got up and headed downstairs and out into the street. It's a fine day, very crisp, with maybe a hint of snow in the air. I opened the door to the marshal's office and stuck my head in. "Anybody work here," I said. Virgil was up out of his chair and met me halfway across the floor. He slapped me on the shoulder and said the only work they were doing was playing nursemaid to those damn Cowboys. It seemed that Ike Clanton was always causing a problem of some kind.

"Is that never going to go away"? I asked. By then Wyatt had gotten up and was on my other side. "It's good to have you and Mollie back in town," he said. "Are you going to stay with us a while this time"?

I allowed as how we would probably be leaving the day after tomorrow. I had thought about letting them in on my dilemma with my father, but thought better of it. The fewer people who knew that William Lawrence was really my father, the better. It was not something I was proud of. We made small talk, me asking about the digging going on along the streets.

"Why that's the new water system," Virgil declared. "They say that San Francisco will have nothing on us in a few years". I just shook my head. I asked about Morgan and Doc and was told that Morgan was out running errands for Louisa. They said Doc was probably already in one of the saloons looking for a game. We talked for a few minutes about nothing in particular, then I told them I was going over to the saloon to see Doc.

I found Doc in the Oriental. He was sitting alone playing solitaire. I thought I might walk around to his side without him noticing, but no such luck. Without looking up, he said "What the hell are you doing here Bogardis? Pull up a chair ." Doc Holliday has not lived as long as he has by being unaware of his surroundings.

I pulled out a chair beside him, and he stuck out his hand. I don't usually shake hands. It's a custom I do not approve of. Doc and the Earps being the exception to that rule. I grasped Doc's hand and was reminded of his grip.

Doc was a small man, even frail looking, but shaking hands with him was like putting your hand in a blacksmith's vise.

"Did you bring your lovely consort with you", Doc asked. I told him I dropped Mollie off at Morgan's house on the way in, and that we would be around for a couple of days before heading back to Contention. He said to be sure that Mollie looked up Kate while we were in town. He didn't know why, but Kate sure took a liking to Mollie.

He asked if I had any plans for tomorrow. I told him I had some personal business to take care of. "Personal business," he said. "Do you need any help with it?" Doc had no idea what I might be up to but was willing to jump in with both feet.

"No thanks, Doc," I said. "This is just a meeting I have been postponing." "If you change your mind, you know I am ready," he said.

I nodded and got up. How many people do you know who would be willing to stand up and fight, risk their lives, over something that meant nothing to them? If it means something to a friend, it means something to them. That's what you get with the Earps and Doc.

I took my time and walked back over to the hotel. I was lying on the bed when I heard the key in the lock. Mollie charged in, jumped on the bed, and told me we were having dinner with Morgan and Louisa and probably some more of the Earps. I should get dressed as we didn't want to be late.

I got up, washed my face, combed my hair, and was ready to go. I had nothing to eat since we had arrived in Tombstone. It just slipped my mind. But at the mention of food, I realized how hungry I was.

Tombstone has some really good restaurants. Doc's favorite was Nellie Cashman's Russ House. He said no one had better say one word against the food in that place, or he'd shoot 'em on the spot!

By the time we got to the Russ House, all three Earps and their wives, and Doc and Kate were already there. They had arranged for a big table, and Mollie and I were sitting across from Kate and Doc. I probably ate more than anyone else, as the gathering had seemed to give me some relief from my thoughts of my father. We all laughed and talked for over an hour. I did notice that Kate would often look at Mollie and smile. When Mollie would see her, it was obvious that it made her somewhat uncomfortable. All good things must end, and the Earps and Doc had business to look after. I walked Mollie back to the hotel and told her I was going to swing by the saloon. I enjoy watching Doc gamble. You may think he is drunk and does not know what he is doing, but he lets nothing get by him. Wyatt has said that Doc is the best gambler he has ever seen, and I tend to agree with him.

I watch Ike Clanton in a game with Doc and several others. Ike is drunk and loud, as I am told he usually is. Doc seems to think he is funny. But I have to get an early start tomorrow, so I go on back to the hotel.   I remind Mollie that I will be leaving before dawn in the morning. She asks if I am going to take someone with me, and I tell her no. I know that she is concerned, yet she says nothing more about it.

As I lie here in the dark, I can't help but wonder if my father will give me any of the answers I seek, or if he will take them to the grave with him. I will know soon enough.

*   *   *   *   *

I let on as if nothing was wrong with me as we rode into Tombstone. I have even pretended that Mr. Bogardis' visit with his father tomorrow is not concerning me. I must not wear my feelings on my sleeves anymore and be more protective of the emotions I show. A woman who cannot have babies with her man will be looked upon as weak and bitter. That will not be me. I will not allow it. Mr. Bogardis thinks of me as a strong woman, and a strong woman he will have!

I did feel better once we arrived in Tombstone. I was looking forward to getting away and seeing the girls. Mr. Bogardis went on ahead to the hotel while I stayed with Lousia at her home. Later tonight, we will will dine with the other wives and their husbands.

It wasn't long before I opened up with Lou and told her of the Scarlet Fever. She hugged me for a long time, and I felt tears wet my cheek. Although I wasn't sure if they were her tears or mine.

She had so much to tell me as well. It seems that Ike Clanton came into town last night. "He's nothing but trouble, Mollie!", Lousia contended. "He's got it out for Virgil and Morg, and Wyatt as well. Seems everywhere we go, Wyatt drags us all into some kind of trouble! He hangs out down there at that saloon with Holliday gamblin' all night and congregating with Clanton and his gang. Clanton's been rantin' and raving about how he's gonna kill 'em all. I wish Virg would just throw him out of town and be done with him. Morgan would, if he was marshal."

"Alright, Mollie, enough about that! How about you and me checkin' out a few of the boxes I pulled out for Lilly? Now you tell me everything the two of you are gonna need. A weddin' is a big event, Mollie. I'm so happy for Lilly and Zack! Now, just when are you and ol' Bogardis gonna tie the knot?".

I knew in a way she was just teasing. It didn't matter to Louisa one way or the other if we were married. Mr. Bogardis told me long ago that Louisa and Morgan didn't certify their relationship with a written bond. I'm not sure if any of the wives were legitimate spouses, but that didn't mean they weren't married in their hearts. They all went by "Mrs." and no one ever inquired as to one way or the other. But just the same, one day I would like to have a wedding and actually be married to Mr. Bogardis.

We spent the afternoon going through boxes and deciding on what I should take back home. Finally, Lou heard the clock chime four-thirty and declared it was time we both got the men folk and went out to eat a nice dinner. She said she would send for Morgan, and I should go catch up with Mr. Bogardis, and we'd all meet at the Russ House at six o'clock.

I took my time walking to the Grand Hotel. The new scenery was doing me good. So many folks walking about. The Grand Hotel was beautiful. I liked it here. But, Mr. Bogardis told me never to go downstairs to the bar. Apparently, the miners have their own underground entrance to the bar where they can come for a drink anytime and then go back to work without ever going above ground. Mr. Bogardis had told me to ask for a key to our room when I walked in the lobby.

There were three men in the lobby registering when I arrived. All three wearing the ragged red sashes around their waists that I have seen many times before. I waited in a chair while the desk clerk took their money and handed them their keys. I recognized their names from Louisa's conversation earlier. One was Ike Clanton, and the other two were Frank and Tom, the McLaury brothers. All three of them smelled like whiskey as they walked by me. I saw Clanton's bloodshot eyes glaze over my torso, and it made me feel dirty inside. I was glad when they finally walked up the stairway and left the lobby. I quickly asked for our room key and hurried to our door.

I was happy to see Mr. Bogardis in the room. Relieved was more like it!

"Get up and get your britches on, darling!" I told him. He was lying on the bed, and I pounced down nearly on top of him. "We are having dinner with the Earps." He told me he was hungry and for me to just "hold my horses" he'd be ready when he was ready.

"You seem mighty chipper, Mollie! Did you and Lou have a nice time this afternoon?", he asked, poking fun at my demeanor. I guess I did appear happier than I did this morning on the ride to Tombstone.

"Well, we are certainly not done, Mr. Bogardis. Tomorrow, Lou and I are shopping for wedding supplies at Summerfield Brothers. She says they have just received a new shipment of oriental lace that I must see! She says it is as soft as a patch of new grass in the sunlight!"

I watched as Mr. Bogardis pampered himself up, shaving and splashing scented water on his checks and neck. Hmmm..... he smelled so good! He changed his shirt , putting on the light blue one, which was my favorite. He tied a black string tie around his collar and grabbed his coat from the door hook. He took my arm in his as we walked out of the hotel. I was glad we did not run into the three men I saw earlier.

Mr. Bogardis and I were the last to arrive at the restaurant, as the Earps were already seated and waiting for us. Seemed they had invited Doc Holliday and Kate as well.

Dinner went well. I saw Kate glance over at Mr. Bogardis a few times during the evening and order Doc a few more drinks than he should have had.

After our goodbyes, Mr. Bogardis walked me back to the hotel room. Again, we did not see Clanton or the McLaurys. Maybe by some chance they were still sleeping off their drunkened binge or perhaps decided to leave town.

I expected Mr. Bogardis to go on over to the saloon and meet up with the Earps and Doc, as that is where they were going after they took their wives home. He kissed me good night, said he'd be in early and locked the door on his way out. I prayed gunshots would not intrude in my dreams tonight.

CHAPTER FIVE

I arose early this morning as I wanted a good start for my ride to the Circle L. Mollie was still asleep, and I got dressed without the lamp so as not to wake her. She looked so peaceful with the cover pulled up under her chin. I bent down and kissed her gently on the cheek. She mumbled something that sounded like "please be careful" before falling back asleep. Or was it, "please don't go". I wasn't sure.

When I got to the Dexter Corral, everything was ready to go. My rented horse was saddled and waiting for me. I had procured some hard tack to carry with me as I did not want to take the time to eat before leaving. The ride was cold, with a smattering of snow on the ground. It had snowed a little overnight and was still spitting snow. I was careful on the ride with an unfamiliar horse as I did not want to strand myself in this kind of weather.

I arrived at the Circle L with a clear mind. I did not know how this was going to go. I wanted answers, but I was prepared if I did not get them. A group had gathered as I rode up. Not as many as the first time. As I walked up on the porch, the half-breed came out and met me. I told him I was there to see William Lawrence. He explained that he was occupied with a visitor at the present time. I told him I didn't care. "Please come in out of the cold and rest," he said. "Senor Lawrence has ordered me to make you comfortable at any time you may visit. I believe he is looking forward to seeing you again." I could not imagine my father looking forward to seeing me, but I followed him into the house.

The half-breed pointed to a chair, and I sat down. So far, he had not asked for my gun. "What is your name?", I asked. He replied that his name was Paco, and that he had worked for Lawrence for about 15 years. I asked what he did. "Senor Lawrence is my Patron. It is my duty to protect him and make sure he has what he needs," he answered. I asked if he was Mexican. He smiled and said only half. His mother was Mexican and was taken prisoner by the Apaches. He is the son of his mother and one of the Apaches. He and his mother lived with the Apaches for several years, so he is familiar with the customs of both.

I started to ask about the numerous scars on his face, but thought better of it. Best to leave a man some privacy.

I changed the subject. I did not see as many Mexicans around when I came in today so I asked about them. He smiled a crooked smile and made a noise in his throat.

"Many have gone back to Mexico," he answered. "They were afraid, many things cause them to fear."

"What do they have to fear?" I asked.

"They fear El Diablo de la Barranca", he replied. "Senor Lawrence has lost many men around the Barranca. Then many more that were sent out by Senor Harvey. Then Senor Harvey himself. They say El Diablo de la Barranca took them, and they were afraid he would come for them as well."

I knew enough of his language to know he was talking about "the Devil from the Canyon". I wonder how they put that together. "What do you think, Paco,?" I asked.

"It is true what they say, but I have no fear. El Diablo de la Barranca took them, but I am not afraid." Our eyes locked. "How could I sit and talk to El Diablo if I were afraid of him?", he said.

At that moment, the door to my father's office opened and a well dressed man with a case came out. My father motioned from behind his desk for me to come in. Before I could get through the door, Paco stepped in front of me. "Your gun senor," he pointed to my holster. I took it out and laid it on the same table I had used the first time I was here.

I walked in not really knowing what to expect. My father remained seated behind his massive desk. "I'm glad you came back," he said. " I expect there are a lot of things that you want explained, especially if you plan to kill me."

"How could I kill you?" I asked. "Paco takes my gun before he allows me in."

"You and I both know that taking your pistol means nothing. If you want me dead, I'll be dead. I have never doubted that if we should meet, you might very well kill me. But I am grateful that at least you are willing to talk with me before you do."

I reached inside my coat and produced the .41 caliber Remington Derringer that I had given Mollie. I laid it on the table. "You're right. I could kill you anytime. But before you die, I want some answers.

He looked straight into my eyes and said, "I'll tell you anything you want to know". For some reason, I knew that he would.

*　　　*　　　*　　　*　　　*

There was frost on the window glass and a chill in the room when I awoke. Mr. Borgardis was already gone. I knew I couldn't stop him so why should I try? This was going to be a long day waiting for him to return, if he does. No good could come from this day, no matter what the outcome would be.

I laid in bed longer than I should have and before I knew it, it was almost time to meet Louisa for a late breakfast. I dressed warmly and left for the diner.

I waited for her at the diner for nearly an hour before she arrived. Looking a little peaked, I asked what was wrong.

"It's that damn Ike Clanton!", Lou muddled out in a panicked voice. "Virgil stayed up all night at the Marshal's office and didn't go home 'till almost morning. Allie said Wyatt came pounding at their door just after he had fallen to sleep tellin' Virg that Ike Clanton was huntin' him and was gonna kill him on sight! Well, Virg didn't take it too seriouly and went on back to bed. Wyatt came and got Morgan and talked him into goin' over and convincing Virg to go find Clanton before Clanton finds him. I don't know why Morgan always has to be part of everything his brothers get into!"

Lou rubbed her forehead in a worried manner. I knew what she was going through. I thought I should just keep my worries of Mr. Bogardis to myself.

Neither one of us ate much, mostly just drank several cups of coffee and glared out the window onto Fourth Street. A light sprinkling of snow had fallen earlier this morning, something that Lou said rarely happens around here. The mud in the street became uneven frozen ruts and caused the wagons to have a hard time passing through. We were both watching as a wagon going a little too fast almost ran down a couple of kids playing in the dirty snow. The driver veared the wagon just in time and the kids ran out of the way, hollering curses back at the driver. Lou sipped on her coffee and took another look out the window.

"Now where the hell are they going!" Lou sat down her cup and continued to stare out the window.

It was Morgan and Virgil. They were walking side by side and heading towards the direction of the hotel on Allen Street. They had very determined looks on their faces. It didn't leave us with a good feeling.

"Let's go, Mollie", Lou announced, rising from her chair. "Let 'em get themselves killed, neither one of them got the sense that their good momma gave 'em". I knew she didn't mean it. She feels the same way I do about Mr. Bogardis. You can't change them, you can't stop them.

I followed Lou to Summerfield Brothers Dry Goods on the corner of Fourth and Fremont Street.

CHAPTER SIX

Standing in front of the man I know as my father, I asked him what I needed to know. "The most important thing to me is why you left my mother alone to die of a broken heart. She would never have believed that you could be alive and not come home to her," I said.

"The answer is long and complicated, but I am going to give it to you straight," he began. He jestered with a wave of his hand that I should take the seat before me.

"I was in a field hospital in Texas recovering from two minor wounds. A group of men came to camp that were not regular Confederate troops. I learned that they were Missouri irregulars under the command of Captain William Quantrill. I liked what I knew of them, that being that they took the war to the Yankees. He and his men ambushed Union patrols and supply convoys and occasionally struck towns on either side of the Kansas-Missouri border. One of his men was wounded and was quartered in the same tent as me. After talking with him for a few days, I asked if he would introduce me to Captain Quantrill. I met the Captain the following day. He was a lean, pleasant looking fellow. His eyes were what really grabbed you. They were the darkest eyes I had ever seen. We talked, and I told him of my interest in joining in his outfit. He explained to me that they were always short on supplies, had no medical assistance unless they could get to a Confederate hospital and were always on the move. I told him I didn't care as long I could do something to make this war end. He got permission from my commanding officer for me to join their group. As I talked with him and his men over the next few days, I learned that they had raided a town in Kansas back in August. They all said it would be a raid that the Kansas Red Legs would remember for a long time."

"I was surprised to see a black man in their outfit", he continued. "His name was John Noland and was one of the Captain's best scouts. He had joined because of the abuse his family had suffered at the hands of the Union forces in Kansas."

"Things did not go well for us over the winter. We made several raids, but it seemed that the Confederate government wanted nothing to do with us. Some said it

was because of the Lawrence, Kansas raid. Which is how I got my name. I used William in honor of Quantrill and Anderson, while Lawrence was to remember their greatest raid. Early in '64 the outfit split up into separate bands and returned to Missouri.   I joined up with Captain William Anderson's bunch, better known as 'Bloody Bill'. When the war was over, some of our men went in to surrender. They were shot. The amnesty did not include any of the raiders that rode with Quantrill or Anderson. I could have stayed on with Archie Clement. He kept a pretty good gang together after the war.   They harassed the government of Missouri for a while . After he got killed, the gang eventually became the James-Younger gang. I guess you heard about them."
"Many of the things you probably heard about us were true, but many were not. When there is a war, the winning side gets to write the history.   They have made a hero out of General Sherman. He burned his way through Georgia. Burned farms and homes that were of no military value. He put innocent families out.   It's easy to make war on civilians. Don't get me wrong. I know we got out of hand sometimes. But Sherman had a plan to do exactly what he did, and he will always be a hero".

   "So, I figured if I came home it wouldn't be long 'till someone figured out who I rode with. When you ride under the black flag they will never forget you". He paused and bent his head down just a little. Then took a big breathe and continued, "They would have hung me, burned the place down, and possibly harmed you and your mother. I could not take that chance. General Joe Shelby took his troops into Mexico rather than surrender. I started to go with him, but to be honest, I had enough of the war. So I came out here and started over. I did not expect to build up a place like this. Just lucky I guess."

   "Lucky!" I said. "How lucky was my mother crying herself to sleep at night over the likes of you. You could have sent word. She would have left everything behind and come to Arizona to be with you! And I reckon it's just luck that you and Harvey Gaines ran roughshod over good decent people and took their land."

   He hung his head and replied, "I know this will be

hard to believe, but I did not know what Harvey was doing. He knew I wanted to buy up as much territory as possible, and I was actually giving Harvey the money to pay people for their land. Somewhere there is a lot of money in a bank or under the ground that Harvey saved up. I should not have trusted him, but I did."

He had been looking down but raised his eyes. "The man you saw leaving here today was my lawyer. I am in the process of trying to make right some of the wrongs that have been done. It is all I can do."

"How do you make right the killing of a man, sending his family into a life of hardship so that you could have more land?" I asked. "How do you give it back when you have destroyed families?" I went on, "Do you know that your crew killed a man, his wife, and their young daughter just to get you a few more acres of land that wasn't fit for anything to begin with? How do you make that right?"

Again, he hung his head. When he looked up, he began to speak. "You are right. There are things that I can never undo. But there is one thing I would like for you to understand. We all have a past. Some things we can change, some we can't. But the past is just that, the past. You have one. Are you proud of everything you have ever done? I doubt it."

"You are very lucky," he said. "You have a woman who may care for you as much as your mother cared for me. But don't let the past ever change your future. Take life and run with it."

He leaned forward and looked me straight in the eye. "If you are going to kill me, go ahead. I don't care anymore."

I picked up the derringer from the desk. "Do you have any kind of records of your business dealings for the past fifteen or so years?", I asked.

"Yes, I have most of the property acquisitions," he answered.

"Then get them together so I can make some sense out of them. We will see what we can do about trying to undo some of your misdeeds," I told him. "But don't think that will set things right between me and you. I still intend to kill you for what you did to my mother. But I will allow you some time to try to fix some of your mistakes."

I turned and walked out the door. Paco was waiting. I did not realize I still had the derringer in my hand. "Sorry Paco," I said, "I must have forgotten that I had this with me." He smiled his crooked smile and said, "It does not matter Senor Bogardis, when El Diablo de la Barranca comes for him, there is nothing that can save him".

*   *   *   *   *

Lou was right, the oriental lace was soft! Softer than any other lace I had ever felt. We were told it was made from rich silk threads. I bought a few pieces for Lilly as a wedding gift. Summerfield Brothers had a large variety of just about everything, velvet ready made skirts, silver plated tableware, and corsets all the way from France. When I paid for the lace, I received ten per cent off the price because I paid with cash. The clerk handed me a ticket that he explained was for a drawing on Christmas Day. I thanked him and handed the ticket to Louisa for safe keeping. Maybe today wasn't going to be as bad as I thought it would be!

Lou suggested we then visit Allie. She might have something to contribute to Lilly's wedding box of supplies we started yesterday.

Allie was standing in the doorway when we approached her house. She held her shawl tightly aound her arms and shoulders and looked a bit frightful. Louisa noticed it as well.

"Whatever is troubling you, Allie, put it aside. We have wedding business to discuss", Lou insisted, trying to make light of her and Allie's worry over their husbands.

Allie followed us inside and shut the door. "Morgan came and got Virgil a little while ago. Poor man can't even get any rest!", complained Allie. We could tell she was definitely not in the mood to discuss wedding particulars with us. ! "They went out looking for Clanton and found him down on the corner of Fourth and Allen", she continued. "That witless Clanton was carrying a rifle and had a loaded six shooter stuck down his britches! Virg hit him upside his head and took the firearms from him.

Morg and Virg dragged him down to the magistrate court and fined him for carrying deadly weapons in the city. Then, the damn fools just let him go! They shoulda run him out of town while they had their chance!"

"I told Morgan the same thing myself", interrupted Louisa. "I was hoping this thing with Clanton would die down, but I think this will only make things worse. Did Virgil say what they were planning to do now?"

"I haven't seen Virgil since he left with Morgan this morning", Allie said as she seated herself in a chair beside us. "Mattie came and told me about what happened. She said Wyatt came home afterwards, took some ammunition out of the cabinet and left again. That's all she knows."

I knew this wasn't good. Mr. Bogardis is at the Circle L Ranch, and Lord only knows what is happening out there, and now this confrontation between the Earps and Clanton has my stomach tied in knots with worry!

Allie offered us a cup of tea or coffee, and we both accepted. While she was preparing the beverages, neither Louisa or I spoke a word. We just sat there, absorbed in our own harrowing private thoughts. Lou began fondling a hankerchief with her fingers that she had removed from her purse, rubbing the edges like it was a hard knotted piece of dough.

"I've never liked it here", complained Allie, as she handed each of us a hot cup. " I wish we never came to Tombstone".

I imagined the three of us appeared like we belonged in a funeral parlor rather than the parlor of Allie and Virgil's home.

I didn't want to stay there with Allie and Louisa, but I also didn't want to go back to the room alone and wait for Mr. Bogardis to return. I told the girls that I should leave and resume my shopping for Lilly. Allie offerred me the use of her wool cloak when I left saying that it was an exceptionally chilly day, and I ought to stay warm. I thanked her, and we all bid each other goodbye.

I strolled slowly along the sidewalks of Allen Street, not sure as to where I wanted to go. The wind was blowing harsh and caused me to shiver. As I approached the barber shop, I noticed that a crowd of men had congregated inside and outside the shop. I stopped and pretended to peer into the window of the adjacent store. I saw Sheriff Behan as he jerked a towel from around his collar and proceeded to leave the shop followed by a couple of other men. I watched him cross the street headed toward Hafford's Corner, where several men had gathered about. Three or four other men from the shop, including the barber holding Behan's towel, stood in the doorway and continued to ramble.

"There's gonna be trouble", one of them said.

"Yeah, and more than he can handle", laughed another.

I was close enough to hear some of their conversation. They were talking about Clanton and the Earps. Seems that talk is all over town about how Virgil Earp pistol whipped Clanton today and took away his guns. Then, someone saw Clanton over near the O.K. Corral, along with a couple of the McLaury's, saying that they were looking for a fight. One of the men stated that Sheriff Behan was on his way to find the marshal and see what all the excitement was about.

I glanced over in the direction of the marshal's office. Virgil had stepped outside and met Behan on the sidewalk. Both their voices were raised, and their arms were showing their tempers had been aroused. Not much could be heard from across the street, but after a minute or two, Behan walked away and headed towards Fourth Street. Virgil left going in the opposite direction.

All this tension in town reminds me of Prescott. The red sashed cowboys in the saloon that night, brawling in the streets, fighting like a pack of animals.

I then remembered that I had written a letter to Aunt Polly back in Prescott and had been carrying it with me for days now. Although Aunt Polly was Lilly's aunt, she took good care of me after the accident that night. I wrote and told her about Lilly's engagement to Zack and let her know that Lilly and I were doing just fine.! I pulled the letter from my purse and walked to the post office to mail it.

Upon leaving the post office, Morgan and Doc Holliday walked right past me! They appeared real serious, like they had somewhere crucial to go. Doc was dressed in a heavy overcoat, a smoking cigarette dangled from his lips. The wind caught one side of his coat and blew it open. I saw the handle of his revolver tucked into the waist of his pants.

I walked back across the street, and without looking where I was going, I almost bumped into Martha King. I had met Miss King at the dress shop on a previous visit to Tombstone. I said hello and asked how she had been. She probably didn't remember me, but said that it was a mighty cold day and that she was on her way to Bauer's Market to purchase meat for tonight's supper.

If only Mr. Bogardis and I had a home of our own instead of

living in a hotel, I could be buying meat and preparing evening suppers like I did back in Prescott. I missed our little cottage on Gurley Street. I missed the walks Mr. Bogardis and I would take across the Granite Creek bridge under the starlight. But, I don't reckon I missed Prescott. I was certainly glad to be back in Contention where it all started. We're close enough to visit the Earps in Tombstone any time we have a notion to. My dear friends Louisa and .... I had temporarly forgotten about Louisa! Perhaps I should return to Allie's house and let Louisa know that I saw Morgan and Holliday together a few minutes ago.

I was walking back towards Allie's house when all of a sudden a rush of gun shots blast through the air like fireworks on the Fourth of July! One right after the other, sounding like a box of bullets exploding all at once. It echoed in my ears like it was close by. It must have lasted a good part of a minute. Thank goodness, I knew it couldn't involve Mr. Bogardis. He must still be at the Circle L Ranch.

Morgan! The Earps! Those men at the barber shop did say there was trouble coming!

What could have happened?

CHAPTER SEVEN

I was not sure where to go or what to do! Then suddenly, the man I recognized as Ike Clanton came running from around the corner just ahead of me. He was running like a wild banshee when he turned and ran up Tough Nut Street.

Everyone was coming out of their houses and running out into the streets. Within moments, crowds of men, women and children were running in the direction of Fourth and Fremont Streets. I turned and followed, running as fast as I could. The crowd had all gathered around a vacant lot near the O.K. Corral.

Smoke from the gunshots was still lingering thick in the air, floating high above the crowd looking like dirty ribbons weaving through the sunlight. I breathed in deep, and the taste of bitter sulfur filled my mouth.

I couldn't see much of what was going on, people were everywhere. The ladies were screaming, and the men were yelling. It was chaotic!

I pushed and shoved my way through the horde of gawking people. I saw a man on the ground..... It was Morgan! He was on his knees holding a bloody hand across his shoulder. Beside him was Doc Holliday. He looked like he'd been hit too, blood was seeping through his trousers. One of the McLaury brothers that I saw in the hotel lobby last night was lying face down and most likely dead. The ground around him was muddled in red. Mattie ran up from out of nowhere and ran to Wyatt. He was standing with Virgil, who was shot in the leg and leaning on Wyatt for balance. I heard Louisa scream when she ran to Morg. He was still on his knees, and she was trying to help him up. Kate appeared from the door of Fly's Boarding house and ran to Doc, kissing his face, muttering something in her Hungarian accent and throwing her arms around him. A couple of other men were on the ground and not moving.

Allie was the last of the wives to make it to the alley. She pushed Wyatt out of the way and grabbed hold of her man. Panic was everywhere!

Forcing her way through the crowd from behind me was the woman named Josephine, Behan's lady friend who Mattie thought was trying to lure Wyatt away from her. I watched her as she started to run towards Wyatt but thought against it when her eyes locked with Mattie's.

Sheriff Behan walked up to Wyatt and told him he was going to arrest them all. Wyatt looked him square in the eyes and told him that he was not going to be arrested today! Spit projected from Wyatt's mouth when he said that Behan had deceived him.

"You told me you disarmed those men!", he shouted at Behan.

Louisa was still trying to help Morgan stand. She told him she intended to take him home and examine his wounds. I went over to assist her, and she told me sharply, "I can handle it!"

A couple of men in the alley were trying to break up the crowd. Others were picking up bodies and carrying them away.!

Just then, another loud noise startled me! I almost wet my undergarments! It was the shrilling blow of the miners whistle. Within seconds, miners were out of the mines and out into the streets. In their hands were weapons, guns, axes, picks.... and they approached the alley like an invading army of helmeted men!

Scared, I hurried back to the hotel. I ran up the stairs, unlocked the door and slammed it behind me. I stood leaning against the door trying to catch my breath, confused and frightened, 'till my body finally gave out. I slid down onto the floor .... and collapsed.

*   *   *   *   *

The chilly ride back to Tombstone went by before I knew it. I kept turning everything over in my mind. The past six or eight months have been like trying to break a mustang. Every time you think you got him lined out, he'll twist and turn and all you can do is try to hang on. I would have never believed that I would one day find my father alive, let alone that he would be in the center of all this. I truly wish that I had never found him.

Of course, they say you can't change one thing in your life without changing everything. No matter how bad it gets, there is always sweet Mollie. As long as she is there, I can handle anything else.

It was getting dark as I rode into Tombstone. I dropped off my horse and headed for the hotel. When I entered the lobby, I noticed that the old man behind the counter was awake. That's strange. I don't recall ever coming in after dark when he wasn't asleep. Before I can speak, he tells me that Mollie is not here, and that she wanted me to meet her at Virgil's house. I figured they were probably having a get-together, but the old man could not contain himself. He said there was trouble today, and Mollie is down there helping tend to the wounded.

"Wounded! What happened?", I demanded.

"There was a gunfight in the street today," he explained. "Ike Clanton, his brother Billy, and the McLaury brothers went up against the Earps and Doc Holliday."

"Are they alright?" By now I had grabbed him by the shoulders. "Who is wounded? Are they alright?"

"Virgil was hit in the leg, Morgan in the arm, and Doc was grazed. Billy Clanton and the McLaury brothers are dead," he replied.

I had heard enough. I was out the door and headed to Virgil's house at a run. Before I got there, I could see some men milling around in the street. I didn't slow down but put my hand on my gun. The men were armed with rifles and shotguns. They brought their weapons up but as soon as they saw who I was, they dropped them to their sides. "They are inside," one of the men said.

As soon as I went through the door, I saw Mollie. She ran to me, and I held her close. "Are you alright?" I asked. She started rattling off the day's events to me so fast I could barely keep up. I felt I should have been there to help. At least Morgan, Virgil, and Doc were going to be okay. There was plenty of protection both inside and outside the house, and the doctor had already patched everybody up. I told Mollie I wanted to speak to the men in private, and then we'd go back to the hotel for the night. If necessary, we could stay on a few days in Tombstone. I offered my help to the men, but talking would have to wait 'till morning. I took Mollie, and we headed to the hotel.

As we walked back in the cold darkness, she asked me if my father was still alive. I told her that he was, but I did not know for how long. I told her there was more I would tell her when we got to the hotel. The room was welcoming. We immediately propped ourselves upright in the bed and shared each other's warmth as we talked of the events of the day.

Mollie told me how scared she was. She almost didn't have the strength to go to Virgil's house and help out Allie and the other wives. I know she's a strong woman, but it must have been hard for her to see the husbands of her friends almost die. I began explaining the exchange between me and my father, but Mollie fell asleep in my arms before I had finished.

I knew the Cowboys were registered and staying at the Grand Hotel, as they usually did while they were in Tombstone, but I didn't think we would have much trouble from them tonight. Everyone was either licking their wounds or making arrangements to bury their dead.

All in all, October 26, 1881 would certainly be a day to remember.

CHAPTER EIGHT

I must have laid on the floor of the hotel room for almost an hour last night before I came to my senses.   What was I running from, what was wrong with me! The Earps needed me, just like I would need them if anything ever happened to Mr. Bogardis.   I got up and walked back out of the room. No one was in the lobby when I left. I had to stop and ask one of the men on the Citizen's Safety Committee, who was still trying to disband the disorderly townfolks, where the Earps were. I was informed that they'd been doctored in the drug store and just left in a wagon going to Virgil's house.

I didn't know what to expect when I arrived. The door was partially open. I walked in, and Virgil was on the couch, Allie by his side with a bowl of bloody water near her on the stand. Wyatt, Morgan, Mattie and Lou were all there. Allie was cussing at Wyatt, blaming him for the condition they were all in. Morg was in the chair, wrapped with bandages across his chest and shoulder.   Red colored stains were escaping through the white cloth faster than Lou could cover them. Morgan was in conversation with Wyatt, who was talking with Virgil, all at the same time.

I asked Allie what I could do to help. She told me there was a bottle of alcohol in the next room, and I should go get it. I handed it to her, and she poured some of the contents onto a cloth and touched the gaping hole in Virgil's leg.

"Damn   doctor", she fussed, "he could of done a better job than this!"   She re-positioned the bandages, and Virgil moved in an effort to get up. "What do you think you're doing! You're not going anywhere!", she yelled.

Wyatt told him to calm down. There would be plenty of time for retaliation.   Allie told Wyatt he should go home and leave them alone. Morgan told Allie she needed to keep her nose out of their business! Everyone's   nerves were at their peak. The tension in the room was thicker than the blood seeping through Morgan's wounded shoulder.

Sherriff Behan had walked in without anyone noticing. Wyatt almost drew his gun on him when he turned and saw him. Wyatt asked him what he was doing there. He said he had come to check on Virgil. Wyatt told him, "Well, you checked on him, now get your lying tail out of here!"

"Virgil, you did perfectly right", Behan said and nodded in Wyatt's direction as he left the room in a hurried fashion.

Finally, Mr. Bogardis came through the door! He was alive... my man was alive! But was his father? At that very moment, I couldn't care one way or the other. I ran to him, and he squeezed me tight. I told him I was alright, no need to worry about me. He walked over to Wyatt, said a few words I couldn't hear, came back and took me by the arm. "Come on Mollie, enough for tonight. We'll be back in the morning."

Later in the room, exhaustion overwhelmed me. Mr. Borgardis told me we should stay on in Tombstone a few days, and I agreed. He described to me what happened at the Circle L Ranch, the explanations of his father's actions. That was all I needed to know. I fell asleep contemplating that life and death are only separated by the good aim of a lead bullet.

*   *   *   *   *

Mollie and I slept a little later than usual. We both had a hard day and were pretty much worn out. We got dressed and headed for Virgil's house. There were still plenty of men standing guard outside. They moved aside and allowed us to walk up on the porch. Before I could knock, Doc was out on the porch with us. He grabbed my hand and shook it. I shake hands with very few people, but Doc is certainly one of them. As he reached over to give Mollie a quick hug, I asked if he was alright. He nodded and said that Frank McLaury's bullet had just barely grazed his hip. Nothing to worry about. I asked about the Earps, and he told me to have a seat in one of the rocking chairs. Mollie excused herself and went on in to see if she could help the ladies.

I asked Doc how things got so far out of hand. I knew there was always friction between the Cowboys and the Earps, but I never expected anything like this. He just shook his head and allowed as how things were a lot more on edge than folks realized. It seemed that Ike was always trying to get things riled up. Once he started drinking, his mouth would get away from him. I cocked my head, and Doc caught my meaning. "Yeah," he said. "I know I do the same thing. That's what makes it so bad. Ike wants it his way, and so do I. When he starts talking about Wyatt and the boys, I lose my temper and things go downhill from there." Well, at least Doc could admit that he and Ike were somewhat alike. I wouldn't want to be caught between them. Doc will look you in the eye and drop the hammer, but while Ike might certainly kill you, I don't figure him to be looking you in the eye when he does.

I asked how the Earps were doing and was told that everyone was going to be fine. There was already some talk about trying to bring him and the Earps up on murder charges. That don't seem possible, charging a marshal and his deputies with murder for trying to enforce the law. Doc asked about Zack and then got to the part that I knew would be coming sooner or later. "You shot that son-of-a-bitch Lawrence yet?" I just shrugged and told him I was taking care of it my own way. Doc is enough of a southern gentleman to let it go at that.

I asked if Wyatt was inside, and Doc said he was down at the office taking care of town business. About then, Mollie opened the door and stepped out. "Did you want to come in?", she asked. I told her that since they were okay, I thought I might drop by Virgil's office and see if I could help Wyatt with anything. I would wait for her there, and we could go get some breakfast when she was through.

I told Doc to tell Morgan and Virgil I came by and if they needed me for anything, all they had to was ask. Doc nodded, and I headed on up the street to the office. I did not mention it, but I do not like to go in to see sick folks or the dead. I don't know why. If someone is wounded, I can patch them up without a thought. If someone is killed, I can load them up or bury them. I guess I just can't deal with the formalities of sickness and death.

When I got to the office, I knocked twice and opened the door. Wyatt was seated behind the desk with one hand on a Colt's revolver and the other on a cup of coffee. He relaxed when he saw it was me. "Mind if I get a cup of that stuff?", I asked. He just smiled and nodded at the pot sitting on the stove.

I poured myself a cup and sat down across from him. "You ok?" I asked. He replied that he was fine, and his brothers were both doing well. I told him I had stopped by the house that morning. He just nodded and said, "Thanks". I asked what he thought might happen next. He told me that they certainly had enemies in town, and that there was already talk of bringing them up on charges. All I could do was shake my head. He went on to say that his first priority was the safety of his family. I asked how things got so bad so quick. He gave pretty much the same answer as Doc. Things had just been building between them and the Cowboys, and yesterday they reached the breaking point. We talked for a short while, and I was relieved when Mollie appeared in the doorway. Wyatt had not gotten around to asking about William Lawrence. Wyatt stood when Mollie walked in and asked her how she was doing.

I told Wyatt we were going to eat and asked if he wanted to come along. He thanked me but said he would hang around the office for a while. I asked if there was anything either one of us could do. He replied that everything was being handled, but he appreciated the offer. I told him we would stay until tomorrow just in case, and then we would be going back to Contention.

We made our way to the restaurant, sat down, and ordered. We talked a little about the events of yesterday. When we had finished eating, I was on my last cup of coffee when I overheard three men at the table next to us. I did not get everything they said, but I did hear that the Earps had pushed for the fight, and it was a shame that all the dead were the harmless ranchers.

I stood and turned to them. "Gentlemen, you can think anything you want to think, but it is not wise to let me hear any disparaging remarks about the Earps or Doc Holliday."

With that, I took Mollies arm, and we walked out.

During the day, Mollie went back to the house several times. I mostly hung around the saloons to see what I could hear. It sounded to me like the town was split pretty even concerning who the good guys were in the street fight yesterday.

I saw Mayor Clum on the street and asked him if he expected any trouble. He told me not to worry. If there were charges brought, he was sure Judge Spicer would handle it correctly.

I made arrangements to pick up the buggy early the next morning so we could be on our way. I slept fitfully, and I don't think Mollie rested well either. I had that dream again. Mollie was in trouble, and I couldn't help her. I wake up in a sweat when I have that dream. I don't like it, and I sure as hell don't know what it means.

CHAPTER NINE

We rose early Friday morning. It was a melancholy departure. I hated to leave Tombstone with all the turmoil between the Earps and the Cowboys, but I also wanted to return home to a peaceful Contention with Lilly and Zack. During our lunch stop, Mr. Bogardis questioned me more of the events from Wednesday, but there was not much I could tell him that he didn't already know. I know he feels remorseful that he was not there when Doc and the Earps needed him. He told me if he'd only known, he wouldn't have been so selfish and left out that morning for the Circle L.

I told him that it seems to me the Earps and Doc did just fine. Four against six, and they were all alive. Yeah, a few wounds here and there, but it could have surely been worse! They could have been the men laid out for display in the window of the Ritter and Ream Funeral Parlor.   Those dead Cowboys were dressed in fine store bought clothes and placed in expensive caskets for a public viewing. There was a large sign tacked up above the bodies that read, "Murdered in the Streets of Tombstone".   Everyone in town traipsed by and stared at the sign as if Wyatt, Virgil, Doc and Morgan started the fight in the first place. I'm glad to be out of Tombstone just so I don't have to see that aberrant spectacle again!

When Allie and Lou saw the display, they cussed and hollered for half an hour, saying that their men lie home suffering with bullet holes because of those lousy swine they were making such a fuss about.

Mr. Bogardis told me he talked with Mayor Clum before we left. He says they will be relieving Virgil of his badge tomorrow, pending the investigation of the charges against him. He heard talk in the saloon that Ike Clanton was filing murder charges against them all. Mr. Bogardis says that it's all a bunch of hogwash!

Finally, we arrived back in Contention.   Mr. Bogardis took me back to the hotel to unload the boxes I brought back from Tombstone.

"Damn! Mollie", he moaned, straining just a little, acting as if the boxes were heavy. " What did you girls put in these boxes! Iron ore is what it feels like!"

As Mr. Bogardis hauled the boxes up the stairs to our room, he was interrupted by Mr. Crain bellowing for his attention from somewhere in the back. "Mr. Bogardis, did you hear what happened over in Tombstone!" Mr. Crain almost tripped over a chair trying to get to the hallway to see him. Mr. Bogardis ignored him, as usual, and left the boxes in the room for me to do with as I pleased. He kissed me good bye and said he was going to return the horse and buggy, and that he'd be back a little later.

Word gets around fast, especially since we were only ten miles from Tombstone. Lilly and Zack must be worried about us as well. I thought it best that I go find Lilly
and let her know we arrived safely home. I didn't have to go very far, Lilly was running towards me as I walked out the hotel door.

"Oh, Mollie, I'm so glad you're back!", Lilly grabbed me, I could see she was in a tizzy! "We all heard about the shootings in Tombstone. How are Wyatt and his brothers, Mollie? Were you there, did you see the gunfight? And what about Mr. Bogardis, is he alright?"

"Hold on, Lilly! So many questions", I answered. "I have so much to tell you and show you. Remember the reason I went to Tombstone anyway!"

Arm in arm, Lilly and I re-entered the hotel just as Mrs. Marks was calling my name from across the street. I decided to be like Mr. Bogardis! I tugged on Lilly's arm, moved a little faster, and we ran up the stairs!

I spent the next hour re-telling the events of the last two days to Lilly. Eventually, we got around to sifting through the box of items I brought back from Lou and the girls. I watched as Lilly wallowed in all the pretty lace, the colorful candles and the dress she would wear on her wedding day. She adored the neckline of the gown saying that she would feel like the queen of France in something as elegant as that!

Lilly told me Zack has been concerned about Mr. Bogardis and his return to the Circle L. He hasn't wanted to talk wedding arrangements since we left. I told her that Mr. Bogardis and I will probably ride out to the ranch and see Zack tomorrow and explain everything. Lilly reminded me that since there were very few days left until the wedding, that she should ride out there with us. "I don't even know if Zack has the proper suit of clothes for the ceremony! He has been so worried about Mr. Bogardis that he says he hasn't the mind to think about it", Lilly grumbled. "Why, he hasn't even allowed me to come and cover the windows with new curtains!"

Laughing and acting like juvenile girls, we jumped when we heard a knock at the door. "Mollie, it's me, Mrs. Marks". Neither myself nor Lilly moved. We sat on the edge of the bed, surrounded by lacey objects scattered like a whirlwind had transpired. Another knock, just a little louder this time. "I know you're in there! I want to know all about the gunfight in Tombstone. Mollie, let me in so you can tell me everything. I just have to know!", she pleaded.

Lilly and I just looked at each other and couldn't help the giggles that burst out of the silence. We were enjoying each other's company and didn't want Mrs. Marks to spoil the mood. With broad smiles on both of our faces, we supposed that the busybody Mrs. Marks would just have to read the story in the newspaper!

*   *   *   *   *

Neither of us were very hungry at breakfast, but when you start out on a ten-mile trip, you had better eat something just in case things take a bad turn. We both ate light but had several cups of coffee. I had asked the cook to prepare something we could take along for lunch on the trail. He had boiled some eggs, cut up some chicken, and packed some bread. I paid our tab and took our lunch with us to pick up the buggy. Mollie had arranged for it to be loaded the night before with all the things she had rounded up for Lilly and Zack's wedding and my saddle as well. Today would be the funeral for Frank and Tom McLaury and Billy Clanton.

I had no desire to stay and neither did Mollie. We eased out of town and headed for home. Home. Funny that we would consider a hotel room in Contention home, but I reckon we both do. Neither of us had slept well, and we rode in silence for a good part of the morning. I was pondering my recurring bad dream, and I guess Mollie had thoughts of her own. I know she is excited about the wedding, but today she seems lost in thought. I don't understand all this hoopla about a wedding. Looks to me like they could just get married and be done with it.

By noon, we were both ready to stop and stretch our legs and see if our lunch was fit to eat. Mollie threw a blanket on the ground, and we sat and ate quietly. I thought the eggs were good, but the chicken was not something I would want to feed to anyone. It didn't really matter as we were not in the mood to eat. I was thinking of my father, the trouble in Tombstone, and my dreams. I just can't seem to shake it.

Mollie was just as quiet as me. I can only imagine what thoughts she may be dealing with. I'm sure at least part of it has something to do with the street fight the day before yesterday. She talked a little when I questioned her again of any thing she may have forgotten to tell me. Mollie is no stranger to violence, and she knows how fast things can turn. I know it weighs on her because she cares for me and worries that I may be displayed in the Undertaker's window someday. It certainly is possible, but I don't intend to volunteer for any such show.

As we close in on Contention, Mollie seems to be in better spirits. We can rent the buggy again tomorrow and go out to Zack's place and take them all the stuff from the ladies in Tombstone. All this loading and unloading is a pain in my back!

I dropped Mollie, our bags and the boxes off at the hotel and went down to the saloon for a drink. I got my usual spot, back to the wall, and tried to forget the bad thoughts. That's pretty hard to do. The last time I was in here, I killed two men. All because of my name. Maybe my father was right to leave his behind. Of course he just built himself another name that would have brought shame to my mother.

After I had had enough for the day, I go on back to the hotel to lie down a bit, maybe get some sleep if I am lucky. As I turn down the sidewalk, I catch a glimpse of someone I have seen before. I believe it was Jenkins, the man who did not draw when his two partners did. He turned the corner and was gone. When I got to the corner, I eased around it. He could have been waiting to ambush me. But no, the alley is clear. I am not sure I like the fact that he is back in town. But like the marshal said, he did not draw, and he has not broken any laws nor made any threats. Still, it makes for an uneasy feeling. I take care in going on to the hotel, but nothing causes me alarm.

Lying in bed, I think about Lilly and Zack. I like both of them and wish them the best in their life together.

Maybe Zack has settled down early enough that he does not have too many bad habits, nor too many men wishing him dead. I wish things could have been different for Mollie and me. I wonder if we will ever have a settled life. Mollie deserves it, but I don't know if I am the one who can give it to her.

CHAPTER TEN

It has been a long week. Mr. Bogardis and I constantly worry about our friends in Tombstone and what must be happening since the shooting. He says as soon as this wedding is over, we will ride back to town for another visit. He says maybe we can stay a few days and offer to help out in any way we can.

I shouldn't feel this way, and Lord knows I love Lilly like a sister, but I will be glad when tonight comes and it will all be over. It's just that all this turmoil in Tombstone is hanging over me like a black cloud.

Lilly interrupts my thoughts by reminding me that all the guests haven't arrived yet, and the wedding will start in less than half an hour! I step into the bedroom that once was occupied by Zack's parents and notice all the fresh lumber in the walls. Zack has been steadily busy over the past month or so refurbishing his homestead for his new bride. He built a small stoop outside the door for Lilly and him to sit out on warmer evenings and gaze at the stars. It reminds me of the nights when Mr. Bogardis and I would walk under the stars on Gurly Street, hand in hand.

"Mollie, would you please help me tuck this comb right here", Lilly asked, showing me where to place the hair comb with a point of her finger. She bent her head down just a little as I pushed the comb under several layers of hair, wound tight around her head in braids. "My mother used to fix my hair like this when I was a child", Lilly reflected. "She had beautiful hair herself, long golden locks that my father used to say was his pride and joy! Sometimes, I watched as he washed her hair for her. He would heat a pail of water so it would be warm as the morning sun. She used to love that."

I could see that Lilly wished her parents could be here, to know that she was happy and getting married. I'm sure Zack felt the same way about his parents, but this was no time for bad memories.

"Lilly, you look very charming in that dress. I hope you haven't left this room to let Zack catch a peak of you!", I teased.

"Why, heavens no, Mollie! I wouldn't dare", replied Lilly. "Zack and Mr. Bogardis have been out in the barn for almost an hour. Lord only knows what they are doing."

"I think Mr. Borgardis is giving a talk to Zack", I laughed.

I heard another carriage ride up and looked out the window as Mr. Bogardis appeared from the barn door to take charge of the horses and the buggy. It was Mrs. Marks and Mr. Crain. I told Lilly to stay put, I'd greet the guests and keep everyone busy while she finished preparing herself for Zack.

The main room of the house looked more like a church sanctuary than Zack's ranch right now. Lace flowed from the ceiling and draped down to the floor, making an archway in front of the fireplace for Lilly and Zack to stand beneath and repeat their vows. Ten or eleven town folks came out for the festivities, making the room appear quite small and tight. Preacher Jefferson Cook, from the Methodist Church in town, was dressed in his Sunday clothes and and held a worn Bible in his hand. He told Mrs. Marks he sure was ready to get on with the ceremony so he could dip into the pot of boiled chicken and dumplins she brought!   The wedding cake, covered with rich frosting dripping from the edges, was placed in the center of the table and caused everyone to drool with hunger just thinking about how it would taste in their mouths.

"It's time, Lilly", I walked back into the bedroom to fetch the bride when Zack and Mr. Bogardis came through the door. Zack was dressed mighty fine in a black string tie, a pressed white shirt and black coat.   His hair was smoothed back off his face, showing a high forehead I hadn't noticed before. Zack's not a big man, average height and willowy, but strong as an ox. He'll bulk up as he gets older, a man tends to do that. Zack's not too much on words, like Mr. Bogardis, and he looked more like a bashful boy than a man standing there holding his hat in his hands, fumbling it with his fingers.

"Gimme that hat, son", Mr. Bogardis said as he took the hat from Zack's sweaty hands. "I swear, you're as fidgety as a cat in a tub of cold water."

Zack looked at Lilly like he had never seen her before when she walked into the room. His smile went all the way from one side of his face to the other. Lilly blushed when their eyes met.

They held hands and Preacher Cook read from the Holy Book as I moved to stand beside Mr. Bogardis. I took his hand in mind, squeezed it and wiped a tear from my eye as I listened to Lilly and Zack say they would forsake all others until death do them part. Mrs. Marks, with a flirtatious look on her face, grabbed hold of Mr. Crain's arm and gave him a little wink.

When it was all over and Zack finally kissed his new wife,

Preacher Cook was the first one to serve himself some warm chicken and dumplins!

Mr. Bogardis and I stayed a while after the ceremony to help Lilly clean up the place. We then said our goodbyes and left the happy couple to tend to their first night together.

We managed to ride back to the hotel before darkness hit. Mr. Bogardis was acting a little frisky himself, a mood he has rarely been in these days. He slapped me on the rear as we walked up the steps to our room. "Get along up there, Mollie, we got business of our own to take care of", he taunted.

Once inside the room, he couldn't wait to pluck the cloak from my shoulders and toss it on the bed. "I want you, Mollie", he moaned, kissing my cheek. My breathing got heavier as I felt the wetness of his tongue glide slowly along the neckline of my dress. I arched my back towards the door, leaning against it for support. He loosened my dress tenderly, all the while looking into my eyes. It didn't take long before a stack of clothing was cluttered in a pile on the floor. He moved me to the bed and laid me down with my legs and feet dangling over the edge, just inches off the floor. I could feel part of my cloak wedged under my back, still cold from the chilly ride home.

His silhouette projected a dark masculine figure in the dimness of the room. He didn't say a word as he leaned in closer to my body, close enough for me to feel his need.

I let out a stifled scream when I felt his body and mine join together. His cold hands were beneath my bare hips, holding them in place while he immersed deeper, causing my groans to get louder. My hands reached for the edge of the cloak, and I squeezed it between my fingers. I felt his body become tense and stiff, as if in pain, when he finished. He took a deep breath and let out a sigh as he laid down on top of me. He kissed my face, my neck and finally his mouth found mine. As we kissed, we rolled over and laid side by side.

! "I love you, Mollie, you know that", he whispered. "You deserve more than me. You deserve a fine house and a decent man to love you. I don't know if I'm that kind of man or not. I don't know what kind of life you will have if you stay with me. All I know is that I can't make it without you. Seeing Zack and Lilly so caught up with each other today, well, it makes me think I want the same thing. I ain't never said this to anyone, Mollie, I reckon I thought I never would, but......"

He paused, contemplating what to say next, " I....I ....want to marry you, if you'll have me".

I wish I could have seen his face, but the room was too dark. I imagined he must have looked like a bona fide dapper, all romantic and sincere and such! I threw my arms around his neck and held him tight .

Finally, I thought, I'm going to make a husband out of him!

*   *   *   *   *

I'll be glad when all this wedding stuff is over. I think Mollie is ready to move on as well. She loves Lilly like a sister, and Zack knows he is one of the few people in this world that I place any trust in, but there has been a lot going on.

This business with my father has weighed heavier on my mind than I like to admit.   I have tried to leave Mollie out of it. It's not that I don't trust her, the woman has saved my skin more than once. But I do not want to burden her with my problems. As far as we both knew, my father was dead when we got together.

Now to bring him to life with all the hurt of the past is something that Mollie should not have to deal with. I will handle it myself, in due time.

Mollie has her own problems. Now she is doing for Lilly like a mother. I guess someone has to take charge of the wedding. And Mollie is certainly not one to retreat. She has been torn up since the street fight in Tombstone. I know she thinks a lot of the Earps, both the ladies and the men. But I also figure she saw what happened up there and puts it together with what the two of us have already faced. She knows how fragile life can be out here.

Mollie has spent a lot of time out at Zack's place helping Lilly decorate. Zack has spent a lot of time trying to stay out of their way. Can't blame him for that. Me, I am just content if I don't get drug into too much of it. Don't see why they can't just stand up in front of a preacher and get it over with. That's too simple for the ladies.

I will say that they have pulled it all together, and it looks like it will wind up before you know it. I told Mollie I would take care of the horses and rigs of the guests. At least that will get me out of the house. On my way out to the barn, she pulled me to the side and told me to take Zack with me. I guess she read the question in my eyes. "So you can give him a talking to about being a husband," she said. "What can I tell him? I ain't never been one," I replied. She gave me her "look" so I knew there was no point in arguing. Zack and I headed to the barn.

There were not many guests, but once they all got in the house it looked like a big crowd. While we waited in the barn, Zack paced back and forth with his hands in his pockets. I finally asked him if there was anything he wanted to talk about. He looked at me like he just realized I was there. He mumbled something about not being sure he could take care of Lilly, how was he supposed to act, just all kinds of stuff that I sure couldn't help him with. I finally told him that we had been up against a dozen bandits at a time and even trapped a few right here on this very place. How hard could getting married be? I did mention that if I ever did, I would just go to the preacher and get it done. None of this all week preparation and having all these people come to watch. Naw, not me.

When Mrs. Marks and Cornelius Crane arrived in their buggy, they were the last ones we were expecting. I took care of the horse while they went on in. Mollie had said when the last guests arrived to bring Zack on in. I looked at him and said, "Well, come on son, let's get it over with." He looked at me, and I swear I didn't know whether he was going to pass out or throw up. He caught his breath for a minute, and we headed for the house. When Mollie saw us come in the door, she went to get Lilly from the bedroom.

I was surprised that the actual ceremony did not take very long at all. Mollie reached for my hand and squeezed it hard as they said their vows. I looked at her, and she had a few tears running down her cheek. I pushed my elbow into her side and whispered, "They ain't dead yet." She gave me that look again.

When things were done, Mollie helped clean up a bit and we said our farewells. She asked me what I thought about the whole thing, and all I could do was shake my head. "Seems like an awful lot of doings when everything came down to a couple of minutes," I said. After that we just rode pretty much in silence back to the hotel. I admit I had thought a lot about this whole thing. Of course, that means I was thinking of Mollie.

As we walked up the narrow stairs in the hotel, with Mollie in the lead and her bustle in my face, I couldn't resist giving her a little whack on her behind. I reckon all this wedding hoopla kinda got to me. I used to get so feverish every time I looked at Mollie, but I'd admit that I haven't been much of a comfort in the romance territory lately. Just too much on my mind.

As soon as the door shut behind us, I had her cloak off and my hands all over her. My lips played with her neck and cheeks. I couldn't wait any longer. The desires I remembered had come back with a vengeance. We got out of our clothes, and I placed her on the bed. Her low moans and suppressed screams only excited me more. Neither of us could be considered quiet or passive when entangled together. I am sure half the hotel knew exactly what we are doing. After all the passion played out, we lay on the bed and I began to tell her that she was too good for the likes me. Rather, I wound up asking her to marry me! She answered "yes".

CHAPTER ELEVEN

The air was crisp and clear Monday morning when we rode into Tombstone. Not like it was the night before. Midnight rains made for mud spattering off the wheels of the buggy as they turned. The bottom portion of my dress was torn and ragged and discolored with shades of gray. Clumps of dried dirt lay on the floor board beneath my feet.

The seat rocked back and forth, swaying with the rhythm of the horse's trots. I saw the newly risen sun reflecting off a metal bar on the front of the buggy, It looked peaceful. It was a good morning for traveling. Mr. Bogardis sat straight in his seat, mindful and alert, with the reins weaved through his fingers. Ocassioanally he would turn his attention to me, glance over and smile, sometimes resembling the old Mr. Bogardis I used to know!

The city of Tombstone could be seen along the horizon for at least a mile before we arrived. I kept my eyes on it as it appeared to get larger the closer we got. As if in spite, a church steeple rose up above the roof tops and cast a faint shadow of a cross along the corrupted Allen Street.

Mr. Bogardis stopped the buggy in front of the Grand Hotel. I fell in love with the Grand Hotel the first time Mr. Bogardis and I saw it. It's only been open for a little over a year, and I imagined it looks like something you'd see in San Francisco.

Mr. Bogardis extended his hand to help me down from the buggy and escort me into the lobby. The beauty of the wide staircase, covered with thick elegant carpet and trimmed in rich black walnut wood, overwhelms your sight! Mr. Bogardis checked us in a room while I glided my fingers across the expensive furnishings and admired the costly oil paintings adorning the walls. I peeked into the dining room and couldn't wait until we freshened up and ate our noon day meal on their fine china under the sparkling chandeliers.

"Mollie!", he called to me, "we have a room". I followed him as he carried our bags up the stairs. There are sixteen rooms in the main corridor, the first one being the bridal chamber. Our room further down the hall was just as nice, silk curtains, plush carpet and wall paper.

"I want to be married here", I blurted out. We hadn't spoke of his marriage proposal since the night he asked me.

"Anything you want, Mollie. But now is not the time", he told me, placing the bag on the spread that covered the spring mattress. He took the gun rig he had hidden away in the carpet bag and hung it on the front poster of the bed. "I need to go see Wyatt and Doc and find out what's going on. You need to see what you can do for Allie and Louisa, that's what we came for."

"I know that. I didn't mean 'now'. I only meant when we do get married, I want to be married here at the Grand Hotel." His mood had changed and I'm not sure he heard what I had said.

I watched him take the pistol from the holster and check his load. He stood at the window holding the gun in his hand, looking out onto Allen Street then back at the gun. "Everything has changed, Mollie. That gun fight last week changed everyone and everything here forever. I can feel it." His eyes drifted off like he was seeing the future, and it wasn't something he wanted to know.

"I'll leave you to tidy yourself up. Meet me in the dining room in an hour or so and we'll eat", he told me as he walked out.

I set out to find the girls and see how Morgan and Virgil were recovering from their wounds. In the lobby, I overheard a few old men discussing Virgil's dismissal of being Chief of Police. "D'you hear that Virg is hiding out at the Cosmopolitan?", one of them asked the other. "Somebody went and tried to kill 'em over at his place, and he got scared is all I hear'd".

I gasped, thinking that someone would try to kill Virgil at his own residence!

I ran over to the Cosmopolitan Hotel and saw armed men guarding the lobby. I asked them where I could find Virgil and Allie. I was directed to a room quite small and not as elegant as ours in the Grand. Virgil lay in the bed as Allie opened the door to allow me to enter.

"Oh, Mollie!", she cried out and hugged me. "Wyatt and Doc have just been arrested and taken over to the Sixth Street jail! Judge Spicer has been conducting a hearing since last week. Then Friday, another one of those McLaury boys rode in from Texas. He's been talk'in around town that he's fed up with 'Earp Law' and he's gonna make sure someone pays for the death of his brothers. Wyatt started this whole thing and pulled Virg and Morgan in with him! Him and that good for nothin' Holliday. Why does he have to be so damn hellish?", she raged. "Poor Virg can't leave the bed and Mattie's been sick with one of her headaches for three days and ...." Allie paused and broke into tears.

Bessie, Jame's wife, came over and told her to stop crying, everything was going to work out. James was over at the jail right now seeing what he can do to get them out.

"Do they have a lawyer, Allie?" I inquired. "They need a good lawyer!"

"Yes, we hired Thomas Fitch. He's a personal friend of Governor Freemont. He's been down at the courthouse everyday. They are out for blood, Mollie, it's worse than we thought! The only reason Virgil and Morgan aren't locked up is cause they can't get out of bed. Mollie, I can't leave Virg, but you could go down to the courthouse today and listen in. See what you can hear and come back and tell me. Would you do that, Mollie?" Allie pleaded.

"I will, but I hate to leave you when I just got here. Are you sure you'll be alright?" I asked. With a slight nod of her head, she gave me permission to leave. !   "I'll be back as soon as I can", I told her and left promptly.

The courtroom was brimming with spectators! I had to nudge myself in tightly between two older gentlemen on a bench in the back row. They looked like they hadn't had a bath in a year and smelled to high heaven!   I turned my attention to the front of the courtroom. I thought I recognized the plump older woman wearing a wide brim hat who sat in the witness chair.

A man dressed in a dark gray suit with his back facing me was questioning the woman. He was pacing the floor directing his conversation towards the woman and the judge.

"I saw a man. It was Mr. Holliday", the woman told the man in the black robe. "He had a gun. I know the difference between a gun and a pistol, Judge!   I just don't know whether it was a rifle or a shotgun." She went on to testify that she saw Doc Holliday and the Earp brothers. They were walking near the butcher shop and post office when she saw them.

Then I remembered!   The woman in the witness chair was Martha King! I saw her that day in the butcher shop. I stopped to speak a word or two with her when I was walking out. If I hadn't been in such a hurry that day, I might have been more aware of what was happening around me!

"Mrs. King", the suited man continued, "Did you hear what the men were saying?"

"Let them have it", she answered quite matter-of-factly.

He went on to ask her several more questions. Even prodding her as to if she was scared when she saw them.   She didn't appear frightened when I spoke with her just minutes prior! They should put me in the witness chair! I'll tell them what I think!

Finally, the judge told Mrs. King she could leave the chair and resume her seat back on the bench. She stood and nodded a thank you to the judge, holding her head high in a prideful manner.

"The Prosecution now calls Mr. Wesley Fuller to the stand".

The old men who were seated on each side of me began mumbling between each other. "That ol' drunkard!", the one on my left told the other. "Why, he ain't nothin' but an old card cheat! I seen him down at the Oriental bending his elbows plenty a times. He ain't got nothin' to say but pure bosh, pure bosh I tell ya!"

"Shhhh....", I told them both. "I can't hear what they are saying."

Mr. Fuller told the judge that he was in the back alley, near Fly's Gallery when the shooting began. He says he was on his way to warn Billy Clanton and to tell him to get out of town. But he didn't get the chance to tell him because it was at that time he saw the Earps. He stated he heard Wyatt Earp tell Billy to "throw up his hands" and Billy did so. Billy told him not to shoot him, that he didn't want to fight. It was then he said he witnessed all the shooting taking place.

The old man on my left stretched his head out in front of my chest to talk with his companion on my right. "I told you he wan't nothin' but an old four-flusher!"

"And I told you both to stop talking!" I looked directly at the old man and gave him a stern look to be quiet. He raised one eye brow and wrinkled up his dirty nose. He slowly sat back in his seat and appeared to be pouting like a scolded child.

Mr. Fuller continued to speak. He accused the Earps of firing the first shots. He said that Billy still had his hands in the air and was shot at several times before he drew his pistol with his left hand. When Billy was hit and lay dying, he claims to have never left his side. With that statement, we could hear sighs and murmurs in the court room coming from sympathizers of the Cowboys.

Mr. Fuller testified well into the afternoon. He went on and on about how the Earp's confronted and bullied the McLaurys and Ike Clanton. He was just about to be cross- examined when I noticed the old man beside me retrieving his watch from his vest pocket. "Dag-gum-it, Cotton! We'd best be gettin ourselves back to the hoosegow. We's gonna miss that ol' galley-wagger playing to the gallery!", the old man grumbled in a not so low tone. Both of the men looked at each other and reluctantly rose from their seats. It must have been getting late in the afternoon for my stomach let out a rumble as the men squeezed by me. Lunch! I had forgotten to meet Mr. Borgardis for lunch! He must be half sick worried about me!! I got up and followed the old men out the court house door.

I ran swiftly to the Grand Hotel dining facility to look for Mr. Bogardis.

*   *   *   *   *

We left early Monday morning for Tombstone, again renting a buggy. I much prefer to ride my horse, but Mollie is not much on riding. At least more than just for fun. The time passed quickly. We did not talk a lot, my mind being preoccupied with other things. But it was a beautiful day, not too cool, very pleasant.

As soon as we got into town, I dropped off Mollie at the Grand Hotel and carried our things inside. I reminded Mollie that we were here to see how the Earps were doing. She said she was leaving promptly to go see Allie.   Since I am not much on the sick and dying, I told her I needed to go find Wyatt or Doc and see what was going on.

I went down to the marshal's office expecting to find Wyatt. Instead it was Dave Neagle wearing the badge. I met him a time or two around Tombstone, and he seemed like a good man. He's a little on the short side, but he didn't let that bother him. Probably made himself a better man for it. He told me I could find Wyatt and Doc over at the Sixth Street Jail. I proceeded on over, wondering what might be going on. As I entered, I saw another man with a badge, but this one I did not recognize. When I told him I was looking for Wyatt or Doc, he gave me a hard stare. "I ain't gonna have any carrying on around here!", he bellowed. "They already had one visitor this morning." But, he said I could go back to see them as well. He opened the door to the back room where the cells were located. As soon as I walked in, I could see Wyatt in one cell and Doc in the one beside him. Both of them were stretched out on cots. When they saw me, they both got to their feet and walked to the bars.

"What are you two doing in jail?", I asked. Doc just shrugged, and Wyatt began to tell me how the cowboy faction was going to try to make it look like the Earps just gunned everyone down without a chance. They had filed charges and were demanding a hearing. That's one of the reasons I gave up on being a ranger. It seemed it had gotten to the point that the lawman was accused of being too hard on the lawbreaker. You go out and risk your life to enforce the law, and instead of appreciation, you always have someone questioning the how and why of everything you do. Who would have thought that there would need to be a hearing because the lawmen killed some lawbreakers while trying to disarm them?

I asked how Virgil and Morgan were doing and was told they would both make it. The only reason they weren't in jail was because of their injuries. I also asked Doc about his hip. "Just a graze," he said. "Barely broke the skin, but a nice grove in my holster."

The deputy, who had not left the room, said it was time for me to go. "Visitation for murderers is kept short," he advised. I gave him a hard look and told Wyatt and Doc if they or Virgil and Morgan needed anything, all they had to do was ask. The deputy and I went back into the front office, and I headed out into the street.

I decided to walk around town, more to stretch my legs than anything else. After the ride from Contention, I needed to move around. As I passed Fourth Street, I heard someone call my name. I spun around with my hand already on my Colt's revolver under my coat. The man's hands went in the air and he said, "Whoa, don't you remember me?" I looked close at his face, and I did recall him, from Texas I believe. I relaxed a little, and he lowered his hands as he quickly walked over. "It's me, Red" he said, as he stuck out his hand. He realized that I don't shake hands and drew it quickly back.

Now I did remember him. Red, from south Texas. I asked what the hell he was doing in Arizona. He just smiled and said it was a long story. At the moment, he had just picked up his S&W revolver from Spangenberg's Gun Shop. It had given him some trouble on the trip, and he had left it with the gun shop when he got into town yesterday. Turns out it was only a bad spring and was already fixed. I remember that Red was quite a cowboy down in Texas. He was cowboy, not a gun hand. He only carried one for protection, a last resort. He asked if he could buy me a drink. I said, "Why not", and we headed for the saloon. Mollie and I had agreed to meet at the diner around one o'clock, so I had a little time to kill.

Just as we reached the saloon door, he mentioned that it was really a surprise running into two people that he knew. As we sat down, I asked him who else he had seen from Texas.

"You remember that Jenkins bunch you had all that trouble with out from Waco?", he asked. I thought a minute about the trouble, which I remembered. There were three of them. The old man and two boys. They liked to play fast and loose with other folks' cattle. But the old man was killed in a stampede, one of the boys died when I tried to bring them in, and the other was tried and hanged right there in Waco. I told him I thought all of the Jenkins in that crowd were accounted for.

"Naw, the youngest boy was only fourteen when all that trouble took place," he told me. "He always swore when he got big enough he would get you for what you did to his brothers. He's nineteen or twenty now. I saw him earlier this morning, but I don't think he recognized me. He had three men with him. Two looked like saddle-tramps, but the other looked like he might be a gun hand." He went on to tell me that he had been on a trail drive to Wichita and got offered a job up there. Since there was nothing holding him in Texas, he accepted. As time went by, he had to keep moving west to stay ahead of the quarantine line. Folks up there were not happy taking Texas cattle in their state. They had already had too much trouble with Texas fever.

He said he would be leaving by first light, headed for California. I wished him luck and thanked him for the information about Jenkins. I reckon I better be on my toes. I had that little confrontation with those boys in Contention. The one that lived through it was named Jenkins.

We nodded to each other, and he was gone.

I looked at my watch, and it was already past one o'clock. I better get on over to the diner, or Mollie will be all over me.

CHAPTER TWELVE

I arrived at the Grand Hotel diner about one thirty in the afternoon. Half- starved and half-an-hour late. I thought Mollie would skin me, but she was not there. I asked the waiter, and he said she had not been in. The drinks had taken the edge off my hunger, and since the diner was not crowded, I decided to wait around for her. I was not too concerned. I just figured she was tangled up with the Earp ladies and would be along soon enough.

After a while, I got pretty restless waiting around. I had noticed a bench on the sidewalk near the door of the diner. I moved on outside. At least the scenery would be changing out there. I have developed the habit of watching what goes on around me. Especially the people. Sometimes you might pick up on something important, other times it's just interesting to watch folks living out their lives. And, it'd take my mind off thinking about where Mollie could be.

I sat there thinking about the Earps and Doc, and all the trouble they were in over just doing their jobs. I looked over and glimpsed four men crossing the street at an angle to me. They were caught up in their conversation and did not look my way. Three of them I had never seen before, but the fourth man I recognized. It was Jenkins, the kid whose friends I had killed in Contention. Could this be the youngest member of the Jenkins bunch from Texas? Red had told me that he saw the kid in Tombstone. It might be a coincidence, but I have always found that it's better to never assume something is harmless. If this is the kid Red was talking about, there is sure to be trouble sooner or later.

They entered the diner without looking toward me. I waited several minutes, then got up and walked over to a roof post and leaned against it with my shoulder. My face would be hidden, but I could turn slightly and see through the diner window. They were all sitting at table, with Jenkins doing most of the talking.

I agreed with the way Red had sized them up. Two of them were what I call saddle-tramps. The third tried to look like a gunhand. He was wearing a fancy studded holster tied down with his coat pulled over it. He was dressed too good to be a working man.   I had seen the type all over these parts.   He probably has practiced his draw and his shooting, and maybe even got to be pretty good. But I doubt he has ever stood looking into a man's eyes when that man intended to kill him. No, there's a lot of difference in practice and knowing your life is really on the line.

One thing is for sure, I am going to wait here until Mollie shows up. I don't want her going in there alone. For all I know, they may know who she is by now. And I don't think it is wise for us to go in to eat while they are still in there. I'm glad Mollie is running late, else we would have been in there when they came in. Maybe it's nothing but maybe not.   I have not stayed alive this long by taking unnecessary chances.

I checked my watch, and it was coming on two-thirty. Where could she be? I don't want to be confronted by this bunch while she is with me. I glanced back into the diner as the four of them got up from their table. I looked around, no sign of Mollie. Good. I turn my back to the door just before they come out. But by turning my head, I can see their reflections in the window. They don't notice me and head across the street and back in the direction they came from.

I kept my eyes on them 'till they turned into a side street. Now I wanted to find Mollie and make sure she was alright. I didn't know whether to go looking for her or wait for her. A few minutes later, she made up my mind for me. I saw her coming, running down the street.

She ran up and started apologizing for being so late. She told me how Virgil, Allie, James and Bessie had all moved into the Cosmopolitan Hotel. They were still tending to Virgil in the bed. Allie had asked Mollie to sit in court today and listen in on what the cowboys were telling.   I told her that I didn't think she should be sitting in the courthouse alone with all the trouble that was going on.

Ignoring my comment on her safety, Mollie allowed as how she was starving and wanted to eat. I saw no harm in going in the diner now, as it would be unlikely that Jenkins would return anytime soon. I opened the door and said, "After you, madam." I neglected to mention that I was also late.

As we walked in the diner, Mollie was gawking at the dangling candeliers. "They're beautiful!", she exclaimed. "Oh by the way, I forgot to tell you!", Mollie added in a rush. "As I was running back from the courthouse, I passed four men. One of them looked like I'd seen him somewhere before. They seemed up to no good and I think they may have been armed."

"Not nothin' for you to worry about, Mollie", I told her. No need for her to be involved. "After all, there is a law against carrying firearms in the city limits." I smiled. Yeah, I don't have a holster or gunbelt on, but I am armed at all times. It just doesn't show.

It was the middle of the afternoon, between dinner and supper, so the diner was pretty much empty. I picked us out a table that put my back to the wall, where I could see both the front door and the rear of the diner. The waiter had been sweeping up, so he leaned his broom in the corner and came over to see what we would have. Given the turn of events, I wanted to eat light. I ordered three eggs and some biscuits. Mollie liked the sound of the biscuits, so she ordered some with butter and molasses. We both ordered coffee.

Our coffee was out in just a minute. Brought to us by a man I had seen cooking when I was in there before. As it turned out, he was the owner but also helped with the cooking when the diner was busy. He had recognized both of us, as we had eaten there before on our visits to Tombstone.

I asked him what was going on in town. Every lawman I saw was someone new to me. He shook his head and explained that since the street fight between the Earps and the Cowboys, nothing had been the same. I just pretended not to know much and let him ramble on. He told us that a certain group in town had managed to get Virgil replaced, and Wyatt and Doc jailed. They were going to charge the Earps and Doc with murder.

I prodded him a little and asked how they could charge a lawman for murder when he was enforcing the law. He just shook his head again and told me that I did not understand what was really going on in Tombstone.

When I asked him to enlighten me, he looked around to make sure no one was there. "This whole damn thing is just a fight for power," he said. He went on to explain that there were people in town who wanted to be rid of the Earps. Maybe the Earps enforced the law too hard, maybe not hard enough. But there was a faction in town that wanted rid of them once and for all. What better way than to convict them of murder.

With that, he said he had better check on our food and left us. He was back with it in a couple of minutes, and I must say we were ready to eat. It had been a long time since we left Contention that morning. He left us to eat in peace, which we wasted no time in doing. While we were eating, Mollie mentioned that Bessie and Allie did not really know what was going on, but they had the feeling it was something deeper than what showed on the surface. She asked me what I thought, and I told her we would talk about later. She knows I don't like to talk much in public. As we were finishing our meal, the owner came out and said he had a fresh baked apple pie if we wanted some. Mollie and I just looked at each other and smiled. I told him to bring us one piece, and we would share it.

When he brought our pie, I took a chance and asked him if he knew the four young men who were in here before we came in. He said he only knew three of them. They were local boys, two of them did odd jobs on ranches and in town. The third one liked to think he was a gunslinger. He said folks who knew him and had seen him shoot said he was very good. Very fast. But he mostly just strutted around town and tried to look the part. The fourth one was not from the area, as he had never seen him before.

I did not like the way this was playing out. It sounds like Jenkins is trying to get some help, probably to kill me. I believe that was their plan in Contention, but it did not work as well as he had hoped. My guess is that Jenkins' two friends were supposed to goad me into a fight. When the fight started, it happened so quick that it was over before Jenkins knew it. He probably allowed right then that he would not be any good in a real fight, so if he wanted me dead, he would have to get somebody faster than the two he had in Contention.

I thanked the man and paid up, leaving him a good tip. As Mollie and I reached the door, he said there was one more thing that I should know. A lot of people around town knew that I was friends with Doc and the Earp brothers. It would probably be well if I didn't say much about what was going on. You know, not draw any attention to myself. And certainly not cause any trouble, as they would no doubt have me in jail with Wyatt and Doc, or worse. Well, I think it might be too late for that since I visited them in jail this morning, and Mollie has been over to the Cosmopolitan Hotel and courthouse.

I thanked him again, and Mollie and I started to return to our room. I gave her the short version of what had happened since the fight in Contention. I explained that I figured Jenkins was meaning to see me dead and had some folks who might help him here in Tombstone. I also allowed as how if I got into a shooting scrape here, it might not matter if it was self-defense. I might wind up in a cell with Doc and Wyatt.

No. If they want me, they can come back to Contention to get me. At least there I know I'll get a fair shake from the law.

*　　　*　　　*　　　*　　　*

Lunch was well worth waiting for! Both Mr. Bogardis and I were hungry and enjoyed our meal. As we sat down, I told Mr. Bogardis of the four men I'd seen while I was running back to the hotel diner. I probably wouldn't have noticed them at all if it hadn't been for the youngest one. I have seen him somewhere before, maybe in Contention. Mr. Bogardis didn't take much mind to it and told me not to fret about it.

He says we need to head back to Contention soon. I told him we just got here, why do we need to rush back? I hadn't even had the chance to see Louisa! He said we'd stay one more day and leave bright and early Wednesday morning. He sounded as if it was cut and dry, and I knew better than to dispute his decision.

I wanted to spend tomorrow sitting back at the courthouse so I asked Mr. Bogardis if we could visit Morgan and Louisa this evening. He said that was his plan and just as soon I was ready to leave, we would walk over.

Louisa let us in after several knocks on the door. She had it bolted and barred for protection. Morgan was still resting in bed. Louisa was in the process of changing his bandages when we arrived. Mr. Bogardis excused himself and went to pour himself a drink in the parlor. Morgan's shoulder wound looked a little on the infected side. Redness surrounded the skin that still laid opened from the gunshot. He didn't flinch an inch when she poured raw alcohol on it.

Morgan was my favorite of the Earp brothers. Like all his brothers, he was even tempered, except when riled. Most people just liked Morgan right off. When he smiled and laughed, it was contagious! He was one of those folks that people felt they could trust and depend on. He wasn't afraid to show his affection for Louisa either. Sometimes it caused her to blush!

When she finished dressing his wound, Mr. Borgardis re-entered the bedroom. He told Lou and I to boil a pot of coffee and leave the two of them to catch up. We shut the door on our way out.

I told Louisa about my day in court and all I heard. She asked me not to mention it to Morgan, it would only upset him more than he already was. Then she asked about Lilly and Zack's wedding.

I gave her all the details, and she seemed delighted that Lilly was happy to use everything she and Allie lent her. I said I would be getting her things back to her next time we came to Tombstone. "Something has come up and Mr. Bogardis said he thought we should be getting back to Contention", I grumbled. Lou surmised that all men are like that, can't make up their minds if they are coming or going! The mood was lighter once we got to laughing.

Morgan called for Lou to bring him and Mr. Bogardis another drink. We sat and visited for several hours, and Mr. Bogardis said we best get back to the hotel for the evening. I whispered to Lou that I plan on sitting in the courthouse again tomorrow. Billy Claiborne was set to testify, and I wanted to know what lies he had to tell. She whispered back to me "be careful".

CHAPTER THIRTEEN

The first thing I did Tuesday morning was go see Allie. We stayed so long at Morgan's last night, I hadn't the chance to tell her about the hearing yesterday. Bessie answered the door and said Allie was at Morgan's. I asked her to tell Allie that I'd return to the courthouse today and stop by again on my way back to the hotel.

I saw an empty seat closer to the front of the room when I walked in and started toward it. But remembering what Mr. Bogardis had said, I changed my mind and sat on the back bench instead.

The same two old men were seated in the back row. They smiled a wrinkled smile and slid over when they saw me. I gave them my "you better keep it hushed up" look. I think they knew what I meant!

I was just in time to hear Billy Claiborne being called up to the witness chair. He was sworn in and repeated his name. He proceeded to testify that the Earp brothers and Doc did all the shooting! He was sitting up proud in that chair, his back arched tight against the straightness of the wood like he was a king or something.

He rose from the chair long enough to make a show of how Tom McLaury threw open his coat to reveal he was unarmed. He says during all the commotion, Behan shoved him inside Fly's Photography Studio. He claims he saw it all from there. Seems in all the remembering he done of that day, when asked, he couldn't even recall what Doc was wearing! Heck, I could have answered that question!

He got up again in an attempt to show how Morgan poked his pistol around the corner of the house next to Fly's to shoot Billy Clanton. He says Billy fell backwards after he was hit and slid down the window beside him. I saw a few women in the courtroom cringe when he told how "poor" Billy was shot.

I felt an elbow poke in my side and turned to the old man on my right. "You's Bogardis' woman, ain't ya?", he asked. "I seen ya'll walking over to Morgans Earp's place yesterday", he went on speaking in a low mangled voice. "We're for the Earps, me and Cotton over there", he said pointing a boney finger towards the man on my left. "Yep. We think they're gittin' a raw deal. Wish there was sump'in the two of us could do." He shook his head and I patted his hand and told him that I was sure that the Earps appreciated their loyality.

I excused myself, told the old fellows goodbye and left the courthouse. I told Mr. Borgardis I wouldn't spend a lot of time here today. He seems to be worried about me being on my own here in Tombstone.

I walked to the Cosmpolitan Hotel to give my account of the hearing to Allie like I said I would. She had prepared a mid-day meal so I stayed and ate with them.   Virgil seemed to be doing better, but Allie said he was still in a lot of pain.   He was angry over the arrest of Wyatt and Doc, which didn't help his disposition any.

I told Allie we would be heading back to Contention in the morning.   She asked why so soon. I explained that I had hoped we'd stay longer, but Mr. Bogardis thought it best that we should be gettin' on home.   She said she would write and let me know what was happening in town. I told her I would do the same.

When I got back to the hotel, I was surprised to find Mr. Bogardis in the room. I had figured he'd be with Morgan or sitting in one of the saloons in town. He said he thought we'd have a quiet evening all alone and order room service for supper tonight.

I jumped on the bed, kissed him and told him how sweet he was! I put my hand on his chest and slid my fingers between the buttons on his shirt.   A few strands of chest hair mingled with my finger tips as I kissed the side of his neck.

I was caught off guard when he sat up straight, rejecting my moves and causing my arm to fall away from his chest. He picked up his Colt's revolver, which lay on the bedside table. He spun the cylinder a few times and checked his load. Again, I watched how he stared out the window and then back to the gun in his hand. He had the same look in his eyes as he did the morning we arrived. That look of doom.....that look of death.

*   *   *   *   *

Mollie busied herself today with sitting in the courthouse. I didn't see the point in it. I told Mollie everything seemed one-sided to me. Tombstone was pretty much torn in half between the Earps and the Cowboys. But she was trying to find out what she could so she could report back to Allie. I leisured around town all day alone, with Wyatt and Doc in jail and Morgan and Virg in the bed. I wanted to try and see if I could catch up with Jenkins and his men. I looked around, but didn't see them at all today. Being too late to start back to Contention, I thought we'd stay out of sight at the hotel until morning. We ate dinner together in the room, just the two of us.

Mollie filled me in on everything going on with the hearing, and I told Mollie all about Jenkins and the fight in Contention. I also explained everything Red had told me on Monday about Jenkins. It all fits. He had to be the younger of the boys and was now old enough to carry out his vengeance against me. He was old enough, but I think he found out in Contention that there is more to killing someone than just hiring a couple of cowhands who claim to be able. I am afraid that this kid in Tombstone, the one who fancies himself a gunfighter, may have convinced Jenkins that he is up to the task. Especially if he has some help from those other two. I hope they change their minds before it is too late.

We slept late in the morning. I got up and went down to the livery to have the buggy readied for the trip. I stopped by the diner in the hotel and asked if we could get something to eat for the journey. Mollie loves this eatery, but I think it's more so the interior, not the food. The owner said he would fix something up, and I could stop by and get it in a half hour.

When I got back to the room, Mollie was dressed and ready to go. As I started to open the door to leave, she put her arms around me and smiled. "We need to come here more often," she said. "And do what? Sleep late?", I replied. With that, she laughed and gave me a kick in the leg. We both smiled. I kissed her softly, patted her rear, and said, "Let's go."

We walked down to the livery, stopping by the diner to pick up whatever the owner had prepared. The buggy was ready, and we were on our way to Contention. Funny, after the Sam Fisher fight, I thought I wouldn't care if I never saw Contention again. But, there is a certain safety in the familiar. I just have to remember that it is never wise to let your guard down. Especially now that I have Mollie to worry about. But I'm not complaining. I wouldn't have it any other way.

After a while, we stopped by the road and opened up the food sack. We had biscuits and ham. Not a big meal, but certainly enough to get us to Contention. Mollie got started talking about Lilly and Zack. She sure thinks a lot of them. And I would trust Zack with my life. They are young, and I'm sure they will have their share of hard times. This is a hard, unforgiving country. But I know Zack is dedicated to providing the best he can for Lilly. And I think she would stand behind him as best she could. It will be hard making a living on his parents' ranch. He knew that going in and was willing to do what he had to do to make a place for them. I told Mollie I would help anyway I can.

We arrived in Contention mid-afternoon. I got our bags in our room and the buggy back to the owner. When I got back to the hotel, Mollie, Mrs. Marks, and Mr. Crane were all in the lobby. Those two busybodies wanted all the news from Tombstone. We gave them a brief summary, and I was glad to note that Mollie had not gotten too carried away. She told them enough to satisfy their curiosity, but not anything that was not already public knowledge. Good girl!

Mrs. Marks told Mollie that a bolt of new fabric had come in, and that Mollie must see it. She was going back to the dress shop and if Mollie wanted to walk with her, she would show it to her. Of course that suited Mollie. I told her I had some things I needed to see about and would meet her for supper. "And this time don't be late," I teased. She threw her head back and said, "Why? You'd wait for me anyway."

I walked over to the marshal's office. He was sitting behind his desk trying to read the paper. The paper was flat on the desk, and he was leaning over it, his eyes just a few inches above it. I asked him why he didn't just see about getting some glasses. He said he didn't need them. He could see fine as long as he didn't have to read.

I explained to him about what had happened years ago in Texas with the Jenkins clan. I also told him that I met a man who identified "Jenks" as the youngest of the bunch, and that he had always said he would see me dead. The marshal rubbed his chin and asked me what I thought. I told him about the crew that Jenkins had put together in Tombstone. I assured him I didn't want him to do anything, other than keep his eyes open if they showed up in Contention. I had no doubt that they would be there soon.

CHAPTER FOURTEEN

I wished we could have stayed in Tombstone longer. Although I had never actually been in a courtroom before, I always thought that one day I would be there to testify against my husband Sam Fisher! All his thieving and killing with his family back in Texas, I just knew one day it would all come to a head. I just didn't foresee that it would end like it did, me having to kill him to save Mr. Bogardis' life.

Yesterday, Mrs. Marks and Mr. Crane questioned me about the happenings in Tombstone. I told them just enough to satisfy their gossiping intentions. When I told them Mr. Bogardis had asked me to marry him, I thought I heard Mr. Crane almost choke on his own spit! Mrs. Marks hugged me and said, "well, it's about time". She told me we needed to start making plans on fitting me for a wedding dress.

Mrs. Marks had been tending her store pretty much on her own these past few weeks, and she let me know she was plumb tuckered out! Mr. Crane says that working so much has made Mrs. Marks entirely too ornery lately, and that he sure does appreciate me helping her whenever I can. I never minded working for Mrs. Marks. She gave me my only opportunity when I first came here, and for that I will always be grateful. She still is the town busybody, but I suspose every town has their share of those! And she truly is happy for me and Mr. Borgardis.

Zack and Lilly are due to come into town today. They had ordered some provisions from Tuscon, and they arrived on the same train as Mrs. Marks' fabric did yesterday. I couldn't wait to see them! As I left the hotel, I asked Mr. Crane if he would please let them know that I would be over at the dress shop if they stopped by looking for me. And If I know Lilly, our room would be her first stop!

Mr. Bogardis came in the lobby just as I was about to leave. He almost tripped over Littlefoot who was running out as he was walking in. "Damn cat!", he muttered. "He's always right under my feet."

"Don't forget Littlefoot helped save your life!" I reminded him, smiling.

I told him where he could find me today if he was bored. He said no need to worry, he had the notion he would be rather pre-occupied today as well. He said he had an invitation to go out to the Circle L Ranch to visit his father. Something might be going on out there, and he ought to ride out and investigate. He knew I didn't approve of him going there alone, but taking my advice was something he wasn't about to do. He told me I should go back up to the room and slip the derringer in my purse. He wanted to make sure I had protection and reminded me that the men who were looking for him wouldn't think twice about harming me.

He kissed me goodbye and said he'd most likely miss dinner. He teased and said I should fend for myself. I kissed him back and said I supposed he would do well from missing a meal every now and then. I ran out the door as swiftly as I could when I saw him narrowing his eyes at me!

*　　　*　　　*　　　*　　　*

I had planned on doing nothing today, but Paco showed up and told me Senor Lawrence had requested that I come by at my earliest opportunity. I did not like that. I am not someone he can summon whenever the mood strikes him. I told Paco to tell him I might be out in a few days. Paco did not seem near as menacing away from the Circle L. Here he talked softly and held his hat in his hand. He then told me that he thought it might be very important. Then he said something I never expected to hear. "Please come soon Senor Bogardis," his voice almost a whisper.

I told him to go on back, and that I would be there later in the day. He thanked me and left quickly. I wondered what my father had up his sleeve. I almost wish things were different between us, but that will never be.

Mollie said she was helping Mrs. Marks today. Something about the new cloth shipment she had in the store. I also thought Mollie mentioned that Lilly and Zack might be coming to town today as well. In any case, I am sure she can find plenty to do without me.

I told her of my intent to visit my father. She looked like maybe she didn't approve, but did not bother to argue with me. I cautioned her to carry her pistol with her today, and if anything looked suspicious, she should get word to the marshal. I would prefer she took the cut-down Colt with her. There are four men who want to do me harm and getting to her would be a sure way to do so. She could even put the Remington derringer in her breast fold, and the Colt in her purse. She does not like the weight of the Colt but understands the importance of being ready and able. Unfortunately, she learned that from me. She has learned lessons that I wish she didn't have to know, and she learned them because she was with me. Sometimes I really feel bad that all I brought her is violence, but we have to accept what we are and go on living.

I saddled up and headed toward the Circle L. Truth be known, I was not anxious to see my father. There was not much he could say to me that I cared to hear. I know he had hard decisions to make after the war. All of us did. But his were just plain wrong. I could forgive just about anything that he did during the war, but I will never forgive his actions since. The war has been over for sixteen years now. We did what we had to do, but when it was over, most of us came back and shouldered our responsibilities. But he ran and hid from his. That was not the way he raised me in the short time we had together.

When I topped the rise and the ranch house came into view, I stopped and just looked around. Southeastern Arizona can be pretty desolate, but the enormous ranch house and all the out-buildings sure made you think you were somewhere else. The old man had really been busy the past sixteen years.

I rode on in and as usual, Paco met me as I stepped onto the porch. "Thank you for coming", he said. "I will tell Senor Lawrence you are here." With that, he disappeared into my father's office. A moment later, he opened the door and motioned for me to go in. I held out my Colt for him to take. He raised one hand and shook his head. Well, I guess my father decided that maybe I would not kill him just yet. He shouldn't be so sure.

My father was seated behind his desk, as before when I was here. He motioned for me to sit, and I did. "Paco said you wanted to see me," I said. He nodded and thanked me for coming. I told him not to expect me to make a habit of running whenever he called. He let out a big laugh. That's the first time I had heard him laugh. "No, I expect you won't," he said.

"I wanted to talk to you about the possibility of you coming to work at the Circle L," he said. Then it was my turn to laugh. "Me work for you?" I asked. Now that would really be something. I told him there was going to be no talk of that, as I would never be interested in coming to work here. "Not really working here," he said. "I want you to take over and run the whole show. You would be in complete charge and could do anything you want. There are quite a few bank accounts that you would have say over, and you could do whatever you felt necessary to try and remedy any of my misdeeds."

"There would only be two conditions," he said. "One, that I be allowed to live here on the ranch until my death, and the second that when I die, you will take me back to Georgia to rest beside your mother."

I could feel my face turning red with rage. "I don't want to run this ranch, and I sure as hell don't care where you live, or die for that matter. And as far as taking you back to be buried beside my mother, the buzzards will have your bones picked clean before I will ever allow you to be laid to rest with her."

He hung his head, and I could see the sadness as his shoulders drooped forward. He told me to look around this room. It was the first part of the ranch to be built. The rest of the ranch-house was built around this room. "I have spent a lot of time in this room," he said. "Many nights I fall asleep behind this desk."

It was gloomy in there, it gave you the feeling of despair just being in the room. I asked him why he didn't just get up and walk out into the sunshine instead of staying in this dark room all alone. He just laughed and said, "Come around the desk. I want to show you something."
I walked around the corner of the desk. It was the first time I had seen him from the waist down. He pulled back the blanket covering his legs. Both legs were gone from the knees down. "What happened," I asked.

He explained that about eleven years ago, he was stringing some wire for a horse corral behind the house. He had the wire spools on a wagon and decided to continue working while Paco went to get some water. A big rattler crawled out from under a rock outcropping and spooked both him and the horse. He lost his footing and fell. The horse bolted, pulling the wagon across both of his legs. Paco was back in minutes, but back in those days the closest doctor was in Prescott. They tried to set the broken bones, but after a few days gangrene had set in. By the time they got him to the doctor, both legs had to be cut off just above the knee.

He laughed, "I survived the war to be crippled by a fluke accident." He just shook his head. "If that is your last word on my offer, I will not trouble you further," he said looking down at a stack of papers on his desk. "I told you I was working on some things to try to make right my mistakes. I will let you know as soon as I have them finalized. It will be soon."

I turned and headed for the door. I passed Paco without speaking and was on my way back to Contention. Should I put him out his misery? Somehow, I felt no compassion for this man, and I'm not sure if that's his fault or mine.

The ride back to Contention seemed longer than usual. I got to thinkin' that maybe I should have killed my father the first time I saw him. Should I really take over his operation and try to undo some of the things he has done? It is tempting to think that I could make a difference, and I'm sure Mollie would eagerly jump in to restore what we could. I just don't think I could bear to see and deal with my father every day. It's too much. But he did say he has something working that should be in place soon. I think it best to wait and see what that might be.

It is getting colder every day now. I pulled the collar of my coat up closer to my neck to keep the chilling wind from seeping into my skin. I do not like the cold weather, but I can adapt to anything. I wish we would have some warm sunny days so that maybe Mollie and I could go out for a buggy ride and spend the afternoon together. That is the only time that we seem to be at peace. This thing with my father occupies my mind constantly. It seems there is always someone like Jenks either trying to kill me for revenge or sometimes just to make a name.

And it seems like they are getting younger, and I am getting older. I know age will slow down anyone. I wonder how long I can stay sharp. Then I had to go and ask Mollie to marry me. It's not like I'm a storekeeper, and she is a dressmaker. Just because we get married does not cause people to leave us alone. What worries me most is that being with me puts her in danger. It wouldn't be hard for someone to figure out that the worst thing they could do to me would be to harm Mollie. Like it was with Sam Fisher when he snatched Mollie and came after me. He meant to kill her that day and would have, but Mollie is a brave woman. Someday she may come up against more than she can handle. And I know it will be my fault. That old dream of her being in danger and me being unable to help her happens about once a week. I don't like it, but there is not much I can do about it.

As I ride into Contention, I keep a sharp eye out for Jenks and his boys. They missed a good chance in Tombstone, but they did not know I was there. Even if I had won the fight, I might be in jail waiting for a noose. No thanks. I believe I am better off in Contention where I know my way around better.

When I dropped my horse off at the livery, I asked if any strangers had shown up lately. No one had seen any, but I took the young kid who worked there aside. He is the one who does most of the work. I told him if he would get word to me of any strangers coming in, I would take good care of him. I gave him a silver dollar, which may have been a week's pay for him and told him it was very important. His eyes got about as big as the silver dollar and said he would be sure to keep a good watch.

I walked on over to the marshal's office and asked if he had seen Jenks or any strangers. No luck there. I checked in at the saloon where the shooting with Jenks' friends had taken place. Nothing there either.

Well, I better find Mollie. She gets real nervous when I don't check in. She always wants me to take Zack with me. I have told her it is not his problem. She's probably still at the dress shop with Mrs. Marks burning her ears off with more questions about Tombstone. She'll be grateful for my rescue!

The dress shop is empty except for Mrs. Marks. She said Mollie had gone back to our room, but that she wanted to talk to me. When Mrs. Marks wants to talk to you, it translates into her wanting to ask a bunch of questions. I closed the door behind me and asked how I could help her. "Well, for one thing," she said, "you can tell me when we are going to have another wedding." She said she had been asking Mollie, but she would only tell her that we have not yet decided on the date.

I told her that I had thought about a Christmas wedding, maybe even having it the afternoon before the Christmas dance. That was a very special time for Mollie and I last year. She said it sure was a special time! We had the fastest gunfighters in the country right there in Contention City, and the whole town was afraid to take a deep breath. We both laughed and agreed that everything had worked out well in the end.

But I told her that Mollie really wanted to marry in the spring. I don't like the cold weather and neither does Mollie. She'd had enough of the cold living up in the Ohio Valley. In the spring, maybe Mollie and I could take a trip somewhere for a couple of weeks. A real honeymoon. With that, she just smiled, and I knew I was off the hook for the moment.

I bid her good-day and walked on over to the hotel. Cornelius was behind the desk. He smiled and asked if I had a minute. What is this, question and answer day?   I stopped to see what he wanted, and of course he started stumbling and stuttering. He still gets that way around me sometimes. What he wanted to know was the same thing Mrs. Marks had wanted to know. When is the wedding?   I just told him he needed to check with Mrs. Marks, as she had the latest news on that subject.

I went on up the stairs and to our room. I opened the door to see Mollie lying across the bed, drowsy but awake.   "Are you going to sleep all day?" I inquired. She just smiled and reached for my hand. She pulled me down on the bed beside her, which was not hard to do. We just lay there a few minutes looking into each other's eyes. I told her that old man Crane and Mrs. Marks were looking out for her. They wanted to know when the wedding was going to take place. I told them in the spring. She smiled and said it was fine with her. I rolled over onto my back, bringing her head to my chest. In minutes, we were both asleep.

CHAPTER FIFTEEN

The past few weeks have flown by. It's been a struggle to keep myself from worrying about the Earp hearing in Tombstone, but Mr. Bogardis says we can't keep running off and traveling ten miles every other day. He says we shouldn't get too much involved in all the mayhem at the courthouse. He was certain that the Earps and Doc would be exonerated from the murder charges when all is said and done. He still couldn't believe that lawmen could be arrested for doing their jobs. He says what a pathetic world this would be if that was the case!

I recieved a letter today from Louisa. I'd rather hear the news straight from Lou or Allie instead of reading about it in the newspaper. It was a long letter explaining the last few days of the hearing. With Morgan and Virgil still in the bed, they were made to give their testimony straight to Judge Spicer at their bedside.

Lou says that Bessie went down to the courthouse last Monday and listened to her friend Addie Bourland testify. Addie's house is next to the empty lot where the shooting took place. She went to the window when she heard men talking, but ran to the back of her house after the shooting began. Bessie said she wished Addie had seen everything, she would have told them what the truth really was! Addie's a fine woman and one of the best dressmakers in Tombstone, according to Bessie.

Finally, Judge Spicer made his final decision. Lou said he talked for a good part of an hour before he finally pronounced that there was no sufficient cause to believe that the Earps and John Henry Holliday were guilty. He then ordered that all charges against them were to be dismissed. Half the people in the courtroom let out a holler of disbelief, and the other half cheered in agreement to the judgement! Wyatt and Doc walked out of the courthouse free men again.

Lou said Wyatt came straight over to the house and told Morgan. He carried a bottle in the bedroom with him, and he and Morgan drank half of it before ten minutes had passed. When he left, he went over to the Cosmopolitan Hotel to see Virgil. All the while, poor Mattie waited for him at home and he didn't even show up 'till past dark and half-drunk. By then, she had one of her headaches again and emptied a bottle a Laudanum before falling asleep.

On the last page of the letter, Lou wrote, "Wyatt is going to be the death of Mattie for sure, the way he does her. He was probably over at the Oriental all evening keeping company with that woman who lives with Behan. She has had her eyes on Wyatt since she came into town. She looks down on us, but she's one to boast about her lifestyle! Living with Behan and carousing around all hours of the night in the saloons. No wonder Mattie has her headaches!"

Lou finished the letter by saying that Morgan thinks that it is not over in Tombstone yet. He told her that just because Wyatt and Doc are out of jail, Ike Clanton will never let it rest. Lou says she still keeps the door locked and bolted, and the guns are always loaded and within reach.

I plan to write her back tomorrow when Mr. Bogardis and I return from Zack and Lilly's. Lilly is all excited that she has set up housekeeping as "Mrs. Blade", she can't wait to have us over as guests. They arrived in Contention just a few hours ago, and we plan to follow them back out to the ranch. This will be good for Mr. Bogardis as well. He always has so much on his mind. He isn't the same man I first met a year ago in the streets of Contention. He was running from his demons, or rather he was running to find them. Either way, the demons were not far behind.

So much has transpired this past year. Sam came looking for me and intended to take me back to Texas, dead or alive. Somehow I found the strength to kill a man I used to love, to save the life of the man I now love. I look back and wonder what my life would be like if I wasn't standing on the sidewalk that day, stopping to feed Littlefoot. If I didn't look towards the street and see a stranger riding tall in the saddle. If I didn't take a chance and write him all those letters. No use wondering now. My life is as it is, and I wouldn't have it any other way.

*　　　*　　　*　　　*　　　*

It's been a few weeks, and I have not heard anything from my father regarding his "plans" to remedy any of his past mistakes. If I don't hear something soon, I will have to ride back out to the Circle L and stir things up a little. Just because he's a cripple does not give him the right to run roughshod over hard- working, decent folks. I am determined to hold him to it.

Zack and Lilly were in town today and asked us to have dinner with them this evening. Mollie and I could stay the night and come back in the morning. They came into town in their wagon so I suggested that Mollie ride back to their ranch with them, and I could bring a buggy out later in the day. I don't think Mollie particularly liked the idea, but she knows I do not like to be penned in with folks for long at a time. Even Zack and Lilly. So she agreed, and they headed on back to the ranch. At least this will give me some time to check around town and see if anyone has seen anything of my "friends."

I dropped by the marshal's office to check with him, but he said he had neither seen nor heard anything about Jenkins. When I stepped out of the office, I saw the kid from the livery running toward the hotel. He saw me and turned to meet me. "Mr. Bogardis," he panted, "four men just rode in. They left their horses, and one of them asked if I knew you." I let him catch his breath for a moment before he continued. "He told me to go find you and tell you that he wanted to see you in the saloon, the one where you do all your killing." I thanked him, handed him a few loose coins from my pocket and told him to go back to the livery. "One other thing," he said, "when they walked down the street, I saw two of them go in the saloon and the other two went down the alley next to it." Well, it looks like they finally got their courage up.

I turned around and went back in the marshal's office to fill him in. No one was there, and the back door was standing open. Contention seems to have a problem getting a lawman who is willing to stick his neck out, even if that is exactly what the job is all about. Zack is well out of town with the ladies by now, so I won't get any help from him. At least Mollie was out of harm's way.

I went out the back door of the marshal's office and headed for the hotel. I needed a plan, and one part of it was what I called "Mollie's Shotgun". It's the sawed- off ten gauge double that Mollie saved my life with when I was under Sam Fisher's gun. I have carried it often since, using it at Canyon Diablo and Zack's ranch. I guess I think that it brings me luck. I slid in the back door of the hotel and when I started to go up the staircase, I almost scared Cornelius Crane out of his skin. I told him I needed to pick up something and would be going out the back way. He just looked at me without a word.

When I got to our room, I checked both my Colt's and decided to load the empty chamber in each one. I always leave the hammer down on an empty chamber for safety.

This time I may need all six. I grabbed the shotgun from under the bed, checked to be sure it was loaded, and put a few shells in my coat pocket.

When I got back outside, in the rear of the hotel, I tried to picture where the two men who went down the alley might position themselves. They had to expect me to come in the front of the saloon, so being on the side or out back would do them no good. The only thing that made sense was that they were going in from the back door. They were figuring I would not expect anyone to come out of or shoot from the back of the saloon. Well, let's see if I can cut the odds a little.

I moved along behind the row of buildings until I got next door to the saloon.

I slowly approached the rear door, which was slightly ajar. I carefully looked in and saw the two men standing behind the door leading out into the saloon proper. Now, how am I going to get them out of there without alerting the two in front! I had an idea. When someone whispers, you can't recognize their voice. All whispers sound pretty much the same. At least that's what my mother used to tell me. Thought I might as well give it a try.

"Hey, one of you come here," I whispered loud enough for them to hear, but not loud enough to be heard in the front. They looked at each other, then one of them walked to the door and eased it open. As soon as he was outside, I whacked him on the head with the shotgun. He went down, and I took his pistol and put it in my belt. I eased on in with the other man not turning around, probably thinking I was his partner. When I got beside him, I laid the barrels of the shotgun against his neck. His eyes went big, and I motioned with my head for him to move on out the back.

When we were outside, I took his gun and told him to help his friend, who was just coming around, to his feet. I marched them quietly behind the buildings to the marshal's office. We went in the back door, and I motioned to a cell. The one who had not been hit in the head must have wanted something to show for his trouble, so he tried to break away. The butt of the shotgun caught him under the chin, and he went down like a sack of nails. The other one was back to his senses so I told him to drag his partner into the cell with him. I locked the door and threw the key into the front office.

"I am going now to introduce myself to your friend, as I have already met Jenks. If anyone comes in here, you might be able to talk them into letting you out. But I must warn you, if I see either or both of you outside this cell, I will kill you where you stand. No questions, no quarter. Do you understand?" I asked. The one who was the most conscious nodded and said they were through. All they wanted was to leave. "We'll talk about that after I see your friends," I said.

I don't think Jenks and his pal will have figured out that the boys in the back are gone. They expect me to come in the front, and the boys in the back can back the gunhand. Sounds like a good plan if the boys in the back were still there. I think I will just go in the front and let them think everything is as they expect it to be.

As I start out the door, the marshal turns the corner. He did not expect me to be in his office. I told him I had a couple of bad boys in a cell, and I would appreciate it if he kept them there 'till I confronted their friends. I told him their guns were in his desk, and the keys were on the floor. I said I might have two more guests for him. I think he knew it would be unlikely.

I walked slowly down to the saloon, keeping my eyes peeled for anything unusual. Just 'cause I think I have everything figured out, don't always make it so. I stopped at the edge of the door so I could get a look inside. Jenks and his gunhand were sitting at a table with a bottle and two glasses in front of them. I propped the shotgun against the wall and went on in.

They both looked up and smiled when they saw me. Jenks said he decided he would come back and visit me one more time while I was still alive. I told him I knew who he was, and that he should just go on back to Texas or wherever. He laughed and said he intended to do just that, right after I stopped breathing.

They both stood up and moved a few steps away from each other. I noticed that Jenks had a gun. So I have to figure that he is a player. I said, "Who's your friend?" Jenks smiled again. The gunhand said, "My name is Jim Rogers, but they call me 'Pistol'. And I aim to make my reputation off you Bogardis." With that, the few people who were in the saloon backed away to get out of the line of fire.

"I've seen him shoot, and he's the fastest thing I've ever seen," said Jenks. "Why they say he is faster than Wild Bill Hickok. What do you think about that, Bogardis?"

"Well, there's a few things you ought to consider," I said. "One, Bill Hickok's been dead for five years now. So I reckon how fast he could or couldn't shoot doesn't matter much. Two, I'm assuming both of you are going to draw, so I'll be going for both of you. Oh, and one more thing. Those two boys in the back room, well, they ain't there no more."

Their eyes glanced at each other. I could see Jenks swallow hard. I said "Pistol, you don't know me, and Jenks is using you to do a job that he ain't got the cohones to do himself. You can still walk out of here."

"I can take you," he said, with a little too much confidence. His hat was pulled down over his forehead casting a shadow across his cold blue eyes. His hand went for his gun, and I drew and fired two shots. One ripped through Pistol's chest, and the other hit Jenks in the right eye. I immediately knew I had been hit. My left shoulder was burning, and I could see the fabric of my coat torn. Pistol was still moaning so I walked over and kicked his gun away. I bent down, and he looked at me. "I almost got you!", he sputtered. He tried to say something else, but there was too much blood gurgling out of his mouth. He went limp and died.

The old bartender ran out from behind the bar and asked if they got me. I allowed as how they did, but they didn't get me good. He said he would go get the Doc for me, but I told him no need. I'd just walk over to his office. I picked up the shotgun as I went out the door.

Doc had heard the shooting and was already heading out of his office. I told him I was the only one that needed anything. We went back inside, and I slipped my coat off. There was a fair amount of blood on my shirt and running down my arm, but not enough to worry about. The wound was just a graze, so at least he didn't have to dig a slug out.

He had me cleaned up and bandaged in a few minutes. The marshal came in. He had already been to the saloon. I told him what I had learned about Jenks, and that it appeared to be a revenge thing. He just shook his head and asked what I wanted him to do with the two in the jail. I told him to hold them 'till Doc was through with me, and I would come by and see them. He nodded and left.

I walked down to the jail and told the marshal I was ready to see the prisoners. He walked into the back with me. They both went a little pale when they saw me. "Your partners are both dead," I told them. I got up close against the bars, allowing my breath to weave through the iron rods. "The marshal is going to let you out in the morning, but if I ever see either one of you again, I'll kill you." I turned and walked out.

I went straight to the hotel, put on a clean shirt, and headed down to the livery. I gave my young friend another silver dollar and told him he probably saved my life. It sure made him happy. I had to laugh to myself cause I don't know if it was because I was still alive or because he made another dollar.

He got my buggy ready, and I was off to Zack's. Mollie's gonna fuss when she finds out what happened, but at least I won't be late.

CHAPTER SIXTEEN

I arrived at Zack's in plenty of time for supper. I pulled the buggy up to the barn and unhitched the horse. I glanced around and saw Mollie standing on the porch watching me. Of course she had no idea that anything had happened. I got the horse put up and started walking towards the house. She stepped off the porch to greet me when she saw my coat sleeve. The coat was black and most of the blood had run down my arm, so all she could see was the tear.

"What did you do, fall asleep and roll out of the buggy?", she teased. I just smiled and said, "Something like that." We laughed and hugged each other, then turned and went into the house. Lilly was in the kitchen. Zack greeted me at the door. We nodded to each other, and I yelled into the kitchen, "Hope you girls got something good whipped up for supper. I'm starving, and Zack here don't look like he's had a decent meal in quite a while." Mollie bumped my shoulder, which gave me a start, and Lilly came out of the kitchen waving a big ladle at me. "I'll have you know he's the best fed he's ever been," she laughed.

I guess I would have to admit that they both looked happy and content. I know it's not easy out here trying to make a living with just the two of them. But they sure look like it agrees with them. I'm certainly no farmer, nor do I care to chase cattle or horses all over God's creation. But sometimes in the hours between the dark and the dawn, I wonder what it would have been like for Mollie and me if we had not lived the lives we have lived. I guess it all comes down to the fact that our lives came together because of who we were and where we were. Change anything for either one of us, and we would have never met.

We had a fine meal, and I ate more than usual. Afterward, we sat in the parlor while Lilly and Mollie sang the songs they remembered from their youth. Zack tried to sing a little, but I knew better than to try. Nobody can do everything well, and singing is something that I do not do well. But I did enjoy listening to them. Mollie and Lilly were quite good, but poor Zack needs to get a fiddle 'cause he sure can't sing a lick.

The house being small, Mollie and I slept near the

fireplace. Lilly and Zack rounded up plenty of stuff to make a nice pallet on the floor. I made sure to position myself so Mollie could not see my shoulder. Everything went well until she laid her head over and touched the bandage. She immediately got up and turned up the light to see what it was. Of course she demanded an explanation. I told her what had happened, and she accused me of planning the fight while she was gone. I told her she could check with anyone in town, I did not know anything was amiss until her and the Blades were well out of town. Then she fussed because she thought I should have left without confronting Jenkins. Of course I explained to her the danger of letting something like that go. As it was, I knew where they were and pretty much what their plan was. To postpone it would be to give up the advantages that I had. She finally calmed down and accepted it for what it was.

We got up the next morning, had a good breakfast and started getting ready to head back to Contention. Zack walked out to the barn to help me get the horse hitched up and everything ready. I told him about the events of the previous day, and that Mollie was a little upset, but that it just worked out that way. He told me again that if I ever needed him for anything, he would not hesitate to lend a hand.

As we drove back to Contention, we talked more than usual. I have had so much on my mind lately that I have not been good company, so I allowed Mollie to have her say.

We started talking a lot about the future. If I am going to make an honest woman out of her, I reckon we need to make some plans about where we are going to live and what we intend to do. It seems that most of our conversations get side- tracked because Christmas is coming in a hurry. Mollie can't wait for the Christmas dance, and to tell the truth, I am looking forward to it as much as she is. Last year's dance was very special for us. It's hard to believe we've been together that long. And this year, she does not have to worry about people looking down on her.

So, I allowed her to talk on and on, discussing her

plans for her dress and the entire evening for that matter. Only half hearing what she said, I told Mollie that whatever she wanted was fine with me. Just tell me when it is and what to wear, and I promise to dance her feet off!

*   *   *   *   *

All the way home from Zack and Lilly's, Mr. Bogardis and I talked about the Christmas dance. It was just a week or so away, and my dress wasn't finished yet. I told Lilly she should have Zack bring her into town this week, and we could work on both her dress and mine at the same time.

Of course, I still have the dress I wore last year. I added some lace and crinoline to it, but this year I thought I'd rip it out and start all over again. Mrs. Marks gave me some colorful ribbon and decorative sewing beads that would be taking its place.

I only wish the Earps could join us again this year. What a surprise to meet them at the dance last Christmas! I remember how Mr. Borgardis had it all planned out. It caused everyone in the entire town to drop their jaw! But, Morgan and Virgil are still in the bed recovering from their wounds. It would sure do them good to get out and celebrate Christmas and forget their troubles for the night. Mr. Bogardis says that is not gonna happen. They cannot leave their guard down for even a few hours.

When we arrived back at the hotel, Mr. Crane informed me that Mrs. Marks was searching for me. He says she has volunteered my services with the Christmas dance committee to help with decorations! He also asked Mr. Bogardis if he could spare a minute of his time.

Mr. Bogardis raised his eyebrow and snickered, but motioned for Mr. Crane to step over to the side of the lobby with him. "What is it, Mr. Crane? Has Littlefoot been in your stash of ....." Mr. Crane hurriedly "shussssh"ed Mr. Bogardis before he had the chance to finish! "No, Mr. Bogardis. It's just that.... it's ... It's just that I think Mrs. Marks is anticpating something from me after the dance this year, if you get my meaning." I could almost see Mr. Crane's face blushing! I had to hold back a giggle with the cuff of my hand. "Well, Cornie", Mr. Bogardis told him as straight-forward as he could, "I'm not sure there's anything I can do to help you out with that."

"I was just gonna.... you know.... ask you....", Crane was

stuttering so badly that I wasn't sure Mr. Bogardis would have the patience for him to finish. "She, Mrs. Marks that is, has given me the notion that she wants to ..... uh....", he confided as quietly as he could, embarrassed that I was only a few feet away.

"Well, Cornie", Mr. Bogardis told him, "Why don't you just haul yourself over to Po-Mo-Sang's laundry and ask about his Chinese friends in town. I believe those Chinese folks have a concoction that might suit you, in one form or another".

"Oh, thank you, Mr. Bogardis! I"ll do that! I'll do it right now!" And having said that, Mr. Crane snatched the door open and leaped across the street like a boy chasing a frog! Mr. Bogardis grabbed my hand, and we laughed all the way up the stairs!

CHAPTER SEVENTEEN

Well, all of the plans concerning the Christmas dance had come together. Mollie had been busy working on her dress for the dance, as well as helping Lilly with hers. They are like a couple of little girls when they get together. When all four of us are together, sometimes Zack and I just look at each other and shake our heads. But neither of us would change a thing.

At first, Zack was a little nervous about the dance and asked a lot of questions. I would bet he has never been to a dance. I told him about last year and how Doc, Wyatt, and Morgan showed up with their ladies, and how they had the whole town convinced that they had known Mollie forever. I'll never forget the look on Mollie's face that night.

Lilly and Mollie have even been trying to teach Zack to dance, at least well enough so Lilly won't be sitting on the side all night. They need to be working with me too, as I just barely got by last year. I probably would not have even tried had I not known how much Mollie was looking forward to dancing. Nobody ever accused me of being graceful on the dance floor.

Zack and Lilly arrived in town early afternoon. We got them a room in the hotel so they would not have to ride home late. Mollie went down to the dress shop to pick up a piece of ribbon or something that she decided, at the last minute, would look good on her dress. I wish I could have gotten her a new dress for the dance, but she seemed pretty content with just fixing up the one from last year.

It sounded like a herd of horses in the hall! I looked out the door to see Mollie, as well as Lilly and Zack, stomping all the way up the stairs. Mollie explained that she ran into them in the lobby. I told the girls to get their things put away, and we would all go get something to eat, then we could get ready and head on over to the dance. As soon as the girls were out of sight, I reached in my coat and brought out a bottle. I told Zack maybe we should have a drink before we left. He looked like he could use one. We sat and talked while we were drinking, about nothing of any importance. I told him about old man Crane asking me what to do with Mrs. Marks after the dance. That got a good laugh out of both of us! We passed the time pretty quick 'cause it seemed like just a few minutes went by, and the ladies were ready to go.

We ate quickly, got back to our rooms and commenced to changing clothes and getting all spruced up. Zack told me they'd go on and get down there, since Lilly was in such a rush. According to him, she'd been ready for days!

Walking down the street arm-in-arm was just like last year. We could hear the fiddle tuning up as we walked. This time when we got there, people actually greeted us and seemed to be happy we were there. Big change from last year. I had sent word a while back to Doc and the Earps that we would be happy to have them again, but they replied that with all that had happened of late that they might better stay close. I could certainly understand that.

The music had cranked up by the time we were inside and said our hellos. Mollie grabbed me, and there we went - gliding across the dance floor! I glanced at Zack and Lilly each time we took a turn by them. Zack was a little slow, but I ain't got much room to talk. I still had the bottle in my coat, and everytime we went to the punch bowl, I would add a little whiskey to mine and Zack's. By the time they were ready to shut down, Zack had come alive and was really showing his stuff. Of course Lilly was thrilled.

There was not much conversation as we walked back to the hotel. I was thinking about last year and suspected Mollie was doing the same. We said our goodnights in the lobby, and Mollie and I walked slowly to the door of number ten.

"Do you remember what happened in here last year," I asked. She looked up at me and smiled. "I know what's going to happen in here this year," she replied.

*   *   *   *   *

410

My dress caught hold of a loose nail in the door frame as we left and caused the seam to rip all the way to my calf. "Dang it!", I cried. "I wanted everything to be perfect for tonight!" Mr. Bogardis squeezed my hand and assured me I looked wonderful in spite of the torn dress. No one will notice, he said, no one will be looking down towards the floor!

I spent several days hanging ornaments and making paper flowers as decorations for the dance. When Mr. Bogardis and I first walked in, he said he was truly amazed at what a good job I had done. Practically everyone in town was there. But, it seemed that a few of the older fellows had stopped by the saloons for a party of their own before attending the dance. They were escorted out with the help of the town deputy!

Lilly and Zack were already at the dance when we arrived. They had come to town earlier and were staying in a room near Mr. Bogardis and me. Mr. Bogardis and Zack disapeared for what seemed like an hour while Lilly and I put ourselves together. Looking at our reflection in the window pane, Lilly and I fancied ourslves as the queen of England going to the Grand Ball. We were laughing and giggling like school girls and hardly missed the men at all!

"Mrs. Blade", Mr. Bogardis said in such a cavalier voice, "May I say that you look splendid this evening." He tipped the edge of his hat with his fingers acting like a proper gentleman, but Lilly grabbed him and gave him a big hug anyway. "Save one of those waltzes for me, will you?" Lilly nodded and answered, "If you can pry me away from the man who loves me long enough!"

Mr. Bogardis and I danced almost the entire evening. There were a few minutes when he and Zack went missing again, but Lilly and I assumed they were outside for a breather or smoking one of those cigars they seem to like. Zack took to the dance floor like he'd been doing it all his life by the end of the evening! He was sweeping Lilly off her feet, and I must say she really enjoyed it.

My memories of last year's Christmas dance kept coming back to me the entire evening. It was the first time I met the Earps and their wives. Doc kissed my hand, and Morgan whirled me off the floor like he'd known me for years! What a night that was. I also remember how Kate was flirting with Mr. Bogardis.

Before we left the dance, Mr. Bogardis excused himself. He said he had to speak with Mr. Crane for a moment. They talked over in a far corner of the room and when he came back, I asked him what it was all about. "Oh, nothing for you to be concerned about, Mollie", he said with a twinkle in his eye. "I think Mr. Crane and Mrs. Marks will be continuing to 'dance' after they leave here tonight!"

I smiled. I was just thinking the same thing about Mr. Bogardis and myself.

CHAPTER EIGHTEEN

All the excitement of Christmas is behind us now. We need to just settle in for the winter. I do not favor cold weather, but I can stand all southern Arizona has to throw at me. Mollie and Lilly have started to plan our wedding. Mollie says she wants to honor my mother and have us wed on her birthday, May twenty-fifth.

She left this morning to see if some item she had ordered at the store had come in. I told her I would stop by the saloon and then meet her for lunch. I had no sooner put my chair against the wall, when two men who I had seen, but did know, came in. They ordered drinks and when they saw me, they approached my table. "You're Mr. Bogardis, ain't you?", one of them asked. I replied that I was. They commenced to tell me what an awful thing it was about Virgil Earp. I asked what they meant. They allowed as how Virgil was shot from ambush last night. "Is he alright?", I asked. They said a shotgun blast nearly tore his arm off, but the word was he would probably live, but without that arm.

I went immediately to the telegraph office and wired Wyatt in Tombstone. I asked if he needed me.

I told the operator that I would be in the saloon, the diner, or the hotel. If I got a wire back from Tombstone, I expected him to send someone to come find me. I waited in the saloon until time to meet Mollie. As I was walking to the diner, the telegraph operator's son ran up to me with a paper. It was from Wyatt. Virgil would make it, but he would be crippled for life. No one had been apprehended, but Wyatt said he was pretty sure who was behind it and would be filing papers. He thanked me for my offer to come to Tombstone, but said it would not be necessary at this time.

I saw Mollie as I was putting the paper in my pocket. I walked across the street and took her arm. "I saw you slipping that note in your pocket," she smiled. "I bet that's from one of your admirers." I explained that it was bad news from Tombstone. I guided her over to a bench on the sidewalk, and we sat down. I told her the whole story that I had heard and let her read the wire from Wyatt.

She was very upset and said that we should go on to

Tombstone just in case the Earps needed our help. I told her to calm down, that I had already offered my services but would not go sticking my hand in it until Wyatt asked me to. He knows what he is doing and is trying to keep everything legal. We need to just wait.

We walked on down to the diner and had us a good lunch.   As we were headed back up the street, I saw a familiar face coming to meet us.   It was Paco from the Circle L. I knew that this probably bodes ill.

By the time he got to us, he already had his hat off. He greeted me and bowed his head to Mollie without really looking at her. "What is it this time, Paco," I asked. He would not look me in the face but began stammering and stuttering. I managed to figure out that he wanted me to come out to the Circle L. I told him to tell Senor Lawrence that I would see him soon enough. He explained that it was not his Patron who wanted me. It was him. "What can I do for you there that I cannot do here?" I asked. All he would say was that it was mighty important, and I should come with him immediately.

I told him I would go by the hotel and then meet him at the livery. Mollie and I walked back to our room, and I could tell she had some concern about this. "Don't worry," I told her and assured her it would not take long. I stuffed an extra Colt under my coat, took my rifle, and threw some spare cartridges in my saddle bag. "If this is nothing to worry about, why are you so well armed?" she asked. "You know me. I like to be ready," I replied.

I gave her a kiss and a pat on the bottom and went out the door. This will be the last time that I go running out there for my father. That's for sure.

Paco was waiting for me at the livery. I got my horse saddled, put the bags on, and slid my rifle in the scabbard. "Let's go," I said. Paco had nothing to say, so we made pretty good time getting out there.

When we rode up,   I could not tell that anything out of the ordinary was going on. I guess I would find out soon enough. When we went through the front door, I expected to either have to sit and wait for my father to see me or perhaps go right into his office. Instead, Paco motioned me to follow him down the hall. I had never been anywhere in the house other than the office and the front room.

We walked past two doors and stopped at a third. Paco knocked twice and opened the door. Inside was my father, lying naked on a table, dead, with a towel across his loins. Two Mexican women were bathing him. I could tell right off that he had been shot in the head. They had already cleaned him up, but blood was still seeping out from behind his head.

For a moment I was speechless. I had no love for the man, but I did not expect to see him dead, unless by my own hand. "What happened, Paco?" I asked. He told me that the cook had heard a single gunshot early this morning and ran to find him. He went into my father's office and found him slumped in his big chair. He had put a pistol in his mouth and pulled the trigger. I was dumbfounded for several minutes, finally telling Paco I wanted to see his office.

We went back through the house and entered the office. It was as Paco had said. There was blood and brains all over the back of the chair. In the floor by the chair was a Colt '51 Navy. I picked it up and looked around for something to wipe it off with. Paco handed me his bandana. The only way a southern soldier would get a Colt would be to own it before the war or take it off a dead Yankee. The south had some guns patterned after the Colt, but this was the real thing. Sam Colt did not sell arms to the Confederacy. The grip had CSA carved into it. My father probably carried this gun in the war and then used it to end his own life.

I walked over to the chair that I had sat in when visiting my father before. I had to sit down and think. Here was a man who had wealth and just about anything he wanted that money could buy. True, he had no legs and nobody who cared anything about him except Paco. Maybe the sins of his past caught up with him, and he did not want to live with them anymore. What was it he told me once? "Everyone has a past. And that's all it is, the past." I looked over at Paco and asked "What now?" He said Senor Lawrence had picked out his burial spot many years ago and had given Paco instructions for his funeral. Paco also said that his Patron had written a letter for him recently with other instructions. He said he intended to follow them. He also told me that he knew Senor Lawrence was my father. He had told him before I ever came to the ranch. He also said that my father had been planning something to do with the business and had left instructions with his lawyer.

None of this means anything to me. "When do you plan to bury him, Paco?" I asked. I guess the least I can do is see him put in the ground. Paco said they would leave the house with him about noon tomorrow. His burial would only be about a mile from the ranch house.

Before I knew what I was saying, I asked if there was anything I could do. Paco just shook his head. I thought I saw a tear roll off his cheek. I told him I would be back in the morning for the funeral.

The ride back alone seemed to take a long time. I had vowed to kill my father, but he beat me to it.

*   *   *   *   *

There's not much for me to do. Mr. Bogardis felt that the funeral of his father's was not a place I should be. He said there were a lot of rough cowhands and other sorts that he didn't want me exposed to. He said with the exception of a few Mexican women, I would be the only lady there. So, best I just stay here and not attend. Besides, he wasn't sure what to expect himself.

I don't think Mr. Bogardis knows how he is obligated to act or feel. He has been without his father for so long, believing he was dead in the war. And then to find him alive! He has built up a hatred towards him that scares me. Now even in death, he cannot find a way to forgive him.

Yesterday, he told me of Virgil being shot. It sounded serious. I told him I thought we should go. Allie will need all the help she can get. But he declined, saying that if he was needed, Wyatt would let him know.

I am considering renting a carriage tomorrow and riding to Tombstone alone. He will not miss me since he will be at his father's ranch for the funeral. He has said he may spend the night, that there were some papers he wanted to sift through in his father's office. I could ride out as soon as he left and come back bright and early the next morning. Allie is my friend, she would do the same for me.

Mr. Bogardis has been spending his time in the saloon since he came back from the ranch. He came to the hotel only long enough to tell me what had happened, then he was gone. I can't help him when he is like this. He shuts me out, and I feel helpless.

I needed to talk with Mrs. Marks and let her know I will not be assisting her in the shop tomorrow. As I left the hotel, Littlefoot was right behind me. Always hungry and expecting food from either myself or Mr. Crane. I bent down and patted him on the head. His fur was so soft! He purred and rubbed his hairy body against the bottom portion of my dress.

When I stood up, I felt the eyes of a stranger upon me. Just a few feet away, stood a man with a red sash around his midriff. His eyes was fixated on me. Tobacco ran down his chin, and his tongue extended and licked it off. I turned quickly and walked towards Mrs. Mark's home. I turned and looked back down the street when I reached her door. But he wasn't following me, no one was there. I remembered the man in the red sash in Prescott, the one who kicked me outside the saloon. I will never forget that night! I feel nervous and shakey now each time I see one of those cowboys. All those feelings from that night come rushing back.

Mrs. Marks invited me in when she answered her door. She made a pot of coffee and offered me tea cakes while we sat. She was sure in a blissful mood and her eyes wrinkled like little slits when she spoke. I explained that I would not be able to help her tomorrow in the shop. "Why, Mollie", she declared, "no need for you to worry about that! I was thinking about closing the shop for a few days. Taking a little time for myself, maybe spending a few days with Corne...., I mean Mr. Crane." She blushed when she said his name.

"Alright, Mrs. Marks", I answered, not knowing exactly what to say. "Is everything alright with you and Mr. Crane?" "Oh, it's heavenly!", she replied. "We just had ourselves a fine time at the dance the other night. Didn't you and Mr. Bogardis, as well?"

"Yes, we did. A fine time, Mrs. Marks". I felt a little out of the conservation. Mrs. Marks was in her own world, her mind re-visiting the night of the dance. I thanked her for the coffee and tea cakes and said I should be getting back to the hotel. It had become dark since I arrived, and I was a little worried I might run into the man in the red sash.

I kept my eyes open all the way home and saw nothing of the man I had seen earlier. Littlefoot was waiting for me in the lobby, and Mr. Crane was asleep in the chair behind the desk. His mouth partially open and making sounds resembling a horse's nicker. Littlefoot followed me up into the room, expecting to receive his nightly scraps. When I opened the door, I found Mr. Bogardis sprawled across the bed, still fully dressed. The smell of whiskey emitted from his body as I pulled off his boots. He never made a sound.

I went to the table and cut the end crust from a piece of bread and poured a bowl of water for Littlefoot, which he quickly lapped up.

I went back to Mr. Bogardis and finished removing his clothing. The Colt's revolver he carried with him to his father's was loaded and tucked inside his pocket. I took the gun and placed it in the bedside drawer beside my cut down Colt. I gazed down at his peaceful face and knew it was deceiving. I covered him with a blanket, hoping he would sleep through the night.

CHAPTER NINETEEN

When I got back to Contention, I explained to Mollie about my father taking his own life. Although she had never met him, she was shocked and surprised that he was dead. And at his own hand. Each time I went to the Circle L, I think she expected me to come back and tell her that I had killed my father.

I told her about the funeral arrangements for tomorrow. I suggested that she stay in Contention. After all, the only person from the Circle L she had ever seen was Paco. Mollie wanted to go. I think she just felt like I needed her with me. She is rarely wrong about that kind of thing, but I told her no.

I was exhausted, but I needed a drink. I left Mollie in the room, told her I'd be back later and went down to the saloon. I ordered a bottle and a glass. The last thing I remember is stumbling a little as I walked up the stairs to the room.

I got up and got an early start. I kept thinking that I have no obligation to this man and if I did not attend his funeral, it would not matter. But I reckon my mother raised me better. Good or bad, he is my father. I will attend, but he already knew that I would not honor his request to be buried in Georgia beside my mother.

I arrived early, and Paco was taking care of last minute arrangements. He told me the grave had been dug, and the stone marker was at the gravesite. I asked how he had a marker prepared so quick. He told me my father had the stone carved several years before, with all the information on it that he wanted known.

He also explained that he had sent other vaqueros out to notify certain people and set some things in motion. All of that was specified in the letter my father left for Paco. Everything was as my father had requested of Paco. The doctor had been a longtime friend and listed the cause of death as heart failure. The lawyer would be in attendance to be sure my father's wishes were carried out. A minister would also be there. A plain coffin had been procured.

Seems like he had been thinking of this day even before I made an appearance in his life. If he had done it sooner, he would have saved no telling how many innocent people a lot of grief and heartache. But that is over and done.

At shortly after noon, some of the hands loaded the coffin into the back of a wagon. The wagon led the procession to a small grove of trees by the creek. The grave was indeed ready, and the coffin positioned on boards over the grave. The minister read some verses from the Bible and spoke for just a few minutes, although I can't remember much that he said. He led a short prayer, and the service was over. The coffin was lowered into the ground and covered.

It was then that I noticed the gravestone. It was made of stone and looked to have been done by a craftsman.

It read:
William Lawrence
And
Dent Bogardis
Two Sides of One Man
May They Both Rest in Peace

I told Paco that I was sure my father would have approved of the funeral, and that I would be headed back to Contention. I told Mollie yesterday that I would stay the night, but thought it not to be necessary now that everything was done. He told me there was one man I needed to see before I left. He took me back towards the wagon and pointed at a well dressed gentleman. I walked up to him, introduced myself, and told him Paco had said I should speak with him. He put his hand out and said, "My name is Colonel William Herring. I practice the law in Tombstone and was Mr. Lawrence's attorney." I merely looked at his outstretched hand and shook my head. "I do not shake hands," I said.

He withdrew his hand and explained to me that he knew that William Lawrence was my father. He said that he had several matters of concern that he needed to discuss with me at my earliest convenience. I told him I occasionally travel to Tombstone and would look him up the next time I was there. He nodded, then told me it was a matter of some urgency that I meet with him. "Next time I'm in town," I said and walked over to my horse.

I rode out from the ranch. I stopped somewhere a few miles from Contention and just sat alone on a creek bank. I couldn't think. My mind was jumbled and blank. I guess I just wanted to be alone for a while. Before darkness sat in, I rode on into Contention.

I was looking forward to getting back to Mollie. Although I would never admit it, I leaned on Mollie more than I should. I had a lot to think about in one way, yet on the other hand, one of my problems was solved. That's a hell of a way to feel about the death of your father. But then we did not have a typical father/ son relationship.

When I got back to the room, Mollie wasn't there. She was most likely still working for Mrs. Marks. I thought I'd have a drink to finish out the day. Mollie wouldn't be expecting me tonight anyway, it'll be a suprise when I do come in. I then walked on over to the saloon and ordered a bottle.

*   *   *   *   *

He didn't know I was awake when he left. I reached in the bedside table drawer and took out my Colt's revolver. I slipped it in to my purse, just in case. I waited 'till I knew he had ridden out of town before I left the hotel. I walked to the livery and rented a buggy. Told the boy where I was going, and that I'd be back late tomorrow morning.

It was a cool morning, and I was glad I'd worn the wool cloak. I was going along on a full trot when I thought I'd seen a rider. He was a little ways out, about a quarter mile behind me. I almost dismissed it in my thoughts, but then I remembered what Mr. Bogardis has told me time after time..... "always be aware of your surrounding, Mollie!"

I took the gun from my purse and tucked it in the folds of my skirt, between my legs. I jerked the reins and told the horse to "giddy up". The rider was approaching closer. I looked back and saw a red cloth swaying from his side.

My heart sped up, and I began thinking that leaving this

morning was not a good idea. I was on the road to Tombstone alone, and Mr. Borgardis was not even aware of what I was doing. He would not like this!

Within seconds, the Cowboy was in front of the buggy, riding beside the horse. He reached out and grabbed the horse's reins and slowed the buggy to a stop. I saw my breath in front of me as I spoke and asked him what he wanted.

"Looks like the little lady is all alone without her man", he sneered and spit out a wad of tobacco, aiming it towards the buggy.

"I wouldn't put it that way if I were you", I answered, trying to be as calm and in control as I could. Actually, I was thinking about how fast I could pull the gun from between my legs if I needed to. "I'll ask you again, what is it that you want?"

"So, where is Bogardis?", he inquired. "Why isn't he with you?"

I figured this was as good a time as any to show the Cowboy I was armed. Besides if I told him the truth, that Mr. Bogardis didn't know where I was, well ... no tellin' what he might do. I looked away from the Cowboy, as if I was watching someone coming from behind him. He took the bait, turned around long enough for me to pull the gun. The barrel was pointed directly at the Cowboy's face when he quickly turned back to me. I held the Colt with both hands, told him it was loaded and I knew exactly how to shoot a man.

He raised his arms slightly and blurted out, "Whoa!", while shallowing a mouth of chewing tobacco. I moved the gun an inch and shot a load off at his side. I'm sure he heard it whisk by his ear!

"I know you have somewhere else you need to go", I told him with all the confidence in the Arizona. He answered a "yes ma'am", kicked his horse in the shank and galloped off. I sat there watching him ride out of sight before I jerked the reins on the buggy. I kept the gun in my hands as I held on tight to the leather straps. Every few seconds I would look back. Not knowing whether I should turn around and go back to Contention or ride hard and fast in the direction of Tombstone. Without realizing what I was doing, I had chosen the latter.

My heart was still pounding by the time I saw the hills of Tombstone. I slowed the buggy down to a trot, took a couple of deep breathes to compose myself and headed towards the Cosmopolitan Hotel. I figured that is where I would find them.

I thought I better not mention the ordeal that just happened to Allie or any of the Earps. No need to stir up any more trouble. No need for Mr. Bogardis to find out.

CHAPTER TWENTY

I took one drink and gave the rest of the bottle to an old hard case sitting at the table beside me in the saloon. He gladly took it from me and got up and left the bar in a hurry as if I was gonna take it back. I missed Mollie, so I wanted to get back to the hotel and hold her.

She still wasn't in the room when I got there. It was late, and I began to worry. I had an idea she may be at Mrs. Marks. I started back out of the hotel and walked past Mr. Crane. "Evening, Mr. Bogardis", he said rising from his chair. I stopped and took a step backwards, asking Mr. Crane if he'd seen Mollie. He answered that yes he had, only it was way early this morning. "Early? How early?" I questioned him. "Well," he started, thinking back trying to remember, "I reckon it was just past sun up. I seen her down at the livery, leaving in a buggy. I figured she was headed out to meet up with you some where."

I bolted out of the lobby and walked quickly to the livery. I doubted anyone but the boy that stays out behind the stables will be there this time of night. I saw a light burning in the shed so I called out for the boy, so as not to startle him. He came to the door when he heard me calling. I asked the young fellow if he'd seen Mollie, the woman who's with me when I rent the buggies from him. He mumbled that he had.

"What?" I said. "When did she leave?" He told me that she left in a buggy early that morning going to Tombstone. Damn that hard-headed woman. She knows I don't like for her to be out and about alone especially on the ten mile trip between Contention and Tombstone. Anything could happen. Lose a wheel, horse break away, or worse. There are still a lot of men out there who I would not want Mollie to have to deal with alone. But she is so independent that she thinks she can do as she pleases. I hope she took the Colt with her.

I thanked the kid and asked him to put my saddle and gear on a fresh horse. I headed over to the hotel to pick up a few things. First, I wanted to be sure Mollie had left armed, and I wanted to pick up my ten gauge. There is plenty of bad stuff going on in Tombstone, and it would be wise to be ready. It appeared that she carried her short Colt, as it was not in the drawer. I have extra cartridges in my saddle bags, my rifle is in its scabbard, I have two Colt's, and my shotgun will go across my saddle horn. Yeah, that ought to be enough, at least for a small war.

I was on the trail about dark and had to temper my desire to get there quick with the knowledge that it is dangerous to try to move too fast once the sun is down. But, I arrived in Tombstone before midnight.   I went straight to the Grand Hotel, as that is where we always stay in Tombstone. I had to wake the clerk, and he grumbled a little 'till he realized who it was.

"Why good evening, Mr. Bogardis. Would you be needing a room?", he asked. I told him I was there to meet Miss Mollie and thought she might already have a room. He said he had not seen her, and she was not registered.

I went straight over to Cosmopolitan Hotel thinking I might find them there. I was not surprised to see three men outside guarding the entrance. I could see that one of them was Texas Jack.   "Jack, it's Bogardis," I called out. With all that's been going on, I sure don't want to get shot by mistake. "Come on over," he replied. We nodded to each other, and I looked at the other two. I don't recall ever seeing them before, but if they were on guard with Jack, they must be ok.

Before I could ask if he had seen Mollie, he grinned and said, "I reckon you're here looking for that pretty lady that lets you hang around."   I nodded, and he told me she was inside asleep. I asked if she was alright, and he told me she was just fine.   "But if she ever runs you off, there's gonna be a line from here to yonder wanting to take your place," he said. I would have thought that too familiar from most folks, but not from Texas Jack. I took it as a compliment.

I asked about Virgil's condition, and he explained that it was pretty serious as far as the arm was concerned. The doctor wanted to take it off, but Virgil would not let him. Other than his arm, he was doing fairly well.

I told him I thought I better put my horse away, then if it suited them, I would come back and stretch out on the porch.   He motioned with his head, and one of the men said he would take care of the horse. Jack told me there were some blankets in the lobby,   and I was welcomed to catch some rest before morning.

I spread out a blanket on a bench and got as comfortable as I could.   I couldn't help but think how surprised Mollie would be in the morning. Knowing that she was safe was all I needed. I was asleep in no time.

*   *   *   *   *

Allie was surprised to see me when I arrived. I knew better than to say anything to Allie about the Cowboy along the trail. I acted as calmly as I could when she asked if I had a pleasant ride. I also hesitated to tell her that I had come on my own, but thought I'd best get it out in the open.   She raised her brows and said she thought Mr. Bogardis wasn't going to be taking it too kindly when he found out. I told her I'd planned to leave right after breakfast and get back to Contention long before he ever found out.

It was a good thing I had come. Allie was at her wits end. There was plenty of chores to keep me busy all day! Wyatt had been staying over at the hotel since Virgil was shot. Allie said he was on her last nerve. "Damn Earp men!", she kept saying. I asked about Louisa and Mattie, and she told me they had their hands full as well. Lou waits on Morg hand and foot and has to deal with Wyatt coming and going, stirring things up all the time. Mattie says that Wyatt is hardly in her bed at nights, and she suspects as to where and who he is with.

Wyatt told Virgil that he wants all of them to move into the Cosmopolitan Hotel. He says none of them are safe in Tombstone any more. "There's safety in numbers, Virg! It ain't gonna get any better. Ike ain't giving up 'till we're all in the ground", Allie heard him tell his brother. Allie shook her head saying that it would never be over until "Wyatt" said it was over. I told her maybe he was right about the safety thing, seems that moving into the hotel was a good idea. I know that they have men posted in front and behind the hotel, not even a mouse could slip by them. She just complained that everything had to be Wyatt's way. He makes all the decisions, and Virgil and Morgan follow along. Now, Virg's arm is hanging on by a thread, he may never have use of it again, and Wyatt is still handing out orders.

The rest of the evening I did some laundry for Allie, made coffee for the boys outside and fetched clean water for Virgil's dressing. Allie always re-wound the bandages herself even after the doctor had just left the room. She said Virg was her man and she didn't trust no one taking care of him, she'd do it herself.

Before I fell in for the night, I checked to see if my Colt was still in my purse. I would need it come morning when I headed back to Contention. Allie fell asleep sitting in the chair by Virgil's bed. I threw a blanket over her and tried to get comfortable on the floor. I was so worn out from the events of the entire day, but all I could think about was if Mr. Bogardis was alright after his father's funeral today. It must have been hard on him today, whether he admits it or not.

CHAPTER TWENTY ONE

Texas Jack and his partners were still there when I awoke. I asked if he stayed around the clock. He told me that they would be relieved shortly, but that they would hang around to get breakfast. He'd sent one of the men to get some biscuits and coffee from the diner.

We talked for a few minutes about the ambush. I asked if they had come up with the shooter. Jack said it was pretty sure there was more than one person involved. Maybe just one shooter, but probably several lookouts. Everyone on the Earp side of things was sure it was Ike Clanton's doing. Ike always had a big mouth, but when it came to gunplay he would more than likely do it from the shadows.

We heard the front door rattle as someone inside was trying to open it. I reached over and gave it a push. It swung open, and there was Mollie. She nearly fell over when she saw it was me. "Good morning," I said. "Have you started makin' house calls since the last time I saw you?" She blushed and told me she was just trying to do what she could to help out. "Yes, I can see that," I replied. From the expression on her face, I think she knew I was not happy about her coming to Tombstone alone. Of course, she knew when she left Contention that I was not going to be happy about it, and it certainly did not stop her. She had made up her mind, and that was that.

I asked Mollie if Virgil was awake, and she said she didn't think so, but that Wyatt was up. I asked her to tell him I was outside with the boys. In a few minutes, Wyatt came out, smiled, and shook my hand. "I thought I told you not to come running up here unless we sent for you," he said grinning. I told him I had not come because of him or Virgil, but rather because I was chasing a runaway woman. He got a kick out of that, and we both laughed. He asked if we were going to stay, and I told him I had not really thought much about it. He told me the town was going to have some fireworks that night for New Years Eve, and we might enjoy the show. I smiled as I remembered the fireworks on the Fourth of July last year. Mollie and I had also made some of our own. I'm sure she will want to stay. I told Wyatt I had something I needed to talk to him about in private. He suggested we go out back where we could see anyone approaching as we talked. I quickly told him about my father, and that I had just come from his funeral yesterday.

I also explained that I had business in town with the lawyer, Colonel Herring. Wyatt said he was a good man, and whatever he was involved in would be on the up and up. I thanked him, and we walked back to the room.

I asked Mollie if she would be interested in staying for the fireworks tonight. She broke into a grin and nodded quickly. I told her I would go by the hotel and get us a room, as they might sell out if a lot of people came to town for the fireworks. I bent down, kissed her on the cheek, and told her we had something to discuss tonight. I'm sure she knew I was referring to her unscheduled trip. She looked down and nodded her head.

I swung back by the Grand Hotel and arranged for a room. I told the clerk we would probably be staying at least a couple of nights, if not more. I got my gear into the room and put away. Then I decided to walk around town and just look and listen to what folks were saying.

I already knew that there was a pretty large following that believed the Cowboys were murdered by the Earps during the recent street fight, and that the Earps had been pushing for the fight for a long time. It may have been close to half the town who sided with the Cowboys, on this matter anyway. Yep, there are always two sides to every story.

I had lunch alone and went over to the Alhambra just about the time Doc was walking in. He slapped me on the back, asked me about Mollie, and offered to buy me a drink. I took him up on it.

As we sat at a table alone, I asked him who he thought was behind the attempt on Virgil's life. He said a blind man could see that it had to be Ike Clanton. Maybe not the trigger man, but certainly the one behind the attack. I did not mean to get him wound up, but he went on to tell me that he wanted to declare war on the Cowboys and get it over with. This would not be something that would just die down. It should be met head on before anything else happened. Then he shook his head and said that Wyatt wanted to handle this through the law. Doc grunted, "Nobody else gives a damn about what is legal, why should we?" Then he continued, "But you know Wyatt." Yeah, I know Wyatt. And if he can do it within the law, he will. But if it ever gets to the point that he gives up on the law, look out.

Doc and I played some low stakes poker the rest of the afternoon. I lost three dollars to him and considered myself lucky. I told him I was going by to see Virgil and see if Mollie was ready to go. He asked if we were staying for the fireworks, and I told him we would. He said he and Kate would be in the street in front of the saloon just before midnight if we wanted to join them. I thanked him for the invitation and left.

When I got to Virgil's room, Wyatt was in the hallway. "You come after that woman?", he asked. "Yeah, guess I will take her off your hands," I replied. Just then, Mollie stuck her head out the door and smiled. She said she would just get her bag and be back out in a moment. She was true to her word, and we said goodbye to Wyatt and headed to our hotel.

I could not keep my mouth shut any longer. "Mollie, whatever possessed you to ride off to Tombstone alone?" I asked. "Don't you realize how dangerous that was? Anything could have happened! Your horse might have bolted, you could have lost a wheel on the wagon, to say nothing of the fact that you are alone with some mean folks running around. What if you ran up on a Cowboy who knew who you were?"

She looked at me for a moment and said that she was armed, and it would not be the first time she had ever killed a man. I shook my head, "Mollie, what if it had been three men, or seven men, or ten men?" She looked as if that had not occurred to her. I stopped walking and turned her to me. "Don't you understand that I am only trying to protect the one I love?", I asked.

"Yes I do, and I'm sorry I caused you to worry," she replied. "I won't do it again."

Of course I know that she means she won't do again unless she needs to, but I thought it best to let it go at that.

We continued on our way to the hotel. "Are you excited about the fireworks?", I asked. She smiled and asked me if I remembered the last time. I replied that I did, and that I expected to make some of our own, again.

*   *   *   *   *

Well, I guess my plan of being back in Contention long before Mr. Bogardis found out I had gone, had back fired on me. He told me that Mr. Crane had seen me leaving town, and he figured out the rest from the livery boy. He gave me a good talkin' to, but didn't seem to know about the Cowboy trouble on the way. I didn't mention it or else he wouldn't turn me loose on my own ever again.

Mr. Bogardis says we're gonna stay in Tombstone a few days since we're here anyway. Seems his father's attorney is in town, and he wants to meet with him and talk. He hasn't told me much about the funeral, only that Paco had everything taken care of. That's why he didn't feel the need to stay at the ranch, that and the fact that he says he wanted to be sleeping in the bed with me.

Allie lent me one of her dresses to change into. Mine had some blood stains on it from Virgil's wounds. As I changed into the dress, I overheard a conversation between Wyatt and Morgan. Wyatt told Virgil that he got approval to deputize a posse. He was leavin' right after the election for City Marshal in three days. I shuttered to think that he might ask Mr. Bogardis to go along! Virgil said something back to him that I couldn't quite make out, and Wyatt left the room.

Allie told me to have fun watching the fireworks. I wish she would come along with us, but I truly understand her not wanting to leave Virgil, let alone being in a festive mood. Just then, I heard Mr. Bogardis in the hallway talking with Wyatt. I grabbed my cloak and opened the door. I forgot my purse so I had to go back and retrieve it. I asked Allie one more time, "Are you sure you wouldn't want to come along?" She answered no, but that we should all be careful. Ike and his men are out there somewhere. I then remembered the Cowboy yesterday morning. I was lucky, it could have been a bad situation.

The fireworks were wonderful, though not anywhere as grand as the ones we saw in Prescott. We stood with Doc and Kate near the sidewalk at the saloon. Although Kate's arm was wrapped around Doc's arm, her eyes ocasionally drifted towards Mr. Bogardis. "That's a fine man you have there, Mollie", she commented. Doc looked at me and smiled. I guess he didn't mind it at all when Kate flirted. Mr. Bogardis tightened his arm around my waist, letting me know that I had nothing to be concerned over. I smiled back at Kate, thanked her and said , "Yes, he is."

In front of us on the street was one of those red-sashed Cowboys. He apparently had been watching the fireworks from some place near us. I had seen Doc glace over in his direction a time or two during the display. "Holliday, how'd you like them loud explosions?", the man said with a snicker. His face was dirty, as well as his clothes. He gripped a liquor bottle in one hand and stumbled into a light pole. He'd obviously had drank more than his share.

"Assuming that you are sober enough to have witnessed the light show this evening, let's just say I like explosions very well", answered Doc. Kate laughed and told Doc to come along, no cause to get into a squabble out here this evening. "Don't you worry your pretty little head, Kate darling. Mr. Brocius and I were just discussing the fireworks. Isn't that right, Mr. Brocius?"

"Yeah, that's right, Holliday". The man walked off, laughing and staggering. He joined a group of other men on the opposite side of the street. Mr. Bogardis told Doc that it was time to get back to the hotel, and he ought to be thinking about doing the same thing. Kate kissed Doc on the mouth, right in front of us, and rubbed her hand on the mid-section of his trousers, just under his belt. I turned away, a little taken back with her boldness in public. Mr. Bogardis told Doc and Kate good night and to be careful walking home.

When we arrived back in our room, Mr. Bogardis teased me by saying that I should take a lesson from Kate. "Hummmm", I whispered, "maybe I already have".

CHAPTER TWENTY TWO

Well, I guess we managed to get 1882 here on time. Mollie and I were out in the street with Doc and Kate. There were a lot of fireworks, real fireworks, and of course everyone was shooting guns into the air. I take it New Year's Eve is a time when the local officials turn a blind eye to the firearm ordinance. As long as it does not get out of hand.

We just laid around New Year's Day and recuperated. But now it's time to get back to the business at hand. In my case, I need to see Colonel Herring and see what he wants with me. Mollie decided not to go with me, preferring to visit with the girls instead.

I walked into the Colonel's office at just the right time. He was there alone. He stood immediately and attempted to shake hands, which of course did not work. He went to the front door, locked it, and hung up a sign that read "Back Soon." He motioned for me to follow him into what must have been his private office. I sat down and waited for him to start the ball.

He began by explaining that on the day I saw him at the Circle L, he was putting together some things for my father. I said nothing. He went on to say that my father had left everything he owned to me. That took me by surprise. "What do you mean, everything he owned?", I asked. He nodded and repeated, "Everything". He said the ranch, all the property throughout the territory, the money, everything. To do with as I pleased.

He stood up, walked over to a large safe, and withdrew a stack of papers from it. He said that the papers were deeds and various other legal instruments that my father had signed over to me. He suggested that I let them remain in his safe, at least for the time being. He took an envelope off the top of the stack and handed it to me. "This will answer some of your questions, but may bring up more," he said. He told me that the letter was written to me from my father, shortly before his death. "You should read the letter carefully and think about its implications before you start making decisions," he advised.

He offered to leave me in the private office while he went back out front and opened for business. It seemed a good idea, as no one would be bothering me while I read my father's last communication with me. I was a little nervous when I opened the letter, not knowing what he might have to say.

I unfolded the letter, smoothed the paper, and started to read:

Son,

If you are reading this, I am no longer of this earth. Although you would not permit me to lie beside your lovely mother now, I can only hope that I will see her again and that she can forgive me.

I assume the Colonel has told you everything I owned is now yours, to do with as you see fit. He has the bank information for several accounts in different places. There is a large sum of money that belongs to you.

Paco has been loyal to me for at least ten years. He can be trusted to do as you instruct him, and he will never lie to you. I wrote Paco a letter as well. I am sure he will not let you down.

You may have wondered how I could ever accumulate what I have with no seed money. That was easy. Back in '71, I was wandering around the mountain that you can see from the porch of the ranch. I discovered a small, but very rich vein of gold. This was years before Ed Schieffellin made his big silver strike in Tombstone. I chose to keep mine quiet, as I did not want to draw attention to myself. Anytime funds get low, we mine enough to replenish the bank accounts. Plus, there is considerable gold and silver coins hidden in the ranch house. Paco knows. I must warn you that you need to stay conscious of your need to access the gold in the mine. Paco will handle getting it out, and we send it to a buyer not around these parts. He is honest, we let him have a good price, and he keeps what he knows to himself. And really, he does not know a lot. Only that once or twice a year, a seller offers him some gold at a very good price.

Although I have accumulated considerable wealth, my life has been a failure. Use what I have given you to help rather than hurt.

I hope you can make right some of my wrongs. I have tried to make my peace with you and with God. Remember what I told you about the past. You can't undo the past, but you can change the future.
I wish you and your lady happiness and love.
I Am
Your father
Dent Bogardis.

I laid the paper down on the desk and just stared at the wall. This is not what I expected. I need to think. I need to talk to Mollie.

I folded the letter and put it in my coat pocket. As I went out through the front office, I thanked Colonel Herring and told him I would be back in a day or so. He nodded and smiled and wished me well.

    *   *   *   *   *

Mr. Bogardis left to see his father's attorney this morning. I wanted to spend some time visiting Louisa and perhaps see Mattie as well. Mr. Bogardis hasn't told me how long we are staying, so I thought this was as good an opportunity as any. !

As I walked to Lou's house, a group of men with the red sashes were in front of the general store. I passed by trying not to look up in their direction. One of the men poked his leg out, causing me to have to step over it. I heard a few comments under their breath, and it caused my heart to race. Without thinking, I raised my eyes and looked into the face of the man I met along the road. I gasped for air, as he smiled and tipped his hat in my direction. The men were laughing and cussing as I walked quickly away. I was almost in a panic. I still haven't told Mr. Bogardis of the incident. I was starting to think maybe I should. As I approached Louisa's house, I saw a few men with guns on the porch. I told one of them who I was, and he said he would see if the Earps were accepting visitors. The man returned and said it was alright for me to enter.

Lou was at the door with a warm welcome. We sat and talked for a long while about the tension in Tombstone. Nothing was the same since the street fight. There was no glow in her face or sparkle in her eyes like before. She was full of worry and sadness. In a matter of minutes, the lives of the Earp family were forever changed that day. I offered to help Lou in any matter of need she may have. She declined and said she would be fine, Morgan would be fine. I knew she didn't actually believe what she was saying, but I couldn't press the issue. I hugged her and told her I was going to check on Mattie. She asked if Mr. Bogardis would be riding with Wyatt in the posse he was forming. I said I didn't know, but that he seems to be pre-occupied with the death of William Lawrence and was right now at the attorney's office.

I then walked to Mattie's home. I kept a watchful eye for any men with the red sashes. Mattie was home alone, of course Wyatt was at the hotel with Virgil. She was pleased to see me and offered refreshments as we sat on the sofa and talked. She said she is tired of living in Tombstone and had begged Wyatt to leave town before all this Cowboy hatred came to a head. Wyatt refused to leave, and now it has done nothing but tear the family to pieces. She said he rarely comes home at nights. She looked as if she was about to shed a tear from her eyes, so I looked away. I noticed an almost empty bottle of Laudanum on her beside table. I asked if she was still having those terrible headaches.

"Oh, they are nothing, Mollie", she answered. "They come and go. I only take the medicine when I need it."

I could tell this was a subject she did not wish to talk about. An unexpected knock on the door startled us both. Mattie opened it to find an associate of Wyatt's asking her if everything was alright. She told the man that all was well. "We'll be outside if you need us", he told her, all the while looking at me. Mattie shut the door almost before the man had entirely removed his boots from the door frame. "I hate the fact that we have to be protected 'round the clock!"

"I should go," I told her as I stood and moved towards the door. "Mr. Bogardis is at the attorney's office and will be expecting me to be back in the room when he gets there." I hugged her, feeling as if it were to be the last time I would ever see her.

"I understand", she said quietly. "Ask one of the men out front to walk you back to the hotel if you want."

I took Mattie up on her offer for an escort back to the Grand. Mr. Bogardis was already in the room when I got there. He was holding an envelope and a piece of writing paper in his hands. "I'm glad you're back, Mollie. I have something to show you."

CHAPTER TWENTY THREE

The paper Mr. Bogardis was holding was a letter from his father. That letter changed everything. He explained that his father had given him his entire estate. Soon after we got back to Contention, we moved out to the Circle L Ranch and began calling it our home. Mr. Bogardis says we have plenty of money, and that I could redecorate the ranch to my liking.

There are two other women living at the ranch, although both are limited to broken English. They tend to the housekeeping and cooking and have very little interaction with Mr. Bogardis and myself. Perhaps that will change as we get to know each other better.

Mr. Crane was very saddened to see us leave. Mr. Bogardis says it is because he will be missing our money! But, I think he was in the habit of having us around. Mrs. Marks said for us to be careful out here with all the Mexicans on the ranch. She said they cannot be trusted. Mr. Bogardis told her not to be looking down her nose at anyone when she didn't even know who she was talking about! Her face became red like a little child's when scolded.

She and Mr. Crane promised to come visit once we got settled in. I said perhaps we could all have a party, like we did the day Lilly and Zack were married. Mr. Bogardis reminded us all that there would be time enough for a party when we have our own wedding day. Mrs. Marks asked if we had changed the date due to our new circumstances. !

"Oh no, Mrs. Marks. We chose that day because it was Mr. Bogardis' mother's birthday." I explained. "And even though we are living at the Circle L, I still intend for the wedding to be at the Grand Hotel in Tombstone. I want to say our vows under those graceful arches and sparkling chandeliers! I knew the first day I entered that hotel that I would want our wedding there. And in just a few more months, I shall get my wish!"

It has been several weeks since we moved into the ranch. I was beginning to miss Contention. I told Mr. Bogardis that I wanted to go back and check in on Littlefoot. He shook his head and said he was sure Littlefoot was well taken care of. I suppose he knew I was just eager to go into town.

He surprised me this morning and told me the buggy was ready to leave, and I should get my "rear-end moving", as he put it! Although it was a crisp February morning, the ride to Contention wasn't at all bad. Perhaps due to the fact that I was itching to get out of the house. !

451

After Mr. Bogardis loaded our supplies from the store into our buggy, I told him I would be visiting Mrs. Marks. He said he never thought the day would come when I would be rushing off to visit Mrs. Marks! He yelled out to me to meet him at the diner for lunch.

I found Mrs. Marks at the dress shop, covered with fabric from head to toe. She said she had several special orders and no help worth any count at all. She laid it all aside and said she had a good bit of gossip to tell me. She proceeded with all the latest news from the big city of Contention!

Time flew by, and I remembered a letter I wanted to mail to Louisa. I had written it a week ago and have been waiting to come to town to mail it. Lou, Morgan, Mattie and Wyatt have all moved into the Cosmopolitan Hotel. I felt badly for them, with all the trouble in Tombstone.

I told Mrs. Marks I must go and left walking towards the post office. From there, I was to meet Mr. Bogardis at the diner for lunch. I was hungry so I was hurrying along. Mr. Bogardis told the Mexican ladies not to pack a meal for us this morning, that we would be eating in town.

When I turned the corner to walk towards the diner, I was startled when I saw the red-sashed Cowboy from the trail to Tombstone. He blocked my path for a second before he took his time moving slowly around me. His cold bloodshot eyes were staring directly in mine, and his puckish smile revealed brown discolored teeth. Several days of hair growth protruded from his dirty chin, and he had an odor like a three-day-old dead animal. He mumbled and asked me where Mr. Bogardis was, just as he had that morning. He said something about how he would take me to the hotel and see how I liked it. He leaned in close enough to my face for me to smell his foul breath.

I glanced behind him and saw Mr. Bogardis approaching us from behind on the sidewalk. Finding instant courage, I told the Cowboy that he would see Mr. Bogardis sooner than he had planned, and he wouldn't like it so well. He had just enough time to let out a little chortle before Mr. Bogardis caught him off guard.

Mr. Bogardis grabbed him on the shoulder, whirled him around and landed his right fist on the Cowboy's jaw! When he was down, Mr. Bogardis kicked him right between the legs. The Cowboy whimpered like a bleeding pig on the way to the slaughter house! A few kids crossing the street stopped to watch the spectacle and ran off giggling as the Cowboy rolled himself into a ball.

I heard Mr. Bogardis threaten him as he took my arm to walk away. I thought this might not be a bad time to tell him the whole story about the cowboy he just injured. Mr. Bogardis said if I could wait, we'd just as well go back to the ranch to eat. At least there, there wasn't trash laying on the sidewalk. He helped me into the buggy, and I proceeded to tell him everything from the beginning.

*   *   *   *   *

I had to think about things before I started making decisions after I received my father's letter. Mollie helped by assuring me that I could do more good with what my father had given me than I could ever hope to do without it. I had not mentioned it to Mollie, but before this happened, I was beginning to look for work. Our bank account was starting to concern me.

We decided that we would move out to the ranch and see how things would go. So before my father had been buried a month, we made the move. It was not really much of a move. We had been living in hotel rooms for so long that we did not have much to move. I did have some hardware stored around town. Mostly guns and such.

I had told Paco of our plans and advised him what day to expect us. When we arrived, he met us at the door, just as he always did when I went to visit my father. He showed us around our new home, which was very well decorated. I could tell Mollie was impressed as well as surprised. We have a large bedroom with its own doors to a private patio on the back side of the house. We were introduced to Magdelena, Paco's wife, and to her sister, Maria. They were the two women I saw preparing my father for burial. They would do the cooking and cleaning and help with anything we needed. They all lived in two rooms attached to the main house. There were two other bedrooms on our side of the house that were not in use. Don't know why my father built so large a home. And of course, I now had my father's old office.

We settled in easily, and Mollie started making the

place her own. I had told her that she could do whatever she wished with the place, and we certainly could afford anything she might want.

Things went very well, considering. I used my time to go through anything I could find of my father's. He had built quite an empire out here, and very few people even knew his name, much less what he looked like. I had asked Paco how the hands took to the idea of me taking over. He said most of them were relieved, but some had decided it would be a good time to move on. That suited me. Chances are, the ones who wanted to move on would have been the trouble makers.

Mollie and I went out riding a couple of times, but the weather is still a little sharp for her. I promised her that we would check out all the property come spring, and that seemed to please her. Always ready for another adventure. I reckon the fact that we needed some supplies was as good as any excuse to make the trip into Contention. Mollie and I decided to take a buggy and ride in together.

Our first stop was the general store. When we got through, Mollie wanted to see Mrs. Marks, and I said I would swing by the marshal's office and probably end up in the saloon. We could meet up around one o'clock and eat at the diner. If I ate Magdelena's cooking at every meal, I would soon have to have some bigger clothes.

When I went in the marshal's office, he was all laid back with his feet on his desk. That could mean that nothing is going on, or it could mean he just didn't care to get involved in anything that might be going on. I asked if there had been any excitement, and he said not until today. Ike Clanton had showed up with a few Cowboys. It seems that Ike is trying to get another murder charge against the Earps and Doc by coming to Contention and filing the paperwork with this judge. The marshal laughed and said you could file papers on anyone, but that didn't mean you could make it stick.   Never-the-less, he says Wyatt and Doc will be picked up and jailed again until the mess is sorted through. I left and headed over to the saloon. I have plenty to drink at the ranch, but I seem to enjoy it more in a saloon. Must be the atmosphere. I put my chair against the wall and ordered coffee and a bottle. It was a very slow day, but then it was still pretty early.

When it was finally time to meet Mollie, I paid up and started down the sidewalk. A Cowboy with a red sash walked out of the saddlemaker's shop and turned down the sidewalk in the same direction as I was headed. When he came out, he turned before he saw me, so he did not realize I was behind him. I could see over his shoulder that Mollie was coming down the sidewalk toward us. As he got to Mollie, he side-stepped in front of her.   When she tried to go around the other way, he again stepped in front of her. By now, I was almost on him and could hear what he had to say.

"Why if it ain't ole Bogardis' woman again. We just keep running into each other. It's a shame he ain't never around. I sure would like to see his face when I take you over to the hotel."

Mollie could see me right behind him. She smiled and said, "You're gonna see his face one of these days, but it may not be as much fun as you think."

I grabbed him by the shoulder and spun him around. My fist caught him under the chin, and he went down hard. It took a few seconds for him to realize what had happened.   When he tried to get up, I kicked him as hard as I could between the legs. I must have got it right 'cause he turned white as a ghost and started throwing up. When he finished retching, I told him if he ever insulted Mollie again, I would kill him on the spot.

Mollie put her arm in mine, and we left the Cowboy moaning on the sidewalk. The events of the morning had caused me to lose my appetite, and I told Mollie we'd eat at home instead of the diner. She agreed saying she had things she needed to tell me on the way back to the ranch anyway.

CHAPTER TWENTY FOUR

Because of the warmer weather, Mr. Bogardis and I have rode the ranch borders more than once. I am feeling more like the Circle L is our home, and Mr. Bogardis and I are happy to be here. More happier here than we ever have been! I am working on learning Magdelena's language, and she is slowly acquiring more English words for us to communicate better. "Buena manana, Magdelena, cual esta para el desayuno hoy?" I ask her each morning when I walk into the kitchen. She answers, "Manana Miss Mollie, we aw havin' eggs, be-can and fla-jak's". I smile and tell her she is improving very much!

I received another letter from Louisa this week. She is in Colton, California with family. Morgan was concerned with her safety and thought it'd be good for her to get away from the tension in Tombstone for a while. She said Morgan's health was improving, but she missed him very much. She wrote that Virgil lost the use of his arm after an ambush. Allie is so distraught, but it could have been worse and he could have lost his life instead of his arm. A few days after Wyatt was released from jail, he organized another posse and went out after a man who robbed the stage back in January. Wyatt was back in Tombstone, and he told Morgan that he'd heard the Cowboys were plotting more revenge against them. Lou wrote that she was worried about Morgan wanting to stand with Wyatt, against Ike and his men.

I started writing a letter back to Louisa, but I keep getting sidetracked with all the things to do around here! I told Mr. Bogardis that I wanted to ride to Tombstone to see about the Earps, but he says now is not the time to be in Tombstone. Ike and his Cowboys are like a loose cannon running around town, anything could happen. He says soon, when things settle down, we'll invite them here to the ranch. Besides, we will be in Tombstone for the wedding in May, just nine weeks away! I sure hope that Louisa will be back by then.

Mr. Bogardis had news to tell me Saturday night. He said he was planning to ask Zack and Lilly to move in with us at the Circle L. He said Zack could tend to some of the work load, and Lilly and I could spend more time together doing what ever it is we wish to do. He said we would have to ask to see if they were interested, but in my heart I knew that they'd say yes!

We rode out to the Blade ranch the next day. I was thrilled at the prospect of Lilly and Zack living with us, it couldn't be soon enough for me! Lilly came running up to the buggy, and we were giggling in no time. I couldn't wait until Mr. Bogardis made his announcement.

Then I heard Zack telling Mr. Bogardis the news he had just heard from Tombstone. At first, I couldn't believe it.

"Murdered! No, it can't be!" I started crying. Lilly grabbed me and guided me into the house. I was still crying when she poured each of us a cup of hot coffee to settle our nerves. Morgan was shot while playing pool, and he is dead. Poor Louisa, she is still in California, so far away! Her heart must be broken into many pieces. I wish I could be there to help her. Zack and Mr. Bogardis were making plans to meet in Contention tomorrow when the Earps come to the train station. You can bet I will be there as well.

That night, I barely rested at all. I was up before dawn and ready to ride into Contention. Mr. Bogardis did not want me to go along. He said there could be trouble, that I should stay here. He could see no need for me to tag along. I told him that he could ride out without me, but after he was gone, I would leave on my own. He mumbled and cussed a few seconds, but he finally turned to me and said to get a move on it, he'd be leaving shortly.

When we got to the train station, Virgil and Allie were surrounded by several armed men. We couldn't get close enough to talk to them until Mr. Bogardis recognized one of the men, and they let us through. Virgil looked ill, and Allie was sobbing.

There was so much chaos and commotion, it was hard to see what all was happening. The train whistle blew, and it sounded like a screaming banshee. I had only enough time to tell Allie how sorry I was to hear about Morgan. I asked about Mattie and Bessie, but I couldn't hear her response. The men were yelling and telling them to board the train.

Mr. Bogardis grabbed me and told me we needed to get out of the way. It wasn't safe there. I looked back toward the train and waved goodbye to Allie, for what I suspected would be the last time.

*　　　*　　　*　　　*　　　*

It seems that Mollie is more like me than I thought. She seems to be making herself quite at home here on the Circle L.

"What would you think about us hiring Zack to sort of ramrod the ranch?", I asked while laying in bed one night.

460

That made her sit up and take notice! I explained that Paco would still take care of everything around the house. She allowed as how that would be a very good idea, but not very fair to Lilly. She would see very little of Zack. "Not if we let both of them move in the ranch house," I replied. I thought she was going to jump out of the bed. I don't think anything could have suited her more. I told her that tomorrow is Sunday, so if she would like, we could ride over to their ranch and see what they have to say. I should have known better than to get her all excited when we are getting ready for sleep! I just hope she doesn't keep me up all night.

At breakfast, I asked Paco to have one of the men get the buggy ready for the trip. I had gotten up some arms, just in case. As we boarded the wagon, Paco gave us two canteens of water and a blanket to cover our legs. Paco had told me before that no one should ever go out in this country, even for a short trip, without water. I know he is right.

We arrived at the Blade ranch in no time at all. Zack and Lilly were both out the door before we could get on the ground. Lilly ran to hug Mollie, as women will do. Zack came around and nodded to me and asked if I wanted to put the horse up. I told him we had just stopped by for a few minutes. With a grim look on his face, he said he was glad we came because a rider had just come by and brought news from Tombstone. "What's happened now?" I asked, expecting to hear of more trouble out of the Clanton gang.

"Morgan Earp was murdered last night," he said. I was speechless. Mollie stopped her giggling and turned to me, a look of disbelief on her face. I inquired how it happened. Zack said the word he had was that Morgan was shooting a game of billiards. and someone shot him through the window. Of course they had not caught the shooter, but he said that Wyatt and Doc had no doubt who was behind it.

They were going to put Morgan's body on the train in Benson to go to California, where his parents and wife are. James was going to accompany the body. Virgil and

Allie would be catching the train in Contention for Tucson on Monday. They were also going to California. I told Zack I would be in Contention tomorrow to see if there was anything I could do. He said he would meet me there.

Poor Mollie was crying. She thought a lot of Morgan and Louisa. When we got settled inside, I told Zack that this may not be the proper time, but I wanted to talk to him about a business proposition. He leaned forward and listened.

"As you know, I am the new owner of the Circle L Ranch. I want you and Lilly to move out there with me and Mollie. You would be in charge of running the cattle operations and some 'special projects' that need taking care of. You would have no expenses of any kind, and I'm sure we can agree on suitable compensation. You can keep this ranch, and the Circle L will buy any livestock you have. What do you think?"

Zack and Lilly looked at each other. "We're gonna have to talk about this," he said. "But what did you mean about 'special projects?'", he asked.

I asked him if he remembered Mrs. Pryer and her two kids. The ones we met on our way to Canyon Diablo. He nodded that he did. I told him the first thing I wanted done come warmer weather was for him to track them down. All she said was she was going back to Illinois, once they made it to Tucson. I told Zack he could start in Tucson, but even if it meant going all the way to Illinois, I wanted him to find her. I know we can't replace her husband, but if she wants her land back, that can be arranged. And with the water flowing again. If she wants to come back, we will outfit her and get them all back here safe and sound, at no cost. If she does not, then I am to pay her a fair sum, and I mean a generous sum. It might take some time to find her, so if Lilly wanted to go with him that would be fine. What I want to do is make right as much of the Circle L's misdeeds as I can.

I looked over at Mollie and told her we should be getting on back. I told Zack I would meet him in the morning in Contention. Mollie jumped in and declared she would be going as well.

The next morning as planned, we met in Contention in time to see Wyatt, Doc, and Virgil, and a group of guards probably twenty strong. Wyatt explained that he had received word that the Clanton group wanted to wipe the Earps out and would be waiting on the train in Tucson. They wanted to get Virgil, Wyatt, and Doc all at one time. From their point of view, that would be a good idea. If you leave Wyatt or Doc alive, you will probably not live long.

I asked if they needed me to go with them. They allowed as how they had over twenty hands that would be scattered throughout the train. Texas Jack was going to remain in Contention with their horses, so if they needed us, they would wire him from Tucson, and he could round everybody up. "Just so you know that I'll be there if you say," I said. With a nod of his head, they boarded the train and left.

CHAPTER TWENTY FIVE

I still feel saddened when I think of Louisa having to bury her husband. Lord knows how I would do if I was in her situation. I haven't heard from her since it happened, but Mr. Bogardis says to give her time. It may take her a month or so before she feels she can write and talk about it. Mr. Bogardis receives news quite often about Wyatt and Doc and their killings of the men involved. I don't blame them at all. Mr. Bogardis says they are going outside the law, and it's gonna come back to haunt them someday. I just wish this whole thing was over, or that it never happened! Now, the way it is, the Earps will not be able to attend our wedding, and Louisa is without a husband.

But at least Zack and Lilly said yes to Mr. Bogardis' proposal. They have moved in the Circle L. Zack and Mr. Bogardis are busy during the days, and Lilly and I have things of our own to do. Magdelina is teaching Lilly her spanish words, and it is very amusing. Magdelina has run off on more than one occasion, frustrated with Lilly's pronunciations! "Doy para arriba!", Magdelina would scream, throwing her hands in the air, "Esa mujer cabelluda amarilla nunca aprendera!"

Littlefoot, or rather some wandering yellow-haired cat he found, had a litter of kittens in Mr. Crane's storeroom a few weeks ago. He was furious! Lilly and I gathered them all up into a box and brought them back to the ranch with us. Cute little things, six of them in all. Maria does most of the cleaning, and she is not pleased to have animals in the house. Mr. Bogardis hasn't said anything, but he tends to avoid the room where we keep them. Lilly and I will name them just as soon as we can think of six names to give them.

We are also busy thinking about our wedding. At least it will be a date that Mr. Bogardis can remember. His mother must have been a lovely woman. I know he deeply loved her. This is our way of honoring her, being married on her birthday, May twenty-fifth. I will be wearing her gold cameo locket that Mr. Bogardis gave me around my neck. In some small way, she will be with us on that day.

I have chosen my dress. Lilly and I have spent a lot of time preparing it. A high lace collar and several rows of ruffles across the breast will proudly show off the gold locket. I was thinking about adornment for my hair, but Lilly says I should keep it simple, maybe a few tiny white flowers stuck here and there. I still have my mother's tortoiseshell hair comb, so Lilly can braid my hair and use the comb to hold it in place.

Although I was married to Sam, we never had much of a married life. Sam and I were married in a small church, with a few friends and a couple of his family members. I never knew his background or where he came from until it was too late. I later found out that Sam and his cousins intended to rob the local bank in town until he met me. I think Sam loved me, or at least he tried for a while.

His family had deep ties in the corrupt business of cattle thieving and horse stealing. His cousin King Fisher would never allow him to leave the "family". Sam wanted to, and I think he gave it his best shot. It didn't last long, and he was back to running with the "family". I just couldn't live with a fugitive wanted for stealin' and killin'. I tried to leave once or twice, but Sam wouldn't hear of it. He became violent and angry, telling me I belonged to him and I would do as I was told.

The best thing that could have possibly happened for me was to run out of money and end up in Contention City. I was fortunate the day I stood on the sidewalk and watched Mr. Bogardis ride into town. I thought I was foolish to write all those letters to him, which he still keeps folded up in his saddle bags! But, fate was looking out for us, and now here we are about to be married. About to be spending the rest of our lives together! I couldn't be happier!

Zack and Mr. Bogardis are leaving to spend the day in Tombstone. He wouldn't hear of the idea to allow Lilly or myself to go. I conceded, allowing to the fact that the Earps will not be there so I have no reason to go. He says he needs to speak with his father's attorney again and secure the hotel rooms at the Grand Hotel. He is going to secure the bridal suite that we saw the last time we were there. The door was ajar, and I peeked inside. It will be our honeymoon room.

We will come back to the ranch the afternoon following the wedding. Magdelina says she will prepare a feast for us to celebrate with everyone here. Lilly tells me that our honeymoon holds many "surprises", and then she giggles 'till her face turns red! I know she has a secret, but for now she is doing her best not to tell me! All she says is that we will 'all' have a reason to celebrate!

With Zack and Mr. Bogardis out of the house, Lilly and I spent the rest of the day chasing loose kittens and cleaning up messes before they returned to find the evidence on the floor!

*　　　　*　　　　*　　　　*　　　　*

Zack and Lilly settled right in almost as easily as Mollie and I. Zack has been getting the feel of all the ranch operations. Surprisingly, there is no where near the head of cattle that one would expect on a ranch this size. According to Paco, my father would buy cattle and almost immediately turn it for a profit. Most of the hands were involved in transportation rather than the usual branding, weaning, and everything else that goes with the day-to-day operations of a cattle ranch. Without the constant need to move cattle, most of the vaqueros were not needed. To be sure, there was still a lot going on, but from now on the cattle trade would be more normal.

The government was in the market for cattle, but more so for horses. Zack and I agreed that we had rather deal in horses than cattle. We could maintain a herd of cattle sufficient to supply any government needs, but we would focus on the horse trade. While horses are a necessity, the lack of feed is always a problem. With the kind of acreage we have, we should be able to maintain a large remuda.

Lilly and Mollie are busy in the ranch house. Zack and Lilly took one of the spare bedrooms and made it their own. As for me, if things get to be too much for my peace of mind, I can always retreat into my office. There it is quiet, and I have no concerns about anyone coming in uninvited. Paco takes care of that. It seems like all is well for us, and sometimes that makes me uncomfortable. When things are going too well, it is often a sign that something bad is on the way.

We heard through Texas Jack that there was an ambush planned at the train station in Tucson when they left Contention. It sounded like someone wanted to do away with all the Earps and Doc at one time. Wyatt killed Frank Stillwell, and from what I hear, he made sure of it. He was hit with both barrels of a shotgun and had at least six pistol bullets in him. They think Ike Clanton and Pete Spence were in on the ambush, but got away. Wyatt took many of the men with him as a posse to track down anyone who had a hand in Morgan and Virgil's shootings. So far, they have killed Indian Charlie at a wood yard in the mountains and Curly Bill Brocius and Johnny Barnes at Iron Springs. The stories are that Wyatt is serving more as an executioner than a lawman. I guess that's understandable when a group is trying to wipe out your entire family. I understand it, but it don't make it legal. But, I'm not sure I'd do it any different.

Mollie and Lilly have been busy fussing over the wedding stuff. I told her to do whatever she wanted to, as far as the wedding was concerned. I had just as soon do what Zack and Lilly did and invite a few friends to the ranch and get married here. Mollie will not hear of it. She has always loved staying in the Grand Hotel in Tombstone and insists that we get married there. I won't put up much of a fight about it, I'll let her have her way. I smiled as I told her we should have our party at the Birdcage. She made a face, as she knows that no decent woman would be seen even going by the Birdcage. I laughed and told her I would go ahead and get our rooms reserved in the hotel. I told her that Zack and I would ride into town and pick up some supplies, and I would make the arrangements for the rooms since the wedding is only a month away.

Zack was quite eager to go to town when I told him I had business there. I don't think he has been off the ranch since he and Lilly moved out here. The morning we were to leave, he asked if I wanted the wagon hitched up to pick up the supplies. I smiled and shook my head. "Let's just go in on horseback," I told him. "We can let someone pick up supplies latter, I have to ride in that wagon too much with Mollie," I explained.

We got saddled up and on our way. Zack asked what we were going to do since we sure couldn't bring much back. I told him I needed to make reservations at the hotel for the wedding. I also need to stop by Colonel Herrings office and sign some papers. Other than that, why not just hang out in the saloon for a few hours and head on back to the ranch. Zack grinned and said it suited him fine.

As we rode into town, we could not tell that anything much had changed. Of course all the Earps were gone. Virgil and James to California to bury Morgan, while Wyatt and Doc were out tracking down the suspects in Morgan's murder and Virgil's shooting.

I told Zack to cut loose if he had anything he wanted to do. He said he might stop by the store and see what they had that Lilly might take a fancy to. I told him I would be through in about an hour and would meet him at the saloon.

We parted company, and I started making my way to the Grand Hotel. Mollie and I were well known there, so the clerk greeted me by name. I told him that I would need two rooms for May twenty-fourth through May twenty-sixth, as well as the parlor on the evening of the twenty-fifth for the wedding. That would give us time to settle down before the wedding, as well as give us a place to stay the next day. I had not mentioned anything to Mollie, but I let Lilly in on my plan. Lilly would pack some things for Mollie, besides what we would be taking to the hotel. The day after the wedding, we would get Zack and her to take us to the train station in Contention. From there, we would head to San Francisco for a rest. We could stay a week or two, see the sights, and come back as husband and wife. Still sounds funny, I never thought I would be a husband. I left the hotel and walked over to Colonel Herrings office. Again, he was alone and asked me to step back in his private office. He is getting used to me. This time he smiled and nodded but did not extend his hand. He brought some papers from his safe and told me I was welcome to use his office to read over them. I accepted and read each one carefully.

When I finished, I stood up and walked to the door. He came back into the inner office and asked me if everything was to my satisfaction. I told him it was, and that I was ready to sign them. We went through each one, and I signed where he indicated. I thanked him and left. I ran up on Zack as I was walking to the saloon. "Suit you to ride on to Contention before we get a drink?", I asked. He nodded, and we headed out of town. We covered the ten miles in a hurry. I told Zack I was going by the marshal's office just to check in and would meet him in the saloon in a few minutes.

No one was around at the marshal's office, so I

headed on over to the saloon. I got there before Zack and found a table to my liking and ordered a beer. I was waiting for the bartender to bring it when one of the old timers that I had come to know poked his head in the door. "Mr. Bogardis, I think that friend of yours is in a little trouble out here", he said. I walked to the door to see Zack in the street confronted by four cowboys. It was easy to see they were looking for trouble.

I walked out into the street and stopped about ten feet to Zack's right. The one doing all the talking said he was going to show Contention what "fast" looked like. I shook my head. "If you try, he will kill you before you clear leather," I told him. "Best just to let things go, nobody wants any trouble," I said. One of the others spoke up and said, "You're Bogardis, ain't you?" I nodded. "I guess you think you can walk away," he said. "Not anymore," I replied.

He went for his gun and about the same time the other three pulled. I got the one I was talking to, Zack got the one who thought he was fast, and we both fired at the other two. Who hit who I don't know, but they all went down. As is my habit, I did not take my eyes off them until I was sure the fight was over. When I looked over at Zack, he was holding the side of his head, and I could see red. Blood was trickling down the side of his neck. I holstered and went to him to see if he was okay.

About one-fourth of his left ear was gone. Shot plumb away. I told some of the bystanders that we were going to see the Doc and to tell the marshal what happened. The doctor looked at Zack's ear and chuckled. "Well son," he said, "I can't put it back on, but all it will do is look a little strange." He bandaged his ear up and gave him some ointment to put on it. "Just keep it clean, and it will take care of itself," the Doc told him.

I told Zack that we should go on and get our drink, then start back to the ranch. The marshal did not come around, but the bodies were gone when we got back to the saloon.

Well, this ought to be good. I have to take him back and explain to his wife, and Mollie, how he got his ear shot off. At least he ain't dead.

CHAPTER TWENTY SIX

It was such a beautiful day to travel! We were packed and almost ready for our ride into Tombstone when I heard Lilly speaking to Mr. Bogardis. She looked a little frazzled, almost in a panic. Mr. Bogardis shook his head, and I heard him say, "Never mind, Lilly, I might as well let the cat out of the bag".

He walked over to me and said he had a surprise in mind for us. I glanced at Lilly, who was about to explode with excitement, and then back to Mr Bogardis. I suspected that this could be the big secret Lilly had been trying so hard to keep the last weeks! Mr. Bogardis put his hands on my shoulders and a broad smile consumed his face. "Mollie, I'd do anything to make you happy", he began. "I've arranged to take you on a trip to San Fransico after we are married". Of course, I gasped with delight! He continued, "Zack and Lilly will ride with us to Contention to catch the train after we leave Tombstone. They'll be there to pick us up when we return. I know you have always wanted to see San Fransico, Mollie, and I wanted you to have the opportunity. Now that money is not a problem, it's the least I can do".

I think I had tears in my eyes before he had finished. All I could do was hold him tight. I whispered "thank you" in his ear. It was all I could manage to say. I told Lilly that she wasn't one for keeping a secret. "You're wrong Mollie!" She gloated. "You don't know everything. It's hard for me not to tell you my secret, but it'll have to wait until after you are married."

We had two trunks packed and loaded within a matter of minutes. Zack and Mr. Bogardis loaded them into the wagon, and we were on our way.

Tombstone wasn't the same without the Earps. Who would have ever imagined that it would all play out like this? It seemed the town was still a little discorded, but calmer than the last time we were here. Mr. Bogardis and I strolled around town arm in arm, just like we had when we first stayed there. Tonight, just a few hours away, we were becoming Mr. and Mrs. Bogardis, and it seemed like we have come full circle.

Lilly and Zack had dinner with us earlier, but they were now venturing off on their own. Lilly was still bursting to tell me some enormous surprise, and Zack had to keep giving her a "look" to restrain her. I think the romance of our wedding was causing them to be a little syrupy! They took the wagon and headed down Fourth Street seeing what adventure they could find. As I waved and told them to have a good time, I noticed that Zack did not have his ear bandaged.

Lilly has gotten over the fact that Zack lost part of his ear last month while he and Mr. Bogardis were in Contention City without us. But, she was making him wear some sort of patch over it 'till it healed up. He keeps pulling it off and teasing her by saying that she should love him with or without a left ear attached to his face. Earlier in the hotel room, he was chasing her around the bed teasing her, trying to make her kiss it. She ran screaming out into the hall causing a ruckus! Finally, Mr. Bogardis had to tell him to contain his silliness until after they get back to the ranch.

Mr. Crane and Mrs. Marks said they wouldn't be traveling into Tombstone for the wedding tonight. Mrs. Marks is a little under the weather, and she has been running Mr. Crane ragged the last few days. He has been fetching her hot water bottles and making trips to the drug store for some assorted remedies for her ailments. I will miss them badly, but I understand. We sent word to them that we shall invite them to the ranch for Magdelina's feast when we return from San Francisco.

Back in the bridal room, Mr. Bogardis laid out his black dress suit and tie on the chair. My dress was hanging on a rod behind the door. I was wearing his mother's cameo locket. I rarely take it off and find myself opening it often. He came towards me and laid me down on the bed. He held the locket in his hands and opened it to read the inscription, "In Omne Tempus". They are words he had a jeweler engrave on it before he gave it to me. Of course, Mr. Bogardis didn't know Latin, but Doc had mentioned they were the words he had written in a letter to a woman back in Georgia. And now, those words belonged to us. He kissed me saying, "We will be together forever, Mollie, I promise."

Before I knew it, we were both asleep in each other's arms.

I woke suddenly to Mr. Bogardis calling my name, telling me to hurry, that we had to get out immediately!

He opened the door of our room and bright red and orange flames raced across the front of his body.... it was just like the first time I saw him, his dark silhouette against the sunset of the Arizona sky.

The Grand Hotel was on fire! He told me we had no choice but to try and escape by going down the stairway. I looked at my wedding dress hanging on the back of the door, it was engulfed with twisted halos of grey smoke. Mr. Bogardis threw a blanket over my head and told me we had to move fast. The air was thick and heavy as we stumbled down the staircase. I couldn't breathe, we were both gasping for air.

"Hang on Mollie", he tried to say between breaths. "We're almost there."

The lobby was dark. I couldn't quite make out which direction it was to the outside. The blanket had caught fire, and I dropped it where we stood. He told me to get down on the floor and crawl to the door. We then heard a loud noise, a crackling sound coming from above. Mr. Bogardis threw himself on top of me, trying to shield my body. For a moment, I thought I felt the taste of his lips. I closed my eyes, coughed and tried to take in a breath of smoke favored air.

* * * * *

I was starting to get a little nervous. I'd only been to one wedding, and now I'm having one of my own. I sure wish Mollie had been content to have the wedding at the ranch. Lilly is beside herself. It's almost like she is getting married all over again. I think Zack is starting to get a little excited too.

Today is the day! We are all in Tombstone to prepare for the wedding. I had that same bad dream again last night. The one where Mollie is in trouble, and I can't save her. That dream always puts me on edge.

The Grand Hotel has assured us that everything is ready for the wedding this evening. I know Mollie and Lilly have both driven the hotel manager crazy. It seems that every time he sees one of them coming, he tries to go the other way. I keep telling her it will all work out fine, and if not, I will shoot the manager. Mollie does not quite get the humor of that remark, but Zack almost laughs out loud every time I say it.

Mollie and I decided to go get something to eat, and then come back to the hotel and rest a while before we start to get ready. Zack and Lilly were going to tour the town. As we walk back to the hotel, Mollie tells me that this is the happiest day of her life. "Sure," I said, "bet you tell that to all your husbands." She "lost her footing" and stomped my foot. We both stopped on the sidewalk, looked at each other, and laughed.

The town is about as quiet as Tombstone ever gets. There is always some noise coming from the saloons, wagons and horses coming and going, and sometimes a fist fight between two saloon patrons who have taken their disagreement out into the street. Just another day, except this one will end with Miss Lewis becoming Mrs. Bogardis. When we get to the room, I pull my boots off and stretch out on the bed. "Wanna have a little fun before you get married?", I asked. She jumped down on the bed beside me and laid her head on my chest. "No, I think I'll wait for my husband tonight," she said.

We both fall into a light sleep. The next thing I knew, I could smell smoke. At first I didn't pay it much mind, but the smell was getting stronger quickly. I sat up and saw smoke coming from under the door of our room. I could hear people yelling and screaming. I looked out the window, and flames were already crawling up the outside wall.

I shake Mollie awake and tell her we have to get out. I grab her arm and head for the door. When I open it, it's like the whole hallway goes up in flames. I pulled her back into the room and stripped a blanket off the bed. I threw it in the floor and poured the pitcher of water on it. I picked it up, threw it across my back, and told Mollie to get under it with me. I quickly explained that we were going to have to go down the hall to the staircase, then down the stairs, and out the front door, and we were going to do it in a hurry.

As we started down the hall, we were both coughing and could hardly see where we were going. We had to stay against the wall and use it to guide us to the stairway. We made it down the stairs, but once we reached the lobby, we couldn't see and could barely breathe. "On the floor Mollie, we can crawl out," I yelled.

We were both on our hands and knees, and we could almost see the daylight outside the door. Just a little farther. Then I heard a sharp crack, and pieces of the ceiling started falling on and around us. When I heard a loud snap, I threw my body down on hers. It must be the second floor coming down! I turned her head to me and looked into her eyes one more time. "Mollie, I.........................

EPILOGUE

It has been a couple of weeks since the fire. Neither Lilly nor I can believe we have really lost them. Some say the fire started in the Tivoli Saloon, but no one knows for sure. It was like a wildfire and destroyed most of Tombstone in less than an hour.

Lilly and I were at the other end of town when it started, but we ran for the hotel as soon as we realized what was happening. I got in a bucket brigade to try to help the fire department control the blaze. The hotel just collapsed on its self. When the fire was out and cooled, I started looking through the rubble. I found Mollie and Bogardis about fifteen feet from the front door. Bogardis had tried to cover her, but when the upstairs fell through, a large beam fell across them. At least their bodies were not burned. Either the beam killed them or they couldn't breathe through all the smoke.

When we brought them out, Lilly went to pieces. She would not turn loose of Mollie. I pulled her away, and she held tight to me screaming their names. We got the wagon and wrapped them as best we could for the trip home toContention. I thought, this was not the way they intended to leave Tombstone.

Just before we left, a man came up to me and introduced himself as Colonel William Herring. He said that he had been working on some papers for Mr. Bogardis, and he had already checked his office. He had invested in a safe that was supposed to be fireproof after the last Tombstone fire. It was indeed fireproof, and everything inside had survived. I asked what that had to do with me, and he explained that Mr. Bogardis had made a will which left everything to Mollie. But one of the provisions of the will was that if Mollie was no longer alive, everything would go to me, with a share to Paco.

He explained that there was nothing for me to do right now, but he thought I should know that everything Mr. Bogardis owned was now mine and Paco's. I just shook my head. I had rather have the two of them back than any amount of wealth in the world.

We got them to Contention, and I was about to arrange for them to be prepared for burial. Paco was there at the hotel with Mr. Crane and said that someone had brought him word of the Tombstone fire. Neither he nor Mr. Crane could believe that Mollie and Bogardis were dead. Paco said to bring them back to the ranch, that his wife and her sister were experienced in preparing folks to be buried. Before we left, I purchased two of the best made coffins I could find to be delivered the next day.

When we got to the ranch, Lilly had regained her composure somewhat and took charge of choosing what they would be buried in. Paco's wife removed the locket that Mollie wore around her neck and asked if she should be buried with it. I said no, and gave it to Lilly, as Mollie had always said it should go to Lilly if anything ever happened to her. Lilly put her hand on her stomach and told me if our baby was to be born a girl, she would name it after Mollie, and the locket would be hers one day as well. Lilly never had the chance to tell Mollie and Mr. Bogardis that she and I were expecting a child. We'd planned to tell them right after they were married. It was the big secret that Lilly had been keeping from Mollie.

The next day, we laid them to rest in the little grove of trees by the creek. Several people from Contention came, including Mr. Crane, Mrs. Marks, and some of the folks on the town council. None of the Earps or Doc Holliday could make it, they being pretty much on the run now.

Paco, Lilly, and I came down here today to put up the grave marker we had made. We tried to keep it simple, as we thought that would be their wish.

It reads simply:

Nathaniel Bogardis &   Mollie Lewis
May 25, 1882
In Omne Tempus

As we stood looking at the marker, Paco asked me if I had anything planned now that I was in charge of the Circle L. I nodded my head and slipped my arm around Lilly. I knew what I had to do. "Yes, Lilly and I will be leaving for Tucson soon," I said. "We have to find a woman named Pryer that we met on the trail a while back. It's what Mr. Bogardis and Mollie would expect us to do."
Lilly looked down at the headstone and smiled. "We'll be back soon, Paco", she added. "I will be in need of Magdelena to help deliver our little 'Mollie' or 'Nathaniel' Blade".

THE END

ACKNOWLEDGMENTS

As we were writing the books, it was easy to believe that there could have been a "Mollie" and "Bogardis" who actually lived in Contention City in 1881. We almost felt that it was their transending thoughts that appeared on the pages we typed. We took their 'fictional lives' and intricately wove historical events and legendary people into their story.

Although the books would be fiction, we began the adventure to research all we could find about Contention City, Arizona. I explored the pages of Prescott's newspaper, "The Weekly Arizona Miner" and Tombstone's "Epitaph" from 1881-1882. I read the transcripts of Judge Spicier's hearing that took place regarding the gunfight at the O. K. Corral. T.B. roamed the internet for articles and essays on the lives of the Earps and Doc Holliday, along with the local towns that sprang up the the area. We asked questions from western historians when we couldn't get enough.

Jim Dunham was gracious to lend us his expert knowledge on western history. Jim is a well-known accomplished gunslinger (gun spinning and fancy gun handling) and historian who has worked with 20th Century Fox and the movie "TOMBSTONE". He helped to make sure we told the proper facts and had our events in order. Jim can be seen on the History Channel series, "Tales of the Gun". He is the Director of Special Projects and Historian at the Booth Western Art Museum in Cartersville, Georgia.

When each book was completed, we chose a scene that we felt 'defined' the turning point in that part of the story. We sought out an expert photographer who could take our visions and transform them into a book cover. We looked no further than fellow SASS member, Don Contresas. Don's photographs have enriched the pages of several magazines, as well as his own 'coffee table' style books titled, "We Dance Because We Can (1996)" and "The Cowboy Way (2002)".

Unfortunately, T.B. and I realize how badly each of us are at spelling. He says I tend to "make up words that only I seem to know what they mean". We'd like to thank our editor, Lana D. Greene, for all her long hours and hard work at correcting our mistakes.

For posing for the cover of **Time in Contention 3 - The Trouble in Tombstone**, we would like to thank Derek Burton. He is portraying

"Pistol" from the story, and we think he made a fine cowboy! Thank you, Derek, for playing along with us!

In this day and time, it's difficult to get recognition and exposure once the books are written. We would like to give credit to Red Doc Entertainment for helping to promote our books to the public. T. B. and I continue to present our program for book clubs, organizations and libraries free of charge. To book us at YOUR next event, please contact us through reddocentertainment@yahoo.com.

And last, but not least, we each have a few special folks we would like to thank. Some of our fictional charactors in the books were named after our family and friends. Thank you all for lending us your names (we hope you all become famous one day)

To both mine and T.B.'s family, friends and fans, we greatly appreciate you when you show up at our book signings and special events. Thank you for your continued support and encouragement! WE LOVE YOU!!!

Cindy's Thank you's.....

When I was a child, my dad would allow me to stay up late (on school nights) and watch westerns on TV with him. We would sit silently on the couch in front of a black and white 19 inch screen. It was our "time" together. During the midnight movie, sometime around 1968, I heard Glen Ford annouce that they were riding to catch the "3:10 to Yuma" train in Contention City, Arizona. I almost felt like I was there. Although I could never find much information on the city of Contention, I never forgot it. Even then, I knew that one day I would write a book about Contention City.

In November 2008, I emailed T.B. a short story about two stangers and their meeting of chance. I wrote how fate lead a woman, standing alone on the wooden sidewalks of Contention City, to fall in love with an unknown cowboy. I asked for his opinion on what I had written. T.B. responded with an email of his own, but this time, it was in the viewpoint of the "cowboy" instead of the woman. I thought, this is it! It was the perfect opportunity to do what I have always known I would.

To Destiny ~ who patiently read my ramblings and offered to refine my "inaccurate" words.

To Paden ~ who constantly "brags" on his mom!

To Gabe ~ my little buddy who says he's my number 1 fan!
To Gary ~ he continues to tell me "I can do anything".
And to my dogs, Sammy and Pollyanna, who kept me company many nights while I stayed up 'till dawn writing.

T.B.'s Thank you's.....
Thank you to my family and friends who supported us. To those who could have but didn't, looks like we got it done without you!

TIME IN CONTENTION
The Ballad of Mollie and Bogardis

He rode into the town that day, one more stranger, no one cared.
But fate had Mollie look his way, their eyes met and they stared.

They were two people all alone, with secrets they won't mention
about to gamble the unknown, as they spend Time in Contention.

She was a lady by all rights, she was prim and she was proper.
She longed for more than lonely nights, some day no one will stop her.

He came to town to fight his fight, with colt pistols made for kill'in
He knew that he was in the right, still there's blood that would be spill'in.

Under the cold December moon, arm and arm they walk together.
Two shadows in the dim lit room, now their hearts would bond forever.

But happiness is all in vain, Mollie writes a good-bye letter.
Bogardis drinks away his pain, when Sam Fisher comes to get her.

The time has come the fight is here, it's Bogardis 'gainst the seven.
With Mollie gone he feels no fear, now let's see who goes to Heaven!

The bullets fly the shots repeat, and one by one the bad men die.
But Mollie's back just up the street, to save Bogardis she must try.

She aims the gun to save his life, with deliberate intentions.
The story ends where love begins, cause they spent Time in Contention.

"TIME IN CONTENTION"
The Ballad of Mollie and Bogardis
by Cindy Smith and T.B. Burton.

THE RANGER and ZACK BLADE

Down an alley in Contention on a cold dark winter night,
He was calling for a lantern when a young man brought the light.
No time to draw conclusions, no time to stop the raid!
The Ranger felt inclined to trust the young man called Zack Blade.
In the town they call Old Tucson, there they would meet again.
The Ranger hired the Blade boys, Zack and brother Ben.
If they could stop the bandits then they'd be highly paid,
So into northern Arizona rode The Ranger and the Blades.

Near the Canyon of the Devil where the bandits robbed the stage,
The Ranger had a plan that was sure to earn their wage.
Through gunfire and commotion they thought they had it made,
Till the Ranger saw the bullet hit the brother of Zack Blade.
When the shooting had all ended and the land was full of lead,
The sand in that desert place had turned to crimson red.
They loaded up the bandits and formed a death parade.
Thirteen horses bore the bodies of twelve outlaws and Ben Blade.

Zack returns home to Contention, finds his family in the ground.
The Ranger swears to help him, their killers must be found!
They learned about Will Lawrence and the folks that he betrayed,
When the Ranger goes to face him, he's alone without Zack Blade.
The Ranger can't believe it but the truth's before his eyes.
He will make the grim decision about who will live or die.
That day of confrontation is one that will not fade!
And therein lies the legend of the Ranger and Zack Blade.

THE RANGER and ZACK BLADE
by Cindy Smith and T.B. Burton

song inspired by TIME IN CONTENTION 2,
The Return from Prescott
Available on CD

THE GUNFIGHT

Leather hangin' from their hips as they rode into town
Drinking and carousing in the bar where they were found
Threats were made, and plans were laid,
Ill tension filled the air
Trouble was a comin'~soon death would be everywhere.

Restless hands were fondlin' the triggers on their guns
Gathering their courage but they weren't the only ones
Down the street, the men would meet,
Out where the cold winds blow
Three men would die that day ~ cause they drew their gun too slow.

Cowboys gathered in the street each with a loaded gun
Commence to fightin' or get away and three began to run
Thirty rounds of bullets blast there wasn't time to pray
Unprepared to meet their Maker, on this their Judgement Day.

White smoke swirled high in the air while people gathered 'round
Staring at the chaos and the bodies on the ground
Some men bled, and some were dead.
It's not the right or wrong
What it all comes down to is ~ which side of the gun you're on

THE GUNFIGHT
By: Cindy Smith and T.B. Burton